"A book to keep you up at night, turning the pages. Katharine Swartz skilfully moves between two protagonists. She brings alive with her writing a past in which racism was the norm and one's conscience was the only ethical guide. Both protagonists are three-dimensional, and the reader is drawn into their dilemmas and can feel the changes they are going through. As I am myself descended from slaves who survived the horrific Middle Passage from Africa to the Caribbean, I was particularly intrigued by Abigail's story."
- Sharon Maas, author of *The Quint Chronicles* series

"Katharine Swartz weaves an enthralling dual timeline story with a truly unique premise that takes the reader on a journey from some of the most beautiful Northern coastlines into the Georgian drawing rooms of England. I was truly captivated by this heart-wrenching historical novel set in a dark time in British history and interwoven expertly with a poignant, yet uplifting, modern-day narrative."
- Suzanne Kelman, author of *A View Across the Rooftops*

ABOUT THE AUTHOR

After spending much of her childhood in Canada, and then three years as a diehard New Yorker, Katharine Swartz lives in a small town on the Welsh border with her husband – an Anglican minister – their five children, and an assortment of pets. She writes contemporary fiction under the name Kate Hewitt and historical fiction under her own name. She loves hearing from readers, and you can sign up to her newsletter or her Facebook book group on her website: www.kate-hewitt.com.

Other titles by Katharine Swartz

Far Horizons
Another Country
A Distant Shore
Down Jasper Lane
The Other Side of the Bridge

In the Tales from Goswell series

The Vicar's Wife
The Lost Garden
The Second Bride

THE WIDOW'S SECRET

Tales from Goswell

Katharine Swartz

LION FICTION

*To Rachel Walker and Sophie Wrigley, for being
such good Cumbrian friends! Love always, K.*

Published by
Lion Hudson Limited
Wilkinson House, Jordan Hill Business Park
Banbury Road, Oxford OX2 8DR, England
www.lionhudson.com

ISBN 978 1 78264 281 7
eISBN 978 1 78264 282 4

First edition 2020

Acknowledgments
Extract on p. 278 from "silently if, out of not knowable" by E.E. Cummings.
Published by Liveright Publishing Corporation in SELECTED POEMS by E.E.
Cummings, edited by Richard Kennedy. Reproduced by permission of W.W.
Norton & Company, Inc.

A catalogue record for this book is available from the British Library

Printed and bound in the UK, April 2020, LH26
by Clays Ltd, Elcograf S.p.A.

Acknowledgments

The title of *The Widow's Secret* came to me before the idea. I knew I wanted to write a book about the Whitehaven slave trade, which I'd read about, and as I was ruminating on potential plot points, the title came to me, and I immediately began to wonder – what is her secret? It took me much thought, research, and several years to find out.

I have many people to thank for this book, as the subject matter both past and present required much research. I am grateful to everyone who offered their expertise – my sister-in-law, Lynn Swartz, who advised me on matters of marine archaeology; Whitehaven archivist and friend Elizabeth Norton, who helped me with matters related to eighteenth-century Whitehaven, and the lovely staff at The Rum Story, who let me look around, recommended books, and answered questions.

I am also grateful to my editor Jess Gladwell, who was very patient with my needing to extend deadlines and always wonderfully encouraging of my work, as well as my current editor, Eva Rojas, who took up the manuscript mid-production and has also been patient and wonderful!

My friend Jenna Ness was a great encourager as well, and listened to me moan about the endless research into eighteenth-century manners. I am so thankful that she is always available for an online chat – or a glass of wine in Paris!

I'd also like to thank my family, who are always patient and (generally!) understanding when I am up against a deadline and lost in the world of my story, accepting when I am not quite present, and then happy when I "return".

The Widow's Secret was a long time in the making, and I am so thankful to readers who have patiently followed the *Tales from Goswell*. I hope you enjoy the latest instalment!

Prologue

The sea is calm tonight. He stands at the prow of the ship, the dark water lapping gently at its worn and weary sides. The still night air possesses a bite; it is cold, but he does not feel it. Already he is becoming a ghost. Soon he will slip beneath these waters, yes, as quickly and easily as that. Or so he hopes, although perhaps he is not deserving of such a respite.

The moon is still high in the night sky, a blank-faced ivory oval, as milky-white as his beloved's skin. But when he closes his eyes he sees skin of another shade, and it torments him. How it torments him, even though he has tried so hard to pretend that it doesn't.

Alone in the dark, he tries to banish the many dark faces with their desperate, accusing eyes, their silent, pleading voices. *Don't think of them. Don't think of them.*

And yet he must. He must, because he has come to this moment. He can see the rough shape of the Head now – a darkened hulk in the distance, the pleasant green of its contours hidden by the black night. He is so close to home, and yet he has never felt so far away.

Forgive me.

Who is he asking? His God? His wife? Or the hundreds, perhaps even thousands, he cannot bear to see behind his lids any longer, always rising up to accuse him the second he closes his eyes?

All of them. *All of them.*

A shuddering sigh escapes him, halfway to a sob, and he feels the ship start to list beneath his heavy feet. He can bear no more. If he had been a more courageous man, he would have ended this long ago, before the arduous journey from the West Indies to here, across stormy seas, battling both the waves and his own inner agony, knowing what he needed to do and yet unable to do it.

Or perhaps he would have had the strength to sail onwards, into the harbour, to face his love as well as his guilt, and find a way forward somehow, if such a thing were even possible.

But he wasn't a brave man – he's discovered that now – so he'd journeyed on, both desperate and defiant, refusing to acknowledge the guilt that rode and rode him. But he accepts it now, he takes it as his due, a burden far too heavy to bear, and he bows beneath it.

Silently he turns from the prow, from the lights of the harbour twinkling in the distance like a promise he can no longer keep.

Forgive me. Please, please forgive me.

CHAPTER ONE

....

Rachel

The insistent buzz of her mobile startled Rachel Gardener out of a restless doze just after seven. Next to her, her husband Anthony lay on his back, breathing heavily in a way that was not quite a snore.

Rachel swung out of bed silently, already alert, reaching for her phone.

"Hello?" Her voice was a husky sleep-laced murmur as she pushed her hair out of her eyes and her feet into slippers. Outside the May morning sparkled like a jewel, sunlight glinting off Bristol's floating harbour, everything fresh and damply new, glinting with the expectation of another spring day.

"Rachel? Sorry to ring so early."

"I was up." Leaving Anthony now snoring gently in the bedroom, Rachel clamped her mobile between her ear and shoulder as she threw on her dressing gown and headed towards the kitchen. "What's going on, Izzy?" Her colleague at Bristol Centre for Maritime Archaeology wouldn't ring at such an hour if it wasn't important.

"Something's come up, surprisingly urgent."

"Urgent?" Rachel switched on the kettle, her interest already piqued.

"Commercial work," Izzy explained. "Up in Cumbria."

"Ah." Rachel had been working for Bristol's Centre for Maritime Archaeology for five years, ever since she'd received her PhD, but she often freelanced for commercial developers and county councils when they were in need of a maritime specialist – usually when something unexpected, and often unwanted, turned up during a property renovation or development. That was when things became urgent.

Rachel put two heaped spoonfuls of ground coffee into the mini-cafetière. "That's rather far," she remarked. She should know; she'd grown up in Cumbria, although it all felt a lifetime ago now. For a second she let herself recall the forbidding façade of the house made of Lakeland stone where she'd grown up, halfway between Windermere and Kendal, with nothing but the lonely sweep of empty fells visible in every direction, and the relentless howl of the wind often the only sound. She saw the empty rooms, heard the ringing silence, the disappointment and grief seeming to shroud the house in fog even on a sunny day. Then she pushed it all firmly out of her mind.

"Yes," Izzy agreed, "it is quite far, but I thought since you were from there, you might fancy a visit? Go see your mum while you're at it?" Rachel didn't reply and Izzy continued, "Besides, it's your speciality. Shipwreck in shallow water – well, relatively shallow. Around fifteen metres. Probably not much left, but still something. Enough to warrant an initial investigation, at least."

"I'm all ears." Rachel leaned against the counter as she waited for the kettle to boil.

"So, here's the story," Izzy stated as she riffled through some papers. "Some sort of wreckage from a ship has been found buried in mud a quarter of a mile off the coast of Whitehaven, in about fifteen metres of water. It was discovered when Copeland Mining Company did some offshore test drills. They're scheduled to reopen a mine for coking coal there next year. Nothing had come up with the remote sensing they did earlier, but when they started the drills a few bits and pieces were caught in the core matrix.

9

They reported it and now intend to move on to another area for the tests, but they'd like to return to the area of the shipwreck as it's important to their development, so they want an immediate investigation to see if there's anything that needs to be excavated."

"Okay." The kettle switched off and Rachel poured water on to the coffee grounds, breathing in the comforting aroma. "Any idea about the ship?"

"Not really. Old, certainly, based on what they discovered, which admittedly wasn't much – just some iron bits, I think. Afterwards they sent an underwater drone down and what they saw looked substantial enough to warrant investigation – a few timbers from what looks to be the hull." She paused. "They're dotting all their i's and crossing their t's on this one, because it's very important this mine is reopened. Apparently there has been some opposition from the local community, environmentalists, et cetera."

"There always is."

"So they want a prompt and proper investigation, everything done by the book. They'd already done both a DBA and an EIA, and nothing was flagged up. This shipwreck has come as a complete surprise to everyone, especially since there are already some documented wrecks in the area, and this definitely isn't one of them."

"Interesting," Rachel murmured. Archaeological desk-based as well as environmental impact assessments would have been an important part of the mining company's planning stage of their project, along with the remote sensing. This unexpected wreckage must have thrown quite a spanner in the works.

"So it's a yes?" Izzy asked, clearly already knowing Rachel's answer.

"Yes, of course it is."

"I thought so. Will Sayers is your liaison at Copeland Mining Company, and Mark James is with Cumbria's Historic Environment Service, available for advice. You should contact them both when you get there. The bits that have been salvaged so far were bagged and are currently being kept at a local museum by the harbour."

"Okay." Rachel could feel her pulse start to speed up. She loved this part of the chase – the clues, the mystery waiting to be unravelled underneath the ocean's waves. Admittedly, with the mining company eager to continue with its work, she would undoubtedly face pressure to evaluate the wreck as quickly as possible, but she still loved to wonder. To dream.

"All they want to do is determine that the wreck contains no heritage assets so they can continue their work."

"Right."

Rachel took her first sip of coffee, savouring the rich taste. Outside a seagull skimmed the glinting water before soaring up into the still-blue sky. "If it's as old as they think, there's unlikely to be much left, so they shouldn't be too worried. I doubt there will be the interest or the funding for a full-scale exploration."

"Like I said, they're dotting all their i's. And it has been submerged in clay-based mud. There's a good chance something of interest remains, but whether the Secretary of State determines it's worthy of conservation is another matter."

Having worked on dozens of shipwrecks off Britain's shores, Rachel already knew the drill. A previously undiscovered shipwreck could only be protected if the Secretary of State for Digital, Culture, Media and Sport decided it was a designated heritage asset. Considering there were at present over forty thousand wreck sites in the UK's coastal waters, and only sixty-two were protected, she wasn't holding out much hope.

"And there's no clue as to what ship it might be?" she asked. "If it's so close to the coast, surely its sinking was recorded at the time?"

"Nothing found yet, but as you know there were loads of wrecks. In any case, I'm sure you can figure it out," Izzy answered cheerfully. "Spend a day trawling through the local archives, or head to Kew?" Rachel had spent many a dusty afternoon in the national archives in Kew. "Always fun. Can you head up to Cumbria today?"

"Today? It really is urgent, then." Rachel took another sip of coffee as she mentally went through her week. She and Anthony were meant to be having dinner with friends tomorrow night. He was working throughout the weekend, catering for private dinner parties both nights. "All right."

"It's all a bit delicate from what I gather," Izzy explained. "As I said, there has been some environmental opposition to the coal mining operation, although it was approved by the local council earlier this year. People are keen for the jobs it will bring to the area, but others would like to see the whole thing stopped."

"Surely a shipwreck isn't going to stop them. They could just test in another area."

"It will slow things down, I suppose. So you'll go today?"

Rachel pushed aside the thought of the missed dinner. "Sure."

"Thanks, Rachel. I knew you could do this. Do keep me in the loop after you've talked to Sayers and James, and you've had a look at the drone footage. Ally and Dave are planning to come up the day after tomorrow, to have a first look with you."

"Okay, sounds good." After she'd finished the call, Rachel stood sipping her coffee and staring out at the sunlit water as she ran through a list of things to do before she left for Cumbria. She supposed she should ring her mother to let her know she'd be in the area, although Whitehaven was over an hour from her family home.

It wasn't close enough to call yet, Rachel decided. She could leave that for after she'd arrived, seen the site, and talked to the people she needed to. The thought brought a flicker of relief she chose not to acknowledge.

She was just rinsing her coffee cup out in the sink when Anthony came into the kitchen, yawning widely and raking a hand through his wavy dark hair.

"Did I dream your phone ringing at an ungodly hour?"

"I'd hardly call half past seven ungodly." She hadn't meant to sound quite as tart, but somehow, as it did so often, it came out that way.

Her husband registered her tone with a tightening of his mouth, a flickering of his eyelids, no more.

"Sorry, I'm in a rush," Rachel said as she edged past Anthony, who was blocking the doorway of the galley kitchen, to head to the shower.

"A rush? Why? Who was on the phone?" Idly he scratched his stomach as he wandered towards the kettle.

"Izzy." She paused, then decided she might as well tell Anthony now, although she knew he wouldn't like it. He never liked her travelling, especially when they had plans. "A shipwreck has been discovered up in Cumbria. I need to leave this morning."

"What?" Anthony turned to face her. "You're going all the way up to Cumbria?"

"It's urgent. A mining company is involved. They discovered the ship during some offshore test drills, and they want the situation resolved quickly."

Anthony shook his head slowly, reminding Rachel of a bear. Everything about him reminded her of some big, lumbering, shaggy animal – his size, which was a solid and muscular six three, his dark hair, kept a little too long by her reckoning, as well as his beard, trimmed close. His slow, deliberate movements, the back and forth of his head, when he was shaking it as he was now.

When they'd first met three years ago, she'd liked the comforting bulk of him – he felt like someone solid and substantial, the kind of man she could depend on, an anchor in a life that sometimes felt like the shifting sea.

She'd let that feeling carry her away, and they'd married after knowing each other for just over a month, but three years on it all it was all beginning to grate on her, even though she tried not to let it. She knew it was unfair, just as she knew she was far more of a trial to Anthony than he was to her.

"But what about our dinner tomorrow night, with Ken and Elspeth?" he asked. "It's been scheduled for months."

"We can reschedule, surely."

Anthony kept shaking his head. "You know how busy they are. And you are, as well," he added; it sounded like an accusation.

"I'm sorry, Anthony, but what can I do? Work is work." Rachel heard the annoyance in her voice, like needle pricks in a cloth. Make enough of them and even the thickest, most sumptuous fabric would tear.

He sighed. "Do you have to take every job?"

"I was asked for in particular." She folded her arms, impatience adding to her irritation, although she did her best to tamp both down. "If it was you, I wouldn't make such a fuss."

Anthony's face drooped into familiar lines of disappointment, wide shoulders slumping, which felt far worse than his annoyance. "I know you wouldn't," he said quietly as he turned away from her.

Rachel bit her lip, feeling as though she should apologize, but for what? Work was work. She also couldn't keep from feeling relieved that he was letting it go so easily. She'd expected more of a fight. A few months ago, maybe, she would have got one.

"Is there any coffee?" he asked tiredly.

"I'm sorry. I only made enough for one." A habit she couldn't seem to kick after fifteen years of living on her own. "Sorry," she added again, and she hoped he knew she was apologizing for more than the lack of coffee. At least, she thought she was. "I'll call you when I get there."

"Fine." Anthony shrugged as he refilled the kettle, and after another second's hesitation, wondering if she should say something more, Rachel headed for the shower.

An hour later she was on the road, her dive kit packed in the back of her SUV along with a case of everyday clothes. The sun was high in the sky, the whole world bursting with verdant green, as she left the city behind for the open stretch of M5, heading north. It was a little over five hours to Whitehaven, on the coast of Cumbria, halfway between Carlisle and Barrow. If she was lucky, with little traffic, she'd be there before three o'clock.

Her heart lifted as she sped down the road, pushing away the memory of the rather tense farewell she'd had with Anthony. She would have preferred for him to be annoyed rather than disappointed, but he'd been silent and sorrowful-eyed as he'd hugged her goodbye. She'd offered her cheek for a kiss, pretending that this was a sign of intimacy rather than a way to avoid something more.

Anxiety cramped her stomach at the unwelcome and ever-present thought. What was *wrong* with her? Why couldn't she love her husband the way most women seemed to, with effortless ease, as natural as breathing? They were practically still on their honeymoon. It wasn't supposed to be this difficult yet. But Rachel had to acknowledge that it had nearly always been difficult.

She'd met Anthony while on a research grant in Florida, excavating a newly discovered Spanish galleon off Key West. He'd been the chef and owner of a seafood place on the beach where she'd eaten most nights. She'd been drawn to his easy expansiveness, so different from her own quiet containment. She'd been fascinated by how relaxed he was, and longed for it herself.

And he had brought her out of herself a little, made her smile, made her laugh. Made her start to think, amid the tropical glow of Florida sunsets and sea breezes, that they could be happy together.

Don't think about it, she instructed herself. *You have a project to focus on, and there's nothing you can do about all that right now anyway.* The tension in her stomach eased as she purposefully focused on the shipwreck waiting to be discovered. Already Rachel imagined it shrouded in mystery – an unknown wreck so close to the coast? Most wrecks in sight of the coastline would surely have been recorded at the time.

Perhaps this one had been, and Izzy simply hadn't discovered the record yet. Rachel would find it somewhere – in the Customs House archives or the ship registers in the archives at Kew. With enough time and attention to detail, most things could be discovered, and if the wreck itself offered up a precious clue…

The possibility and even the promise of such a thing made Rachel's spirits lift, and she pushed away her last lingering thoughts about Anthony and his disappointment. When she got back to Bristol, she'd make it up to him. Dinner out or, even better, in – a romantic night together. Somehow she'd manage it.

Five hours later, she was driving down the steep hill towards Whitehaven's waterfront, the elegant skeleton of a once-thriving Georgian town visible beneath the modern marks of petrol stations, superstores, and shopfronts of plastic and neon.

She followed directions to the town's main museum on the waterfront, where Izzy had said the pieces of wreckage that had been caught in the core matrix were being kept.

During her brief drive through the town, Rachel could see why the jobs the mining company provided might be needed there. Whitehaven looked like a place that was struggling and had been for some time, with several boarded-up buildings scarring the elegantly proportioned streets, as well as many of the warning signs of any town's declining prosperity – charity and betting shops, and too many empty storefronts, amid the cheerful hanging baskets of flowers and the bustle of a market in one of the town's small squares.

The waterfront seemed a bit more commercial and cheerful, Rachel noted as she parked her car by the museum, taking a moment to survey the graceful curve of the town's harbour, the water between the old stone quays now bobbing with various sailing boats and other small vessels.

Once, hundreds of years ago, it would have held huge merchant ships, and these quays would have been used to load and unload vast amounts of coal, iron, wool, sugar, and other goods.

For a second, Rachel could picture it – the huge ships, the smell of coal smoke clogging the air, the harbour bustling with activity and commerce, sailors and stevedores lifting and hauling crates and barrels. High above, the Georgian townhouses that had once belonged to Whitehaven's wealthy merchant class would have reigned supreme. Now they were divided into shops and flats, or even empty.

With a nostalgic sigh, she let the vision recede and headed into the museum. One of the staff ushered her into the office of the museum director, Anne Barton, a friendly woman in her fifties with a head of curly grey hair and a Cumbrian accent stronger than any Rachel had heard since her childhood.

"It could be anything, of course," she said as she sat behind her desk. "There's no obvious record of a ship sinking there, but of course a hundred years ago or more, ships were sinking all the time. Wrecked on the rocks, cargo lost."

"But it wasn't near any rocks, was it?" Rachel asked as she took the chair in front of the desk. "A quarter of a mile out?"

"Yes, that's true. And we do have commercial records going all the way back to the 1600s, when Whitehaven's harbour was first used for shipping coal to Dublin. You can see them in the archives, if you like."

"Thank you," Rachel murmured. "I will take a look."

"There have been quite a few shipwrecks in the area over the years," Anne continued. "The SS *Izaro* being the most notable, perhaps. And there are at least four wrecks off the coast nearby that are marked by buoys… You've probably heard that it's important to ascertain if this wreck contains any heritage assets, so the test drills can continue as soon as possible. The mine is set to reopen next year."

"Yes, I'm aware, thank you," Rachel said. "I'll be meeting with Copeland's liaison tomorrow. Could you tell me what has been discovered so far?"

"Not very much. When the first borehole was drilled, a bit of iron was caught in the core matrix, and it was enough for Copeland Mining to send an underwater drone down. The footage showed a shipwreck, mostly submerged in mud. They halted drilling until the wreck could be evaluated, but it doesn't look like there's much left."

"And you have the item that was caught in the matrix here?"

"Yes, we put it into storage as soon as possible. I'm afraid I can't identify it, but it looks interesting, perhaps some part of a tool? Would you like to see?"

Rachel felt that familiar lick of excitement inside as she nodded. "Yes, please."

"I'll show you the way."

Her heart started to beat a little harder as Anne led her to a storage room at the back of the museum, away from any sources of light and heat. Even though she knew whatever fragment had been caught would most likely reveal little about the mystery ship, she couldn't keep from feeling that flare of anticipation, the intoxicating what-if she was always pursuing beneath the sea, coaxing it to give up some of its many secrets.

"I double bagged it," Anne said as she put the object on an examining table. "I hope that was correct procedure. I don't actually have a background in archaeology."

"Yes, thank you." Rachel took the pair of latex gloves Anne handed her and pulled them on.

Carefully she undid the bag, knowing she would need to keep whatever object she found exposed to air for as little time as possible, even though by the sounds of it, it had already been somewhat compromised.

Gently she lifted out a small twist of iron, almost in a heart shape, that looked, as Anne had suggested, as if it had been part of a larger implement.

"It's interesting, that, isn't it?" Anne remarked. "I wish I could say I knew what it was."

"I think it must be the head of some sort of tool, as you thought," Rachel said slowly. "The bottom of the heart shape looks as if it was screwed into something else." She felt a flicker of some memory at the back of her brain, but she couldn't hold on to it. Had she seen something like this before? Probably, but she'd seen so many bits and pieces over the years. It was incredibly difficult to remember each and every one.

"Is it possible to date it?" asked Anne.

"Not on its own, not without knowing anything else." Yet the bit of iron intrigued her, just as it had Anne, the shape of it suggesting something sentimental, although Rachel knew that was unlikely to be the case. In all likelihood the heart shape was similar to the top of a pair of scissors – a way for whatever implement it was to be held by a finger and a thumb. Still, alone, it looked almost like the keepsake of a sweetheart.

Knowing she couldn't do much more until she'd actually seen the wreck, Rachel rebagged it before heading back with Anne for a cup of tea in her office to view the underwater drone's footage.

"I'm afraid there isn't much to see," Anne said as she turned her computer screen towards Rachel so she could view the footage. "Most of the shipwreck is still covered in mud, or rotted away. I think Copeland Mining would have preferred it to stay buried." She made a face, half grimace, half apology. "It's slowing them down, and Copeland have promised the area over five hundred jobs. People are counting on them."

"I understand," she told Anne neutrally, and the museum director pressed Play.

Rachel squinted, adjusting to the dark murkiness of life fifteen metres below the sea. The ground was grey and softly undulating, and as the camera moved around, Rachel saw a shape emerge from the mud – the sinuous curve of a hull, poking through the seabed like a hip bone. A plaice swam lazily in front of the camera, making her smile as she leaned forward, searching intently for more clues.

Through the ghostly grey murk of the sea, the skeleton of a ship emerged – the rotted timber, the iron bands, barely visible through the drifts of mud and sand and time.

"What's that?" she asked, her tone abrupt as she leaned forward, jabbing a finger at the screen.

"What's what?"

"That iron bar." She frowned as she studied the iron bar resting gently on the seabed.

"I don't know." Anne sounded mystified. "Some part of the ship, perhaps?"

"Perhaps," Rachel allowed. She needed more information before she started making guesses. Still, her heart flipped over and her mind raced as the sea and its secrets proved as alluring as ever.

CHAPTER TWO

Abigail

Whitehaven, 1763

Abigail Heywood pressed her nose to the glass of the upper storey window of her house on Duke Street, the chilly waters of the Solway Firth in the distance ruffled and grey on this cold winter's day.

The paltry flames from the morning room's coal fire barely penetrated the room's icy chill; winter in Cumberland, with the winds off the sea buffeting the townhouse, invariably brought a bone-deep cold that didn't thaw until June, if not later, or even at all.

Abigail drew her shawl more firmly around her shoulders as she surveyed the scene in front of her: the harbour in the distance, bristling with the masts of its many ships, and below a few people hurrying here and there, heads tucked low against the wind – servant girls intent on going down street on an errand for their mistress, and merchants striding self-importantly about their business on one of the town's many quays or in its smoke-filled coffee houses.

Whitehaven was a town that positively seethed with determined prosperity, with its new-money merchants rich in coal and tobacco presided over by the Lowther family who had dominated the trade for nearly a century. Once a forgotten fishing village, Whitehaven had been turned by the Lowthers into an elegantly planned town three times the size of Carlisle – one they boasted could rival Liverpool for its port, or York for its society.

Up here, in the solitary confinement of the parlour of her father's house on Duke Street, Abigail did not think either was true. Whitehaven was miles from anywhere, cut off from the rest of the world by the unforgiving fells, the only turnpike road going to nearby Goswell for coal and no further, and the stage coach having to go up to Carlisle before down to Sheffield and London, taking over three days.

While Whitehaven possessed two assembly rooms, as well as an impressive theatre, its society was small and forever turned inward, focused on a few seemingly important families – the Lowthers, the Jeffersons, the Speddings, the Gales. Abigail's own family, despite its substantial wealth in the wool trade, was not counted in that number.

And most likely never would be, thanks to an unfortunate summer in Harrogate six months ago. Today, like nearly any other, Abigail knew she could look forward to nothing more than needlework and letter-writing to her relatives in Kendal, perhaps taking tea with one of her mother's few friends, listening to their idle and speculative chatter about the grand doings of one of the town's important families. Another dreary day of waiting – but for what? Surely there was nothing more to wait for. It had already gone.

"Abigail, my dear, come away from the window." Caroline Heywood bustled into the room, her hands laced over her floral-patterned stomacher, her robe cut away to reveal an excessively frilled petticoat underneath. "The last thing we should want is for you to catch a chill. A reddened nose is so unbecoming."

"Who is there to see my nose, red or otherwise?" Abigail returned as she sat down by the fire and eyed her half-completed sampler with some distaste. She was a mediocre needlewoman at best, and didn't see the point in so much stitching. She much preferred books to the domestic arts, but she'd just finished the latest novel, *Sophia*, and had nothing more to read.

"All of polite society, I should think," Caroline replied in a voice laden with triumph, and Abigail turned to her mother in surprise.

"What can you mean?"

"We have been invited," Caroline said in the voice of one who is making a grand pronouncement, "to a musical evening at the Tamworths' tomorrow night."

"We… have?" Abigail stared at her mother blankly. She had not been invited to a single event in Whitehaven's scant social season all winter, despite her mother's desperate and increasingly obvious contrivances to obtain such an offer.

She'd avoided the monthly gatherings at Whitehaven's assembly rooms as well; her parents had thought it best for her to lie low, at least for a little while. But now it was January and things had changed, just as the tide had turned, bringing new possibility and prosperity to the town's shores.

Before the summer, Abigail had been a nodding acquaintance of all the genteel young women of Whitehaven. She had been invited to the few card parties, musical evenings, and even the summer ball that comprised the town's season, although not, perhaps, as an honoured guest.

Abigail had never been under any illusion regarding her status – she was the plain daughter of a middling merchant who had made a respectable fortune in worsted cloth. She was no particular prize for the discerning bachelor, nor was she the most desirable companion for the young women of Whitehaven who aspired ever higher – to wed local gentry, or merchants' sons in

Liverpool or even London. Still, she'd been respectable, so she'd been included, her name had been on every list, if rather far down.

Until it had been struck off.

"How has this come to pass?" she asked as she watched her mother fuss around the room, as she often did when she was either anxious or excited, picking up a tasselled pillow and putting it down again, flicking an imaginary speck of dust from the arm of a chair.

"What does it matter how it has come to pass? It matters simply that it has." Caroline gave her what Abigail suspected was meant to be an airy smile. "Now what should you wear? I think your pink robe is lovely, but perhaps a bit too summery for the season. I shall have to have Jensen iron your new petticoat. She must take care with the frills –"

"Mama." Abigail's voice came out in a strident command, and Caroline's fluttering stilled.

"My dear –"

"How has this come to pass?" she repeated, her tone demanding an answer. "I have not been invited to a single occasion since we returned to Whitehaven in September, and well you know it."

Mother and daughter stared at each other for a long moment before Caroline looked away. "Abigail, your stubbornness shall surely be the demise of all our hopes."

Their hopes, Abigail rather thought, had already come to an end. "I would like to know."

"What does it matter?" Caroline repeated. "You are invited and you must go. There will be many gentlemen in attendance…"

All of whom had already passed her over as a potential wife, or with whom she would be out of favour regardless, thanks to a single moment's indiscretion while taking the waters in the north's only spa town.

"It matters," Abigail said in a hard voice, "because I thought it impossible. What have you done?"

"I? I have done nothing –"

"Papa, then."

A look of guilt flashed across her mother's face, rendering her like a child for a moment, and Abigail steeled herself. What new indignity would she have to face now? She'd already had her behaviour raked over in every genteel parlour in Whitehaven, her shame whispered and tittered about behind far too many manicured hands.

"Your father agreed to buy into John Tamworth's latest venture," Caroline finally said. "He's had trouble obtaining investors. Tobacco is all going into Glasgow these days, and the rest, it seems, to Mr Martin." Mr Martin, Abigail knew, had the majority of the tobacco trade in Whitehaven, and had for some years. "It is uncommonly hard for a man to make his fortune when there are so many others vying for the same trade."

Abigail sat heavily in a chair by the fire, barely noticing its comforting, if negligible, warmth.

"And you said this musical evening was at the Tamworths'?" she recalled quietly.

"Indeed, yes. But what does it matter how you procured the invitation, Abigail? Surely the thing is that you will be in attendance –"

"Everyone will be whispering about how I procured it. My father had to *buy* it for me." She could not quite keep the sharp edge of bitterness from her tone.

"Your father made an investment, that is all –"

"That he wouldn't have made otherwise?"

"Let us not descend to talking of business! It's so common."

"You know the truth of it, Mama," Abigail said despairingly.

How could she walk into that evening with everyone knowing how she had come to be there?

"Even so," Caroline protested, hands fluttering at her sides once more. "Even so, my dear –"

"It won't make any difference to my prospects, Mama. Surely you can see that." Over the last six months, there had been no talk among her family, not even a whisper, of her being ruined; her parents had too many hopes for their longed-for and much-awaited only child to use a word such as *that*.

It had all been bright, breezy chatter about how things blew over – how this time next year people wouldn't even remember Harrogate. Her father had blustered that in any case he thought the town was going to seed; its purging waters smelled so dreadful, who in their right mind would want to take a glass? Next year they would try Tunbridge Wells, or even Bath.

All of it had made Abigail ache with both guilt and regret; she could suffer her own great disappointment in silence, but to face her parents', day after endless day, and all for a naive mistake she'd made, believing a man was a gentleman simply because he'd held a title. What a fool she'd been. What a silly little fool.

"Abigail…" Caroline knotted her hands together at her waist, her chilblained knuckles swollen and red. "Please don't make a fuss about this. Your papa has gone to such effort."

"I won't make a fuss." Abigail forced a smile even though her heart felt like a stone inside her. She could not refuse her parents an occasion to hope, even if it all came to nothing, as it surely would. "And I think I shall wear the rose."

"Oh, thank you, my dear! It does suit you."

It did not, but Abigail forewent saying such a thing. Her mother was pleased, and that was all that mattered. She could endure an evening of acute embarrassment for that. Although how excruciating it would be she did not realize, until Caroline added happily, "And you'll take part, of course. I told the Tamworths that you would sing 'The Lass of Richmond Hill', with their daughter Georgiana accompanying on the pianoforte."

"Mama, you didn't!" Abigail stared at her mother in dismay. "You know I can barely carry a tune."

"Nonsense, you sing very well. And you must perform, Abigail. All the young ladies will."

Abigail shook her head, knowing there was no point in protesting. The thing was already done; to refuse now would be nearly as bad as the performance surely would be. Still, the evening, which had, to her own shame, shimmered with the faintest promise of interest despite all her pragmatic assertions, had now lost all its lustre, and was only something to dread.

The next evening Abigail walked into the murmuring crowds of the Tamworths' house on Argyll Street, lifting her chin and trying not to notice the various stares and whispers – just as she was trying not to be aware of how ill-suited she was to wear a robe of pale pink with a petticoat underneath sporting far too many ruffles. Her mother insisted on choosing what she considered to be the very latest fashions for her, even though Abigail knew her square jaw and straight body did not do well with such an excess of frills and lace.

The shade of pink, so becoming on a young woman with fair or dark hair, clashed impressively with Abigail's auburn. She suspected her mother chose it as a wilful denial that the shade of her thick and unmanageable locks was anything close to ginger, just as she'd insisted Jensen, the maid of all work who helped them dress, should powder her hair and fashion it into a towering style, even though Abigail suspected it was going out of date. She felt ridiculous, but she still attempted to walk with pride.

The two parlours on the Tamworths' first floor were full of Whitehaven's polite society, everyone murmuring and mingling, and Abigail recognized nearly all of those in attendance, just as she recognized that each and every one would have heard of her indiscretion at Harrogate; the whispers had travelled all the way over the fells, turnpike road or not.

Now she smiled at one acquaintance, and then another, their dressed hair and fine clothes blurring in front of her proud stare. Next to her, Caroline fluttered nervously, caught between anxiety and excitement, so wanting this evening to be a success when Abigail knew it would be anything but. And, she acknowledged wryly, she hadn't even sung yet. That humiliation, at least, would be saved until later.

"The Tamworths…" Caroline murmured, looking rather wildly around the room for the family purported to be their social saviours. Their generosity, however, did not seem to extend to socializing, for when Abigail caught Georgiana's eye, the young woman, thought soon to be engaged to the Jeffersons' second son, turned away.

It was like that. It was, Abigail reflected, *always* like that, no matter how hard her parents tried, how determined they were. Her grandfather had been a husbandman with fewer than forty acres; their beginnings were humble, and even though most of Whitehaven's merchant class had similar stories, the Heywoods had somehow never quite risen above the stink of the sheep pen next to the house. In fact, even now her father's warehouse was attached to their home, just as many other merchants' were, with a door between them.

Since the summer, her parents' determination had given way to desperation, and that only made things worse. If Abigail had had some small chance of procuring a husband of some description before the summer, it had faded to insignificance since because of her parents' obvious contrivances, as well as her own woeful misfortune.

The evening was, just as she'd expected, endless. They remained on the edge of the room, sipping lukewarm tea and straining to hear the nearby idle chatter and gossip. Abigail only hoped her own name was not mentioned.

Her father, at least, had been spared this embarrassment; he had gone into another room, with the other fathers and older sons, to talk business out of the ladies' hearing. Trade, it thankfully seemed, was not affected overmuch by society's whims.

At least when the music began, she had something to divert her attention, as well as everyone else's away from her; the assembly of guests seemed to spend an excess of energy in being seen to ignore her.

Of course, there was her own unfortunate rendition to suffer through. Abigail knew her parents were proud of her mediocre accomplishments; like her needlework, singing was not something she professed either to enjoy or to excel at, but her doting papa and mama had convinced themselves it was.

Soon enough, it was her turn to stand in front of the narrow-eyed audience, the unfriendly murmurs dying down to a gleefully expectant hush.

Colour surged into Abigail's cheeks as she stood by the pianoforte, a sullen Georgiana at its keys. She opened her mouth for the first note, unable to keep from wincing at its flat sound. Heaven help her, why did her mother put her through such a torturous exercise? Not to mention the torture visited on the gathered listeners.

Still Abigail kept singing, her head held high, her chin tilted as if daring anyone to titter behind their hands. "I'd crowns resign to call thee mine," she sang, and then nearly faltered as her gaze, focused blankly ahead, suddenly caught on a smile in the corner of the room – the glimmer of something other than indifference, vindictive glee, or pity.

It was a man, a gentleman Abigail didn't recognize, with hair a similar shade to her own, unpowdered and queued in the back. He wore simple clothes: a frock coat in dun brown, buff breeches, and rather weathered boots. And he was smiling at her.

Abigail nearly stuttered in her wretched song as she met his gaze; the colour of his eyes was startlingly bright. Unlike hers, which were the muddy murk of low tide, his were the dazzling blue of the windswept sea. Or so she would describe them if she were writing a romantic novel, but she'd never considered herself one for such silly notions off the written page.

Yet when he smiled, that tiny quirk of the corner of his mouth, she suddenly felt like laughing. She saw a look in his eyes, in his small smile, that made her feel as if she were sharing a joke rather than being for ever the butt of it.

And so Abigail straightened her spine as she sang, her voice soaring over the gathered assembly, its oft-faltering notes seeming, for once, as clear and pure as a lark's, as her gaze moved over the gathered assembly and then, inevitably, back to that of the smiling gentleman.

CHAPTER THREE

Rachel

Rachel rubbed her eyes wearily as she took a sip of her now-cold coffee. She'd spent the last hour on her laptop in the museum's little café, trying to find a match for the heart-shaped implement whose use she still hadn't figured out. Of course, knowing the provenance of the ship it had been on would have helped, but she wouldn't know that until the day after tomorrow, when her colleagues Ally and Dave joined her for a preliminary dive.

So far she hadn't come across anything online that looked like it, but she'd been distracted by various internet searches into the history of shipping in Whitehaven, scrolling through the online archives for ship registers, only to discover she would have to travel to Carlisle to look at them, and in any case she already knew the records didn't start until 1786, when ships had been required by law to register with a Customs House, which could very well be too late.

There were, of course, the National Archives in Kew, which would have outport records and customs collections for the period in question, as well as the local archives, which would have various records of merchant ships, but until she had more information, Rachel knew she could spend hours if not days or even weeks squinting at endless pages and reels of microfiche, looking for she knew not what. She needed more information about the wreck before she started trawling through various archives.

Next to her laptop her phone buzzed, and Rachel glanced at the name on the screen. Anthony. She hesitated, then turned her phone over. She'd call him later, from the B&B she'd booked into in the nearby village of Goswell, when she had some privacy, and the time and space to chat, although she still didn't know what she'd say.

She shut her laptop, trying not to feel dispirited. She couldn't really do much more today; she had meetings with Mark James of Cumbria's Historic Environment Service and Will Sayers, the liaison for the Copeland Mining Company, tomorrow, and until she talked to them, she was stuck.

Rachel suspected what both of them would say. *As interesting as this could be, there are thousands of wrecks off the coast. Unless you can find the money…*

With a sigh she slipped her laptop into her bag before rising from her chair and rolling her shoulders, which were tense from sitting hunched over for the last hour.

Giving a fleeting smile of farewell to the woman at the counter, Rachel headed back out to the harbourside. Now that evening was approaching, the damp Cumbrian chill in the air was noticeable, creeping beneath her fleece-lined windbreaker. She remembered it well from her childhood, along with the endless wind, constantly buffeting her as she walked along, rattling the windowpanes at night as she huddled in bed, her duvet pulled up to her chin, the house silent and empty all around her. Cumbria was a beautiful place, but as far as Rachel was concerned, the weather was terrible.

Now she hunched her shoulders against the wind off the harbour as she walked back to her car.

She could, of course, take the opportunity to visit her mother, especially if she wasn't going to be staying in the area all that long. Yet Rachel resisted the notion, as she so often did, because her relationship with her mother was prickly at best, and often downright distant. If her father were still alive…

But that was a train of thought she never let herself entertain, because it was so pointless and so sad. She hated the way it made her feel, as if an emptiness were whistling through her. It had been twenty-five years since her father died, and it still hurt, a wound that never truly healed, a scab she kept picking at despite her best intentions not to.

Pushing thoughts of her parents aside, Rachel decided to take a walk through Whitehaven and enjoy its crumbling Georgian charms. Although having lived only a little more than an hour away, she'd never visited the town, and despite the damp chill in the air, she was looking forward to exploring more; perhaps she'd even discover something of use to the shipwreck, although admittedly that possibility seemed slight.

Still, it was fascinating to think that the owner of the wreck had almost certainly walked these streets, and perhaps even lived in one of the elegant townhouses she was walking by now.

Rachel headed down the town's main thoroughfare, the appropriately named Lowther Street. She'd already learned that the Lowther family had engineered the development of the town over three hundred years ago, with a Georgian grid of streets that New York and other American cities had been allegedly modelled on.

She was idly inspecting the window fronts of various shops when, next to a pretty flower shop, she stopped in front of a sign for a museum – The Rum Story, "the dark spirit of Whitehaven", about its association with the shipping of rum and its dependence on the slave trade.

Intrigued, she headed down the little alleyway that led to a courtyard café and the entrance of the museum. She was just glancing at some rusted manacles in a display on the wall when a woman from behind the till spoke.

"I'm sorry, we're just about to close," she said with a grimace of apology.

"Oh, are you?" Disappointment swooped inside her and Rachel stepped closer to a glass cabinet near the till filled with curios of the slave trade – a rusted neck collar, some clay beads used for trading, a scrap of a ship's log detailing the number of human losses.

"Yes, but we open again tomorrow at ten. You're welcome to come then."

"Right." Rachel's gaze trained in on one of the items in the case: what looked like a pair of pliers – with a heart-shaped handle. Her heart felt as if it were expanding in her chest, and then squeezing hard. "Sorry," she said quickly to the attendant who was clearly trying not to seem impatient, "I'm in Whitehaven investigating a shipwreck and I just thought I might have…" She trailed off as she peered closer at the implement, and then glanced at the little plaque beneath, explaining what it was: "A speculum oris, used to force open the jaws of slaves so they were not able to starve themselves while on board ship."

A frisson of horror ran through her at the grim thought. That innocent-looking heart, used for such an inhumane and evil act. But it meant that the shipwreck could very well have been a slave ship, with undoubted historical significance.

"I'm sorry, miss, but I really do need to close up now."

"Yes, yes, of course." Rachel nodded, her gaze surveying the double doors of dark glass that led into the museum; she couldn't see anything beyond them. "Yes, I'll come back tomorrow."

Back outside she headed for her car, deciding there was no point wandering around any longer. She'd check into the B&B, get something to eat, and see if she could find out more about the slave trade of Whitehaven. She hadn't even realized that

Whitehaven, such a small, remote town, had once had a slave trade. She'd assumed that the trade had stayed in the more major ports of Bristol, Liverpool, and London. But if that heart-shaped handle really was part of a speculum oris…

The drive from Whitehaven to Goswell, a village just a few miles away, was lovely, rolling hills giving way to sparkling glimpses of the sea. As Rachel crested the top of the hill leading down into the village, she was struck by its pastoral beauty – a row of pastel-coloured terraced cottages, a plume of smoke curling lazily into the sky; a train pulling out of the station that bisected the village, and a squat Norman church fronting a sheep paddock.

She drove slowly down Goswell's main street, then took the beach road towards the sea until she found the B&B, a Victorian terraced house with flower boxes under every window and an uninterrupted view of the sea, with its long, sandy sweep of tidal beach.

"The rain's held off for you," the woman at the front desk remarked cheerily as Rachel checked in. "I'm afraid I don't do suppers, but there's a lovely pub in the middle of the village. Breakfast is anytime you like between seven and nine."

"Sounds perfect, thank you," Rachel murmured as she took her key and started to lug her bag up the narrow stairs. Her room was small and cosy, with a brass bedstead, a Victorian washbowl on top of the chest of drawers, and a lovely view of the beach.

Rachel dumped her bag on the floor and sat on the bed, soaking in the sight of the slate-grey sea stretching to an unknown horizon. In the distance, she could just make out the hilly, violet haze of the Isle of Man.

She felt a sudden, surprising sweep of loneliness – something she hardly ever felt, because she *liked* being alone. She was a solitary creature, always had been, at least since the age of twelve, when she was forced into it by the death of her father, and her mother's alienation.

Yet for a few seconds, staring out at that endless, empty sea, Rachel felt sorrow roll through her like an echo, and she realized it was, at least in part, because of that heart-shaped handle of the speculum oris. Such a horrible device, and it gave rise to vague and deeply disturbing imaginings of what life aboard a slave ship could have been like, the grief and sorrow of so many that those rotted timbers might once have held – if it really was a slave ship.

Why had it sunk off the coast, so close to Whitehaven's harbour? And who had been on it?

Suppressing a strange little shiver, Rachel opened her bag and unpacked her things. The excitement of working on a new find was tempered by the knowledge of what kind of ship it could have been, and she couldn't quite shake the unease she felt about it all. Now that she was settled in the room, she decided to do a quick internet search on the slave trade in Whitehaven. She was soon clicking link after link, frowning as she scanned the information she'd had no idea about, jotting down the relevant details.

Her phone buzzed, and she saw it was Anthony ringing again. This time she decided to take it.

"Hello, I'm here." She tried to sound cheerful.

"Thank goodness. I was getting worried."

"There was no need."

"I can't help it, Rach. You're my wife. That's the way I am." He sounded light, friendly, but his words still rankled with the things he wasn't saying but she knew he was implying. Still, Rachel let it all pass over her. She wasn't going to be snippy with him now. She *wasn't*. "So what's the wreck like?" Anthony asked.

"I haven't seen it yet, besides some drone footage, but…" She hesitated, unsure whether she wanted to voice her suspicions about the nature of the ship to her husband.

Anthony didn't really *get* what she did. He listened, of course; he could be a wonderful listener. But he didn't understand the logistics, or the legalities, or even her interest in maritime archaeology, the importance of a site or a find. He was a chef; he lived in the present, the tangible, the experienced, and her fascination with the past perplexed him. Really, they came at life from completely opposite ends. But shouldn't that mean they met in the middle?

"Rach?" he prompted, and she let out a weary breath.

"I viewed some of the wreckage and I think… I think the ship might have been a slave ship."

"A slave ship? In Cumbria?"

"Yes, Whitehaven had a small slave trade in the mid-1700s. Nothing to rival Liverpool or Bristol, but still." She checked the notes she'd scrawled on the back of an envelope. "Between 1750 and 1769, there were over sixty ships involved in the trade that sailed from Whitehaven to Africa and then the West Indies, before coming back again."

"Huh. I had no idea."

She hadn't either, really; living in Bristol, of course, she knew all about its horrible history with the slave trade, and how much of the city had been built on its wretched back. But Whitehaven, a forgettable market town in the wild reaches of Cumbria? "Apparently, in the eighteenth century, it was a port rivalling that of Liverpool or even London, although it's a bit hard to see that now."

"So what makes you think it's a slave ship?"

"I found a device." Again she had the urge to shiver, as though something were raking along her skin. "It's horrible. Used to force open the mouths of slaves when they were trying to starve themselves."

"How awful." Anthony paused, and she could picture him shaking his head, that slow back and forth. "I can't even imagine it."

"Nor can I. But if it is a slave ship, it could be an important discovery. Very few wrecks of slave ships have ever been found. The São José off the coast of Africa, the Clotilda in the States – there's a whole group of archaeologists dedicated to what is called the Slave Wrecks Project."

"Then shouldn't they be involved?"

A little stung, Rachel replied a bit sharply, "I was the one the mining company rang. I'm the one here."

"I know, but if there are already experts available…"

Rachel knew he had a point, just as she knew he wasn't really interested in how much she loved her work. What he really wanted was her back home, going to dinner with their friends. She suppressed a sigh. "Did you reschedule the dinner?"

A pause, and then Anthony said in a rather diffident voice, "Actually, no. We decided to go ahead and meet up just the three of us, since it's so hard to find a date that works for everyone." Another pause, this one seeming laden. "I didn't think you'd mind."

"Oh. Right." Rachel sifted through her jumbled feelings and decided she didn't mind. Why should she? Elspeth and Ken were more Anthony's friends than hers; they'd met when he'd catered a private dinner party for them. Apparently he'd stayed afterwards, drinking whisky and chatting into the small hours of the morning. Rachel had been a later addition, the invariable add-on. "Well, I hope you have fun."

"Thanks. I will."

Another silence, this one definitely becoming tense. Rachel felt as if she should apologize, but for what? All she'd done was go to work, just as Anthony did, night after night, and she didn't complain. Yet she knew it was different; that she was different. And she knew Anthony knew it as well.

"I should go," she finally said. "I haven't eaten yet, and I think tomorrow will be a busy day."

"All right. Let me know how it goes."

"I will." She hung up without saying goodbye, not out of pique, but because that was simply the way she ended calls, and as she stared out at the sea afterwards, she wondered how it was possible a conversation with someone you loved could make you feel even lonelier than when you'd been sitting by yourself.

It was her fault, she acknowledged not for the first time as she grabbed her coat and headed out to the pub the proprietor of the B&B had mentioned. The air was still damp and smelled of coal smoke, the main street heading steeply uphill. Rachel walked briskly, her hands swinging at her sides, her head down, as was her way.

Yes, it was her fault. She didn't know how to be a wife. She certainly hadn't learned the art from her mother, and she'd lived most of her adult life alone, moving from place to place, first for her various degrees, and then on different digs and work sites.

She'd never figured out how to share her life, her thoughts, her fears and dreams. Even the prospect of doing so made her wince and cringe. She didn't know how to invite people in, something so many others found easy. She had a few friends, but she kept them at a bit of a distance, out of habit or instinct, and she'd always been okay with that. She hadn't wanted more.

As for her most intimate relationship, she found it hard work. She didn't want to, tried for it not to be, but it was all the same. All too often she prickled, she resisted, she snapped; she knew all that, and yet she couldn't keep herself from doing it.

In a dark, dusty corner of her heart, she feared that Anthony would tire of her one day – tire of her diffidence and distance and the coolness that entered her voice without her even realizing it. He would tire of it all and he would leave her. She wouldn't blame him, either, and part of her wondered if it would come as a relief, even as another part quelled in terror at the thought. She didn't want to be left. Not again.

The pub was full of noise and laughter as Rachel opened the door, ducking her head under the low stone lintel. A fire burned cheerily in a large stone fireplace, and groups of people had moved tables and chairs together to create huddles of bodies and conversation, the clink of glasses punctuated by a sudden loud laugh.

Rachel made her way to a table for two in the corner at the back, trying not to feel even worse than she had alone in her room. At the table near her several women were laughing and talking expansively, gesturing with their hands as one woman stood up and began to top up all their glasses.

"Oh Jane, really, I shouldn't."

"Nonsense, we're celebrating. It's half-term!" The woman who was pouring let out a slightly manic laugh. "All our lovely children home for an entire week. What could be better?"

This was met with a chorus of groans as well as laughter, and the clink of refreshed glasses raised in a toast. Rachel watched them covertly, fascinated despite herself.

They were like an alien breed, these women, with their children and their husbands, their busy lives, full of family and friends and evenings out. They were all dressed up for a night out together, with make-up and jewellery, high-heeled boots and perfume. Rachel's face was scrubbed clean; she was wearing old jeans and a ratty fleece, and her husband was going to dinner without her.

As for children, that was a subject she didn't let herself think about very often. At thirty-seven, it was getting too late anyway – a fact that Anthony had reminded her of more than once. She'd been putting him off for one reason or another – because they hadn't been married for long, because work was so busy – but eventually she wouldn't be able to. He'd want to know why, and she didn't know if she had an answer, or at least one he'd accept.

"Are you really going camping, Ellen?" another woman at the table asked, and Rachel watched out of the corner of her eye as a woman with sandy, frizzy hair and a friendly, open face gave a comical groan. "Yes, Andrew convinced me. I don't know how. Even Annabel has agreed, and you know what she's like."

"Chloe must be thrilled, though. She loves camping. She and Merrie rigged up an old tent in the garden last summer. Do you remember?" the woman who had refilled their wine glasses, Jane, said fondly. "It poured with rain, but they insisted on staying out the whole night, daft things."

"I'm sure it will be fun." This from the quietest member of the group, a dark-haired woman with sad-looking eyes and a thoughtful smile.

"I hope so, Marin. I hope so." Ellen pretended to shudder before throwing back a large swallow of wine.

Jane noticed Rachel and looked puzzled, but then offered her a cautiously friendly smile. Rachel couldn't make herself return it as she looked quickly away, picking up the laminated menu and studying it far too intently. Her cheeks burned as she realized she'd been caught blatantly eavesdropping, and whatever for? She didn't know these women. She certainly didn't care about them.

"What can I get you, love?" a waitress asked as she came up to Rachel's table with a friendly smile.

"Umm… the veggie lasagne, please." Rachel glanced back at the menu. "And a glass of white wine."

"Pinot Grigio do you?"

"Yes, fine, thanks." She handed the woman the menu with a distracted smile, and to her dismay she caught Jane's eye again.

Jane waved her glass merrily at her. "I can heartily recommend the Pinot Grigio."

The other two women with her – Ellen and Marin, Rachel remembered they were called – twisted round in their seats to give her looks of unabashed curiosity.

Rachel managed a tight smile. "Thank you," she said. "I look forward to it."

An uncomfortable silence lingered as they all looked at each other, and with nothing else to do, Rachel reached for her phone. No signal, but she pretended there was, thumbing some random icons and trying to look intent.

After what felt like several minutes but surely could only have been a few seconds, the women turned back around and resumed their conversation.

"Where is it you're camping, Ellen?"

"Near Ravenglass."

"So pretty."

"What about you, Marin? What are you and Joss up to? Is Rebecca back from uni yet?"

"Not yet, but we're driving up to Edinburgh mid-week to fetch her. She's got so much stuff."

Rachel let the conversation drift over her, this impossible, unobtainable world she had never felt a part of – people busy and involved, cheerful and excited.

She thought of her own desperately quiet childhood, silent dinners, empty evenings, her father's absence between her and her mother like an awful, impossible chasm. When she'd left for uni, she hadn't looked back. At least she'd tried not to, and yet when it came to her mother, Rachel always found herself trying. Hoping.

When the waitress came back with her wine, she thanked her and downed half of it in two quick gulps, craving the blunting of all her edges. Her phone had signal now, and she pulled up her internet browser, determined to spend the time researching slave ships rather than listen to a conversation she was not a part of, and that made her feel as if she was missing something, and always would be.

She touched the search bar and started typing: "Slave ships of Whitehaven, shipwrecks" and then waited for the results to load.

CHAPTER FOUR

Abigail

Whitehaven, 1763

"His name is Mr Fenton, and he is a tobacco trader. He was a sea captain at the start, but now he merely invests. He owns one ship, and he has recently moved to Whitehaven from Liverpool. His family is from Furness."

Abigail put down her neglected needlework to stare at her mother in confusion. "Who are you talking about, Mama?"

"Why, the gentleman, of course!" Caroline came into the sitting room, her face alight with purposeful excitement. "The gentleman from the musical evening who could not keep his eyes off you, I might add!"

Abigail blushed and looked away. She knew, of course, whom her mother was talking about, although the description, as it often was with her mama, was exaggerated. Mr Fenton had most certainly been able to keep his eyes off her, and had done so for most of the evening.

And yet, the memory of his smile, that teasing glint in his eyes, had kept her awake for the last three nights, sweetly revisiting it. It was little to build a dream on, but one used what one had, and all Abigail possessed was a smile – and now a name.

"Mr Fenton, you say? From Furness?"

"Indeed. His father was an innkeeper."

"What sort of inn?" Abigail asked. She was not sure how she felt about that; she pictured a brawny man with a red face and sleeves rolled up, rolling barrels of beer.

"Oh la, what does it matter?" Caroline dismissed. "The important thing surely is that he has made his own fortune."

"Has he a fortune?"

"One ship, and," Caroline paused, imparting this bit of information with deliberate relish, "he intends to commission the building of a second upon his marriage."

"His marriage!" Abigail couldn't keep the disappointment from seeping into her voice as it curdled her insides. "He is to be wed?"

"Faith, child, not yet!" Caroline's smile was wide as she plumped herself in a chair by the fire, quite overcome by her verbal exertions. "He intends to be, that is all. He has recently come to Whitehaven to set himself up. He is already three and thirty. I am sure he is quite ready to find a wife."

"He has a house here?"

"He is renting rooms on Lowther Street."

"Rooms…" Not that she minded, of course, but Abigail could see already that Mr Fenton was not quite the brilliant catch her mother made him out to be. The son of an innkeeper, with one ship and a set of rented rooms – Georgiana Tamworth would almost certainly turn her nose up at such an offer. "Where did you learn all this?" she asked her mother.

"From Mrs Tamworth. Mr Fenton has already been introduced to them through a mutual acquaintance, and she will make our own introductions presently."

"She will?" Sourly Abigail wondered how much that had cost her father. The Tamworths' generosity knew no bounds, it seemed, at least as far as her father's purse was concerned.

"Yes, and he shall come to supper." Caroline could not resist bringing her hands together in a little clap. "Abigail, my dear, this could be the beginning of all our hopes."

Which made Abigail both wince and wish, an uncomfortable combination. "We do not even know him, Mama –"

"He is a young gentleman of means! You have taken his fancy! And he is new to Whitehaven."

This made Abigail blush, along with everything else. Yes, Mr Fenton was newly come to Whitehaven, but if he hadn't heard the whispers about her yet, he surely would. "Even so –"

"Abigail, please." Caroline's gay manner dropped as if she'd shed a cloak. "Do not dampen our enthusiasms. This is a great hope."

Tears pricked Abigail's eyes and she bit her lip, determined to keep them back. She could not begrudge her parents such a hope, even if it came to nothing, as it surely would. Still, for all their sakes, she felt she had to issue a warning.

"Mama, if he doesn't know, he will discover it," she said in a low voice. The silence that ensued was heavy-laden, suffocated with disappointment. Abigail glanced at her mother from under her lashes and saw that she was looking weary and drawn as she stared into the fire.

Without the usual animation of her expression, her mother looked old and careworn; she was already well past fifty years of age. Abigail had been an unexpected blessing later in life, after many miscarriages.

"I'm sorry," Abigail whispered, although she did not even know what she was apologizing for. Her foolishness of six months ago, or the reminder of it now? Or the fact that she was unlikely to find a husband, since she possessed no great beauty and an unfortunate past?

Her mother straightened, a flash of determination lighting her tired brown eyes. "There is nothing we can do about what happened in Harrogate," she said firmly. "I think perhaps the wisest way forward is for you to mention it to him directly, yourself."

"What!" Abigail stared at her, aghast. "I couldn't possibly –"

"You must. When the moment is at hand, of course. It is hardly a polite topic of conversation around the table." Her mother's lips twitched in an unlikely smile. "When you are alone with him, of course, and you deem it – appropriate."

"And when shall I be alone with him?" Abigail cried. "I do not know the man, and you know what the dangers of being alone can be…" She trailed off, unable to remind her mother yet again of her own folly.

"Mr Fenton is a gentleman," Caroline stated with conviction. "And if he should wish a turn around the garden with you –"

"Mama, it is *January*."

"Even so. Or if not completely alone, then mostly alone. In the drawing room, while the others play whist, perhaps."

Abigail's face heated with mortification. "Mama, I couldn't."

"You must." An unusually hard note entered Caroline's voice. "You must, Abigail, because we may not have another chance."

Three days later, Abigail stood in her bedroom, gazing worriedly at her reflection. Mr Fenton, along with the Tamworths, the vicar and his wife, was expected in a quarter of an hour.

"You are looking very well, Miss Heywood," Jensen said loyally as she put the hair tongs away. "Very well indeed."

"I do not feel very well." In fact, her stomach was roiling with nerves and her face held a greyish cast that had nothing to do with the white powder Jensen had put on her face, along with a touch of rouge made from beetroot and beeswax. Abigail rarely wore such cosmetics, but tonight her mother had insisted the effort was worthwhile.

Abigail had refused the hair powder her mother had wanted, however; she believed powdering one's hair was going out of style, although her mother disagreed, and in any case Mr Fenton had not worn any at the musical evening. Caroline had, thankfully, let the matter go.

Her dress was in the latest style, at least of those that had come to Whitehaven, with a robe over a frilled petticoat, wide panniers that nearly brushed the doorways, and a stomacher in floral-pattered silk. The colour was far more becoming than the rose of the musical evening; the deep russet complemented Abigail's hair, or at least she hoped it did. This was, after all, their Last Great Hope.

It felt as if a flock of swallows had nested in her stomach and they were swarming towards her throat as she considered the import of the occasion. What if Mr Fenton was not interested in her? What if he preferred Georgiana Tamworth? It had been necessary to invite her, much to both Caroline's and Abigail's dismay. Would Mr Fenton prefer Georgiana's blonde curls and sour face? Perhaps, especially if he'd already heard the whispers about Abigail.

"Abigail!" Caroline came into the room, and immediately began to fuss with her daughter's hair, arranging a curl over one shoulder, another by her ear.

"Jensen's done wonderfully, Mama," Abigail begged. "Please don't fuss." Her hair was styled higher than it ever had been before, with fat sausage-like curls resting on her shoulders.

"I still think some powder," Caroline murmured, and Abigail shook her head, careful not to dislodge her elegantly upswept hair. "Very well, very well. Our guests will be here shortly. Do come downstairs."

Moments later their downstairs maid Lane was opening the door, and although she'd never heard him speak, Abigail felt as if she recognized the voice of the gentleman who entered – vibrant, slightly too loud, with a Lancashire accent. She threw her mother a frightened, excited look, and Caroline's chin lifted, a gracious calm coming over her as she straightened her shoulders and sailed forward to meet their guest.

"Mr Fenton. I am so delighted to make your acquaintance at last."

Abigail watched, frozen, by the drawing room fire, while Mr Fenton bowed low over her mother's hand. "As am I, Mrs Heywood. Assuredly, as am I." As he straightened, his gaze – those blue eyes glinted so – met Abigail's, one eyebrow raised gently in inquiry. Her heart felt as if it had galloped into her throat, and she feared the expression on her face resembled that of a snared and terrified rabbit.

"Please, allow me to introduce our daughter, Miss Heywood," Caroline said, rather grandly, flinging one arm out towards Abigail as if she were presenting the loveliest specimen of womankind. Abigail bobbed a nervous curtsey, her hand near to shaking as she held it out.

Mr Fenton bowed over it, lifting his head to meet her gaze yet again as he remained half bent. "A pleasure, Miss Heywood."

"Likewise," she whispered. Her voice sounded thin and papery, and Mr Fenton smiled.

Afterwards, Abigail did not remember much of the evening; it passed in a blur of both terror and joy as she stuttered through the most basic of pleasantries, her mind feeling as if it had been emptied. She suffered Georgiana Tamworth's snide looks and Mrs

Tamworth's far worse sly innuendoes. "Poor Miss Heywood has not been very sociable this autumn." Abigail held her tongue as her mother gave her an unnecessarily quelling look, forbidding her to be drawn on the wretched topic.

She could barely touch any of the dozen dishes that their mahogany table bowed beneath; Caroline had gaily informed the party that they would be dining à *la française*, with everything brought out at once, which she believed to be the fashion. Abigail did not know if it was any more; Whitehaven's fashions tended to be out of date, her mother's even more so.

"Are you not enjoying your meal?" Mr Fenton asked quietly. He had, naturally, been seated next to her, with Georgiana at the far end, next to the vicar and his wife, who had been invited simply to make up the numbers.

Abigail's startled gaze flew to his. "Wh-why do you ask?"

Mr Fenton smiled down at her, that lovely quirking of his lips making her heart flutter. "Because you are not eating it."

"Oh." Abigail glanced down at her untouched veal cutlet and lamb and salad, blushing. "I…" She could hardly admit she could not eat because she was so very nervous. "I suppose I have other things to occupy my mind."

Too late she realized how forward that might have sounded, and she blushed all the harder when Mr Fenton murmured back, "As do I."

"I hope your thoughts do not trouble you," Abigail managed after a few torturous seconds where she struggled to think of a suitable reply.

"Indeed, they do not trouble me at all. In fact, quite the contrary, Miss Heywood."

She had to look away under his glinting gaze, willing her blush to recede. Why on earth had she allowed Jensen to put rouge on her cheeks? She surely did not need it. She must look as if she were on fire.

"I hope I have not said something amiss," Mr Fenton said after a moment.

"Not at all," Abigail returned, struggling to keep her voice light. With a daring she had not known she possessed, she turned back to him with a smile. "Quite the contrary, Mr Fenton," she parroted his words back to him, and smiled properly, revealing a dimple in one cheek.

"How very pleasant."

She smiled then too, noticing Georgiana's narrow-eyed gaze from the end of the table, where the vicar was boring everyone by talking about the state of his tithe barn. She had nothing to worry about, Abigail assured herself; this was all most respectable – and most thrilling.

"I suppose you think you might catch him," Georgiana said spitefully to her an hour later, when they had retired from the dining room, and the ladies were alone in the drawing room, waiting for the men to return from taking their port and snuff.

Abigail stiffened at Georgiana's words. "I do not take your meaning," she replied coolly.

"I'm quite sure you do. Watching you at table – it was disgraceful. Almost as disgraceful as your antics last summer."

Abigail clenched her hands into fists, hidden by her skirts. She could not believe Georgiana could be so uncouth as to make such a remark. "I think I shall ask Mrs Quimby about her charitable work," Abigail said stiffly, and walked blindly towards the vicar's wife, who was more than happy to discuss the poor folk she kindly visited with baskets of calves'-foot jelly and various liniments.

Abigail's stomach writhed with nerves as she listened to the woman chatter blithely on, one eye on the door, waiting for it to open and the gentlemen to be ushered in. Her stays felt too tight, and her hair, so elaborately and ridiculously curled, was starting to itch. Although she'd barely managed a mouthful at supper, she felt as if she could lose what little she'd had at any moment.

Then the gentlemen came in on a gust of air and a burst of laughter, and her heart rose along with her gorge, so she pressed one hand against her stomacher, willing it all back down. Mr Fenton's gaze met hers directly, surprising her with the intent in his eyes. He had not a qualm as he made his way over to her and Mrs Quimby.

"I trust you've had an agreeable evening."

"Very agreeable," Abigail murmured. She lowered her gaze, unable to look at him directly; it felt like looking at the sun. Of course she knew, in a distant, pragmatic way, that Mr Fenton was not as dazzling as all that. His reddish hair was thinning on top, and his calves, in stockings that certainly could have been a more brilliant shade of white, were slightly scrawny, without the pleasing, muscular roundness current fashion dictated. His manners were refined but clearly learned, and while he was most certainly a member of polite society, it was only just.

And yet. And yet her heart twirled in her chest just to look at him, and when he smiled she felt like singing.

Abigail was not sure how, but Mr Fenton contrived to spirit her away from Mrs Quimby, and while a game of whist started at the table by the window, Abigail found herself sitting on the sofa by the fire with him, her tongue well and truly tied. His attention was so warm and so sure, she did not know what to make of it. Why had he sought her out so directly? What on earth could she possess to recommend herself to him so thoroughly?

"I fear I am a poor conversationalist, Mr Fenton," she managed when they'd sat in silence for a few minutes, the fire crackling and popping near them. "Almost as poor a conversationalist as I am a musician." She felt she had to say it, for he'd suffered through her assuredly mediocre rendition of "The Lass of Richmond Hill".

Mr Fenton let out a low laugh. "I was enchanted by your singing, Miss Heywood."

She stared at him in disbelief. "You surely were not!"

His eyes glinted merrily as he answered, "Indeed I was. For I could tell from your rather pained expression that you were not enjoying the experience one jot, and yet you sang on. It was quite remarkable, Miss Heywood. Quite admirable." He leaned forward so she breathed in the bergamot scent of his pomade. "Even if the tune was not quite…" He trailed off deliberately, his eyes alight with merriment, and Abigail gave a choked laugh, half horror, half amusement.

"Really, Mr Fenton. You should not insult a lady so!"

"I assure you, I meant it as a compliment."

Abigail looked away, fearing their talk was too flirtatious. She did not want to be made a fool of again. It would hurt far worse the second time.

"Miss Heywood? I trust I have not offended you with my jest?"

"Not at all." She swallowed. "I am well aware of my musical accomplishment, or lack thereof." He chuckled softly and she was emboldened to ask, "How long have you been in Whitehaven, sir?"

"Only a few weeks, but I intend to reside here permanently."

"And have you made much of what little society we have?"

"I hope to do so in time. The acquaintances I have made thus far have proved to be quite agreeable." She could not mistake the warmth of his words, and she swallowed again. From across the room she caught her mother's eye and saw her give a meaningful nod. She could not say it, Abigail thought frantically; not on so short an acquaintance! She could not admit her woeful shortcomings, and yet...

Caroline glared from her seat at the whist table. Abigail swallowed hard. Was she to risk everything on this? Jeopardize any happiness she might find?

"I wonder," she said, hearing the false note of jollity in her voice and inwardly cringing at it, "if you have ever taken the waters at Harrogate? I did so last summer, and I thought perhaps you might have heard of it?" She paused, forcing herself to turn back to him, though everything in her trembled. "I must confess, I found it all quite... unpleasant," she said, her eyes firmly on his waistcoat, for she could not bear to look him in the face. "Surprisingly so. People here make such a to-do of the purging waters, but I daresay I would not deign to try them again."

Terrified, Abigail lifted her gaze to Mr Fenton's and was jolted to the core by the compassion she saw there, the softness in his eyes seeming almost tender. She pressed one hand to her throat, overcome by his emotion, as well as her own.

"Indeed, I have heard about Harrogate," he said quietly. "And I must confess, it seems to be quite a palaver over nothing very much indeed. I have no desire to try the purging waters, I assure you."

Abigail sagged against the sofa, her heart thudding painfully inside her. She felt as if she could have wept with relief, and yet she was still afraid to take Mr Fenton's words at more than their mere face value.

"Indeed," she whispered, and found she could not say much more. "Indeed."

Mr Fenton leaned forward. "I wonder, Miss Heywood, if you would do me the honour of dancing with me at the next assembly? I hope I am not too forward in procuring an acceptance from you at such an early date, but I am quite determined to dance the minuet with you."

A blush warmed Abigail's cheeks once again, but this time it was one of fragile, incredulous delight. "I would be glad to do you such an honour, Mr Fenton," she murmured, lowering her gaze appropriately.

When she looked up again, she saw her mother from across the room, her cards quite forgotten, as she flashed Abigail a smile of triumph. Their Last Great Hope was surely being realized.

CHAPTER FIVE

······································

Rachel

"There is most likely nothing significant about that wreck. We've done our duty in reporting it, and we'll fund an initial dive to determine what we surely all know – it's nothing more than some rotted wood and old iron."

As an opening gambit, it was exactly what Rachel had expected. She was sitting at a conference table in a stuffy room of Copeland Mining Company's office in a 1960s box of a building on the outskirts of Whitehaven. Across from her was Will Sayers, whose job it seemed was to get the mining company's work back on track as quickly as possible.

"That is very likely," Mark James, the consultant from Cumbria's Historic Environment Service, admitted with a wry grimace. He was there in an advisory capacity only, as the service did not do commercial work. Rachel would be the one to submit her findings to the Department for Digital, Culture, Media and Sport, and wait to hear their verdict. "Still, it needs to be determined first."

"Fine." Will Sayers rolled his powerful shoulders, his neck giving a wince-inducing crack. He was a handsome man, in a blunt, bluff way, his shirt sleeves rolled up on powerful forearms, his face tanned and wind-burned, despite having an office job. Rachel imagined him fell running at weekends, doing marathons in his spare time. He seemed that kind of man. "Surely one dive will determine whether this wreck has…" He paused to give his notes a brief scan. "Heritage assets?"

"Possibly," Rachel allowed. "In fact, I believe the wreck has already produced a heritage asset." She paused to make sure she had both men's attention. "The piece of iron caught by the core matrix is, I believe, the handle of a speculum oris, a device used to force open the mouths of slaves."

A silence greeted this pronouncement, with Will looking entirely nonplussed, and Mark's gaze narrowing in thoughtful consideration.

"Are you saying you think the wreck is a slave ship?" Mark asked.

Rachel nodded. "It seems likely, considering what was found."

"Speculum orises were also used by dentists," Mark pointed out.

"On a ship?"

He shrugged. "It's not conclusive."

"No, which is why we need to have a preliminary dive."

"What does it matter if it's a slave ship?" Will asked, curiosity warring with impatience. "Especially if there's nothing left."

"There are very few wrecks of slave ships," Rachel explained as evenly as she could. Will's manner grated on her, even as she acknowledged there was something compelling about him with his intense, blue stare and his barely leashed energy. She couldn't really blame him for wanting her to get her job done, so he could continue with his. "So finding one, in any type of condition, could be significant."

"But if there's nothing there –"

"Something has already been shown to be there," Rachel couldn't keep from interjecting. "The speculum oris. And in the drone footage I viewed yesterday, I believe I saw a bar of iron, which often served as ballast in a slave ship, as a counterweight to the human cargo."

"But why would a slave ship founder so close to Whitehaven harbour?" Mark asked.

"Plenty of ships sank there. It's shallow and rocky." Although this was a bit farther out than most, which did make her wonder how it had sunk.

"But it wouldn't have been carrying slaves," Mark ruminated. "It would have been on the third leg of the trade, most likely carrying rum and sugar."

Rachel couldn't argue with that, but Will leaned forward, sensing something deeper in Mark's words. "The third leg? What does that mean?"

"The transatlantic slave trade was a triangular journey," Mark explained. "Ships would have left Whitehaven, or Liverpool, or Bristol, and gone to the west coast of Africa – known as the slave coast – where they traded beads and brass goods and sometimes weapons in exchange for slaves, often captives from wars between various African tribes. They then took the slaves on what is known as the dreaded middle passage, to sell in the Caribbean and Americas. Then they loaded up with rum, sugar, tobacco, and spices, and returned to Britain." He gave a little shudder. "Horrible business. Many died on the middle passage – the conditions were unbearable."

"So why is it significant that the ship would have been on its third leg?" Will asked.

Rachel exchanged a look with Mark, feeling her determined optimism start to leave her in a regrettable trickle.

"Well," he began slowly, "if there were no slaves on board, then it becomes similar to a wreck of a merchant ship, and I suppose of somewhat less historical significance." He gave Rachel an apologetic grimace. "Although still noteworthy for sure, especially if it still had items related to the slave trade on board, which it seems to. Have you read of the wreck of São José?"

Will shook his head; of course he hadn't heard of it.

"It was a very interesting discovery off the coast of Cape Town a few years ago," Rachel jumped in. "Around three hundred years ago, the ship got stuck on a reef and broke apart. Two hundred and twelve slaves drowned, and the rest were sold to local farmers."

"Very sad," Will said with a nod, "but what does it have to do with this?"

"It was the first ship to be discovered to have been wrecked with slaves on board," Mark explained. "Which made it historically significant."

"But this one isn't." Of course he cut right to the heartless nub of the matter.

"But it could be," Rachel protested a bit desperately. "We've already discovered a significant relic, simply by chance. The handle that was thrown up from the core matrix will undoubtedly be acquired by a museum."

"So let's see what you find on an initial dive," Will said. "After that we can talk. We'd like to get the test drills up and running as soon as possible."

Rachel nodded. "We'll know more after I can see what's left."

"If anything much is," Will said with a tight smile.

An hour later Rachel was stepping into the dim interior of The Rum Story on Lowther Street. Her colleagues Dave and Ally would be arriving tomorrow, and assuming conditions were favourable, they would dive the next day. She could hardly wait.

The same woman was at the till of the museum, and she smiled as Rachel came in. "You're back. I wondered if you would return."

"Definitely," Rachel said as she paid for her ticket. "I'm really interested in this period of history."

"You mentioned a shipwreck…"

"Yes, just off the coast." Rachel paused, knowing she shouldn't say too much, considering the sensitive nature of the mining company's work. "It might be a slave ship," she admitted cautiously, as it was still mere speculation on her part. "But nothing's conclusive yet. So I thought I'd have a look here."

"There were a few slave ships going in and out of Whitehaven, back in the day," the woman said. "As you can see from our exhibition. It never rivalled Liverpool or Bristol, of course, but it was still surprisingly significant. Unfortunately. No one likes to talk about it now."

"It is horrible, isn't it?" Rachel said quietly. Her gaze caught on a framed, faded plan of the interior of a slave ship, with its many narrow holds for human cargo. She could not imagine the terrible suffering the people held there would have endured. She felt compelled to enter the museum and discover it for herself, even though she didn't want to.

She walked slowly through the exhibits, from the front room preserved as a wine shop from the 1700s, owned by the Jefferson family, one of the largest merchant traders in Whitehaven at the time, to a replica of the rain forest of Antigua, where many of the slaves ended up.

Particularly grim was the model of a slave ship, with the slaves lying chained next to one another; she read how when the ship left Africa, a whole new deck was put in to cram the slaves even closer, resulting in many of them dying during the voyages. The ones who survived had their hair dyed and their bodies oiled to give the unfortunate illusion of health.

All of it increased her determination to excavate the wreck and learn more. Who had captained it? Why had it sunk? What might she find?

At the end of the exhibit, a staff member offered her a tot of rum, which she took, nearly choking on its strength.

"Goes down a treat, doesn't it?" he said with a smile. She wasn't sure she could agree. Still, she bought some chocolate rum balls as a gift for her mother; she'd told herself she'd ring today to arrange a visit for tomorrow morning, while she was waiting for Dave and Ally.

"So you don't know which ship it is?" the woman asked as she rang up Rachel's purchase.

"Not yet. It's quite old, so there's unlikely to be much left. I'm hoping to go through the records of slave ships coming in and out of Whitehaven, to see if any were wrecked nearby, but I haven't started with the archives yet." Trawling through endless reels of microfiche was not her favourite part of the job.

"Are you going to visit the local archives in Scotch Street?" the woman asked. "I know they have some records on slave ships, although not many."

Rachel had already done a thorough search on all items related to slavery in the local archives' online catalogue, and while there had been many interesting letters and pamphlets, nothing had related to local shipwrecks. She was still planning to visit the centre, just in case.

"The local archives aside," the woman continued, "you might be interested in the Fenton Collection."

Rachel's curiosity was piqued. "I haven't heard of that. What is it?"

"Abigail Fenton was the widow of a slave trader in Whitehaven in the 1760s, and after her death, her daughter donated the letters he'd written to her while captaining a slave ship to the Society for the Abolition of the Slave Trade, as she had requested."

"Really?" Rachel's heart skipped a beat as her interest quickened even more. "And he was a captain out of Whitehaven? Where are the letters now?"

"They're held by the British Library archives now." She made a face. "I think there was a move to bring them up here, once upon a time, but it never happened. You can view them in the library's Reading Rooms, I think, if you have a pass."

"I have a pass." She'd been to the Reading Rooms many times, and had a friend who worked there, besides. "Do you know if any of Fenton's ships were wrecked?"

"Yes, he died on his last voyage," the woman said. "His ship *The Fair Lady* sank somewhere in the Caribbean." She gave a little shrug. "I only know this because I'm a bit of a history buff myself. I saw the Fenton Collection when I was in London a couple of years ago. The letters are fascinating, very personal. There's only a few of them, but they're worth reading."

"I'll have to have a look at them." Although she could hardly hightail it to London now. Still, Rachel was intrigued. The ship off the coast couldn't belong to Fenton, though, and she knew she needed to stay focused. "Thank you," she said to the woman, and took her paper bag of rum balls.

The day was wet and windy, without even a hint of spring in the air, and Rachel decided to hole up in one of the town's coffee shops off the Market Square to do some more research on the slave trade out of Whitehaven. With a latte at her elbow and her laptop in front of her, she started to type in the search bar.

She was deep in the records of an online archive when she heard a voice nearby.

"Oh, hello. It's you."

Rachel looked up, blinking the world back into focus, and saw the woman who had recommended the Pinot Grigio at the pub the night before. "Jane," she said before she could think, and the woman looked understandably surprised.

"You know me?"

"Sorry, I heard the others say your name." Rachel gave a grimace of embarrassed apology. "I must sound rather creepy."

"Not at all." Jane gave her a wide smile as well as a frank look. "You're not a local?"

"No, just visiting the area for work."

"Oh." Jane took a step back. "Sorry, am I interrupting? I'm so nosy, honestly. Never mind."

She started to turn away, and Rachel found herself blurting, "No, not at all. I'm glad of the company. I don't know anyone here, although I'm actually from the Lake District originally."

"Are you?" Jane turned back, seeming happy to keep the conversation going. "You don't have an accent."

"No, it was a long time ago, and I lived in Windermere, not Whitehaven."

"You left and never looked back?" Jane surmised with a commiserating smile. "Honestly, I wanted to do the same when I first moved here."

"You're definitely not local." Now that they were properly speaking, Rachel had registered Jane's American accent.

"Nope, I'm from the States. New York City, as a matter of fact."

"Wow, that's quite a journey."

"One latte," the woman called from behind the counter, and Jane gave an apologetic moue as she went to get her coffee.

"Do you mind if I join you?" she asked when she returned with her coffee. "Or am I really interrupting? Please do tell me to mind my own business if you'd rather. I won't be at all offended."

"No, no," Rachel said. She wasn't used to making chitchat with strangers, but she liked Jane's easy friendliness. She closed her laptop and put it back in her bag. "I could do with a break, actually."

"What work brought you here? Can I ask that?"

Rachel laughed. "Of course you can. I'm a marine archaeologist, and I'm investigating a shipwreck site that was discovered off the coast."

"Oh, wow. That is the most fascinating answer anyone has ever given me to the whole what-do-you-do-for-work question."

Rachel laughed again. "Thanks. I suppose."

"Really. A shipwreck? What kind of shipwreck?"

"I don't know yet. An old one, certainly. Perhaps a slave ship."

"A slave ship? Wow." Jane shook her head. "You forget that sort of thing happened up here. My husband Andrew tells me that Whitehaven was quite the important port back in the 1700s, but I have trouble believing it now."

"I know what you mean, but he's right. It was a very important place, at least for the region, in its own way. But I'm most likely speaking out of turn, because we don't really know what kind of ship it is yet, and we might never know, since there most likely isn't much left. I'll find out tomorrow, when I dive down, and that might be the end of it all."

"My lips are sealed." Jane pretended to zip her lips closed before she took a sip of her latte. "It does sound rather fascinating, though. I'm interested in history myself. We live in the old vicarage in Goswell, and when we first moved there I discovered an old shopping list from the 1930s in the pantry." She made a face. "I know it's nothing on a shipwreck, but it led me to research the history of the house, and who lived there during the war."

"Did you discover anything?"

"Yes, a woman named Alice James lived there. She would never be in any history books, but I think she lived a remarkable life, in a quiet way. She took in a child evacuee while her husband was a chaplain with the army."

"It's wonderful, isn't it, how little clues can give way to greater stories?" Rachel said. "I think that's what got me into archaeology – how something seemingly so small can be part of a bigger story."

"Yes, exactly. It was just a shopping list, and yet it gripped me." Jane smiled in reminiscence. "So have you found anything from this wreck of yours? Are you gripped?"

"I am gripped," Rachel said slowly. "Although I'm not even sure why. I don't know a single thing about the ship – who owned it, what time period it came from, anything. And yet –"

"You'll find out." Jane sounded certain. "Somehow you'll find out."

"Here's hoping. The 1700s is a bit more distant than the 1930s. Like I said, there's not much left."

"When do you think the ship sank?"

"I have no idea, but my guess would be between 1730 and 1769, which is when the slave trade stopped in Whitehaven."

"Is it? I thought it wasn't abolished until later?"

"Not until 1807. It moved out of Whitehaven simply for economic reasons." Rachel sighed. "And that's about all I know so far."

"Well, I'm already intrigued." Jane leaned forward. "Look, if you're in the area for a bit, why don't you come to dinner? If you're at a loose end? Are you staying in Goswell?"

"Yes…"

"Then do come round. Tomorrow, perhaps? Nothing fancy, and my children will create chaos, I assure you, but it's always nice to meet someone new."

Rachel was taken aback by the invitation, and part of her wanted to refuse. She wasn't good with social occasions or children, and yet... she liked Jane, and she still felt lonely.

"All right," she said. "Thank you. That's so kind."

Jane gave her the details and then finished her coffee, wishing Rachel good luck with her research before she left. Rachel didn't feel like scouring online archives any longer, so she left the shop and decided to return to her B&B, where she could ring her mother at last.

The phone rang at least six times before her mother finally answered, her voice sounding a bit thinner and threadier than usual. "Four-seven-nine," she said as her standard greeting, the last three digits of their phone number. It was such an old-fashioned way to answer the telephone, and inexplicably, considering her love of history, it had always annoyed Rachel. Why couldn't her mother just say hello like everyone else?

"Mum, it's me. Rachel."

"Rachel." Her mother sounded surprised, and not altogether pleased, which was all too expected. "I haven't heard from you in a while. Is something wrong?"

"No, nothing's wrong. I just thought I'd ring. I'm in Cumbria, actually, for work. Up in Whitehaven."

"Whitehaven. Goodness. What are you doing there?" Her mother sounded more surprised than interested.

"Excavating a shipwreck, but I've got some spare time before we can do anything, and I thought I might visit." A silence followed this suggestion, making Rachel wonder why she bothered. Too often she didn't, and every time she roused herself to make an effort, she remembered why she generally chose not to.

"A visit? When?" No *Ooh, that would be lovely*, or *Thanks, darling, how kind*. Nothing but a seeming reluctance to see her only child that Rachel had never understood even as she reciprocated it.

"Tomorrow? Unless you're busy?" She almost hoped she was.

"No, I'm not busy. I have an appointment in the morning, but I'll be back by lunchtime. Will you be staying for a meal?"

"I don't have to, if it's a bother."

"I can serve something cold, if you like. It won't be much."

Her mother's usual generous hospitality, then. "That's fine, Mum. Honestly, I don't mind."

"All right." Her mother still sounded uncertain, as if she was half tempted to call the whole thing off. "Tomorrow, then, around noon?"

"Sounds great."

"See you then." Her mother rang off without saying goodbye, just as Rachel always did, but it stung when she was on the receiving end. With a sigh, she put her phone away, the afternoon stretching emptily in front of her, and tomorrow would surely be worse.

CHAPTER SIX

Abigail

Whitehaven, 1763

The wedding was in May, when pale blue skies and a lemon-yellow sun shone down benevolently on St Nicholas Church where the ceremony took place, with friends and family waiting outside to escort them to the wedding breakfast back on Duke Street.

It had been three and a half months of cautious courtship rather than heady romance, with Abigail knowing just how much she was playing for. She knew that if she did not manage to hook Mr Fenton, there would be no hope for her at all. No marriage, no reputation reclaimed, no future happiness for her and her parents.

It was this or nothing, the highest stakes she could imagine, because of course the gossip had swirled around her once more as soon as Mr Fenton made his interest known. Would Abigail make a fool of herself twice? One indiscretion, she knew, could just about possibly be recovered from. Perhaps. Two, never.

Her ever-present fears were only somewhat allayed by the kindly attentions of Mr Fenton who, by all accounts, seemed quite taken with her – something she didn't entirely understand or trust, but which thrilled her mother.

"Why shouldn't he fall in love with you!" she exclaimed when Abigail had dared to voice her own whispering doubts, and she had chosen not to reply with the obvious: because she was plain and dull, and had a reputation.

None of those qualities or lack of them seemed to deter Mr Fenton, who danced both the minuet and a country reel with her at the assembly rooms on Howgill Street in February, and then at Mr Watson's assembly room on Albion Street in March.

Later in the month, much to other mamas' chagrin, he took her and her mother to see his ship, *The Pearl*, laden with coal for Ireland, and wool, clay pipes, and iron for the Americas.

Abigail had stood on the slippery dockside, a chill wind blowing off the harbour, as she'd stared at the huge ship with its many sails and ropes, the rough-looking sailors scrambling over boxes and barrels on the deck with nimble ease, all of it strangely unfamiliar.

She'd lived her whole life in Whitehaven, with only summers in the country, and she was used to ships. She saw their bristling masts from her window; she smelled the exotic and sometimes foul stench of them that wafted from the harbour on a breeze-laden day – spice and sweat, sticky-sweet sugar, and the clogging scent of coal. She knew the oft-treacherous tides of fortune surrounding the trade that had built Whitehaven into a prosperous town; its relentless ebb and flow that could both make and undo a man's fortune.

Yet despite all this, she'd never been this near to an actual ship, had never stood on the seaweed-slimed stones of the old quay, never smelled so close and thick the fetid air of the docks, mixed with the sugary scent of spice and rum and the hint of ever-present coal smoke, as well as the unwashed humanity that hefted and heaved along the quays. She felt quite taken aback by it all, by its uncomfortable nearness, its brutal rawness. This was a merchant's world, a man's world, not hers.

"She'll sail this evening," Mr Fenton told her with obvious pride, as he nodded at *The Pearl*. "It will take three months to reach the Americas, and another three back. With luck and Providence's hand she'll return in September, laden with tobacco to sell at market."

"I thought tobacco was going into Glasgow now," Abigail remarked, more to make conversation than anything else. She knew that the Scottish city's position near the North Atlantic trade winds could cut a journey to the Americas by as much as twenty days, and so the trade was trickling away from Whitehaven. Mr Martin was one of the last to deal in it. For a second after she spoke, Mr Fenton's expression became shadowed, before he gave her a jolly smile.

"Not all of it, surely! There is plenty of desire for the Virginia leaf farther south, I assure you. I have had no trouble thus far, never fear. Come, the quay is no place for a lady." He put the tips of his fingers on her elbow as he guided her and her mother away from the busy wharf, back towards the house on Duke Street where Caroline had invited him to take tea.

He took tea three times at the house over the next few weeks, and danced a minuet with Abigail again in April. Later in the month they walked to Holy Trinity Gardens, with Jensen trailing behind, and the outing was noted by every lady's maid in Whitehaven who had been sent down the street, and every elegant curtain along Lowther Street twitched as they walked along.

"He will offer soon, I know it," Caroline vowed that afternoon, when Abigail had returned both exhilarated and afraid, as well as exhausted, by Mr Fenton's attentions.

She thrilled to his presence even as she feared putting so much as a toe wrong. When he made conversation, her head too often emptied, or even worse she said something that could be considered abrupt or uncouth as her thoughts flew out of her mouth without the necessary careful consideration.

Still he would return to visit her again, favouring her with his smile, the courtly bow that was a touch brash; he held a teacup clumsily, his laugh was a guffaw rather than a titter. Abigail knew these things, and found she did not mind.

As Caroline paced the morning room, Abigail could see how edgy she was becoming. Two dances, three takings of tea, several walks – it was enough to set the tongues of the entire town wagging and everyone wondering when he would declare his intentions. Abigail knew that if he did not propose, she would be utterly ruined.

And then he did. He called on the house one morning in late April, when the sky looked freshly washed and fragile blue, and the first-floor drawing room, the best room of the house, held a damp chill because her mother had seen no reason for a fire. He asked to see her alone, and Caroline had given her daughter a look that was both triumphant and terrified before scurrying away.

Abigail led Mr Fenton into the chilly room, the curtains drawn against the morning sunlight to keep the carpet from fading. The room felt dark and unfriendly, empty and austere, hardly the place for a proposal, if indeed that was Mr Fenton's intention, because even now, alone with him, Abigail could not be sure and did not dare hope.

"I'm pleased to see you, Miss Heywood," he said formally once they'd entered the room, the door a little ajar for form's sake.

Abigail bobbed a curtsey, hiding her hands, damp with nerves, among her skirts. "Likewise, Mr Fenton, I assure you."

He nodded, standing with his legs spread apart, his hands clasped behind his back, as he gazed into the empty grate, swept clean of yesterday's ashes. Abigail waited, barely daring to breathe, to hope.

"I have enjoyed these last few months of our acquaintance," he said at last, and her heart tumbled over.

"As have I," she managed to whisper.

"And it would be my greatest pleasure to deepen it," he continued, finally turning to look at her.

Abigail waited, unsure how to respond to this rather oblique statement, needing more before she framed a reply.

"I am a man of humble beginnings," he continued, his blue eyes gazing at her with that slightly unsettling forthrightness. "And modest means, compared to some, I must confess. But I have ambition and the hope to trade and prosper, and I believe I could provide for you quite adequately, if not even admirably in time." He paused, swallowing, and Abigail put one hand to her throat. She felt dizzy all of a sudden, overwhelmed by the moment, by its surprising sweetness as well as its magnificent importance. "So what I am asking now, Miss Heywood, is will you consent to become my wife?"

Abigail opened her mouth to assent, undoubtedly, assuredly, blessedly, yes, of *course*! Yet somehow the simple yes that she so longed to say would not come.

Mr Fenton frowned at her, a new unease creeping into his expression as she stared at him, open-mouthed and silent. "Miss Heywood?"

"Why?" she finally blurted, before mortification scorched through her at her idiotic shamelessness. Why had she not simply said yes when he'd asked? What a fool she was.

"Why?" he repeated, his frown deepening. "I am afraid I do not take your meaning."

"Why me?" Now that she'd said it, she knew she needed to know, even if it cost her – and it could cost her everything.

"Why have you set your sights on me with such determination, Mr Fenton? I confess I have been flattered and pleased by it, indeed I have, truly, and yet..." Her heart pounded and she bunched her skirts in her fists as she forced herself to go on. "Why me?" The words were stark and painful in their honesty. "I am plain, I know that well, and my wit is far from sparkling. I can hardly have charmed you." She bit her lip. "And I know you have heard about Harrogate, much to my own mortification."

Mr Fenton stared at her for a long moment, and miserably Abigail wondered if she'd lost all chance at a marriage, at *happiness*, with her ill-thought remarks. Why had she felt the need to point out the unfortunately obvious? Why had she been so foolish, *again*?

Yet she still wanted – needed – to know.

"Let me address your concerns in order," Mr Fenton said after a moment. A small smile lurked about his lips, giving her the faintest, most fragile ray of hope. "To the first, I do not find you plain. You are no simpering blonde miss, it is true, and I am glad for it. Your looks are strong, and they please me."

"Oh!" The syllable escaped softly from her as the flush of humiliation began to turn to the faintest pinking of pleasure.

"As to the second, your wit is not sparkling, I admit, and I am glad for that as well. I do not favour the arch comment, the gentle mockery that is so in vogue among polite society but leaves me quite cold." He shook his head firmly. "Your wit is dry, like mine, and your manners are honest and plain – far more plain than your looks, if I may be so bold as to say so!" He smiled then, and Abigail smiled back, her heart becoming lighter and lighter as realization unfurled inside her like a flower. He *liked* her – he actually liked her.

"As to the third," Mr Fenton said, his tone becoming sombre, and she tensed, expectant, afraid again. "Harrogate. You were both honest and bold in drawing the poison from that place upon our first conversing. You had been right in your assessment – I had heard of it, and of you in that regard, I am most sorry to admit." Abigail looked away, unable to face the censure she was sure would be in his eyes. "And what I know is this," Mr Fenton continued. "The man in question – for I cannot call him a gentleman – abused your trust as well as your innocence. And you are innocent, Miss Heywood, of that I am quite sure."

Her startled gaze flew to his, and she nearly wept at the compassion she saw softening his features. How could he be so understanding? "But I was so foolish –"

"No," Mr Fenton said gently, "you were naive. There is a vast difference."

Abigail swallowed, still near tears. "How can you say such things, when you have heard –"

"What I have heard is that a man of suitable means and family made your acquaintance and showed you favour, and asked you to walk with him alone when he should not have, considering his caddish intentions."

Abigail closed her eyes briefly as she recalled the charming, slightly mocking, smile of George Darby, the younger son of a country squire in the West Riding, and how he'd lavished her with attention for a fortnight, asking her to dance, whispering in her ear, making every head turn, including her own.

When he'd asked to walk with her alone among the pleasure gardens of the spa town one afternoon after they had taken the waters, she'd foolishly thought a proposal would be forthcoming. Instead he had tried to kiss her, and after enduring a moment's horrid embrace, she'd pulled away from him, and he'd called her names she could not repeat even in the disquiet of her own mind – names she had not even heard of before.

Horrified, heartbroken, Abigail had stumbled through an explanation of her misbegotten hope that he'd been about to propose, and George Darby had laughed in her face. "What? To you?"

The words had rung in her ears as she ran from the gardens in tears, her bonnet askew, her robe in disarray, and her petticoats spattered with dust. The gossip had swirled around her since that awful moment, the blame heaped upon her and never upon the ne'er-do-well Mr Darby, who had shortly afterwards become engaged to a York heiress, and she had never felt free of it – until now.

"Truly?" Abigail whispered. "Truly, that is how you see it? Even after all that has been said to you? Because I can only imagine –"

"Don't," Mr Fenton said quietly. "Don't imagine it. It is not worthy of your attention, or mine, from this day forward."

"But…" Abigail shook her head, tears she could not hold back spilling down her cheeks, embarrassing her further. "I never thought…" She shook her head again, and then Mr Fenton was before her, raising her hand to his lips as he brushed her knuckles with the barest of kisses.

"Shall I ask again?"

"Ask?" Abigail felt too overwhelmed by everything even to remember what the question was.

Mr Fenton's mouth quirked in that lovely smile. "You to marry me."

"You don't need to ask again!" she cried. "Of course I will. It is an honour, Mr Fenton. Truly, an honour." She was overcome with emotion, with gratitude, with hope.

He was suitable, but more importantly he was kind, and his gentleness had made her fall in love with him. She would have married him regardless, but how much sweeter it was to approach that so very blessed state of matrimony with happy eagerness, and not to trudge towards it with mere weary resolution. How fortunate she was, after feeling so forgotten by God, so cursed by fate. Abigail wondered at it all, wondered and wept, as Mr Fenton kissed her hand again.

"Then I shall speak to your father in all haste, and we shall make the arrangements as quickly as possible."

Abigail's head spun at this. "Quickly, yes."

"There is no reason to wait," he confirmed. "I have already looked at a house on Queen Street that I hope you will find agreeable."

"Oh." A smile broke across her face like a wave on the shore at the thought of her own house; mistress of her own home at last. *At last.* "Oh, yes."

"Then I will not delay. Your father is at home?"

"Yes." She did not add that he was no doubt waiting eagerly in his study, ready to spring out the moment the door to the drawing room opened and Mr Fenton emerged.

"I am so glad." Briefly he took her hands in his and squeezed them; it was the most they'd ever touched, save for when they'd danced, and she thrilled to the feel of his callused palms, his strong fingers. "And I hope, my dear, that now we are to be wed, you might, in private at least, call me James."

"Yes, of course I shall," she whispered. "James." It sounded strange and exciting on her tongue.

"And I shall call you..." he prompted gently.

"Abigail." She squeezed his hands back. "You may call me Abigail."

He turned from the room, and Abigail pressed one hand to her mouth to stifle her laughter as she heard the creak of her father's step, the alacrity with which he spoke.

"You wish to speak to me, sir? But of course! I am most glad to converse with you upon such a personal matter. Most glad indeed!"

A month later, with the banns having been read the necessary three times, they were wed at St Nicholas, where her family had sat in the fourth pew every Sunday for twenty years. Abigail emerged from the church hand in hand with James, flush with both victory and love, a triumphant, married woman, on the cusp of everything.

She had done it; she had rescued herself from ruin, and her family's reputation from being forever maligned. She'd married a man who was perfectly respectable, admirably hard-working, and would now be invited to all the social events the town had to offer.

She would be mistress of her own household – a modest townhouse, it was true, only half the size of the home she'd grown up in, but still very comfortable. Jensen was coming with her, and James had promised to employ a cook and laundry maid as well. They would be well established, and in time who knew how he might prosper? He had ambition, for sure, and a ship; he was already in negotiation to buy a second, which he had promised to name after her.

But most importantly, she thought, as she turned to share a loving smile with her husband, she had found a man who was gentle and kind and *good*, and she loved him. Of that she was sure, and it was a certainty that sent her sailing through their wedding breakfast, still flushed with happiness and triumph, raising her glass and drinking deeply, eager to embrace a future she had once thought quite beyond her.

When the rolls, buttered toast, ham and eggs had all been devoured by their gossipy guests, and the wedding cake was parcelled into careful pieces to send to relatives, Abigail and James set off in their hired carriage towards Keswick, where they would spend the evening before travelling on to York for their honeymoon. Abigail did not think she could have been any happier. She felt as if she might burst with it; her smile could not contain her joy, her whole body humming with a tune she'd never thought to sing.

Everything was ahead of her, shimmering like a promise, golden and perfect, as the sun sank beneath the fells, and twilight stole upon the world.

CHAPTER SEVEN

Rachel

Rachel's stomach cramped as she drove up the sweeping gravel drive, now clumped with weeds, to the imposing house of slate-grey Lakeland stone four miles outside of Windermere.

The house had always seemed forbidding to her, with its blank windows and dark stone, the steeply pitched slate roof. In every direction, there was nothing but the lonely sweep of fells, punctuated by the occasional miserable-looking sheep. A steady rain was falling, obscuring the horizon, and shreds of cloud lay low in the sky, matching Rachel's mood.

When had she last visited her mother? Deborah Barnaby had not been invited to Rachel's wedding in Florida; it had been too hurried, and in any case, she hadn't thought her mother would want to go or even care.

She'd left a voicemail with the news, and then reluctantly brought Anthony for a stilted visit one dark winter, when they'd come up for Christmas after their wedding. There had been thimblefuls of sweet sherry in the sitting room, the fire barely throwing out enough heat to ward off the icy chill that pervaded the huge house with its ancient heating system, and Anthony had done his best to be jovial, while her mother had remained tight-lipped and cool-voiced, as had Rachel herself, because as always they'd played off each other to no one's benefit.

Had it always been that way, or had it started when her father died and it felt as if all the joy had drained out of the house, the glue that had held them together as a family finally coming unstuck?

Except that couldn't be true, because they hadn't felt like much of a family even when her dad had been alive. Even then her mother had been cool and remote; it had just been offset by her father's wonderful, effusive love – bear hugs and bass-toned chuckles, the sound and feel of him filling the now-empty house.

With a sigh Rachel climbed out of her car, ducking her head against the rain before heading to the front door, where she lifted the heavy brass knocker and let it fall once, because even though she'd spent eighteen years in this house she still felt like a guest, and an unwanted one at that.

"Rachel." Deborah opened the door dressed in a pressed button-down shirt and corduroys, her grey hair held back with a velvet Alice band. She let her cheek hover near Rachel's for a moment, in lieu of a kiss or, heaven forbid, an actual hug.

"Hi, Mum."

"I hope you don't mind something cold for lunch. I've been out all morning."

"No, I don't mind."

Rachel took off her coat and then followed her mother into the kitchen, the most comforting room of the house, and yet it still made her feel sad.

Her father belonged here, with his booming voice and extravagant laugh. He had filled up every space he'd ever been in, including this enormous house. Without him, it felt like a mausoleum – big, empty, and cold. It had been twenty-five years since he'd died, and Rachel knew she should be used to it by now, and mostly she was. She was used to grief, felt it almost like a friend.

But coming home still felt like a shock, a remembrance of all that once had been and no longer was – the parent who loved her extravagantly, accepted her unequivocally. Unlike her mother, who always seemed so disappointed. Kind of like her husband.

"Would you like a cup of tea?" Deborah asked, sounding so very polite.

Rachel nodded, holding her hands out to the old Aga's rumbling warmth, deriving some comfort from its ambient heat. "Yes, please."

She watched her mother move slowly to the kettle, noting with a ripple of uneasy surprise how much older she looked. It had been over a year at least since she'd seen her last, and although Deborah was only seventy, she looked older somehow, with deeper lines scored into her face, her hair now almost entirely white.

"How have you been, Mum?" Rachel asked as her mother lifted the kettle and took it to the sink to fill. Her wrist, poking out from the cuff of her shirt, looked twig-like to Rachel and she stepped forward instinctively.

"I can do that, Mum –"

"Nonsense. I can manage perfectly well." Deborah turned her back to her as she filled up the kettle, and Rachel watched, feeling oddly apprehensive. Her mother had always been quietly competent, a bit intimidating in the way she simply *did* things, and expected everyone else to as well. When Rachel had not followed her footsteps in terms of the domestic arts – cooking, cleaning, ironing, sewing – she'd felt the weight of her mother's silent disappointment. And there were other unnamed ways in which she hadn't measured up.

So why was she now thinking her mother couldn't fill a kettle?

"There we are," Deborah said with satisfaction, and Rachel watched as she moved straight back to the worktop, where she began to pour the cold water from the kettle into the old blue teapot that Rachel couldn't ever remember her not having.

"Mum…" She hesitated, second-guessing herself because it felt so strange. "You haven't actually boiled the kettle yet."

"What?" Deborah turned, looking startled, and then realization flashed in her eyes. "Oh, how silly of me. I don't know what I was thinking." She dumped the cold water out of the teapot and put the kettle back on its ring with a little laugh. "How very silly."

"Is everything all right?" Rachel asked cautiously. She didn't know why she asked; her mother wouldn't tell her if it wasn't.

"Yes, of course. Why wouldn't it be? Just having a senior moment. I think I'm allowed at my age." Deborah's lips curved up in a smile, but her gaze was dark and flat. "So tell me again why you're up in Cumbria?"

Rachel hesitated, not wanting to let the moment go. It felt so *odd* – her mum was never spacey or rattled. Was having Rachel here making her nervous? Their relationship had always been so tense and stilted, but never anxiety-inducing. Not for Deborah, at least.

"Rachel?" she prompted, her voice sharpening slightly.

"A shipwreck off the coast of Whitehaven," Rachel said, knowing she had no real choice but to let the whole matter of the kettle drop. It wasn't a big deal, anyway. She herself had done things like that a thousand times – orange juice on her cereal, forgetting to turn the iron off. Everyone did. It didn't mean anything.

"What kind of shipwreck?" Deborah asked, and Rachel proceeded to tell her about what she had discovered so far – the speculum oris, the slave trade out of Whitehaven.

"Such a nasty business," Deborah said when she'd finished. She was getting some cold ham out of the fridge and arranging it on a plate with a few limp lettuce leaves. "Why would you want to dig into all that?"

"Because it's history, and it's interesting," Rachel said as patiently as she could. Her mother had never understood her, or her father's, fascination with the past. Buried things should stay buried, according to her. Don't rake things up. Don't muddy the already-dirty water.

"Interesting?" Deborah repeated. "How innocent people were enslaved, tortured and abused?" Deborah's voice rang out, making Rachel feel as if she had done something wrong.

"Yes, it's all horrible, absolutely, but learning more about the past can inform our future. You know the saying, 'Those who cannot remember the past are condemned to repeat it'," she pressed. She had it on a magnet in her office back in Bristol, a reminder that what she did was important.

"There is a difference between remembering and ferreting about for information that can help no one," Deborah retorted, and Rachel blinked, startled by her mother's tone, sharp even for her.

"I didn't realize you felt so strongly about it," she said after a moment. She'd known her mother didn't particularly rate her archaeological work, but she'd never been quite so openly hostile to it.

"I'm sorry." Words that rarely passed her mother's lips. "I don't mean to sound so argumentative. It's just – why look back?" She shook her head. "In any case, it's been a difficult morning."

"Has it?" Rachel took plates and cutlery to the table, laying it for two. "Why? What's happened?"

"Nothing you need to concern yourself with," Deborah answered, and now she sounded weary rather than sharp.

Rachel watched her for a moment, noting again the deeper lines running from nose to mouth, the look of resignation in her brown eyes that made them appear almost black. "Mum... everything is all right, isn't it?" she asked uncertainly. She wondered if her mother had received some sort of medical diagnosis, and then she wondered how she'd feel about that.

Would she grieve her mother? Certainly not the way she had her father, dead of a heart attack at only forty-six, the matter of a moment, the shining sun of her universe extinguished for ever.

"Everything is fine," Deborah said briskly. "Come and sit down, before it all gets cold."

It already was cold, but Rachel decided not to point that out. She sat across from her mother, and gazed down at the slightly slimy-looking ham, a few sliced tomatoes that looked as if they were past their best-by date, and the lettuce. A cold lunch, indeed.

"Where were you this morning, anyway?" she asked.

Her mother shrugged. "I just had an appointment. Nothing terribly important. But there is something I need to discuss with you, Rachel, so actually I'm glad you're here."

"Oh?" Her mother's tone of brisk resolution made Rachel wary. "What is it?"

"I'm going to sell the house."

"What? But why? I mean…" She'd never liked this house, not since her father had died anyway, and yet something in her resisted the thought of losing it, the only real home she'd ever known. The only place where she could remember her father.

"Why shouldn't I?" Deborah returned with some asperity. "It's far too big for me. I've been living here on my own for nearly twenty years." This was said with a faint note of accusation that made Rachel feel as if she should apologize for growing up. "I should have sold it ages ago. I don't know why I didn't."

Rachel didn't know either, and yet her mother seemed so much part of this house – its dark rooms, its velvet curtains and heavy furniture, its overgrown English cottage garden with the lonely fell beyond.

But it was far too big for one person; it had felt big even when it had been the three of them, with six bedrooms plus attics, and her father travelling so often for work. The house parties and weekend visits her father had once talked about never materialized.

"What will you buy instead?" she asked.

Deborah shrugged. "Oh, I don't know. We'll see."

"But you must have some plan," Rachel pressed. "You could move into Windermere – perhaps a small cottage?"

"I don't think so." Now Deborah sounded reluctant to talk.

Rachel stared at her in confusion. "Mum –"

"I forgot to make the tea," Deborah said, standing up. "The kettle's boiled now, hasn't it?"

Rachel couldn't remember if it had or not. She watched as her mother stood up and made the tea all over again, bringing it to the table while Rachel sat there toying with a lettuce leaf and a piece of ham, her appetite having vanished, her sense of unease and disquiet growing with every moment.

"Here we are," Deborah said with a rather brusque attempt at cheer. "Now let's talk about something else. How is Anthony?"

Rachel hadn't spoken to him since the other night, when he'd told her he was having dinner with Ken and Elspeth on his own. "He's fine, I think."

Deborah raised her eyebrows as she took a sip of tea, her lips pursing for a moment before she put her cup down. "You think?"

Rachel shrugged. "I haven't seen him for a few days, and we've both been busy with work." Which wasn't exactly true.

"Men need attention, Rachel – far more of it than women do. You should remember that if you want to keep him. But maybe you don't."

Rachel blinked, stung all over again by such a brief and scathing assessment. Her mother was no feminist, but Rachel thought the sentiment was antiquated, even for her. "Women need attention too," she said quietly. Although all too often she didn't even want Anthony's attention, which was part of the problem.

"It's not the same."

"It should be."

Deborah frowned, annoyance tightening her features. "Why must you always be so disagreeable?"

"I thought we were just having a conversation." Rachel took a sip of tea, nearly spitting it out when she realized it was stone cold. Her mother hadn't switched on the kettle; had she even noticed she was drinking tea the temperature of tap water?

"Mum…" Rachel began, and Deborah's frown deepened.

"What is it?"

"Nothing." She didn't even know what to ask. Something was going on, but her mother clearly didn't want to tell her what it was. "Perhaps I should look in my old bedroom after lunch," Rachel suggested. "If you're thinking of selling, I could clear out some of my things." Not that she had much left, but still.

"Very well. That sounds like a sensible idea."

They didn't speak much after that, and then Rachel tidied up the lunch things while her mother took her cold tea into the sitting room. Raindrops spattered against the windows as Rachel washed the dishes at the sink, the view of the grey-green fells obscured by the mist and rain.

She had a deepening sense of unease, and as she put away the leftover ham she found herself glancing around the kitchen, looking for clues as to what might be going on in her mother's life. There were no notes on the calendar pinned to the wall, which was on last month anyway. The fridge was nearly empty, with just the ham, and a few old vegetables rattling around in the drawer at the bottom.

Now that she was standing in the middle of the kitchen looking around, Rachel realized what a lonely, neglected feel the house had. It had always been a cold, draughty place, but it felt even more so now, echoing with emptiness.

What did her mother even do with her days? She'd worked at a local library when Rachel was at school, but she'd left that job years ago when the library, like so many others, had closed. She'd never looked for another one; Rachel's father had left her well provided for. Rachel didn't know any of her friends, or even if she had any. Her mother, to her at least, had always been a figure of icy isolation.

She peeked into the sitting room and saw that Deborah had dozed off, so she went upstairs, the steps creaking under her weight.

Her bedroom looked much as it had when she'd left it for university nearly twenty years ago – the pink chenille bedspread pulled up tight, a bookshelf of old revision guides and history books under the window. There was a musty, damp smell in the air, and the desk where she'd studied for her A levels was covered in dust.

For a second Rachel let herself remember how life used to be when her dad had been alive – she pictured him poking his head around the door while she lay in bed reading, waiting for him to tuck her in on one of the rare nights he was home.

Is my princess still awake?

He'd tickled her and given her a smacking kiss on the cheek and then pulled her covers up right over her head, making her shriek in delight. It felt so long ago, it might as well have happened to another person. It *had*.

With a sigh Rachel crouched down and began going through the books on her shelf only to realize she didn't want or need any of them. She sat back on her heels, staring blankly in front of her as the house creaked and settled around her, and the wind rattled the windowpanes. She half wished she hadn't come, even as she recognized that it had been the right thing to do. But how could she get her mother to tell her what, if anything, was going on?

"Rachel?"

She heard her mother's steps on the stairs, and then she appeared in the doorway, her hair uncharacteristically a little messed up. "I must have dozed off for a moment." She glanced around the room, blinking slowly. "I haven't been in here for years."

"Me neither." Rachel stood up, wincing at the pain in her knees. She wasn't getting any younger either. "I don't think there's anything I want to keep, but I can help you shift things if you need to. There will be a lot to get rid of, I suppose, if you're going to sell." The thought brought another pang of resistance. As much as she'd come to dislike this house, she wasn't ready to get rid of it. It felt like the last link to her father – his golf clubs still in the hall after all these years, photographs of him and awards he'd won adorning the walls.

"Yes, I suppose there will be." Deborah's expression was distant as she stood in the doorway, one hand resting on its frame. "I suppose I'll just get rid of it all. It's not as if I'll need any of it."

"All of it? But –"

"I had such plans for this house," Deborah continued, almost dreamily. "Such hopes, once upon a time."

Rachel gazed at her uneasily. She'd never heard her mother talk like this, in this vague, dreamy tone. "Mum –"

"Rooms full of children, of love and laughter, parties and promises." She shook her head slowly as she let out a long, weary sigh, seeming barely aware of Rachel. "None of it happened the way I hoped and thought it would."

Love and laughter? Those were two words Rachel would never associate with her mother. Even when her father was alive, Deborah Barnaby had been cool, distant, always remote. Rachel could remember how Deborah would close her eyes and angle her head away when her father kissed her cheek; the strained silences around the dinner table; how she'd come home from school to find her mother alone in the sitting room, staring into space, a cup of tea going cold by her elbow.

"Mum," she began, but again she didn't know what to say, and in any case Deborah didn't seem to want to hear it. She started back downstairs without looking back at Rachel or acknowledging her at all.

An hour later, Rachel was heading back to Whitehaven, still feeling unsettled by her visit. She'd told her mother she'd come again at the weekend to help clear out, and Deborah had looked at her in surprise.

"Clear out? Why?"

"Because you're thinking of selling," Rachel had begun, and Deborah had made a scoffing noise.

"There's no need to rush ahead, Rachel. You always were so impatient with everything."

Now, alone in the car, Rachel had the urge to tell someone about the strange visit. *I think my mum's going crazy, or maybe I am.* She thought of ringing Anthony, who was the most obvious person to confide in, but as usual she felt reluctant to do so. He didn't really understand her fractured relationship with her mum. *She's a bit prickly, Rach, but she seems perfectly nice to me.* Everyone did, to Anthony. He always saw the best in absolutely every person he met, which was part of his teddy bear-like charm. Rachel didn't.

With a sigh she decided to leave off thinking about it for now. Perhaps her mum had simply been having an off day; she'd come back another day and check on her, not that her mother would appreciate her concern.

As for Anthony, he hadn't rung her, and it felt a bit like a stalemate. Who was going to break first? And why did it always have to be like that, even if neither of them ever acknowledged that it was?

In any case, Rachel knew she needed to focus on the project at hand: the ship currently resting on the seabed, or what was left of it. She didn't want to think about what was going on with her mother.

Her lips twisted wryly as she recognized the irony. She was happier delving into the secrets of the past than thinking about her own present, never mind her future. Both felt terribly uncertain.

CHAPTER EIGHT

Abigail

Whitehaven, 1764

"There she is. Isn't she a beauty? Almost as lovely as you, my dear."

James turned back to Abigail with a loving smile as she pulled her shawl more tightly around her shoulders. Although it was June, the air was chilly, the dark clouds on the horizon threatening rain.

Abigail had been married for just over a year, and her husband's second ship, *The Fair Lady*, built in Whitehaven's shipyard, was now proudly in the harbour, loaded up with an assortment of pots, pans, clay pipes, and coal, headed for Ireland and the Americas. In three months' time, God willing, it would return to Whitehaven laden with tobacco to sell through the county and even the country.

The last year had held many joys for Abigail; James had proved, as she'd hoped and believed, to be a loving and attentive husband, solicitous of her moods and health, expansive in his affection, and grateful for her gentle reign of their domestic sphere.

Their home on Queen Street was a pleasant, welcoming place; every journey from the Americas brought some new treasure to adorn its rooms, and James was forever procuring some new fashion or other, whether it was a Chippendale clock or a cabinet in the latest Chinoiserie style. Abigail laughed that she did not know what to do with such items, and James took her in his arms and swung her around.

"Enjoy them, my dear, just enjoy them. Upon my life, I will give you so much more one day."

And she did enjoy them. She found herself both pleased and grateful to entertain in these fine rooms, her place in their small society now firmly restored. She was a married woman of means, her husband an up-and-coming merchant who hoped one day to rival the mighty Jeffersons or Gales.

They'd had several dinner parties, attended by some of the best families, and her heart swelled with pride whenever she walked into an assembly room or an evening at the theatre on the arm of her husband. Harrogate had been completely forgotten by everyone, Abigail most of all.

The only faint cloud on the horizon of her happiness was that after a year of marriage, she was still childless.

After the wedding, Abigail had not been prepared for the intimacies between a woman and a man, although Caroline had, on the occasion of her marriage, stammered through a vague explanation the night before as to what happened.

"You might find it a bit shocking, but it is ordained by God. Men have certain needs, my dear. I hope you do not find it too unpleasant…"

Abigail had had no idea what she was talking about, and taking note of her mother's blushes, she had not dared to ask. Of course, she'd known *something* went on between a husband and wife; she was not so ignorant or innocent to realize that.

The unfortunate kiss in the pleasure gardens of Harrogate, the whispers of ruination, had informed her of that, along with the vague descriptions found in novels, songs, and plays, and yet she'd had no idea as to its precise nature, and felt apprehensive about discovering it.

The night of her wedding, she and James had stopped at a coaching inn at Keswick and been escorted to the inn's best chamber. The door shut firmly behind them, he'd taken her in his arms. Abigail had never been as close to him, his solid, strong man's body pressed to the length of hers as he'd kissed her, so she could breathe in the pleasing scent of his pomade, feel the scratchy wool of his frock coat. It had felt both reassuring and alarming.

"I don't wish you to be nervous," he'd assured her, which made Abigail more nervous than if he'd said nothing about it. Already she felt quite overwhelmed by his nearness, the sheer physical presence of him.

But in the end, after some awkwardness and embarrassment and rather determined fumbling on both sides, she'd found it not nearly as unpleasant as her mother had professed, although still quite shocking. To think that all these stiff-faced couples engaged in such intimate acts in the privacy of their bed chambers! Abigail felt as if a great secret had been kept from her, and now she could hardly believe she knew it, she *kept* it.

She'd shared the thought with James once, and he'd burst out laughing before giving her a smacking kiss right on the lips, there at the dinner table.

"And indeed you do know it, my love!"

Abigail had blushed, embarrassed but also pleased. Over those blissful weeks of their honeymoon, she'd found it all quite wonderful, and she thrilled to how much James seemed to love her. A child would surely be their crowning happiness, the blessed fruit of their joyful union.

And yet, after twelve months of wedded bliss, Abigail was still waiting, her disappointment matched by James's, which made it all the worse.

So often she wilted beneath his hopeful look, his raised eyebrows, as he asked the question that was so vague as to barely make sense, and yet Abigail always knew what he meant. At least she'd never had to say the words directly, and admit that once again another month had passed without the quickening she longed for.

As the months passed, Abigail had told herself not to worry. Many women did not fall into that blessed state as quickly as all that. It could take a year or more, certainly. Look at her own mother. But that was her very fear: that she would be like her mother, who was barren for years, decades, before Abigail was born. What if she never had a child? What if she couldn't give James the one thing he surely longed for more than any other?

Now, in June, another month was passing with the tell-tale sign of her childlessness, and as she gazed out at *The Fair Lady* ready to sail, Abigail's stomach cramped in an all-too-familiar pattern. Once again James would ask in his gentle, hinting way, and once again she would have to tell him she was not with child. She would watch the disappointment cloud his eyes before he smiled with gay determination and took her in his arms.

"There is plenty of time, my dear," he would say. "Let us not worry about something only God can provide."

And Abigail would feel even worse. If only God could provide it, why was He not doing so? He had blessed her so much already, she felt guilty for wanting more, even as she battled a sense of resentment that she did not yet possess it.

In any case, James did not ask one of his vague, blushing questions. After they'd seen the ship off he'd retired to his study in the downstairs of their townhouse adjoining the warehouse where he kept all his shipping stock, seeming a bit distracted, no doubt by all that rested on the ship's voyage.

Although he had not spoken of it directly, Abigail sensed that the fortunes of *The Fair Lady* were important – more so even than those of *The Pearl*, which was still in dock looking for investors. After the acquisition of a wife and a house with all its many accompanying expenses, Abigail feared the purchase of a second ship threatened to overstretch her husband's finances, although she never asked, and James certainly never offered such information. He was far too assured, too proud and determined, to suggest any concerns or fears to her.

Abigail might possess the keys to the household and manage its accounts, but the realm of her husband's business, its mysterious mutterings of ports and profits, customs and taxes, was not one she took any part in, and James made sure of it.

"You must not trouble yourself over such things, my dear," he'd say when she, so rarely, ventured to ask.

With the excitement of the ship's sailing over, Abigail went to the back parlour to meet with Cook and see about the arrangements for their evening meal, a pleasing habit she'd got into after her marriage.

She'd learned to be mistress of a household in the last year, taking on its responsibilities with a certain, expectant relish; it was so satisfying and pleasant to decide the meals, to manage their three servants, to ensure Jensen polished their few precious pieces of silver to a pleasing shine, and to inspect their stores of linen and lace, checking for rents or tears.

As a married woman, the needlework she'd once found so tedious suddenly became, if not exactly interesting, then at least pleasingly worthwhile. Instead of a pointless pillowcase, she sewed her husband's shirts, surely a satisfying enterprise! Instead of taking tea with her mother's insipid friends, she'd made her own friends, managing the tea table with elegance and alacrity, furthering her husband's social interests over the passing of porcelain cups.

It was a wife's work and she exulted in it.

Now, however, with cramps banding her stomach, she felt a weary discontent settle over her like a cold, unwelcome cloak. Another disappointment. How many more would there be? Abigail had never considered herself particularly maternal; she had very little experience of infants, and in any case she would almost certainly engage a nurse to take care of their child when – oh, please let it be when and not if – it came.

And yet her arms ached to hold that solid, mewling bundle, to present it to her husband, the only true gift she could give him. A child. A son. Or even a daughter. *Someone*.

"I was thinking to serve yesterday's mutton," Mrs Greaves, her cook, said, startling Abigail out of her melancholy, circling thoughts. "Unless you were minded to something a bit fancier? There's clear soup as well, and a game pie."

"That all sounds perfectly adequate." Abigail gave her a fleeting smile. "Thank you, Cook." She watched the woman leave, feeling adrift in a way she had not since her marriage had begun.

Why this month, above all others, should hit her hardest, Abigail did not know. Perhaps because it had been a full year since their wedding; perhaps because her namesake, *The Fair Lady*, had sailed today. James had produced his child, in timber and iron; she needed to produce hers. *Theirs*. And she could not.

"Oh my dear," Caroline said when Abigail worked up the courage to ask her mother about it a few weeks later, during one of their frequent morning visits. Her kindly face was wreathed in both wrinkles and sympathy. "It has not been as long as all that, surely. Just one year."

"I know." Abigail tried for a brave smile but feared she had failed. "It only feels it, month after month. And Mr Fenton is so eager for happy news, as am I."

"Yes, of course," Caroline murmured, looking away, a faint blush tainting her cheeks. "It can be so difficult."

"How did you…" Abigail trailed off, unsure of how to broach such a delicate subject with her mother. She wanted reassurance, but what did Caroline have to give her? In any case, her mother did not like to talk of such intimate things. But Abigail longed for some comforting word.

"We must trust it to God, Abigail," Caroline said a bit severely. "There is nothing else to be done. It is entirely out of your hands."

"I know." But why, she wondered, did they only trust to God the things they had to? "Anyway," she said bracingly, "Mr Fenton has not asked about it overmuch. He is quite distracted with his business of late."

"There has been no news yet of *The Fair Lady*, surely?"

Abigail shook her head. "No, it is still at sea, and will be for some weeks."

"Of course, his distraction is understandable," Caroline murmured. "What with the loss of tobacco. I'm sure there are many who are feeling it sorely."

"What?" Abigail sat forward in her chair, tea sloshing over her saucer. "What do you mean?"

"It's all going to Glasgow now," Caroline explained patiently. "Surely you have heard the talk? The Martins have given it up entirely. Soon, I daresay, there won't be any coming into Whitehaven at all."

"But…" Abigail felt discomfited by information her mother had known and she had not. Of course she'd been aware of the loss of trade, had heard the vague murmurs, but James had assured her it didn't matter – that there was enough for his enterprise – and she had believed him.

"But if he cannot trade tobacco, what will he do?" she said, mostly to herself, and Caroline gave an elegant shrug of her shoulders.

"That is his business, surely? I'm sure he does not wish you to trouble yourself over it."

"Yes, but…" Abigail hesitated. Of course, her mother would not involve herself in business matters. No gently bred woman did; it was, in these modern times, a sign of her esteemed place in society for her not to do so, but to ensconce herself in her home and concern herself with all its simple, domestic matters. Besides, her mother did not know about the winds of fortune that buffeted the shipping merchants of the town.

Abigail's father was in wool, selling it in Cumberland and Yorkshire; he dealt in trundling carts to the worsted market in Rochdale, and stacks of oily fleeces in the warehouse adjoined to their home. To her he was the faint smell of lanolin mixed with cigar smoke. He'd invested in the Tamworths' shipping venture, true, but only once and reluctantly at that, for Abigail's sake alone.

"He'll have to find something else," Caroline said, as if it were of little importance. "Sugar or rum or spices – there is so much to be had, Abigail. Really, there is no end to the profits a man with an eye to the market could make. You should not trouble yourself. Your husband would not wish you to do so. He has two good ships. That is all that matters."

Abigail nodded slowly, knowing her mother was right, just as she knew she would worry, because wasn't that a wife's duty?

And, she was realizing, there was so much she did not understand. She did not understand why the tobacco was going to Glasgow rather than Whitehaven; she did not understand why

The Fair Lady had set sail for the Americas if that was the case. She did not know what James would do if he could not procure the plant that had been the basis of all his trade, but she felt a gnawing fear in her stomach that she could not push away as she returned home and then, after a moment's hesitation, tapped on the door of her husband's study.

"Yes?" James's voice was brusque, and fighting a wave of trepidation she'd never felt before with her husband, Abigail entered the room.

"My dear!" James rose from his desk of deep mahogany inlaid with hand-tooled leather, a look of surprise on his face. "Is anything amiss?"

"No, not at all." Abigail forced a smile. "I only wondered how you were. You've seemed a bit distracted of late, and my mother has spoken of..." Too late Abigail trailed off, realizing James would not be happy to know he had been talked about.

"Oh?" A playful smile curved his mouth as he took her hand and led her to one of the chairs by the fireplace where he welcomed potential investors. "What did your mother speak of?"

"It is of no account," Abigail said quickly. "I only wondered – is everything well?"

A frown puckered James's forehead but he kept his smile. "Well? Why should it not all be well?"

"Of course, of course." One thing Abigail had learned in a twelvemonth of marriage was that her husband did not like to be questioned or doubted, and after a few uncomfortable conversations she'd stopped doing either. He was hurt by any suggestion that he could not make provision, and she didn't want to seem as if she feared that now. In any case, she didn't.

She was merely... concerned, and a bit curious, perhaps. She wanted to share in his worry along with his joy. "I am sure it is all well," she told him as she touched the back of his hand lightly. "My mother spoke of the tobacco trade; that is all," she explained as lightly as she could. "And how so much of it is going to Glasgow now. I wondered why."

"Your mother was speaking of such things?" James sounded surprised, and not entirely pleased. "How surprising. But yes, she is correct in the main – I expect tobacco will fall off completely in the next few years, thanks to the tobacco lords." He made a face. "They are attempting to have the whole of the market for themselves. I have heard talk of their own warehouses in the Americas, filled with hogsheads of the stuff, ready to export." He shrugged, just as her mother had, and Abigail stared at him in perplexity. He had just sent a ship off to the Americas for tobacco.

"Are you not concerned?"

"I believe there should still be some left for one small ship." He smiled. "But when *The Pearl* is ready to sail, I might make other arrangements."

"Other arrangements? But what will you do? Will you trade in sugar?"

He shrugged again. "Perhaps. I am considering all the possible endeavours I might undertake. The world is a marvellous place, my dear. There is so much to be had – to be discovered, to be traded, to be enjoyed." He reached for her hands and drew her up from her chair, their short interview clearly at an end. "But it is not something you need trouble yourself over, not even for a moment. What does it matter what is in the hold of my ships? The important thing, surely, is that they are mine."

"Yes," Abigail said, longing to be reassured. "Yes."

"Look what Mr Jefferson has had back from his last voyage," James said with an impish smile. He took a small wooden figurine off his desk and handed it to Abigail, who examined it cautiously.

"What is it?"

"A figure of a woman from Africa. Quite heathenish, isn't it? Most extraordinary. You would not see the like anywhere in Europe, of course."

The figurine was only a few inches high, the wood smooth and dark, and honed to a velvety softness. It was of a naked woman, a drooping, round-bodied figure, knees drawn up, shoulders and head bowed. The figure's small face seemed to Abigail both placid and dejected. It looked utterly foreign, rather indecent, its nakedness riper and more obvious than any Abigail had seen, of Greek statues and the like. This was a woman – a full-bodied, heavy-breasted woman.

"It was made in Africa?" she asked. She knew nothing of the place except that it was far away and hot and dark, mysterious and impenetrable, or so it was described.

"Oh, surely not. It was found there, but it was most likely made in the East, in one of the Arab countries, and they traded it. The Africans could never make anything even of this quality, or really anything at all, at least of note. They are like dumb creatures. You may keep it, if you like."

Abigail was not sure she wanted to keep it. She glanced down again at the figurine of the woman with its overlarge head, full, drooping breasts and rounded belly, embarrassed by it even as she felt a strange little tug of fascination. Was the woman meant to be with child? Her belly was so round, with her legs drawn up, her chin lowered towards her knees. Abigail could not discern whether the position was abject or reverent.

"Thank you," she murmured, and she slipped the strange figurine into her apron pocket, felt its small, solid weight against her hip every time she moved, pressing against her. She could not decide whether she liked it there or not.

CHAPTER NINE

Rachel

"Come in, come in!"

Rachel gave a slightly tense smile as Jane's husband Andrew beckoned her into the old vicarage. She'd shown up for dinner after driving home from her mum's, and had found herself both looking forward to and dreading the evening in equal measure.

She was still worried and smarting from the afternoon with her mother, half wondering if she'd been imagining her mother's air of dazed distraction, even as memories of her father pulled at her, the way they always did when she went home.

"Shall I take that off you?" Andrew said with a little laugh, and Rachel realized she'd been clutching the bottle of wine she'd picked up at Booth's in Windermere for dear life.

"Yes, of course, sorry," she muttered as she thrust it at him. She wasn't good at social occasions, never had been. She was so different from Anthony, who thrived on socializing – parties, dinners, even chatting in the supermarket queue, always ready and willing to make a friend. It was so alien to Rachel, so utterly other. She couldn't even begin to understand it, and yet her father had been the same. Perhaps that was what had initially attracted her to Anthony, a thought that had occurred to her before and was still unsettling.

"Come through to the kitchen," Andrew said. "That's where we all seem to end up."

Rachel followed him back through a huge foyer, past several doorways to spacious, elegant rooms built with typically Georgian grandeur, to the kitchen at the back of the house.

It was a large, square room with tall sash windows overlooking the church just a few metres away, and a welcoming Aga against one wall in front of which a black lab lay sprawled, his tail thumping against the ground. It was also filled with people and noise, and Rachel hung back instinctively as conversation flew around her.

"Natalie, did you put glasses on the table?"

"Yes."

"Can I go outside? Please? We're not eating yet."

"Daddy, do you want to see my new dance?"

Over the heads of three children, Jane caught Rachel's eye with kindly exasperation. "Sorry, you are now officially part of the Hatton chaos. Natalie, Ben, Merrie, meet Rachel."

Obediently the children turned to her, offering their various greetings – Natalie a quick smile and wave, Ben a jerk of his head, and Merrie a wide grin as she pirouetted over to Rachel on her tiptoes.

"Are you the archaeologist?"

"Well, yes, I suppose." Rachel gave them all a fleeting smile. She wasn't sure why, but children made her nervous, even ones as old as this. Natalie had to be in university or close to it, and Ben, shaggy-haired and topping six feet, looked to be at least fifteen or sixteen. Merrie, the youngest, Rachel guessed to be eleven or twelve. They all regarded her so curiously, as if expecting her to perform. Rachel had the urge to do a little two-step, some jazz hands. Thankfully she didn't.

"I'll be in the garden," Ben called after a second's pause, grabbing a muddy football from a Welsh dresser crammed with china, stacks of post, and a towering pile of folded laundry.

"Ben," Jane called in exasperation, then shrugged. "He's better off getting his energy out, if such a thing is possible. Natalie, did you put the glasses on the table?"

"Yes, Mum. This is only the third time I've told you." Natalie rolled her eyes good-naturedly and Jane smiled a distracted apology.

"Sorry, sorry. All right, let's go into the dining room. It's far more civilized in there."

"Do you want to see my dance?" Merrie asked.

Rachel glanced at the young girl with her rosy cheeks and blonde ringlets, and gave an uncertain smile. "All right, then."

The dining room was enormous, with a bay window overlooking a muddy garden where Ben was enthusiastically kicking a football against a stone wall.

"Sherry?" Andrew asked her. "Or wine? Or something soft?"

Rachel thought of her mother sipping sherry alone in the living room, the lights turned off, as she came home from school. "A glass of wine would be lovely, thank you."

"Come sit," Jane entreated as she led the way over to a loveseat and two armchairs positioned in the window. "At least it's not raining."

The sky was heavy and overcast, swollen with rainclouds, but at least it was indeed dry. Rachel perched on the edge of the loveseat, wondering why she had so much trouble relaxing.

"Are you going to watch my dance?" Merrie asked and Rachel smiled.

"Yes, sorry. Please, go ahead." She watched with deliberately intent interest as Merrie did a few minutes of mediocre ballet.

"All right, Merrie, that's lovely," Jane said as soon as she'd finished. "Change out of your ballet things now, there's a good girl."

"I enjoyed it very much," Rachel called as Merrie danced out of the room, and Jane rolled her eyes with good-natured affection. "So any news on the shipwreck?" she asked. "It's all so terribly exciting."

"I'm afraid not. I'm waiting for my colleagues to arrive tonight so we can dive down and have a look tomorrow, but to tell you the truth there most likely won't be much there after all this time, based on what I've seen from some video footage."

"But you think it really is a slave ship?"

"I can't say anything for certain at this point." Rachel gave her a quick smile. "Sorry."

"It really is fascinating," Andrew said as he came back into the room bearing glasses of wine, one of which he handed to Rachel. "I remember a shipwreck being investigated when I was a kid, but I can't recall its name. It was all the buzz for a bit, though. Or the crack, as we say in Cumbria."

"Andrew grew up in the Lake District," Jane explained. "Didn't you say you did as well?"

"Yes, near Windermere."

"I lived in Keswick. Which school did you go to? Although I'm not sure we would have crossed paths – you must be five years younger than me."

"I went to a private school in Windermere," Rachel murmured. "It closed years ago now. Sorry."

"That's that, then. What's your last name?"

"Gardener, but I'm married." Anthony had wanted her to take his name, and Rachel had decided that was one argument she could choose not to have.

"And your maiden name?"

She tensed for the barest of seconds. "Barnaby."

"Barnaby, like the historian?" Andrew's smile was wide. "Actually, didn't he live in the Lake District –"

"Yes, he is – was – my father." Rachel gave them both a quick smile, almost an apology, although she didn't know why. She'd had this conversation many times before, and it always pleased and hurt her equally. Andrew looked both flummoxed and impressed with her news.

"Will Barnaby was your father? Wow. I feel like I'm meeting a celebrity."

"Not really."

"Here I have to betray my ignorance," Jane said with a laugh. "Who is Will Barnaby? Besides your father, of course."

"He was a historian on telly," Andrew explained. "One of the first to become famous, and one of the best. He had a programme every week – Thursdays, wasn't it?" Rachel nodded. "He explored all sorts of historical mysteries, got his hands dirty. I remember one about a dungeon in a castle. There was a skeleton he found." He turned back to Rachel. "Didn't he feature you on a few of the episodes? I have a memory of something."

"Just one or two," Rachel said quickly. He'd taken her to a dig in Turkey and a shipwreck off the coast of Sicily. She'd loved both trips, although now they were only hazy memories of sun and sky, the smell of the sea. She hadn't even clocked the cameras; all her attention had been on her father. Although now something tugged at her brain, a loose thread she wasn't sure she wanted to pull.

Her father turning away from her, his laugh floating on the breeze, but not for her...

Rachel pushed the memory aside. Her love of history, her choice to pursue archaeology, surely came from him. Her father had fashioned the landscape of her career, just as her mother had done so with the bleak terrain of her emotional life. A double-edged sword.

"Amazing," Andrew said. "He seemed like such a... a character, I suppose. Larger than life. I loved his laugh. I can remember it, even now."

"Yes." Rachel smiled; tried not to feel that flicker of pain.

"Sorry, though, I must be boring you. You must get this all the time?"

"Not too often; not any more." Her father's programmes had, after all, finished when she was twelve. "It's been a long time since he was on telly," she said quietly, and Andrew's face took on an almost comical cast of dismay.

"Oh, I'm so sorry. Of course, of *course*. I should have realized. He –"

"Died of a heart attack," Rachel finished quietly. "Yes. When I was twelve."

"Oh, how terrible," Jane cried. "Rachel, I'm sorry. That must have been so very awful."

"It was a long time ago," she said stiffly. How had they got to talking about her father's death in the space of five minutes? She almost wished she hadn't come.

"Still, that must have been so difficult for you and your mother," Jane said quietly. "To lose your father at such a young age."

"Yes." What else could she say? How could she explain about how empty the house had felt, how empty her life had felt? The endless stony silences between her and her mother, once they didn't have her father to jolly them along? The feeling that a big, bloody piece of her heart had been carved right out and she'd never found it again? Rachel said nothing more and took a large swallow of wine.

The silence stretched on somewhat uncomfortably for a few seconds before Jane changed the subject so blatantly that Rachel could practically hear the screech of conversational tyres as they switched direction.

"So, how long are you staying in the area? You're at the beach road B&B, aren't you?"

"Yes, and I don't know how long I'll be here. My colleagues are arriving tonight, and we'll hopefully do a preliminary dive tomorrow. After that..." Rachel shrugged. "It all depends on the funding."

"Who is funding the dive?" Andrew asked. "I really don't have the first idea about any of this."

"Copeland Mining Company is funding the initial dive," Rachel said. "But after that it will depend on whether there's any interest. If the wreck proves to be something worth investigating, funding could come from a variety of sources – Historic England, a private donor, a university." She smiled and shrugged. "It's always a bit of a scramble to get the money in place for any project."

"I can imagine," Andrew murmured. "It seems as if funding is being cut from everything worthwhile these days."

"Don't get him started on the NHS," Jane cut in with a laugh. "Or he'll bore you for hours."

"I'm sure he won't." Rachel smiled at Andrew as she started to feel herself relax, just a little bit. They'd got the difficult stuff out of the way now, surely. "How long have you been living in Goswell?"

Jane exchanged a questioning look with Andrew, who raised his eyebrows in return. "Coming up on five years now, isn't it?" she said. "Hard to believe. I was a diehard New Yorker once upon a time."

"You still love your lattes," Andrew reminded her.

"Yes, and you can finally get a decent one in Whitehaven, thank goodness. Our first year here..." Jane trailed off dramatically.

"It's quite a change from New York," Rachel said diplomatically. "Did you find it hard settling in?"

Jane pretended to shudder, although Rachel wasn't sure if she was actually pretending. "I found it utterly dismal. The weather alone." She shook her head. "And the remoteness. It felt as if the fells were hemming me in. Do you know there are more sheep in Cumbria than people?"

"I imagine there are more sheep than people in many parts of the UK," Rachel answered with a smile.

"Too right," Andrew returned with a laugh. "See, Jane, it's not that bad."

"I know, I know." Jane relaxed against the sofa as she took a sip of wine. "Actually, I'm having you on, at least a little bit. I did find it difficult at the start, but I truly love it here now. The people are wonderful, the scenery is amazing. Sometimes it feels a bit like stepping back in time, living in a village community like this, cut off from the rest of the world. Where did you say you live now?"

"Bristol. Not quite New York."

"But definitely not Goswell. Do you like it there? You work for the university?"

"For the Bristol Maritime Centre. We do marine archaeology, either commercial work like this or projects of historical interest for museums, councils — whoever wants something underwater investigated."

"Is it mostly shipwrecks?" Jane asked, sounding intrigued.

"Mainly, but there are other things too. Buildings, even whole villages, that have been flooded." Rachel felt herself relaxing even more, and she took a sip of wine as she described a few of the more interesting projects she'd worked on to Jane and Andrew.

"My job in marketing feels positively dull in comparison," Jane said after listening to Rachel. "Truly."

"But you've done a bit of historical digging yourself," Andrew protested. "With Alice James."

"Yes, you told me about that in the café," Rachel recalled. "A vicar's wife who lived here during the war?"

"Yes, I found her shopping list. We've got it framed now. Would you like to see it?"

"Absolutely."

Rachel followed Jane and Andrew out to the hall, where Jane gestured to a small, yellowed scrap of paper framed and hanging on the wall by the stairs. "I know it's not much, but it really spoke to me for some reason."

Rachel stepped closer to examine the elegant cursive of a bygone age: *Beef joint for Weltons, 2 lb, 2s/3d; Potatoes, 5 lb, 6d; Tea, ¼ lb, 4d; Mint Humbugs for David, 1d.*

"Yes, I can see what you mean," she said. "It almost feels as if you know a bit about her, just from the list. Who's David?"

"Her husband, the vicar here at the time, and an army chaplain. He died during the war, sadly." Jane gazed at the framed shopping list for another moment before turning away. "Of course, you must know how it is to find something from the past and feel connected to it. Have you ever found an object during one of your digs that really spoke to you?"

Briefly Rachel thought about the heart-shaped handle; the speculum oris had spoken to her, but in a horrible way, a premonition of something terrible. Just thinking about it made her feel like shivering – she, who through her research had encountered all sorts of atrocities and tragedies. Yet the handle felt like something else entirely, and she wondered what else, if anything, she might find tomorrow, when she finally got a chance to dive beneath the sea. Would the wreck give up any clues, hint at any answers?

"Some things do," she told Jane. "Every excavation I've been on tells a story; some more personal than others."

"And what about this ship?" Andrew asked. "Do you think you'll find out who it belonged to?"

"I hope so."

Their conversation was interrupted by a sudden outbreak of bickering from the next room; Ben sprinted in, muddy and dishevelled, followed by a furious-looking Merrie.

"Ben, you're tracking mud everywhere," Jane cried in exasperation.

"Give it *back*," Merrie shrieked, and Rachel saw that Ben was holding something pink and glittery that was most likely part of her ballet outfit.

"Ben," Andrew said warningly. He gave Rachel an apologetic look before going after his son, who had disappeared into the kitchen.

"I'd better see about supper," Jane said, as she started off after her husband.

"Can I do anything?"

"No, no." She gave Rachel a distracted smile. "Just relax. Finish your wine."

Rachel took another sip of her wine. In the distance, she could hear Ben and Andrew's raised voices, and another protesting shriek from Merrie, along with the rattle of pots and pans. Out of the corner of her eye she saw Natalie in the hall, phone in hand, pouting for a selfie.

It was all so strange and vigorous, she mused, so different from anything she'd ever known. The house she'd grown up in was a lot like this one in terms of its large, gracious rooms and lovably shabby elegance, but her house had always been quiet, dark, sad. At least that was how she remembered it, save for the time when her father had been at home.

The Hattons' house felt like the complete opposite – brimming with life, with all of its messy emotions, bristling with joy. No matter how Merrie screeched, Rachel knew the Hattons all loved each other. It practically oozed out of them; it was the very necessary glue that held them together.

The realization sent a pang through her – of longing or sorrow or something else, she wasn't sure what. She hadn't had that growing up. Yes, she'd adored her father, but it hadn't been a love that had held her family together, as much as she might have longed for it. The three of them had felt like separate, spinning tops, occasionally colliding with one another before spinning off again.

And as for now? She thought of Anthony, waiting back in Bristol, except he didn't seem to be waiting so much as getting on with his life. Did they have that glue? And if they did, was she picking at it with her prickliness, her difficult ways? They were questions Rachel hated to ask herself, because she was afraid of the answers, yet she feared she knew them all the same.

"Sorry about that," Jane said as she brought a bubbling shepherd's pie topped with crispy mashed potato into the room and placed it on the table. "The family chaos never seems to end, no matter their age. Do you have children?" She smiled at Rachel, eyebrows raised expectantly. Rachel could tell she was ready to launch into the expected barrage of questions about names and numbers, genders and ages. She was thirty-seven, after all, and she'd already said she was married. She should have a couple, at least.

"No." She forced a rather tight smile. "No children."

"Oh." Jane rearranged her expression into something like acceptance, but Rachel could tell she was disappointed. Now they couldn't have that conversation, the shared camaraderie of ages and stages that mothers everywhere seemed to enjoy. "I'll just get the salad."

Rachel turned away, struggling with an unexpected sting of tears. Goodness, her emotions were all over the place today. She and Anthony had spoken about having children more than once; if it were only up to him, they'd have more than a couple. He was one of four, and had hoped for at least that many. When he'd told her so, Rachel had been quietly appalled.

Four children? She was afraid to have one. Not that she'd said as much. She'd murmured something about having a honeymoon period first, even though they both knew she wasn't getting any younger. And that honeymoon had lasted nearly three years – not that it had been much of a honeymoon. They would need to have another conversation soon, and Rachel dreaded it.

What was she so scared of? Not children, not the fact of them, or even the inconvenience, expense, messiness. She thought she could take all that in her stride. No, she was afraid of being a mother. Of being a mother like her own mother had been and still was, because although she hated to admit it even to herself, Rachel knew she was far more like her mother than she'd ever wanted to be. Yet how could she explain that to Anthony? He'd just shrug it off, tell her she was being paranoid, that anyone could make their own destiny, that she'd fall in love with her own children, and in any case, her mother wasn't that bad. He wouldn't understand at all.

"I think we're finally ready," Jane announced as she came back with the salad, and the children and Andrew fell in behind her. "Sorry for the wait."

"Not a problem at all. Thank you for having me." Rachel sat down at the table, trying for an engaging smile. She'd thought about herself enough for one day, surely. It was time to focus on other people, let the light in. "So tell me, Andrew, what is it you do?"

CHAPTER TEN

Abigail

Whitehaven, 1764

The Fair Lady sailed into Whitehaven's harbour on a cold day in November, towards the end of the shipping season, with nothing in her hold but some piles of furs and sacks of rice.

"They wouldn't sell to us," James fumed, his cheerful bonhomie deserting him for once, leaving him shocked and pacing. "Fields and fields of the stuff – acres of it, I tell you – and they wouldn't sell us a single leaf!"

"But why?" Abigail asked, unsettled by her husband's unexpected tone, his hands clenched into fists at his sides. She'd never seen him so agitated. "If they have so much of it?"

"It's all been promised," James said bitterly. "To the tobacco lords of Glasgow. Every single stem. All of it taken from plantation to their damnable warehouses. The captain did his best, I know that." He shook his head. "There was nothing he could do. The tobacco trade is finished in Whitehaven."

It was what Abigail had been hearing for months, even years, and secretly she was relieved that James had finally come to accept it. Perhaps now he could find something more profitable to trade – sugar or rum or cotton. He'd assured her there was something, just as her mother had. For a man wanting to make a fortune, the world was wide open.

"We'll be all right, won't we?" she asked cautiously. They were sitting in the morning room to catch the best of the wintry sunlight, a small fire smoking in the grate. Abigail rested one hand on the very faint swell of her middle, so small as to be barely noticeable, trying not to let her anxiety show.

"All right?" James took his pipe out of his mouth as he looked at her, eyebrows drawn deep into a frown. "Of course we'll be all right, my dear. It's but one ship. One voyage."

"Yes, but…" Abigail did not wish to delve into the intricacies of her husband's business, and she knew he did not wish it either. Even so, she was aware that *The Fair Lady* had had several investors; very few merchants could finance a sea voyage all on their own, James included. How would he pay them back?

She did not dare to ask the question, and she comforted herself in knowing that her husband was a clever and enterprising man, and he had surely prepared for such an eventuality. He would not have walked into such a venture blindly. "What will you trade now?" she asked instead, and he shrugged expansively.

"I will consider my options. The world is wide open for a man like me, Abigail, with two ships to his name. Wide open."

"Yes."

"I am thinking *The Pearl* will sail to Africa before winter. I've been speaking to Mr Jefferson of it, and he speaks well of the trade."

"Africa…" Abigail thought of that strange figurine James had given her months ago now, from the very place. She'd been both fascinated and appalled by the statue, although she could not say why. She'd taken to holding it like a talisman, stroking the smooth, polished wood with her thumb. The woman's rounded belly almost looked as if she were with child. And Abigail herself was beginning to believe she had such happy news to share, although she had not spoken of her suspicions to anyone.

"The African trade," she said now, slowly. "Do you mean – slaves?"

James looked up as he drew on his pipe. "Yes, to the West Indies. They are always in need of slaves there. And then sugar and rum back to harbour – it's a triangular trade, and it is quite profitable these days."

Again Abigail thought of the little figurine. Of course, James had told her it hadn't actually come from Africa. Yet she felt disquieted in a way she was afraid to examine too closely.

"I've never seen a black man," she said unexpectedly, and James frowned. "There are some in Whitehaven, or so I've heard. Servants from the Americas –"

"My dear, they're not *people* – not the way you and I are. Their intelligence is severely limited. Some of them can barely speak."

"But they're – they're human, surely. A man or a woman."

"Better to think of them as – as intelligent animals. Work horses of a sort. Really, they are not anything like you or me."

"Have you see one, then?" Abigail asked curiously, and James shifted in his seat.

"Yes, I'm sure I have. As you said, there are some in Whitehaven. And they have them in the Americas, of course. The tobacco plantations are full of them. But I haven't spoken to one, no."

"I thought you said they couldn't speak."

He frowned, and Abigail realized her conversation was displeasing him. She was not used to the sensation; always she'd striven to please her husband, and always it had been so easy. A pleasure and a delight. Why was she being contrary about this, a matter of which she knew nothing?

"Not all of them can speak," James said with an air of patience. "Only a few of the cleverer ones, I imagine. But it is surely nothing to trouble yourself over, my dear. It's quite indelicate to discuss such things." He smiled at her. "And you seem quite... delicate of late?"

The hopeful lilt to his tone made Abigail blush. How had he guessed? How did he *know*? "I'm not quite sure," she murmured, looking down at her lap and the abandoned handkerchief she'd been embroidering that lay across it. "I didn't want to say anything until I was sure."

"Oh, my dear." James rose from his chair to kneel before her as he took her hands in his own, his head bowed as he struggled to contain his emotion. "Oh, Abigail. Even to *hope*." He looked up at her with glistening eyes, making her heart swell with love.

She smiled shyly. "It is still very soon, James. It might come to naught." She felt she had to say the words; she said them to herself every day, just in case.

"But it might come to all." He squeezed her hands before bringing them to his lips. "Oh, it pleases me so to think of it! You are the most excellent of wives, my love. I am more in love with you now than I ever was."

Tears pricked Abigail's eyes and she blinked them back. "And I you. But I do not wish to disappoint you."

"Let us not talk of disappointment. All is before us, Abigail – this child, our home, a new trade. The world is opening to us with possibility. Nothing is beyond us now." His words were heartfelt and assured, and Abigail longed to believe them.

Why should she succumb to fear? She had no real cause to think that this longed-for child in her would not grow into a strong, strapping man or a lovely young woman; no reason to fear that her husband's new trade would not prosper as it had before. He was right; he had to be right. Everything was before them. This was another beginning.

A week later Abigail was taking tea with Georgiana Riddell, née Tamworth; she'd married a year ago, her hopes for the Jeffersons' second son having come to nothing, and had settled into a matronly domestic life with a placid ease. Already her apron hid a small yet noticeable bump, but for once Abigail did not ache with envy when she saw it.

"I hear your husband is going in with the Jeffersons on a new venture," she remarked as she prepared the tea in a handsome new Queen's Ware set made by Josiah Wedgewood, released only this year.

"Yes, to Africa." Abigail watched Georgiana pour the tea and add hot water. James's easy confidence and cheer, restored after the tobacco debacle, had allayed any unease she'd had over the African trade; it seemed silly to worry about what happened thousands of miles away, in a land she'd never been to. James surely knew more about it all than she did. She felt quite content.

"And then to the West Indies, and back home." Georgiana shook her head. "It will take more than a year."

"It is a long time to wait," Abigail agreed. "But he is prepared for it."

"Of course, they can suffer tremendous losses," Georgiana said sagely. "But I suppose the profit makes up for it. There is no other trade like it for that, or so I have heard."

"Losses?" Abigail wrinkled her nose in confusion. "You mean the sugar spoils? Or the rum?"

"No, no, the slaves, of course. They're lost on the way to the West Indies. It's terrible, I suppose, but what can you do?" Georgiana shrugged before holding Abigail's teacup aloft. "Sugar?"

"Yes, please." Abigail watched as Georgiana took a pair of sugar cutters and prised a lump from the sugar loaf on the tea tray, its fine grains glinting in the light. She had not considered the loss of the slaves, and even now she pictured them wandering away, or off the ship somehow. *Lost.* But she was neither childish nor naive; she knew what Georgiana meant. Of course she did.

"Here you are." Georgiana handed Abigail her cup. She took a sip of the hot, sweet tea, savouring its flavour, and pushed all thoughts of losses of any kind to the back of her mind.

"Do you lose many slaves travelling to the West Indies?" she asked James that evening, as they dined on beef and potatoes in a cream sauce, the tall candles casting flickering shadows across the room.

"Pardon?" He looked startled; he had not been expecting her to ask.

"It was mentioned to me today," Abigail said casually. "It is only that I wondered."

"There are losses on any voyage." James's tone suggested that he didn't want to talk about this. "Spoilage, waste, illness, disease. It cannot be helped."

"Of course." Abigail speared a piece of potato, her stomach roiling at the rich cream. Lately she'd been distinctly queasy – a good sign, according to her trusted book *The Whole Duty of a Woman*, although one Abigail was afraid to trust.

"You need not concern yourself with such matters," James said with a smile. "I do not like you to worry, especially in your condition."

"You are kind." She smiled back at him. "I was only concerned for your profit."

Although that wasn't quite the truth. She was concerned for the profit – yes, of course she was – but she could not keep from thinking about those nameless slaves. Like animals, James had said, and Abigail wanted to believe him. Everyone else did, or so it seemed, and yet she couldn't help but wonder if their careless tone was deliberate, the shrug of the shoulders, the glance away. It all seemed as if it were a careful pretence everyone had silently agreed on, ages ago, because it suited. It suited admirably.

"What do you know of the slave trade, Mama?" Abigail asked directly the following day, when her mother paid a visit. *The Pearl* was due to sail in just two days' time, loaded with trinkets and bits of jewellery, brass pots and pans, all to be traded in Africa for slaves.

"The slave trade?" Caroline looked uneasy. "My dear –"

"Mr Fenton's next venture is to Africa," she said matter-of-factly. "And then to the West Indies."

"Is it?" Caroline looked surprised, and even more uneasy. "I had not realized. Of course, with the tobacco –"

"Yes."

"The Jeffersons have been involved with it for years now," Caroline said. "It is very profitable, I daresay."

"Have you ever seen one?" Abigail asked.

"Seen one?"

"A slave. An – an African."

"No, not that I can recall."

Caroline's tone reminded Abigail of James's last night; her questions were not those of polite conversation.

"Perhaps in passing. There are a few servants from the Americas, I think, although from what I hear they can be difficult to train. I believe an acquaintance in Harrogate had a little black boy," Caroline recalled thoughtfully. "She dressed him in a blue velvet suit. He seemed quite docile, by all accounts." Her mother's gaze narrowed. "Why do you ask?"

"I don't know. I only wondered." Abigail did not know why she kept asking. She did not want to concern herself with such things, and yet only last night she'd taken the little figurine from the top of her bureau and run her thumb over the woman's bowed head. Abigail had seen many Arabian artefacts and trinkets – James had brought them home before – and she did not think this little figurine looked anything like them. But of course it had to be; James had said it was. She'd placed it back on her bureau, and then, after a moment, had shoved it in a drawer of handkerchiefs instead.

"If your husband has chosen the triangular trade, then he is surely set to make a fortune," Caroline said firmly. "That is all that matters." She leaned forward, her mouth curved in hopeful expectation. "And I believe there are other matters to concern yourself with – are there not?"

Abigail pressed one hand against her middle. "How did you know?"

"A mother's intuition. You are looking so well, Abigail. You are positively blooming. Does Mr Fenton know?"

"He guessed," Abigail admitted. "Only last week."

"What a clever gentleman! He must be much pleased."

"He is, but I still fear disappointment."

Caroline's expression clouded. "I know it well. But there is no reason to think…"

Abigail nodded slowly. How could she explain her persistent sense of fear, as if a cloud hovered just over her shoulder, dark and ominous? She could not keep herself from fearing the worst on every occasion – whether it was this precious child nestled in her womb, or another pearl, set to sail in two days' time.

"Do not fear, Abigail," Caroline said, patting her hand. "Trust in Providence. All will come aright."

"Yes." Abigail longed to believe her, that it could be so simple and easy. "Yes."

The very next night Abigail woke to moonlight slanting across the floor of her bedroom, and cramps banding her stomach so painfully that she gasped out loud.

Next to her James, who had shared her bedroom since the first day of their marriage, stirred and then fell back to sleep, settling into the feather mattress with a gentle snore.

Abigail slid out of bed, the wood floor cold beneath her feet, as the cramps continued, strengthening in their force. She clutched her stomach as she reached for the chamber pot underneath the bed, praying that it was nothing more than a reaction to yet another heavy cream dish they'd had for dinner. She would have to speak to Cook.

But as she crouched over the pot, her heart thudding, her hands slick with sweat, she knew that the sudden gush was not an unfortunate reaction to her supper. She glanced down and when she saw the streaks of blood on her thighs she let out a cry of pain and grief that echoed through the still night.

"Abigail!" James was up at once, rolling out of bed, instantly alert, for ever a seaman. He glanced down, his face paling at the sight of the blood pooling in the pot. "No!"

"Can you call the doctor," Abigail whispered. "Perhaps something can be done."

But she already knew nothing could. She felt it, in the way her body was being wrenched inside out, in the pains that gripped her stomach like a deadly vice. And deadly it was, for the child they'd both longed and hoped for was surely being expelled from her womb.

"I'm so sorry, James," she whispered, before her body crumpled beneath her and her head hit the floor.

Late the next morning, the doctor confirmed what Abigail had already known. The bloody sheets and nightgown had been bundled away and burned by the laundry maid; with a fire in the hearth and a newly scrubbed floor, the bedroom where she'd experienced agony mere hours ago bore no signs of it at all, everything as fresh as the morning light streaming through the window.

"You are young and hale," the doctor told her briskly. "All will come in time."

Abigail could not summon the strength to reply. She felt empty, drained of life and also of hope, as if there was nothing left inside her at all; she was no more than a husk.

After the doctor had gone, James crept to her side, taking her cold hand in his. "Abigail, my love." She heard the clutch of tears in his throat and could not stand it, so she turned her face away. "You are well, though," James persisted. "The doctor says…"

Abigail shook her head, no more than a tiny movement against the starched linen of her pillow, as she closed her eyes.

"I know this is a great disappointment, my love, but it is one we can surely weather. We are young. The future is still ahead of us. And we must trust all things to Providence. Even this."

"Then why," Abigail asked, her voice scratchy and distant, "do we trust Providence only when we can do nothing about it ourselves?"

James's fingers tensed on her own. "I do not take your meaning."

"Do you trust the tobacco trade to Providence? Or *The Pearl*? Or is it only this, this unfathomable mystery, that we consign to God's hand?"

"Abigail, you are distraught."

"Yes, I am." Her voice choked and she closed her eyes again. She knew she could not begin to explain to James how she felt; how the wild grief was like a storm inside her, and yet somewhere deep within was a strange, icy calm she could not bear to understand. She could not stand the hypocrisy she sensed lurking in her husband, her mother, even in herself, to trust for one thing and not another; to believe what was convenient, what served the best purpose, and she sensed an even greater discontent looming like the darkest cloud of all, if only she would look up and see its dreaded arrival.

"I will return after you've slept," James said as he brushed a kiss across her forehead. "When you are more yourself."

But Abigail was not sure when that would be, or who she even was. Not a mother, no, and yet still a wife, a daughter, a friend – all roles that felt like costumes she put on and took off. Perhaps she'd never known who she was, or perhaps she'd lost it last night, when she'd bled their baby into a chamber pot.

Abigail closed her eyes against it all: her empty womb, her aching heart, the discontent that roiled like the sea's stormy waves, threatening to come ever closer, crash over her head, if she let it. If she let herself think about it.

Eventually she slept, and when she woke, the last of the afternoon's rays were sinking beneath the sea, sending rich, golden light through the crack in the drawn curtains. Abigail heard the mournful peal of a bell, the creak and clank of the ships in harbour, and knew *The Pearl* was sailing on the evening tide, already set towards the sea, and Africa.

CHAPTER ELEVEN

Rachel

"Ready?"

Rachel adjusted her dive mask as she gazed down at the choppy, grey-blue waves churning beneath the boat. Ally and Dave had arrived last night, and Rachel had met up with them briefly, after leaving Jane and Andrew's, to share what information she knew about the wreck. This morning they were set to do an initial exploratory dive. Her heart thumping with anticipation. Rachel could hardly wait to go below the waves, although she was doing her best to keep her expectations low.

As they readied themselves to slip into the water, Rachel did a last-minute check of her gear – her regulator, dive computer, buoyancy control device, or BCD.

"Everything good?" Ally called, smiling, her freckles visible even with her dive mask on. Rachel nodded. On her other side Dave was completing his own checks, looking intent and serious, as he always did when it came to diving. Off the water, he was a barrel of laughs, but not here, when so much could be at stake.

The boat shifted beneath her feet as Ally went first, dropping neatly into the waves before turning to raise her arms in a circle above her head, the universal dive signal that she was safe in the water.

Dave went next, following the same routine, and then it was Rachel's turn. She put the regulator in her mouth and adjusted the air in her BCD to make sure she stayed buoyant upon entering the water. Then, with one hand covering her mask to protect it and another wrapped around her equipment, she took one large stride into the water, letting it envelop her like a cold, liquid blanket.

She gave the okay signal to the other two, as well as the support staff on the boat, and then Ally made the thumbs down signal and they began their descent. Rachel loved this part, as the water closed over her head and the world became silent all around her, everything but this – the sea stretching endlessly in every direction – falling away.

She remembered the magic of it when her father had taken her for her first dive off the coast of Turkey when she was just ten years old. She'd been in awe and a little scared by the huge underwater world that had suddenly opened up in front of her, and her father must have sensed that because he'd given her a big thumbs up, his hazel eyes glinting from behind his mask. Then Rachel had felt as if she could do anything. She could conquer the world, because it was her and her dad, adventuring together under the sea.

Now she began her controlled descent to the ocean floor fifteen metres below them, slowly and carefully deflating her BCD so she could steadily sink, stopping every half-metre to equalize her air.

Finally, through the murk of the Irish Sea, the bottom emerged, a gently rolling plain of sand and mud, interspersed with rocks, all of it reminding Rachel a little of what she thought the surface of the moon might be like.

She looked around slowly, getting her bearings; they'd used the drone provided by Copeland Mining Company to orient themselves, but of course they could have drifted off a little as they'd descended. Ally swam near her, Dave on the other side, each of them communicating by the accepted hand signals to show all was okay.

But where was the wreckage? The bits of rusted iron and timber Rachel had seen on the drone were not visible on the murky seafloor. Then Ally signalled to follow her, pointing towards the north, and Rachel swam alongside as she searched the ocean floor.

Then she saw it – a rusting band of iron, most likely from the bottom of the ship. She swam closer, examining the bit of barnacle-encrusted wreckage, wishing they'd had the use of a dredge engine to remove the sediment on to a floating screen, where they could examine it for smaller fragments and artefacts. If the shipwreck had been funded by a research institution or private donor, they would have one. As it was, they would have nothing more than a look-see now; the mining company had no further responsibility.

Taking a plastic hand trowel from a pocket on the side of her suit, Rachel carefully removed the mud and sediment from around the iron, but as far as she could tell there was nothing more there. The wood had dissolved long ago, leaving nothing but this rusted shell, a ghostly reminder of what had once been.

She continued to swim along, disappointment curdling inside her as she realized how little wreckage was visible. If they'd had more equipment, more time, more money, perhaps they could have investigated what lay buried beneath the mud and sand, but as it was, what was there would not be enough to deem it a heritage site, or procure any more funding, at least not anytime soon. It would take mountains of paperwork, filling out forms and writing in-depth proposals, to get this turned into a proper research project.

It was what Rachel had told herself to expect, and yet she still felt gutted. Ever since holding that heart-shaped handle, she'd been longing for some clue to unravel the mystery that was this wreck, but there was nothing. Its secrets had been lost long ago, when it had sunk beneath the waves.

From a few feet away Ally brandished the slate they all carried to communicate, and Rachel blinked through the gloom to read what was on it: *Found something.* Her heart turned over and she made the okay signal, wondering what Ally had recovered. She'd have to wait until they'd ascended to the surface to find out.

They spent another thirty minutes going over the site; Rachel found the iron ballast she'd seen on the footage, but it was too heavy for her to carry to the surface on her own – part of it was lodged firmly in the muddy seafloor – and she doubted whether anyone would deem it worth bringing to the surface.

Other than that, and whatever Ally had found, there was nothing but bits of wood and iron – the picked-over bones of a ship that had been lost to time and decay, its remnants silent.

Finally Dave made the signal to ascend, and Rachel signalled her agreement. They began the slow, careful ascent upwards, stopping regularly to decompress. Sunlight danced on the waves as Rachel finally broke the surface and started swimming towards the boat. She hoped Ally had found something interesting.

"I don't know what it is," Ally admitted when they were all back on the boat and heading towards the shore. "Something small and circular, made of metal, most likely gold. Hard to tell until it's properly cleaned. It looks grey now. I've bagged it but we should put it in a safe as soon as we can for preservation. Hopefully it will polish up nicely."

Rachel's heart lifted. Gold was one of the materials best preserved underwater; often it only needed a bit of polishing to make it look nearly as good as new. Whether it would offer any clue as to the identity of the ship was another matter.

Back on shore, they stripped out of their suits and showered, courtesy of the museum. A short while later, her hair still damp, Rachel was in one of the museum's back rooms, with the recovered artefact soaking in a solution of water and nitric acid.

"It looks like a pocket watch," Rachel said, noticing the hinge. The chain, if there ever had been one, was gone.

"Perhaps once it's polished we'll be able to tell more. Get a date on it, at least."

"Yes."

"It won't make much of a difference, though," Dave interjected quietly. "It's interesting, yes, and a museum will surely want it, but in terms of the actual wreck…"

"I know." Rachel knew what Will Sayers would say as soon as she'd made her report: *Very good; moving on.* He'd done all he needed to do and even more; the mining company had no vested interest in a barely existent wreck. Based on what she'd seen, Rachel doubted they'd even be able to procure any academic funding. There were simply too many other interesting projects and better preserved wrecks littering the coastal waters around the country.

"I'd still like to know what ship it is," she told Dave and Ally when they'd gone for lunch at a nearby pub as they waited for the nitric acid solution to do its work. "Especially if it really was a slave ship. There weren't too many of those – only sixty or so out of Whitehaven over a period of about thirty years."

"You've got your work cut out for you, then," Ally said cheerfully. "How many sank?"

"I don't know. I've spent some time going through the archives, but as you know it's slow going." Tracing each ship from the motley assortment of ship registers and outport collections, plus the random variety of letters, receipts, and sale records that had endured through the centuries, was a long and fiddly business.

She'd only come across two so far that had been wrecked, neither anywhere near Whitehaven.

"Well, it can be a hobby project, I suppose," Dave said. "You seem to have caught the bug."

"Yes, a bit." They all had hobby projects – excavations that had caught their interest even after the funding had dried up and the Maritime Centre had moved on. But Rachel knew she'd have to shelve her interest in this particular project; she'd already been away from Bristol – and Anthony – for four days, and had no real reason to stay longer.

Once they'd polished up the pocket watch, they'd hand it over to the local council and head back to Bristol separately. Ally and Dave were planning to leave tomorrow, and Rachel supposed she would have to as well, with a stop in Windermere to visit her mother. The prospect brought a sense of both disappointment and dread.

Back at the museum, the pocket watch gleamed dully, almost as if it were new. The hinge was broken and the inner workings rusted, but the smooth surface of the watch suggested it had belonged to a gentleman of some prosperity. The average seaman was not in possession of a pocket watch, and certainly not one made of gold.

"Look." Ally gestured to some fine, barely visible etching on the back of it. "Initials?"

"Could be." Rachel took a magnifying glass to examine the faint etching more closely. Only just could she make out the three letters in the swirling script of a bygone era: JGF.

"So who is JGF?" Ally asked, sounding intrigued.

"I have no idea. But perhaps we can find out."

After two hours of squinting at microfiche, Rachel was no closer to discovering who the mysterious JGF was. She'd made a list of slave ships operating out of Whitehaven compiled from the archives, and of the nineteen she'd discovered, only half of those had named captains. None possessed the initials JGF.

"How are you doing?" Ally asked as she dropped into the seat next to her in the local archives centre.

"Needle and haystack come to mind."

"You've really got a bee in your bonnet about this, haven't you?"

"Yes." Rachel stretched, rubbing the back of her aching neck. "I'm going to have to stop now, though. I've got to write my report for the mining company."

Ally nodded slowly. "I'm sorry there wasn't more to find."

Rachel shrugged. "We pretty much knew what we were going into. Commercial projects usually end this way."

"I know, but it still feels disappointing."

"Yes." Rachel gazed out of the window at the steadily falling rain; spring seemed to have bypassed Cumbria, at least for today. The wind off the harbour had possessed a bitter chill. "Right." She stretched again and stood up. "I'd better head back to my B&B to write this report. What are you and Dave up to?"

Ally shrugged, smiling. "See what nightlife Whitehaven has, I suppose. Would you care to join us?"

Dave and Ally were both ten years younger than Rachel, single and carefree. The last thing she wanted to do right now was head out for a booze-up in some grotty pub or, heaven forbid, a nightclub.

"No, thanks. I have an early start tomorrow. I need to stop and visit my mother on the way back."

"Right, I forgot you're from up here."

"I try to forget myself most days," Rachel only half joked, before heading outside to the rain and wind. Once upon a time, she'd loved Cumbria – fell walking with her father, afternoons on a sailing boat on one of the county's many lakes – she hadn't minded the rain or the wind or the ever-pervasive cold. When the sun was shining, it felt like the most beautiful place in the world, the jagged peaks of the fells leading on and on to a promising horizon.

It had only been after her father's death, when Cumbria had become nothing more than a bleak house in the middle of nowhere, and the rain and wind and cold had been her only companions, that she'd started to hate it. At eighteen, she hadn't been able to get away fast enough, first to sunny Southampton for uni, and then to Bristol for her PhD. She'd come home as little as possible, which had seemed to suit her mother as well as her. If her mother sold the house and moved from the region, Rachel supposed she wouldn't have a reason to come back at all.

Why, after all these years, did that thought make her sad?

Back in Goswell, Rachel changed out of her damp clothes, into comfy joggers and an old hoodie. Tucked up under her duvet, her laptop on her knees, she made her report to the Copeland Mining Company, even though it pained her to admit how little they'd found.

After she'd emailed it to Will Sayers with a cc to Dave, Ally, and Izzy, the director of the Maritime Centre, she stared at the screen of her laptop, the rain a steady haze outside, and wondered how to discover who JGF was, if it even mattered.

Most likely he was just some anonymous merchant, someone who had thought to make his fortune in the despicable trade. Why did she care? Why did she care about *him*?

She didn't, Rachel decided. It was just that she hated a loose thread. She was itching to tug and tug at it until it unravelled completely. Unfortunately, she'd run out of ways to tug at this particular bit of wool.

Deciding she needed to get out for a bit, Rachel threw on her waterproofs and headed towards Goswell's shores, a long, flat, sandy stretch of tidal beach that was perfect for walking.

Despite the rain, several hardy walkers were out, along with their joyful dogs, scampering in and out of the relentless waves lapping at the shore. Rachel walked with her hands in her pockets, her head down against both rain and gusting wind.

Her mind pinged between the present, with all its concerns – her mother, Anthony, even the prospect of children that had been unexpectedly raised by her supper with the Hattons – and the past, with thoughts of slaves and captains and a polished pocket watch. JGF… Why did those random initials have the faint ring of the familiar? Was it just wishful thinking?

It came to her as she reached the far end of the beach, a rocky outcropping preventing her from walking any farther. The rain had let up to a misting drizzle, obscuring everything in a soft grey fog.

Fenton. The name fell into her mind like a memory fully formed. Abigail Fenton, Rachel recalled. The woman at The Rum Story had mentioned her letters at the British Library. Letters to her slave-trading husband, whose ship *The Fair Lady* had been lost in the Caribbean. Rachel had noted the wreck in the archives, although Fenton's name hadn't been mentioned.

Could Fenton be JGF? But why would his ship have been wrecked near Whitehaven and not in the Caribbean, as reported?

Rachel started striding quickly across the beach as the tide began its inexorable return. She was eager to get back to her room and see if she could find out if Fenton and JGF were one and the same, although she didn't even know what it would signify.

It took only a few minutes to find what she was looking for, in an abstract of the Fenton Collection: "Six letters written by Captain James Fenton, to his wife Abigail, 1766–67".

James Fenton. Surely it was not too much of a leap to imagine that he was the owner of the watch? What were the odds? But what was his ship doing there? If his pocket watch had been on it, then surely so must he have been, which meant *The Fair Lady* had not sunk in the Caribbean as reported, but much, much closer to home. *Why?* And why had the fact been covered up, if indeed it had?

Rachel knew it was easy to see mystery and conspiracy where there was none. The report of *The Fair Lady* sinking in the Caribbean could have been nothing more than a clerical error, transcribed through the ages. Still, she was intrigued, even more now than before, and she knew she'd have to make an appointment to view the Fenton Collection at the British Library before too long. Perhaps she could make a stop there on her way back to Bristol after seeing her mother…

The buzzing of her phone interrupted her racing thoughts and reluctantly Rachel slid it out of her pocket, bracing herself for a call from Anthony, and then tensing when she saw it was an unknown number.

"Yes?"

"Is this Rachel Gardener?" an official-sounding voice asked rather tersely.

"Yes."

"You are the next of kin of Deborah Barnaby, aged seventy?"

Rachel's heart felt as if it had suspended in her chest, and her breath caught as her fingers clenched on the phone. "Yes. Has something happened?"

"I'm afraid your mother is currently at Westmorland General Hospital. She's in a stable condition –"

"But why? What's happened?"

"She hit her head and was taken by ambulance to A&E. I'm sure the local consultant can give you more information. She's being kept in overnight for some tests."

Tests? What kind of tests? And how had her mother hit her head so badly that she had to be taken by ambulance? Fear churned in Rachel's stomach and numbed her mind. "I'll be there as soon as I can," she said, forcing the words through lips that felt frozen. "I'll leave right now."

With all thoughts of James Fenton and *The Fair Lady* gone from her mind, Rachel scrambled into her coat and shoes and headed outside.

CHAPTER TWELVE

Abigail

Whitehaven, 1766

The Pearl sailed into Whitehaven's harbour one sunny morning in mid-April, when the daffodils were shyly unfurling their bright heads and cottony white clouds scudded across a freshly washed sky.

In the seventeen months since it had set sail for Africa, Abigail had suffered three more miscarriages, carrying each child just long enough to begin to dare to hope. Each one was a more crushing loss than the last, taking its inevitable toll on her worn-out body as well as her aching heart.

In May, after her second miscarriage, the doctor, who had before been so brisk, kindly advised she have a proper rest. So James rented a house in Bath, and they'd travelled, extravagantly, by hired coach, an expense which would have worried Abigail if she'd had the energy or emotion to care.

As it was, she felt numb to everything – even James's tender solicitude, which had once made her eyes sting, but now just felt like so much fussing that irritated her if it affected her at all.

"My dear," Caroline had said before they left for Bath, pressing her daughter's limp hand between her own, "you have suffered many disappointments, as you know I have, but I pray that your hopes may still be realized." Her smile was tremulous, her eyes tear-filled as she gazed at her daughter. "Truly, Abigail, you have been the greatest blessing of my life. I pray you might know the same. I trust that you will."

Abigail had tried to smile, but her lips didn't seem to be working properly. In fact, she felt as if her whole body wasn't working as it should; she was nothing more than a jumble of disjointed parts, broken bits she didn't know how to put together. And no matter how loving James was, or how desperately he tried to see to her comfort, she feared he did not know either.

They spent three months in Bath, taking the waters and walking along South Parade and in Sydney Gardens, living quietly and avoiding most society. By the end of the summer, Abigail's body had healed, even though her heart was still a wounded, worn out thing.

James was buoyant with determined hope, insisting that this was still only the beginning; how many beginnings they could have, Abigail could not bring herself to contemplate.

"I know this has been so distressing for you," he said one evening not long before they were to return to Whitehaven. "And it has grieved me sorely to see you in such a low state, my love. But I do think the climate has helped you to heal. I trust we will have good news again one day."

Abigail knew he meant the words as encouragement, but they felt like a burden she had to bear; if they did not have good news, if she could not carry a child, it would be her fault.

In September, she discovered she was pregnant again; James's tenderness in Bath had borne the much longed for blessing. And yet within a few weeks of holding this precious realization to herself, half terrified to do anything that might dislodge this fledgling child from her womb, refusing even to tell James, Abigail went through the whole agonizing process again – the cramps, the chamber pot, the blood and bed sheets, the doctor.

"Really, Mrs Fenton, you must take care of yourself with a bit more rigour," he told her, his manner severe, as if she had been cartwheeling carelessly through the house. "You have now had three losses in the space of a twelvemonth. A woman's body, already naturally weak, cannot be so further compromised."

Abigail had stared at him flatly, unable to think of a suitable reply. Did he not realize how careful she had been, how terrified of doing anything that would result in this grim scenario yet again? For the last month, she had subscribed to the lowering diet recommended by the town's best accoucheur, taking no meat, eggs, coffee, or tea, only allowing herself short walks and never riding in a carriage, and going without the whalebone stays that were the fashion for every gently bred lady.

None of it had helped or worked, and now the doctor clucked his tongue and shook his head, insisting that Mr Fenton should have no relations with his wife for at least three months – a piece of advice that made Abigail blush with mortification and shame. Not only was she failing to provide an heir for her husband, but she could no longer give him the wifely comfort he surely craved.

James, however, continued to be completely understanding, which, for a reason she could not fathom, made Abigail almost angry.

"How can you stand it?" she cried one evening in November, a month after the miscarriage, when rain lashed against the windows, the heavy curtains drawn tightly across, throwing the room into an entombed darkness that seemed suffocating. "I have failed you as a wife in every way possible."

"Abigail, do not speak such nonsense," James implored, taking her cold hands in his own. "You are all I want in a wife and more. Yes, I long for children, as I know you do as well. Of course we do, it is a natural desire. But who am I to rail at what God has ordained? If we are to be so blessed, then I say amen; if we are not, I will say the same."

He stared at her earnestly, his dear face full of so much tender concern, and yet Abigail could not let go of her anger; it rose up inside her like some sort of serpent, twisting its coils around every aspect of her life, hissing its venom.

"I do not know why you would say amen to such a thing," she said coldly, pulling her hands from his, and James's face fell.

"My dear, we must accept whatever God deigns to provide. That is the only Christian response."

"Must we?" Abigail had been a churchgoer all her life, reading her Bible and saying her prayers as a matter of duty rather than pleasure. She had always seen God as some sort of impersonal force akin to the tides, exerting an unknown will on her life whether she wished for it or not, but now she imagined Him as a puppeteer, gleefully holding the strings before He snipped them one by one, and left her dangling in mid-air before falling, lifeless, to the hard ground.

"Abigail, whatever happens, we must bow to God's will," James said quietly. He sounded sad rather than stern, which infuriated her all the more. It was easy for him, and it felt impossible for her.

"I see I disappoint you even in this," she snapped, and walked out of the room, despising herself more than her husband or the God she was choosing not to submit to.

All autumn she had eschewed the dances and parties that the season dictated; she'd discovered Georgiana was expecting again, one hand resting complacently on a bump larger than any Abigail had ever been able to have, and she avoided her along with everyone else, shutting herself up in the house in Queen Street, doing nothing more than sleeping or sitting in a chair. Even reading her precious books gave her no pleasure.

"Abigail, you are retreating from all of life," Caroline said in January, when she came to visit and found her daughter sitting listlessly in front of the fire, without even the pretence of needlework to occupy her. "I understand your disappointment, my dear, of course I do. But you are still a wife, a daughter, a friend. You must inhabit the roles God gave you."

Abigail shook her head slowly. "I feel like naught but a cipher."

"But you are not such a thing," Caroline said firmly. "And you must resume your activities and duties rather than waste away to no purpose. There is always charity work to occupy your heart as well as your mind. Do not make your situation even more desolate by refusing to enter into life and all it has to offer. Why don't you accompany me to the almshouses tomorrow? It is so very rewarding."

Her mother had of late taken to visiting the almshouses established by the Lowther family for colliers and their widows, bringing baskets of food and medicines they could never hope to afford. Ever since John Wesley had come to Whitehaven to preach in the open air last year, her mother had become possessed by a new fervour to do benevolent works, although her enthusiasm did not extend to attending the newly opened chapel on Michael Street, attended by the poor and humble of Whitehaven, rather than their parish church of St Nicholas.

Abigail shook her head at her mother's suggestion; the thought of seeing those in even more desperate straits than herself did not enliven her in the least.

"So be it," Caroline said with some asperity. "But mark my words, Abigail, the person you are injuring the most with this behaviour is yourself."

A fact Abigail already knew full well.

In February she fell pregnant for the fourth and last time. She'd barely begun to wonder – hope did not even occur to her any longer – before the cramps started and the doctor was sent for. This loss was the worst of all, wringing her body, it seemed, of every last drop of blood and vigour, and sending her to her bed for well over a month.

"You are remarkably fertile for a woman of your delicacy," the doctor told her, sounding disapproving, as if her fertility were her fault. "In light of such a situation, I advise you cease relations with your husband forthwith. I will advise Mr Fenton of the same. Otherwise I fear not only for your health, Madam, but for your very life."

They had only been married for two years, and now Abigail would no longer be a wife to her husband in any way that mattered. James took the news stoically, assuring Abigail of his love and constancy, but Abigail spiralled into an even deeper depression than before, refusing to rise from her bed even after her body had healed. She preferred to lie in darkness, to block out the world and all its vain, unrealized hopes, while James conducted his business and Jensen slipped in and out of rooms as quietly as she could.

She did not want to entertain; she did not even want to read a book or take a needle and thread. She felt as if life held nothing for her any longer, and she could not shake it. She did not even try.

"I am too worn out," she protested when James drew the curtains late one sunny morning, determined to rouse her from her bed after six weeks of closed confinement. "James, please. You must not aggravate me so. I am not well. You know it as surely as I do."

"*The Pearl* has arrived this morning," he told her, his smile determined if a bit forced. "They are unloading the cargo now. It is a beautiful spring day, Abigail. Come with me to the quay to see it."

"It is no place for a lady –"

"It is the place for my wife! This is our fortune, Abigail, our very livelihood. You need only come for a few minutes, but I wish for you to be by my side."

From her prostrate position in bed Abigail saw the rigid set of James's shoulders and smile, the desperation in his eyes, and something in her relented as she was reminded of a time when they'd been happy, when their affection had been easy and careless, and life had felt so very simple and bright.

"Very well," she said with a restive sigh. "But only for a few minutes. I am still not strong."

"I know, my dear, and thank you." He kissed her hand before turning to the door. "I will send Jensen to you, to help you dress."

An hour later Abigail was walking to the old quay with James's arm tucked through hers as she blinked in the bright sunlight, the fresh air, tangy with brine, like a slap in her face.

She had not been outside in so long she feared she might collapse beneath the onslaught of her senses – the bright light, the sounds of the stevedores' shouts and the gulls wheeling overhead, the oily lapping of the sea against the old stone pier.

"It was a successful voyage?" she asked, and James paused, his mouth tightening before he gave a brisk nod.

"Yes, I believe so, by all accounts."

Abigail angled her head towards him, noting his eyes narrowed against the sunlight as they approached *The Pearl*. "There were not too many losses?" she asked cautiously. Over the last year she had not concerned herself with James's business in the slightest, too overcome by her own private tribulations. *The Fair Lady* was due to set sail in a few weeks' time, when James had secured the investors, but she had not thought overmuch about it, or even at all.

"Losses?" James gave a little shrug. "Oh, there have always been losses, on any sea voyage. They haven't been too worrisome this time, I believe."

They were near the ship, the smell and sounds quite overwhelming Abigail. She might live near the harbour, the centre of Whitehaven's livelihood, but she was rarely on it. She had not been there since *The Pearl* had set sail what felt like a lifetime, or in fact three lifetimes, ago.

"What is that awful stench?" she cried as she fished a handkerchief from her sleeve and pressed it to her nose. It was worse than anything she'd smelled before coming off the ships in harbour.

"It is always the way with slave ships," James answered with a frown. "No matter how many times they wash it down, the ship always carries that smell."

"But what *is* it?" Abigail cried. James did not answer, and she realized what it had to be: the smell of humanity, unwashed, wounded, ill. It was a rank, fetid smell of sweat and blood, pus and faeces. It was everything awful all at once, and she pressed her handkerchief closer to her mouth, wishing she had a pomander.

"When the wind changes direction, it will not be so bad," James assured her. "Now." He rubbed his hands together, looking both pleased and secretive. "They have just finished unloading. I have quite a surprise for you, my dear. It has come on the ship."

"A surprise?" Abigail regarded him warily. The ship had been laden with hogsheads of sugar and rum, as far as she knew; what could James have brought her this time? She did not want another curio or trinket, like the strange figurine she had kept at the back of a drawer, behind several lace handkerchiefs. She had been tempted to dispose of it entirely, but some perverse need to keep it had kept her from such an act.

"Oh, you shall see, you shall see," James said, his face positively alight with enthusiasm. "The captain has assured me all is well. Let me just make a few preparations." He strode off, to Abigail's annoyance, for she did not like to be a woman alone on the slippery quay, the wind off the water chilly despite the spring sunshine. All around her men hefted and hauled and shouted in loud, crude voices that made Abigail flinch as she longed for the quiet peace of her bedroom, the curtains drawn against the world.

She pulled her shawl more tightly across her shoulders, tightening the strings of her calash bonnet, which hid her profile from prying eyes. If only she could disappear completely.

Then she heard James's voice ringing out with his usual cheer. "Mrs Fenton, my dear! Look and see what I've brought you."

Abigail turned, blinking slowly, her mind going blank at the sight in front of her: her husband leading a child by a chain; a child whose skin was darker than any Abigail had ever seen. The lamentable creature was dressed in nothing but a ragged garment of cheap cloth. His or her – for Abigail could not discern which the creature was – hands were cuffed together with iron manacles bound by the length of heavy chain that James held.

The child's head was bowed, shoulders hunched as he or she shivered in the unforgiving wind.

"What…" Abigail whispered, unable to say or even think any further than that.

"She can be your little lady's maid," James explained with a smile. "Apparently if you get them young they are quite trainable. It is all the fashion in London, my dear. You dress them as little lords and ladies – quite the thing. And she is rather sweet, don't you think?" He put his hand under the girl's chin and forced it up, not roughly but not gently either, so Abigail could inspect her face.

The girl's eyes were large and soft and brown, the expression in them utterly blank. Her skin was a deep mahogany, the same colour as that of the little figurine. Abigail saw there were scabbed-over sores crusting her mouth.

She drew a breath and smelled the overwhelming odour of faeces, sweat, and dirt which, she realized, were coming from the girl's clothes – a ragged scrap of a dress made of coarse linen.

Abigail moistened her lips, her mouth quite dry. "What am I to do with her?"

"I thought she could serve you," James said, making it sound so very obvious and reasonable. "Fetching and carrying, helping you with your needlework, perhaps, if she can manage it. She can be a companion of sorts."

"A *companion*?" Abigail stared at him in shocked horror. How could he possibly suggest such a thing? She would have rather had a kitten or a lapdog, or... a parrot! Everything about this child, from her manacles to her poor, chapped mouth, was dirty and foreign and frightening. Abigail experienced the same reaction to the child in front of her as she had to the little figurine: a horrible fascination mixed with an inexplicable terror. She wanted to back away, quickly.

James's smile, once so warm and wide, now faltered. "I tell you, Abigail, it is all the rage in London. I am sure she will amuse you."

"But we are not in London," she said numbly. "And I do not know of a single gentleman or lady in all of Whitehaven who is in possession of such a –" she nodded towards the girl, who had lowered her head once more, "a – creature as this." There were a few slaves, yes, usually brought from the Americas, but they were older and kept to their masters' homes and Abigail did not catch sight of them at all.

"Then let us be the first," James pronounced cheerfully. "Mark my words, we shall start a fascination! Truly, it is quite popular. You can have your mantua-maker come to the house and stitch her a little gown."

Abigail could not imagine such a thing. Was she to have this child, this strange creature, dogging her like a dark shadow for the rest of her days? How could her husband possibly think she would want this?

And yet she knew she could not refuse the gift; she saw in James's eyes, in his whole posture, how much he longed for her to embrace this and thank him for it. He had done it to please her, Abigail told herself. Therefore she must act as if she were pleased.

"You are so kind to think of me," she murmured. "And so clever! I never would have thought..." She could not finish the sentence.

"Then you are pleased?" James looked at her so hopefully that Abigail felt even more wretched, and determined to hide it. This, at least, she could do for her husband, if nothing else.

"Yes, of course I am pleased." She glanced back at the girl. Her head had been shaved quite recently, as it was covered with a fuzz of small, dense, dark curls, like the wool of a lamb. Perhaps slaves did not grow hair the way white people did. Abigail had no idea. "But what – " Abigail turned back to James – "what am I to do with her now?"

James frowned. "You can take her back to the house, I suppose. I imagine she will be docile. She cannot cause trouble, in any case, as you can see." He nodded towards the child's heavy manacles, and Abigail's stomach roiled in protest of it all.

"Surely you will not keep those on for ever?"

"Not for ever, no. Just until we can trust her to behave as we wish."

"*Trust* her?"

"She's so young, I'm sure we'll have no trouble. Some of the older ones – they need to learn their place. You would have thought after such a long journey they would have learned it, but some have more spirit than others." He shrugged, dismissing the matter.

Abigail felt quite faint, and she had to keep herself from swaying where she stood. All of it was far too overwhelming.

"But where is she to sleep?"

"There is space in the servants' quarters, surely?"

"Cook and Jensen occupy both rooms."

"She can share with Jensen," James said. Abigail wondered how her maid would take such news. She glanced back at the child, who had not moved at all during their conversation but simply waited, reminding Abigail of a cow going to slaughter, unknowing yet still resigned to its fate.

"Shall I take her now?" she asked faintly, and James nodded.

"Yes, yes, better to have her begin to settle. I have matters to attend to here, but I shall come home in the afternoon to see how you are getting on. I'm sure you will all be settled in quite nicely by then."

Abigail was not sure of any such thing. She beckoned to the girl, who did not respond. "Can she speak?" she asked James. "Does she understand me?"

"Gibberish, perhaps. Best to take a firm hand." He clapped one hand on the girl's shoulder. "Right, then, young miss!" he said in a loud voice, as if the girl were deaf rather than seemingly mute. "Follow your mistress."

The girl looked up at him, her eyes as blank as before, and after a moment Abigail took her by the shoulder, which felt frail beneath her hand. "Come with me," she said sternly, and the girl only blinked.

Frustrated and deeply uneasy, Abigail took a few steps, propelling the child by her shoulder, and she came slowly, her steps shuffling, her head bowed.

They made an unlikely, uncomfortable pair away from the busyness of the quay, walking down Queen Street. Abigail was angled oddly so she could keep her hand on the girl's shoulder as she steered her forward, step by painstaking step. She was conscious of twitching curtains, the openly curious stare of a maid from across the street, but Abigail lifted her chin and refused to acknowledge anyone at all. All she wanted to do was get home, where she could put this child in the hands of someone else – Jensen, perhaps, or even Cook. Anyone but her, because she had absolutely no idea what to do with the girl, who frightened her, although Abigail could not have said why. Surely she posed no threat, small and shackled as she was.

Finally they were in the hall of their house on Queen Street, the door mercifully closed behind them. Abigail let out a sigh of relief, utterly exhausted by the short journey. The girl stood with her dirty bare feet on the Turkish carpet James had had brought home from a voyage last year.

Jensen rounded the corner, ready to help her mistress, only to stop in horror at the sight of the child. "What," she exclaimed in a shaking voice, "is *that*?"

CHAPTER THIRTEEN

Rachel

The drive to Westmorland Hospital was a blur of rain and fear. Rachel's hands were clenched on the steering wheel, her mind numb. She was shocked, and yet unsurprised at the same time. After her mother had been acting so oddly yesterday, hadn't she been waiting for something to happen? But *this*? And really, she didn't even know what *this* was.

"Mrs Barnaby is sleeping," a nurse told her with a sympathetic smile when Rachel had finally managed to find out where her mother was. She'd been moved from A&E to one of the wards, where she was being kept in overnight.

"What happened? Do you know?"

"A consultant will speak with you shortly, and explain what's going on. I'm sorry I can't say anything more."

This sounded terribly serious for what Rachel hoped was nothing more than a bump on the head. She perched on a plastic chair in the waiting room, cradling the cup of coffee the nurse had kindly brought her, although she barely tasted its acrid warmth when she took a sip.

Part of her wondered why she was so shaken, so afraid. She'd had barely any relationship with her mother over the last twenty years, since she'd left for university, and before that it had been tense and fraught, something both of them endured.

So why did she now feel like a small child inside, crying as she was peeled away from her mother, desperate for her to hold her and tell her it was all going to be all right?

Her phone buzzed, and Rachel saw it was Anthony. She hadn't told him that Deborah was in hospital or had had an accident. There hadn't been time, getting here in such a rush, and she realized that she hadn't even spoken to him in over two days.

"Hey." Her voice came out flat as she answered the call.

"Hey," Anthony answered lightly. "How's Cumbria? Did you learn more about that wreck?"

"Not too much." She wasn't about to go into James Fenton and the pocket watch right now.

"When are you coming back?"

"Actually, I'm waiting at the hospital in Kendal right now. Mum's had a fall. Or something."

"What? Oh, Rachel, I'm sorry."

"I don't know anything yet," she said numbly. She felt the threat of tears behind her eyes, in her throat, and wondered at them. "I'm just waiting to talk to a consultant."

"Do you want me to come up?"

Yes. She pushed the instinct aside, knowing there was no point. "There's no need, really. Not until I know more, at least."

"It's no problem," Anthony said. "I could leave right now, if you wanted me to." She heard the hope in his voice, and closed her eyes. Why did everything have to be some sort of negotiation, a relentless push and pull?

"You have commitments, Anthony." She sounded as if she were scolding him, and she tried to temper her tone. "And I don't know how serious it is yet. Why don't we wait and make a decision when we have more information?"

He paused, seeming to weigh her words, her brusque tone. "All right," he said at last. "But let me know when you know more."

"I will."

"What about the shipwreck? Are you still working on that?"

"No, it's all finished." The words left a hollow feeling in her chest. "There wasn't much there – just as they suspected. I made my report, and once it's accepted, that will be that, I think."

"You sound disappointed."

"It's always nicer to actually find something."

"Still, I'll be glad to have you back."

"Yes."

A pause stretched into something that should have felt natural but didn't.

"I should go," Rachel finally said. "I think I see the consultant coming." She didn't, but Anthony didn't know that. Except, as she heard the sorrow in his voice as he said goodbye, she wondered if he did.

After she'd ended the call, Rachel sat staring into space as she cradled her now-cold coffee. She was thinking about when she'd first met Anthony, back in Key West, sitting at a bar drinking a margarita, the sun setting over the ocean, everything lazy and golden, almost as if she'd stepped into another life for a little while.

She'd already got one margarita under her belt when he'd come up to the bar to take her food order, dark eyes glinting, his smile so open and friendly she felt as if she didn't have to pretend or hide the way she normally did. Although perhaps that had just been the alcohol.

"What do you recommend?" she'd asked, and he'd laughed and shrugged and said, "Everything."

"Seriously." She'd smiled at him, feeling reckless in a way she never did.

"Since I cook it all, seriously. Everything. But if you like seafood, try the shrimp creole with my special seasoning."

"You cook everything?" She'd been impressed, thinking he was just a waiter, or maybe a manager.

"This is my place. I do it all." His smile was definitely flirtatious, but in a relaxed way. "Try the shrimp."

She'd ordered it, and in the middle of the meal he'd asked her what she thought of it, and then sat down on the stool next to her while she told him it was delicious. She thought that would be the end of it, but he'd kept talking, and somehow an hour and another margarita had passed without her even realizing it, and she felt herself start to relax completely.

He'd asked her if he could take her out the next evening, and she said yes, surprised because she didn't think she was that interesting and she hadn't had a date in years. But maybe, for once, it could be easy; it could feel right. She could let it.

And, amazingly, it was easy and it did feel right when Anthony had taken her to a Thai restaurant in the centre of the town the next night, joking that he didn't consider it competition.

Over sticky rice and pad thai they'd chatted about their lives, their past, their hopes for the future. Serious stuff, but Rachel had skated over the big issues – her father's death, her mother's distance, the fact that at thirty-four she had never actually had a functioning dating relationship. Her dates tended to crash and burn after the first one or two, but with Anthony she hoped that wouldn't happen.

Maybe it was the change of location – Key West, where everything was sunny and relaxed and easy-going. Maybe it was that Anthony reminded her of her father, larger than life, the booming laugh, the bone-crushing hugs, making everyone feel welcome, everything seem simple. When she was with him she felt the way she used to, before her father had died, when she'd thought anything was possible, when life had seemed full of promise.

How had it all started to go so wrong? *When* had it? After their wedding, when they'd visited his family back in New York and she'd started to realize how utterly different they were? When, away from sun-soaked beaches, she felt herself fall back into the old, hated patterns? Or when they moved to Bristol, Anthony selling his restaurant, saying it was no problem, and then starting his own catering business while she continued to work and travel, and their lives split even further apart?

"Miss Barnaby?"

Rachel's head jerked up at the sound of her maiden name, her thoughts clearing as she focused her gaze on the serious-looking consultant standing in front of her.

"Yes."

"Why don't we go to the quiet room to talk?"

The *quiet* room? That didn't sound good. That sounded like another way of saying "the bad news room". Swallowing hard, Rachel nodded and rose to follow the woman to a small room with an uncomfortable-looking sofa, a battered coffee table, and half a dozen out-of-date magazines.

"So, your mother fell and hit her head on the pavement," the consultant said matter-of-factly. "It was a bruise to the temple that left her disorientated but didn't concuss her, fortunately."

"Okay." That didn't sound *so* bad.

"However, it became apparent during her assessment and treatment that she had some confusion unrelated to her injury." The consultant paused while Rachel stared, trying to make sense of her words.

"Unrelated…" she repeated after a moment, because she couldn't think of what else to say.

"It is my opinion that your mother is suffering from some form of dementia," the consultant said, her tone quietly direct, but not without sympathy. "We'd like to keep her in overnight to run a few tests and discuss potential treatment options."

"Dementia." Rachel thought of the cold water from the kettle, her mother's air of evasiveness and distraction. "Have you spoken to her about this? Does she know?"

"According to her notes, I believe she'd already been attending a memory clinic. However, today's episode appears to be of a more serious nature than those noted previously, which naturally causes some concern."

"What do you mean?" Rachel was still struggling to keep up with the revelations. "How was it more serious? I thought she just hit her head."

The consultant paused, and Rachel felt the need to brace herself. "She was found wandering along the road," the consultant explained. "Disorientated and inappropriately dressed."

"Pardon?" Rachel could not imagine such a thing.

"In her nightgown, with bare feet, at night. When a passer-by stopped to assist her, she became… aggressive."

"What?" Rachel shook her head slowly. "No. Surely not." Her mother never had a hair out of place, always knew what was appropriate. She would never wander around outside in her nightgown, and she certainly wouldn't become aggressive. Her mother was cold, not fiery. Distant and remote, not in-your-face hostile.

"I'm sorry. I know this can be shocking." The consultant touched her arm once, lightly. "We will do all we can to confirm a diagnosis and start on treatment."

"What kind of treatment is there? It's not as if it's curable, is it?" Rachel heard how hopeless she sounded; she felt as if her mother was already gone, and what was even more upsetting was she didn't know how she felt about that. Grief-stricken, a little bit relieved? *Spinning.*

"Not curable, no. But there are treatments and therapies that can slow any decline."

Decline. What an awful word. Rachel nodded, not saying anything in response, because she didn't know what to say. She felt like howling, and she didn't even know why. There was so much she didn't know.

"May I see her?" she asked, half amazed that she had to ask permission; that it had come to that.

"Of course. I'll take you to her."

A moment later Rachel was poised at the door of a hospital room; her mother was asleep in one bed, and a woman who looked alarmingly decrepit was snoring steadily in the other. Rachel hung back instinctively; the room smelled of antiseptic, and medicine, and age. Funny how that had a smell, but it did, and she didn't like it. It made her want to back out of the room, walk quickly away.

Standing there, knowing she needed to go in, Rachel felt as if she were poised on the edge of a threshold, and she didn't want to step in and enter this new, unwelcome world of hospitals and medication, of illness and mental decline. Of losing her mother, mentally, physically, completely.

The consultant gave her a quick, encouraging smile. "Hello, Mrs Barnaby," she said in an overly cheerful, too-loud voice as she came into the room, and her mother's eyes fluttered open. The milky blankness in them took Rachel by surprise. Surely her mother hadn't looked that out of it when she'd last seen her, just yesterday? She seemed like another person entirely, like a *non-person*. It was incredibly disconcerting.

"You've had a little sleep," the consultant continued in that same briskly cheerful voice. "You're on the ward in Westmorland Hospital, after you had a fall? Do you remember?"

Her mother stared at her for a moment and then gave a small, fearful nod. Rachel cringed inside. That wasn't her mother, looking so scared, so feeble. Her mother was strong – too strong, as if she had never needed anyone. Certainly not Rachel.

"Your daughter Rachel is here to see you," the consultant continued, beckoning Rachel forward. "Do you remember her?"

Deborah's mouth pursed. "Of course I remember my own daughter," she said in a raspy voice. Rachel almost smiled. *That* sounded more like her mother. Amazing, that she could feel relieved to hear one of her astringent barbs.

"Hey, Mum." Her own voice wavered as she stepped into the room. The consultant excused herself, and Rachel and her mum were left alone, the other woman still snoring.

"This is all a great deal of fuss over nothing," Deborah said after a long moment when Rachel struggled to know what to say.

"What happened, Mum?" she asked as she came to sit by her mother's bed. She almost touched one of her hands, folded across her middle, but her mother had never been much of a one for physical affection, and neither had she. Her fingers fluttered nearby and then fell back to her side. "The doctor said you were walking outside at night." *In your nightgown.*

"It's all a big palaver over nothing." Deborah shook her head, her gaze sliding away from Rachel, towards the window, as if she were already dismissing everything, Rachel included.

"Do you remember what happened?" Rachel asked as gently as she could. "You hit your head?"

"I tripped, that's all, and I was a bit disorientated, as anyone would be." Deborah turned to her, eyes glittering fiercely. "That's all it was."

Rachel regarded her mother for a moment, trying to gauge her mood. Was she being so defensive because she genuinely thought it had been nothing, or because she knew it wasn't? "The consultant mentioned you've been going to a memory clinic –"

"*What?*" Deborah bristled, outraged although seeming to try to hide it. "That's private information."

"She was trying to help –"

"I'm going to make a formal complaint. No doctor should be allowed to just *divulge* information –"

"Mum, I'm your daughter." It came out in a soft cry of protest. "Shouldn't I know if something is going on? If something is wrong?"

Deborah pressed her lips together and said nothing.

"When I saw you the other day, I thought there was something, but I didn't know what it was. The kettle..." She trailed off uncertainly.

"The kettle?" Deborah demanded irritably. "Why on earth are you talking about the kettle?"

"Don't you remember? You forgot to switch it on."

"Everyone forgets to switch on the kettle, about twenty times a day. For heaven's sake. Is that all you have to say?" Deborah turned her head away from Rachel, a deliberate snub. "I'm tired. I think I'd like to be alone now."

"*Mum!*" Rachel stared at her mother as she looked so determinedly away, trying not to feel hurt, yet feeling it anyway. "I want to help," she said softly.

Deborah sighed, a breath that seemed to come from deep within her body, exhaled with effort. "No you don't, Rachel. You never have."

"*What?*" The injustice of the remark left Rachel winded, but there was more to come.

"You've left me alone for the last thirty-seven years. I don't know why you have to change now."

"That's not true." Rachel knew that now was not the time to have a row about who had hurt whom in their fraught relationship, but she hadn't been able to keep from stating the obvious. *She* hadn't left her mother alone – it had been quite the opposite. *Hadn't it?*

Deborah was still staring out of the window, pointedly ignoring Rachel, so after another agonizing few minutes where she debated whether to say anything more, Rachel finally murmured her farewell and crept out of the room, feeling as if she had failed.

She didn't know where to go, but eventually drove back to her childhood home in a daze, her mother's words playing through her mind in an endless, unwelcome loop. *You've left me alone for the last thirty-seven years.*

How could her mother blame her for her own neglect? All those years of her mother sitting alone, barely talking to her, hardly interested in her life. What about *that*?

In frustration, Rachel hit the steering wheel, tears smarting her eyes. Even after all these years her mother still had the power to hurt her with a cold shoulder, a single word. Rachel kept telling herself not to mind, never to care, and yet somehow she still did.

The house looked even bleaker and more forbidding when Rachel pulled into the drive with a spray of gravel. The rain had stopped, but the evening sky was full of heavy, grey clouds that seemed to be pressing down on the world, blanketing the fells.

The house was open, which was a good thing, as Rachel didn't have a spare key and hadn't considered what she would do if it hadn't been unlocked. Broken a window, perhaps.

She walked slowly through the empty, night-shrouded rooms, trying to discern something from their familiar features – the floral wallpaper, the overstuffed sofas, the dining table that seated twelve but had only ever held three, and then two, and then none as they hadn't used it at all.

She scoured the kitchen again for clues, but found nothing, not even any food – the fridge was still alarmingly empty, the plants on the window sill withered and dead. The house felt as though it was inhabited only by ghosts.

And Rachel felt her father's ghost as she climbed the steps towards the bedroom, foregoing her own childhood room for one she had rarely ever entered – her parents' bedroom. Her feet sank into the plush grey carpet and she held her breath, as if entering a sacred space.

Her parents' room had been off limits as a child, the door firmly closed at all times. She'd never questioned it; it had been too ingrained in their family life for her even to wonder, and then after her father had died, her mother had closed the door when she wanted to be alone, which had seemed like most of the time.

Now Rachel looked around the room curiously. She moved slowly to the tall chest of drawers that had held her father's clothes. It had been cleared of the masculine detritus she vaguely remembered – a bevelled glass bottle of cologne, a pair of gold cufflinks, crumpled receipts, a pack of cigarettes (her dad had been a smoker, yet somehow, improbably, back then it had added to his charm).

Now Rachel placed one hand on the empty top, spreading her fingers wide. Her heart, she realized, was pounding.

She looked up, and something in her jolted at the wedding photograph hanging on the wall. Her father, caught mid-laugh, staring straight at the camera, possessing it with unshakeable confidence. He looked so vibrant, so alive, that Rachel felt as if she could hear his voice, inviting her to share whatever joke had made him laugh.

Slowly Rachel moved her gaze from her father – who seemed to be bursting out of the photo – to her mother, so obviously overshadowed. Deborah had a pensive look on her face, the slight, smiling curve of her lips seeming sad as she gazed off into the distance, away from her husband.

Rachel stared and stared at the photo, wondering why her mother was looking like that, what she was thinking about, and if she was imagining the wistfulness in her eyes.

Looking at the photo, now forty years old, Rachel felt as if she were looking at a stranger, someone she felt sorry for. *You've left me alone for the last thirty-seven years.*

Staring at the photo, Rachel wondered uneasily if in fact she had.

CHAPTER FOURTEEN

Abigail

Whitehaven, 1766

As soon as she shut the door behind her, Abigail felt utterly lost. The poor child was shivering, her head bowed, her muddy feet staining the hall's Turkish carpet. What in heaven's name was she meant to do with her?

Jensen shook her head slowly, hands on her hips. "What on *earth* —"

"Mr Fenton brought her for me." Abigail tried to smile, though she felt, inexplicably, like crying. "She needs a bath."

Jensen took a step back, shaking her head with grim emphasis. "Not me, Mrs Fenton. That's surely not part of my duties. You can't ask such a thing of me."

Abigail pressed one hand to her forehead, fighting a wave of exhaustion as well as fear. Getting dressed, walking down to the quay – it had been more activity than she'd had in months. Her head was swimming and she had no idea what to do with any of this. She just wanted to walk away from it all.

"I'll bath her, then," she said, dropping her hand from her head and straightening her shoulders. "But you may fill the tub, Jensen. That *is* part of your duties, I assure you."

Her maid, with whom she'd always got along very well, gave her a sullen look. "Fill a bath? Can't she make do with a basin and pitcher like the rest of us?"

"Look at her." Abigail gestured to the girl's mud-caked limbs, the stench still far too present. "She's completely filthy."

Jensen harrumphed, hands still on hips. "Where's she sleeping, then?" Abigail hesitated, and the maid shook her head again, with even more determination. "Not with me, Mrs Fenton. Not if you want me to stay in this household another night."

"Are you threatening me?" Abigail asked, meaning to sound coldly authoritative, but it came out in a cry of distress. She could not believe she'd come to having such words with Jensen, whom she'd always treated as a friend, and all over this strange, shivering child she didn't even want in her home.

"No, Mrs Fenton." Jensen took a step forward, her expression earnest now. "You're threatening *me*. What is she doing here? Can't you send her back to the master? What was he thinking of, bringing her here like this? Maybe if she'd been trained, or could speak proper English…" But even then Jensen would have been entirely doubtful, it seemed.

Wearily Abigail shook her head. As much as she might be tempted, she knew it would only hurt James. He'd given her a gift; she had to accept it, and with pleasure. "Draw the bath, Jensen, please. I'll deal with the rest." She turned to the child, who hadn't moved or made a sound in all this time. "You," she said uncertainly. "Come."

She received no response.

Jensen made a soft snorting sound of derision. "She doesn't understand anything, does she? Dumb, mute creature." She shook her head.

"She doesn't speak English," Abigail answered, a bit sharply. "Why would she?" She turned back to the girl. "*You*." She needed to give the poor creature a name. She put one hand on her shoulder, and the girl flinched, making Abigail flinch as well. Her soft, dark eyes filled with fear; Abigail could see and understand that, and something in her relented, a little twist of her heart. "I'm not going to hurt you," she said softly. "I just want to give you a bath." She turned back to Jensen. "Please go and do as I asked, and make sure the water is nice and hot. She's so cold, poor thing."

Jensen retreated, muttering darkly, and Abigail touched the girl's shoulder gently. "Come with me," she said, and the girl just stared at her with frightened eyes. Of course she didn't understand, no matter how softly Abigail spoke.

Just as she had in the street, Abigail steered the girl from the hall, up the stairs, to her bedroom. There were marks of mud on all the carpets, which Jensen would surely not appreciate; it would be a full day of scrubbing and sweeping with damp tea leaves.

In her bedroom, Abigail let out a soft sigh of relief. Jensen had dragged the copper tub in front of the fire, which was still burning brightly since Abigail had spent so many days abed. Abigail turned to the girl, touching the corner of her stained, sack-like dress of cheap osnaburg cloth. "You must take this off."

Another blank look, naturally. Hesitantly Abigail reached for the hem of the dress, meaning to pull it over the girl's head, but with her hands manacled she couldn't do it, and in any case the creature started screaming, an awful, high-pitched sound, as soon as Abigail attempted to remove the offensive garment.

"Stop – *stop*," she cried as she dodged flailing limbs, the heavy manacles making the whole procedure even more dangerous. "I am *not* going to hurt you."

"She's wilder than an Indian," Jensen muttered as she came into the room with a can of hot water. "A proper savage."

"That's enough, Jensen."

"She doesn't understand you –"

"Still, that's enough." Abigail stepped back from the girl, her heart pounding from exertion as well as alarm. Her head swam and she fought tears. What to do now? At least the girl had stopped screaming and flailing, although somehow the shuddering gasps she was now giving as her whole body trembled were even worse. Abigail felt exhausted, and she hadn't even begun.

Jensen left to get more hot water, and Abigail decided to wait before she attempted to remove the dress, reeking as it was.

"I just want you to be clean," she said quietly, even though she knew the girl couldn't understand her. Perhaps she could understand her tone, and it would help to assuage her fears. "And warm. After your bath, I'll dress you in something soft and comfortable." Although what that would be, Abigail didn't know. Yet she was surprised at how strangely pleasing the thought was, to see this poor child warm and dressed and fed.

Finally Jensen had filled the tub, leaving a can of water heating over the fire in case Abigail needed more.

"Thank you, Jensen, that will be all," Abigail said, aware she was treating her maid with a crisp authority that she rarely used. Jensen gave her another dark look, muttering something, before she left the room.

Abigail turned back to the girl, who had stopped the shuddering gasps, although she still trembled.

"I must get that dress off you," Abigail said gently. She had already decided the easiest way would be to cut it off, but she was afraid of frightening her again. She went to her workbox by the window and took out a small pair of scissors.

"Look." With one hand on her shoulder, Abigail showed the girl the scissors. Her eyes widened, her lips trembling as she tried to back away, and gently Abigail squeezed her shoulder before gesturing to her dress. "Just the dress. It must come off." She nodded towards the tub of steaming water. "So you can wash." The girl simply stared, still trembling, and Abigail wondered if she would ever be able to make her understand.

"Wash," she said again, and took the flannel Jensen had laid out and mimed scrubbing her body, feeling quite ridiculous as she did so. "Clean." She glanced back at the girl, smiling, her hands held out. "See?"

Slowly, warily, the girl eyed the tub, and then Abigail, back and forth once, then twice. Finally she jerked her head in the semblance of a nod. Abigail's heart felt as if it were blooming, hope and something far more precious unfurling inside her. "You understand," she said wonderingly. "*You understand.*" The girl did not reply, and Abigail stepped forward, once again gesturing to the scissors and then the dress. "Cut. I'm going to cut the dress. All right?" The girl didn't nod but she didn't scream or flail either, and slowly, her heart beating, Abigail lifted the hem of the dress and started to cut through the cheap, rough cloth.

The girl flinched and trembled, but she didn't move as Abigail cut the wretched garment from the hem to its top and it fell to the floor, fit only to be burned.

The girl was naked and pitiful. Abigail stared at her for a moment, noting with appalled horror the sharp point of each rib, the painful jut of her hipbones. The girl hunched her shoulders, and that was when Abigail saw the still-raw wounded stripes on her back that could only have been put there by a whip or cane.

"Lord have mercy," she whispered. To whip such a small child… Silently she gestured to the tub, and with one hand on her shoulder, avoiding the painful, oozing marks, Abigail steered her into the tub. The girl flinched back as her toes entered the water. Abigail knelt beside it to check that it wasn't too hot, and gently moved her forward. Finally, the girl crouched in the tub, her arms around her knees, her eyes dark and fearful, as she waited for whatever would happen next, her fate in Abigail's hands.

Abigail dipped the flannel in the water and then gently squeezed it over the girl's arms. She flinched again but didn't protest, which Abigail took as encouragement. Minute by painstaking minute, she gently washed the girl, dabbing as softly as she could over the stripes on her back, the red chafe marks on her poor, skinny wrists from the heavy manacles she still wore.

"You poor thing," Abigail whispered as she washed, her heart so heavy within her it felt like a burden she could not possibly carry. "You poor, poor thing."

When she was finished, she took a towel and wrapped it around the child and set her on a chair by the fire to warm herself through. Then she rang for Jensen, who came reluctantly, clearly still out of sorts.

"I'll need ointment for her sores, and also two cups of chocolate."

Jensen's eyes rounded. "*Chocolate* –"

"Yes, Jensen," Abigail said sharply. "Chocolate." She gestured to the dirty dress on the floor. "And you may burn that as quickly as possible."

Grumbling, the maid left, holding the torn dress between two pinched fingers, and Abigail draped a blanket over the girl. She was still shivering. She would need proper clothes, and soon.

"There." She stepped back with a smile. "That's much better, isn't it?" The girl, of course, did not reply. "You need a name," Abigail decided. "I must call you something." She thought for a moment. "I've always liked the name Celia," she said finally. It gave her a little wrench to admit it; if she'd had a baby girl, she would have named her Celia. She pointed to herself. "Abigail."

Then she pointed to the girl as she stared. "Celia." She repeated the process three times, hoping to make the girl – Celia – understand, but after the third time the girl shook her head.

"Adedayo," she said, and pointed to herself.

Abigail was jolted; part of her hadn't realized the girl had understood anything, despite the earlier nod; she hadn't expected her to. She'd thought her quite dumb.

"Ade…" she began, and then shook her head. "Say it again."

The girl seemed to understand her request, for she pointed to herself again, a new light in her eyes, making her seem almost fierce. "Adedayo."

"Ad-ay-die-oh," Abigail repeated carefully. "That is your name." The girl nodded, and something lurched inside Abigail. She already had a name.

Animals, Abigail thought numbly, dumb animals who couldn't think or feel the way she did, didn't have names. They didn't have mothers and fathers who named them, who called them by that name. The thought was too overwhelming to contemplate, to consider its awful implications. Abigail pushed it to the back of her mind.

Jensen came in with a tray of chocolate and a small pot of the lanolin-based ointment Abigail used on cuts and grazes. She harrumphed as she set the tray down, but Abigail just ignored her.

"Here we are," she said to Adedayo, and held up the small clay pot of ointment. "To help." She pointed to the raw marks on her wrists. "See?" She dabbed a bit of the ointment on her own hand and rubbed it in. Adedayo watched carefully, and when Abigail raised her eyebrows expectantly, she nodded.

Gently Abigail dabbed the ointment on the raw marks on her wrists, and then the terrible stripes on her back, shuddering a little as her fingers gently, so gently, smoothed over the ridged, wounded flesh. How could someone whip a child like this? And yet she already knew how James would respond to such a question: *They're not properly human, my love. The whip or the cane is the only way they can learn to obey.*

And she'd agreed with him; she still had to agree with him, because he was her husband and she loved him. Because he couldn't be so wrong about this. She couldn't think about what it meant if he was.

After all, she told herself rather sternly, possessing a name was no great accomplishment, and Abigail didn't even know if the gibberish she'd spoken was in fact a name. Perhaps it was something else entirely. Perhaps she'd just been babbling. It didn't have to *mean* anything, but as she put the pot of ointment away, Abigail wasn't even sure what it was she didn't want it to mean.

"And now some chocolate," she said with determined cheer, taking one of the bowls of melted chocolate, cream and sugar that had become all the fashion to drink. She took a sip to demonstrate, and then handed Adedayo her own bowl.

The little girl cradled the bowl in both of her small hands, looking apprehensive as she stared down into its dark, milky depths.

"Sip," Abigail encouraged, sipping again, and her heart swelled as the girl finally took a tiny sip. The smile that bloomed across her face made Abigail want to cry or sing, she wasn't sure which. She drank the whole bowl quickly, too quickly, despite Abigail's gentle cautioning to slow down.

"I suppose you were hungry," she said with a laugh, and then Adedayo let out a little moan before she was violently sick all over herself, the carpet, and the chair. "Oh!" Abigail backed away in disgust while Adedayo started to cry, silent tears running down her face as she cowered in the chair. "Oh dear," Abigail said. "Oh dear."

The brief satisfaction and even happiness she'd felt while tending to Adedayo vanished in light of the present reality; so much mess, so much cleaning, and Adedayo needed a bath again, but the water was scummy, black, and unuseable. Jensen, Abigail knew, would refuse to help. To fill a tub a second time for this little slave child was a luxury not to be thought of.

"It's all right," Abigail soothed, because she could not bear Adedayo's silent crying; it was worse than if she'd sobbed or raged. "It's all right."

She rang for more towels, and fresh water, although not enough to fill the tub, and when Jensen saw the mess of sick, her lips tightened, but she wisely said nothing. An hour later, Abigail had managed to bath Adedayo again, and drape a robe around her shoulders, and she was exhausted, wilting in every way, her spirits as low as her body as she struggled to process the day's events.

Then James came home.

Abigail heard his quick steps coming up the stairs. Adedayo had only just fallen asleep in the chair by the fire, wrapped in a blanket, her head drooping.

"How are you finding it?" James asked in a booming voice that startled Abigail.

"Ssh." Abigail met him at the door, even though she longed only to crawl into bed herself and close her eyes to everything. "She's sleeping."

"Sleeping!" James frowned. "I thought she would be helping you, making herself useful."

"She's exhausted, poor thing." Abigail gave Adedayo a concerned look, thankful she'd fallen asleep again. "I gave her a bath."

"Goodness, she's a lucky one, then. But you mustn't be too tender with her, my dear. These creatures need to know their place."

Abigail found herself bristling at his choice of words. "She's just a little girl, James."

He let out a quick laugh. "A little girl! Are you already fond of her?"

Jolted, Abigail shrugged. "Fond? No. I don't even know her. But she…" She hesitated, words and thoughts and feelings that she didn't know how to articulate swirling through her. What *did* she feel about Adedayo? What could she possibly allow herself to feel? "She has a name," she finally said. "She told me."

"A name?" James looked nonplussed.

"Yes. Ade – Adedayo."

"A heathen name, indeed." He frowned. "You aren't thinking of calling her that, surely?"

Abigail faltered. "It is her name."

"Abigail, my dear, be reasonable. The fashion for these things is to give her a proper name, like a little lady. Not some heathenish name no one can say."

"You mean, like a – like a toy." She didn't know why she found the thought so distasteful.

"A useful toy, I hope. Why not Adelaide?" He smiled placatingly. "It has a similar sound, at least."

Abigail hesitated again, because part of her resisted calling Adedayo anything but her own real name, especially when she recalled that fierce light in her eyes, the way she'd pointed to her chest. To take away her name…

Then she realized she was being ridiculous. Adedayo was a slave, no more than her possession, her plaything. And Abigail knew she could not possibly introduce her new acquisition with a name like Adedayo. A heathen name, as James had said, and impossible to pronounce.

"Yes, of course," she murmured. "Adelaide is a good name."

"There. You see?" He patted her on the shoulder. "My dear, you look completely jaded and worn out. Why don't you rest? I'll call Jensen to take her away." He nodded to Adedayo – *Adelaide*. She would need to remember.

"Jensen does not want to have anything to do with her, I'm afraid." Abigail smiled wearily. "She refused to share her room, as well."

"Ah. I suspect she'll come round in time, once the girl's been trained." He glanced at Adelaide appraisingly. "In the meantime, I suppose she can sleep in the warehouse."

"The warehouse?" Adjoined to the house, it was a large, draughty room with no heating or comfort at all, its windows all shuttered against any light.

"I assure you, my dear, she will consider it a palace compared to what she is used to! These creatures slept in the crudest of mud huts, with nothing on. You cannot even imagine the wretched barbarity of it."

"But you haven't seen it yourself," Abigail said quietly.

"Pardon?" James swung around, eyebrows raised expectantly. "I'm sorry, my dear. I didn't hear you."

"Nothing," Abigail murmured. She did not want to argue with James, or cast doubt on what he said. He was her husband, and she loved him. Of course he knew about these things – far more than she did.

"I'll take her down now," he said, and strode towards the slumbering girl.

"Now? But she's asleep."

"I don't want her to disturb you any longer. You need a proper rest."

Abigail bit her lip. "What about her manacles? They're so heavy –"

"I don't think they should be taken off until we can trust her."

"But she's a child, James." Abigail doubted she was more than six.

"Even so. You hear stories. I do not wish to fear for your safety."

"Why not wait until she wakes?" Abigail suggested. She felt, suddenly and desperately, that she did not want James to take Adelaide down to the warehouse, where it was so dark and cold. "Take her then."

"You can hardly rest when she is in here with you!"

"I can," Abigail said quietly, but it was too late. James had woken Adelaide by shaking her shoulder, and Abigail watched helplessly as he pulled her up to her feet before she'd even blinked the sleep from her eyes.

"Come on, now," he said in a firm and cheerful voice. "Down you go."

Adelaide glanced fearfully at Abigail, who tried to smile. "It's quite all right, Aded – Adelaide. Quite all right. I shall see you later."

"She can't understand you," James told her.

"I know."

He began to steer Adelaide towards the door, and the girl let out a high-pitched keening sound that tore at Abigail's heart worse than anything she'd felt before. She pressed her hands to her face.

"James, please let her –"

"Come on, now." He clamped down on her shoulder, forcing her to walk more quickly. "Enough of that racket."

"*James!*"

But he was already gone, steering Adelaide out of the door and down the stairs, and all the while the girl screamed, the sound ghostly and horrible, ringing in Abigail's ears. She feared she would hear it for the rest of her life.

Abigail bit her lip, her hands clenched so tightly together her knuckles were white. Even after James had taken Adelaide to the warehouse and bolted the door, she could hear the awful screaming. After a while it turned to a horrible moaning, and then, finally, it went silent, which was worse, far worse.

Up in her bedroom, with sleep impossible, Abigail wept.

CHAPTER FIFTEEN

Rachel

"I believe your mother is suffering from vascular dementia." The consultant, Miss Jones, used a gentle, sorrowful voice that made Rachel tense all the more.

She'd spent a sleepless night at the house in Windermere before heading back to the hospital this morning. Anthony had rung while she'd been asleep, and she hadn't listened to the voicemail he'd left yet, although the alert for it glared accusingly at her every time she looked at her phone. She didn't have the strength to deal with his expectant concern, the kind that asked for something in return, on top of everything else.

Now, after several hours of waiting for her mother to return from various scans and tests, Rachel was sitting with the consultant and hearing the bad news, except she didn't actually know what it meant.

"What is vascular dementia?" she asked. "I mean, compared to, well, regular dementia, I suppose."

"Vascular dementia accounts for twenty per cent of all dementia cases. It's a form of dementia caused by damage to the blood vessels in the brain, which leads to restricted blood flow and damaged brain cells."

"Okay..." That didn't actually tell her what she wanted and needed to know. "What does it mean practically for my mother?"

"It means she'll have issues with memory loss and communication. You might find her moods changing; she might become irritable or even aggressive."

No change, then. Rachel managed to keep from saying it out loud. "Communication? You mean – she won't be able to speak?"

"She'll forget words, in the main. Eventually it will become more severe."

"And memory loss?"

"Confusion, similar to what she experienced yesterday."

"And the prognosis –"

"Is the same for every person with dementia. Eventually it will lead to death, but that can take years. Decades, in some instances."

"Do you think that will be the case with my mother?"

The consultant shrugged and spread her hands. "It's impossible to say. I do believe, however, that your mother has had dementia for some time."

Rachel nodded slowly, doing her best to absorb it all. "You mentioned treatment?" she asked finally.

"I'm going to prescribe a medication that will help with her blood pressure, and I'd recommend both cognitive and physiotherapy. There is no treatment for vascular dementia per se, but therapies have been shown to help slow decline."

It all sounded so grim. Rachel swallowed. "Is she... do you think she is able to live alone? I mean, independently." She thought of the huge, empty house, with its steep stairs and empty rooms. A death trap now, perhaps.

"At the moment, yes, I think that is possible, perhaps with some help from a carer or family, but that is something that will have to be continually assessed."

And what then? Would she stick her mother into a nursing home like someone who had worn out their welcome, gone past their sell-by date? It seemed so heartless, and yet Rachel wasn't sure she could contemplate anything else.

"Have you told her all this?" she asked. "She's... aware of the situation?"

"Yes, we've had a conversation, and I've given her some literature." The consultant reached for some pamphlets and passed them to Rachel. "I hope these will be helpful for you as well."

"Thank you." She glanced down at a colourful one, "Living with Memory Loss". *No thanks.* You could dress it up with bright colours and smiling pensioners, but it was still awful. "When will she be released from hospital?"

"She can be released tomorrow morning. I want to keep her in for observation for one more night, because of her head injury, but after that there's nothing more we can do." The consultant smiled regretfully. "I'm sorry."

Rachel nodded jerkily. Now what? She had been planning to head back to Bristol soon, but obviously that wasn't going to happen, and she didn't know when it would.

"Thank you," she said again, and left the room to go in search of her mother.

Deborah was lying in bed, the sheet neatly folded down, her hands clasped across her middle as she stared out of the window. The rain had finally cleared and it was a beautiful spring day, the sky a deep, penetrating blue, the sun shining down as if it were trying to make up for lost time.

Lost time. How much more would there be?

"Hey, Mum." Rachel came into the room cautiously; her mother didn't move or even turn her head. "Did you have a good night?"

"As well as can be expected in a place like this."

"The consultant... she spoke to me about your diagnosis."

Deborah pressed her lips together and said nothing.

"I'm so sorry."

Still nothing.

"Mum, please. I want to help."

"How?" Deborah asked flatly. "There's nothing you can do."

Rachel silently acknowledged this before ploughing on. "The house. You want to sell it? I can help with that, at least. Get it ready."

"Very well." Deborah turned to look at her, and the bleakness Rachel saw in her eyes made her want to crumble. She wanted to bridge this awful chasm that had opened up between them decades ago, but it felt too late. Far, far too late, in too many ways.

"What would you like me to do?" Focusing on the practicalities was far easier. "I could ring an estate agent, box some things up. What do you want to do with all the furniture?"

Deborah shrugged, and Rachel realized her mother could hardly make these decisions right now, from a hospital bed, her diagnosis just hours old.

"Sorry," she murmured. "I know that's all a bit much right now."

"How's my favourite lady?"

Rachel tensed at the booming voice of another doctor as he came jauntily into the room. She was used to the quiet, compassionate manner of the consultant she'd spoken to, not this man's jarringly cheerful attitude, big and blowsy.

He smiled at her, his eyes crinkling at the corners. "I'm Dr Taylor. I'm the junior registrar in geriatric medicine. I'm here just to check Mrs Barnaby's sats."

"Sats?" Rachel repeated dumbly.

"Oxygen saturation levels."

Rachel watched as he put a plastic clip on the end of her mother's finger. Deborah turned her head away.

"I'm not talking to you," she stated coldly.

Rachel cringed at her mother's rudeness. "Mum –"

"It's all right." Dr Taylor winked at her. "She confuses me with someone else. We get there in the end."

"What?" Rachel goggled at him, shocked by this seemingly blasé admission. "What do you mean?"

He shrugged. "She calls me Will, and my name's Jack. But it's fine. I'm used to it, trust me. Almost done, love, and you're looking good, I'm happy to say. Going home tomorrow, I hear."

Her mother was confusing this man, with his loud, somewhat brash manner, with someone else? With her *father*? Because who else could Will be? Rachel could not comprehend it. A little disorientation, yes. Forgetting to fill the kettle, fine. But this utter – confusion? This incapacity? It filled her with something like panic.

"Mum," Rachel said, an urgent note entering her voice, "this is the doctor. Dr Taylor. You know that, right? You know who he is?"

"I'm not talking to him," Deborah stated again in that same cold voice. "He knows why."

"Mum –"

"He knows," Deborah said, her voice rising. "He always knows, and never once has he even *tried* to apologize."

"Apologize?" Rachel's mind spun and her stomach churned. She felt faint, and nearly as discombobulated as her mother obviously was. She didn't want to think about what any of this meant.

"Leave it," Dr Taylor said quietly. "It doesn't help correcting them when they're like this. You just have to go along with it until the fog lifts. I'm sorry."

Rachel looked away as she blinked back sudden tears. What was happening?

"All done, Mrs Barnaby. Take care now." He patted her mother's shoulder and gave Rachel a sympathetic smile before leaving the room. She turned back to her mother, at a complete loss.

"Mum…"

"He always tries to make it up to me without ever actually saying sorry, and the truth is, I let him." She turned back to Rachel, irritable now. "Why are you still here? Where's your father?"

"He's…" Rachel swallowed hard. "He's gone now. He'll be back later."

Deborah nodded, leaning her head against the pillow and closing her eyes. "Good."

Fifteen minutes later, with her mum asleep, Rachel left. She needed a break, so she drove back to the house, thinking she could get a start on readying it for sale before her mother came home.

But as she walked through the empty rooms, she realized she wasn't ready to face any of it, and she could hardly make decisions about her mother's things – furniture, photographs, personal belongings. The last thing her mother would want was Rachel boxing everything up without a by-your-leave.

A text pinged on her phone, and her heart lifted when she saw it was from Jane. "*Have you gone already? Haven't seen you around x*"

Rachel was about to text to explain, when she realized she didn't want to do it by phone. She hadn't thought about the shipwreck or Whitehaven or the Fentons once since she'd left Goswell, but now she realized she was still curious – and she desperately needed a distraction from her own complicated life. After a few moments' reflection, she texted, "*Had to see my mum. Bit of an emergency. Coming back to Whitehaven now for the afternoon.*"

"*Fancy a coffee?*" Jane texted back, and Rachel's eyes stung. She was so kind, and Rachel knew she needed a friend right now, more than ever.

"That would be lovely."

Just over an hour later she was sitting in the local archives centre, asking the kindly archivist to pull up anything that mentioned the Fentons, and make photocopies. She'd also sent an email to her friend Soha at the British Library, asking her to photocopy the Fenton Collection and send her the pdfs – a huge favour but one she hoped Soha would agree to.

It felt good to focus on something other than her mother and the half-formed questions that kept flitting vaguely through her mind. Much better, much easier, to think about James Fenton, slave trader, ship's captain, and try to figure out how his pocket watch had ended up at the bottom of the Irish Sea. If there was a mystery there, Rachel was determined to unravel it.

The local archives didn't have very much on the Fentons, but it was enough to pique Rachel's interest yet again: their address – a house on Queen Street that was still standing; Abigail's presence at a meeting at the assembly rooms on Howgill Street; and Abigail's attendance and membership at the Methodist chapel on Michael Street.

"That wasn't built until 1761," the archivist explained. "So it would have been quite new, and as it is not noted that James Fenton or his wife's family were Methodists, I imagine it was something of a dissension. Most of the prominent merchant families of that time would have been staunchly Church of England."

"Interesting," Rachel murmured. She hadn't learned anything, not really, but she still felt as if she had. She'd been given a glimpse into this other world, and she wanted to see more.

She had twenty minutes before she was due to meet Jane, so she decided to walk down Queen Street and take a look at the Fentons' former house.

When she reached it, however, it proved to be a disappointment; it had been made into flats with a modern façade years ago, and now looked sadly worse for wear, with barely a hint of the fine townhouse with warehouse attached, according to the records, that it once must have been.

Rachel stood in front of it for several minutes, trying to imagine what it must have been like once upon a time. Her eyes fluttered closed as she pictured the scene – the horse-drawn carriages, the maids hurrying on errands for their mistresses, the smell of coal smoke and manure in the air, both a hallmark of eighteenth-century life.

She pictured the house – not with its soulless boxy exterior, but having an elegant Georgian façade with large, sash windows and a brass knocker on the smartly painted door.

And then she tried to picture the Fentons, although she'd never seen portraits of them. James, Abigail, and their daughter Adelaide. What had they looked like? What had they *been* like? And how had James Fenton, captain of his own ship, *The Fair Lady*, on a voyage from the Caribbean with a cargo of sugar and rum, foundered off the coast of Cumbria, so close to home?

Rachel's phone pinged with another text from Jane: "*At the café now! Can I order you a latte?*"

"*Yes, thanks,*" Rachel texted back. "*I'll be there in 5.*"

She glanced back up at the house, its mirror-like windows giving nothing away, the door a modern, metal one with a silver handle, a row of buzzers next to it. All so different from what it once was. What it should still have been.

As she was turning away, someone left the house, wheeling a bike out, a woman in Lycra with braided hair and multiple piercings in both ears. She glanced indifferently at Rachel before looking away, and with her heart strangely heavy, almost as if she were grieving the house along with so many other things, Rachel started walking towards the café.

Jane had ordered them both lattes and had nabbed the best table at the back, with deep, squashy armchairs and a low coffee table between them.

"What kind of emergency?" she asked as she handed Rachel her latte. "You poor thing. No emergency is actually small, is it?"

"Well, some are bigger than others." Rachel took a sip of her coffee as her mother and her diagnosis, the hospital – all of it – came rushing back to her. For a few blissful hours she'd been able not to think of it. It had almost felt like forgetting, except of course she hadn't. It was her mother who was forgetting – or perhaps remembering. *He knows why.* What decades-old conversation had she been having with her father? Rachel was afraid to ask. To know.

"Is your mum all right?" Jane asked, blowing on her coffee, her kindly face wreathed with concern.

"Yes and no. She had a fall and was taken to hospital, and that's all mostly fine, but…" Rachel hesitated. "They've diagnosed her with vascular dementia."

"Oh, Rachel!" Jane reached over to squeeze her hand. "How terribly difficult. I'm so, so sorry."

"Me too." Rachel managed a small smile. "We've never had the best relationship, and I have a feeling this is going to make it worse."

"That really is so hard." Jane shook her head slowly. "But why haven't you had a good relationship with her?"

"Oh…" Rachel felt her throat thicken and she strived to keep her tone even, if not quite light. "I don't know, actually." She never talked about her mother to anyone. She'd tried once or twice with Anthony, but he hadn't understood it. *What do you mean? She's a bit British, but she seems nice enough.* Perhaps he hadn't wanted to understand. Or maybe Rachel hadn't been able to explain properly. She wasn't sure she could now.

"You don't know?" Jane frowned. "So nothing happened, precisely? I mean, you know, like an event?"

"No, no event, unless you count my father dying."

"Oh goodness, I'm sorry. I didn't mean to –"

"No, no, it's fine." Rachel waved her apologies aside. "We drifted further apart after he died, but even before that…" She shrugged. "She was never very maternal, I suppose."

"In what way?"

"I don't know." Rachel suddenly felt defensive, although she couldn't say why. "She wasn't the type of mum to give hugs or kisses, or ask how your day at school was." She pictured coming home from school, the house cold and dark, her mother sitting alone in the living room with a glass of sherry, seeming to ignore Rachel along with the rest of the world. "I can't really explain it better than that. She just never seemed particularly interested in me." *And I wasn't interested in her.* Uncomfortably Rachel recalled her mother's weary words: *You left me alone for thirty-seven years.* How could her mother see it that way? She'd been the child; she'd been the one who had been left alone. Hadn't she?

"I suppose some women aren't maternal," Jane said with a little grimace. "And they have children anyway, especially ones of your mother's generation. It was the thing to do."

"Was it? I was born in the 1980s. Plenty of women were having careers, putting off having children to pursue their jobs." But not her mother. She'd never had a career, as far as Rachel knew, although she'd done some secretarial work for the BBC before meeting Will Barnaby. He'd breezed into the office one day, as buoyant and charming as always, and swept her right off her feet to Cumbria. At least, that had been her father's story. Rachel had never asked her mother.

"True, I suppose. In any case, I'm sorry. It sounds like a difficult situation. Is there anything I can do?"

"I don't think so. She's going home tomorrow, and then I suppose I'll return to Bristol once I feel she's settled in all right."

"Oh, really?" Jane looked disappointed. "I thought you were staying around here, you know, because of the shipwreck."

"I'm afraid the shipwreck is going to stay wrecked," Rachel said with a small smile. "Copeland Mining Company has moved on, and no one has the funds or interest to excavate it further."

"But it all sounded so interesting."

"It was. Actually, I'm still looking into it on my own a bit." Afraid she was boring her with too many details, Rachel gave her the potted version of *The Fair Lady*, the Fentons, and the pocket watch at the bottom of the sea.

"That is so intriguing," Jane exclaimed, which gratified Rachel. "Why would it have been reported that the ship sank in the Caribbean when it obviously didn't?"

"Perhaps they were just guessing, or someone reported it wrongly. It was so long ago. Although I must admit my mind jumps to all sorts of conspiracy theories."

"Such as?" Jane asked, leaning forward, her eyes alight.

"Oh, I don't even know. He sank the ship for the insurance? That was known to be done at the time, especially if too many slaves had been lost during the middle passage. There was a landmark case in the 1780s that ruled against claiming slaves as lost cargo, but *The Fair Lady* sank well before that, in 1767, right before the slave trade ended, in Whitehaven at least – although that was for an economic rather than a moral reason. They lost out to Liverpool."

"But if it was for the insurance, why wouldn't he sink it in the Caribbean, far from any investigations?" Jane asked. "And how did he die with it, assuming he did? Surely he wouldn't have been on the ship when it sank?"

"I honestly don't know, and I'm not sure if I ever will. I've asked a friend to send me photocopies of the letters he sent his wife while on that voyage, but I doubt I'll find anything some other able historian wasn't able to."

"Oh, but it really is so interesting. You'll keep me posted, won't you? And you'll stay in touch?"

"Yes, of course." Rachel felt a pang of loss at leaving Jane; she was the first proper non-work friend she'd made in ages.

A few minutes later they hugged goodbye; Jane had to pick up Ben from football practice, and Rachel needed to head back to the house. She was exhausted, even as she was dreading being alone in its empty rooms.

She'd spend the evening tucked up in bed, she decided, with the photocopies of the archived materials about the Fentons. Perhaps there was something she'd missed.

The night was calm and clear as Rachel drove back through the lonely sweep of sheep-dotted fells, struggling not to keep asking questions she wasn't sure she wanted answered.

As she turned into the gravel drive, her heart froze and then turned over; there was another car in the drive, an olive-green Mini she knew well. And then, as she pulled up next to it, a man stepped out of the car, far too big and shambling for such a small car, a slightly cautious smile on his creased and weary face.

Anthony.

CHAPTER SIXTEEN

Abigail

Whitehaven, 1766

The morning after Adelaide's arrival, Abigail woke early, even before Jensen had come in to light the morning fires, and crept downstairs, through James's study, to the door leading to his warehouse. All had been silent from within since late last evening, when James had taken Adelaide an evening meal of bread and water, and left it on the floor.

"Shouldn't she have something more?" Abigail had asked, and James had shaken his head.

"Her stomach wouldn't be used to it, and she'd just be sick."

Abigail thought of the chocolate, and flushed. "Still – she must be hungry."

"She'll do." James had patted her shoulder. "Really, you must not fret yourself over her, my dear. She's meant to help and amuse you, not be a source of worry or concern. She's being treated better here than she ever was before."

Abigail thought of the stripes on the girl's back, and did not think such a sentiment counted for very much. "I know," she said, trying to smile. "And she does... amuse me. She's a lovely gift, thank you, James." James beamed his gratified delight even as something in Abigail cringed and curdled at her own words. Adelaide did not *amuse* her at all.

Now she unlocked the warehouse door with the key she'd found on top of James's bureau, her heart thumping as if she were doing something wrong. Perhaps she was.

It was dark in the windowless warehouse, the smell both stale and sweet. It was also completely silent, and Abigail's thumping heart seemed to still.

What if...

She didn't even want to think it.

"Adelaide?" she whispered, and there was no response. "Adedayo?" Still nothing.

Leaving the door ajar, Abigail went to the kitchen in search of a candle, returning to the warehouse with it lifted above her head. She swept it around the warehouse, now piled with barrels of sugar and casks of rum, the smell sickly sweet. James must have had the cargo unloaded yesterday, while she'd been with Adelaide. Looking at it now, Abigail didn't think it was as much as there usually was after a ship came into port; the warehouse was barely half filled.

"Adedayo," she called again, and then she saw her, curled up against a barrel of sugar, her face streaked with tears, her eyes open and yet blank. "Adedayo!" Abigail dropped to her knees on the hard floor, putting one hand on the girl's shoulder.

She stirred, flinching under Abigail's touch before she burrowed against the barrel of sugar, away from her.

"Oh, Adedayo," Abigail murmured as she took in the girl's wretched state. She hated to imagine her alone in this horrible, dark place all night, terrified and having no idea what had happened to her or why. "Come with me," she murmured, and reached for the girl's hand.

She came docilely, as if all the fight had gone out of her, and that made Abigail even sadder. Not wanting to disturb, or rather alert, James, Abigail took her to the upstairs parlour. From the second floor she heard Jensen stirring, and hoped she'd light the fires soon. Although sunlight was streaming through the windows, the air held a decided chill.

Abigail wrapped Adedayo in a blanket and dabbed ointment on her wrists, which looked even more sore and red than they had last night. The manacles, she decided, had to come off. Today.

A few minutes later, Jensen came in with a scuttle of coal, nearly dropping it on the carpet when she caught sight of them.

"I thought she was staying in the warehouse."

"No, that is no place for a child," Abigail said crisply, although in truth she didn't know where the girl would sleep. "Please make the fire, Jensen. It's very cold."

Jensen was stiff and silent as she went about her tasks while both Abigail and Adedayo watched quietly.

"And please bring us a pot of tea and some bread and butter," Abigail commanded once she was finished, and Jensen gave her a sullen look.

"No more chocolate, then?" she asked, and Abigail lifted her chin.

"Not today."

James came in as Abigail was breaking off bits of bread to feed Adedayo, as if she were a little bird, her mouth opening and closing without a sound. She ate slowly, chewing and swallowing with effort, making Abigail's heart ache.

"My goodness." He stopped in the doorway, smelling of his bergamot pomade, dressed for the day. "What have we here?"

"The warehouse was cold and dark." Abigail tried not to sound accusing. "And she's clearly hungry."

"I see." She could not tell anything from his tone.

"James…" Abigail twisted around to face him. "Please, can you take her manacles off? Look at her poor wrists. They are so raw and sore looking."

James's frown, no more than a faint crease between his brows, deepened into a furrow. "Abigail, my dear, I fear you are being too trusting."

"What could she do? She is but a child. I doubt she has passed her sixth birthday."

"Even so."

"Please, James. It seems so cruel." As soon as she said the words, she knew they were the wrong ones. Her husband would only say she was being too tender, too sensitive. *They don't feel as we do, my dear.* And, she realized, he would not like her implying he was cruel – which he wasn't. Of course he wasn't. But perhaps he was mistaken, at least in this. He had to be.

"Abigail, my dear." He took a step into the room. "I confess she does seem so small and innocent, and heaven knows I would not bring any person or thing into this house that could be a danger to you, but – " he spread his hands – "you hear such stories. Whole plantations in the Caribbean burned to the ground. Masters poisoned. I have even heard such dreadful tales of slaves practising unfathomable dark arts. Voodoo, it is called."

Abigail resisted the urge to shiver. Surely James was trying to scare her. "But she's just a child," she said again. "She could not burn or poison anyone, and as for dark arts…" She gestured helplessly. "Surely not?"

"You cannot imagine, Abigail."

Nor can you, Abigail thought, feeling both uncharitable and treacherous for it. She sensed James becoming intractable in a way he so rarely was, settling into a slightly pompous but well-meaning authority she chafed against, just as Adedayo chafed against her iron bands.

The little girl had gone still when James entered the room, eyeing them both warily, her bound hands resting on her lap. Abigail realized she needed to take a different tack with her husband; she needed to play to his vanity – a thought that made her cringe. Never before had she had to use such artful manipulation, and it felt wrong. He was not that kind of man, he never had been, and yet in this it seemed as if he was.

"Of course, it must be as you say," she said demurely, hating herself for the deceit. "And if you do in fact fear she is capable of some terrible act of violence…" She paused, waiting for the inevitable retraction of such an obviously overblown statement.

"Not as such, of course," he said hastily. "Not as *such.*"

"It is only," Abigail continued, her gaze lowered, "that I cannot possibly begin to train her with her hands bound. It is quite impossible, which makes her rather useless." Abigail gave a pretty little shrug of her shoulders, half amazed that James did not seem to see through her little charade. When had she ever acted like this? When had it ever needed to be like this between them?

He rubbed his chin thoughtfully as he looked at Adedayo. "Yes, yes, I suppose you're right. She does seem quite docile already. I suppose they whipped any real rebellion out of her on the ship."

Abigail flinched inwardly at that, but kept her expression modestly sedate.

"Very well, very well," James finally said, his voice caught between his usual bonhomie and a very slight irritableness. "But at the first sign of disobedience –"

"Yes, of course," Abigail answered quickly. "I do not wish to be subject to any incivility, I assure you. At the very first sign."

She held her breath as James went for the keys and then returned, barking at Adedayo to hold her hands out. She shrank back, and Abigail pressed one comforting hand on her shoulder.

"It's all right," she said softly. "Like this." And she put her hands together before springing them apart, with a smile. Adedayo seemed to understand, for she held them out, and then thankfully the key was turning and the horrible, heavy shackles fell off, Abigail catching them in her hands. She wanted to throw the things away, but she knew James wouldn't countenance it.

"There," she said quietly, smiling at the girl while James tucked the key into his pocket.

"Any sign," he said, a warning, and Abigail nodded.

"Yes, of course. Thank you, James. I shall begin her training directly."

Of course, she realized after he'd left, she had no idea how to train the girl, or even what to train her for. Her main desire was to feed and clothe her, and assure her she was safe. Abigail only hoped she truly was.

A few days later, Abigail had found a routine of sorts; she spent the mornings with Adedayo, teaching her English, and in the afternoons she would read or sew or, occasionally, visit. If she was in the house, she kept the girl in the room with her; if she was out, James had insisted she be locked in the warehouse – something Abigail resisted yet knew she must give in to, and seem as if she did not mind it.

"If she is to be my personal servant, she needs a proper place to sleep," she said one evening when they were dining alone. "How can she learn to serve a gentlewoman in the proper way if she is sleeping like the worst sort of urchin?"

"You are quite right, my dear, but if Jensen refuses to share her chamber, I do not see what either of us can do about it. Good maids are difficult to find, as you well know, and in any case I sympathize with Jensen. The girl is shaping up quite nicely, thanks to all your hard work, but she is still a savage."

"And she will remain so if she is not taught gentle ways, including where she sleeps." Abigail tried to keep the ire and frustration out of her voice. "I have thought upon a solution," she said, striving to sound agreeable. "I think it will be suitable for all concerned."

James stilled, his glass of claret raised halfway to his lips, his eyes narrowed in something almost like suspicion. He had been irritable these last few days, dissatisfied with everything. Although he said nothing of it, Abigail suspected the profit from *The Pearl* was not all he had hoped for, after paying his investors. He'd auctioned the sugar and rum at the marketplace, and had not seemed pleased with the price.

"A solution," he repeated with ominous neutrality. "And what would that be?"

Abigail took a deep breath, gathering her courage even as she tried to sound light, almost dismissive. "She can sleep in our dressing room." The dressing room was a small room adjoining both of their bed chambers; James had taken his own chamber after Abigail's last miscarriage. It was used for bathing and hair dressing, and had a small fireplace. Abigail thought that with some moving of furniture, there would be space for a bed.

"Our dressing room?" James's eyebrows rose incredulously. "Surely you are not serious."

"Why not?"

"So close to where we are sleeping? I could not think of it."

"She is not a danger," Abigail said patiently. "Surely you can see that."

"You don't know –"

"Why did you bring her into the house if you think her such a threat to our safety?" Abigail cried, impatience and anger and something deeper and worse reverberating in her voice.

James stared at her in disbelief. "My dear, I think you forget yourself," he said, a cool note in his voice that made Abigail blink. It felt as if he had slapped her.

She had never been so rebuked, and she blushed with both shame and anger. How had it come to this? And why was she fighting for the wellbeing of a little girl who spoke but a few words of English, who was more than half heathen, a savage as James had said?

Wasn't she?

"I'm sorry," Abigail murmured, looking away. "I do not know what I was thinking of." There seemed nothing else to say that would be acceptable.

"Indeed," James replied, and pointedly began discussing the latest gossip – a pear tree in Mr Fisher's garden that had borne three types of fruit, and a parrot belonging to Mr Peele, which, after being unwell for nearly a month, had laid an egg.

Abigail knew her husband meant to amuse her, but she cared not for parrot or pear. She felt sick inside, with rage and grief and something wilder than both. She could not bring herself to make comment on any of the amusing anecdotes James regaled her with.

At least she'd been able to make Adedayo's sleeping quarters more comfortable. Much to Jensen's ire, Abigail had insisted a mattress of straw ticking and several blankets be brought to the corner of the warehouse where the girl sadly slept, locked in every night after her evening meal of bread and water, eaten while crouched in the back courtyard because neither Jensen nor Cook would have her in the kitchen.

She'd also sewn two plain dresses for her, thankful for her passable skills in needlework. They were far from fashionable, but at least they were not made of that dreadful, rough osnaburg.

Two weeks after *The Pearl* had sailed into harbour with its precious cargo, Adedayo could speak a few hesitant words of English, and was beginning to learn her letters.

She was sitting next to Abigail on the settee in the upstairs parlour, pointing at letters in a chapbook Abigail had procured for the purpose, when James came in, his stride full of purpose.

He frowned as he saw them both. "Should she be sitting next to you like that? She'll get ideas."

"I am teaching her her letters," Abigail answered in the calm and placating tone she'd learned to adopt with him. "Where else should she sit?"

"At your feet, or at least on a footstool. You do not want her becoming rebellious or defiant." So far Adedayo had shown neither of those traits, but to humour James, part of her wondering even now if he might be right, Abigail gestured to the floor. After a moment's confusion, Adedayo silently slipped off the settee and on to the floor, close to Abigail's skirts. James nodded in satisfaction.

"Thank you, Adedayo," Abigail said quietly.

"She is a slave. She doesn't need to be thanked!" James exclaimed, his voice rising. "For heaven's sake, Abigail, you shall give her ideas far above her station."

"Surely Christian decency is available to everyone?" Abigail asked coolly, unable to keep herself from it.

"You mistake my meaning. And you must stop calling her that heathen name. I thought we agreed on Adelaide."

They had, but Abigail was strangely reluctant to call her that. "Her name is —"

"*Adelaide*. Really, do you want to saddle her with such a foreign sounding name? No one will be able to pronounce it, once she can accompany you about in society. It will set her even farther apart than she already is."

Abigail was so pleased with the thought of such a thing that she acquiesced with a stiff nod. "Very well." Gently she touched Adedayo in the centre of her chest. "Not Adedayo. Adelaide. *Adelaide*." The girl simply stared at her with wide, uncertain eyes. "Adelaide," Abigail said again, firmly.

"I am afraid I have some news," James said after a moment, standing with his legs apart and his hands behind his back.

Abigail closed the chapbook. "What is it?"

"The returns on *The Pearl*'s voyage were not all that I had hoped for, especially considering our expenses from last summer, in Bath."

"I thought…" Abigail bit her lip, deciding not to say more. James had assured her they could afford a summer in Bath, but she'd had her doubts. "What shall you do?" she asked instead.

"I am outfitting *The Fair Lady* for another voyage to Africa, but I do not wish to trust the voyage to Phillips, the captain I had before, on *The Pearl*. He didn't procure enough slaves, and the ones he did were far too sickly. I am sure I can do better."

Abigail's eyes widened. "*You* can —"

"Yes, I shall captain *The Fair Lady*," James said rather grandly. "I have sailed in the past, as you know, although admittedly not to Africa. But I am confident in my abilities, as I hope you are, my dear. I will make our fortunes secure."

Abigail's hand fluttered to her throat as she considered the implication of his words. "But the voyage takes over a year."

"I should return next summer, all being well. I trust my fate to Providence."

Abigail wondered what Providence had to do with the capture and sale of slaves, but it was too strange and unwelcome a thought to voice out loud, or even examine in the disquiet of her own mind.

"That is a long time to be away," she said finally. She realized she did not know exactly how she felt about James's departure; amid the fear and sorrow was a treacherous flicker of relief – something else she did not wish to acknowledge or understand.

"Yes, it is," James agreed, "but necessary in this case." He strode towards her, taking her hands in his. "I will secure our fortunes, Abigail. Everything will come right. Just wait and see."

CHAPTER SEVENTEEN

Rachel

Anthony.

Rachel climbed out of the car slowly, her mind spinning. What was he doing here? Why hadn't he told her he was coming? And why, when she so wanted to run straight into his arms and have him enfold her in one of his big, bear-like hugs, did she hold herself back so they were having a staring contest, the tension ratcheting up before they'd even spoken?

She stood by the car, wishing relationships weren't so complicated, wishing *she* wasn't. It always ended up being this way, and she didn't know how to change it. Change herself.

"I thought," Anthony said after a moment, smiling wryly, "if the mountain won't come to Muhammad…"

"Right." Rachel heard how flat her voice sounded and briefly she closed her eyes. She could do better. "Sorry, it's been a long day."

"Were you at the hospital?"

"This morning, yes, but I've just returned from Whitehaven." He frowned. "I thought the project was finished?"

"It was. Is." She felt bands of tension tighten around her forehead as all the problems she'd been trying to forget for an afternoon came toppling back on to her, too heavy a weight, and she gave a shrugging sort of grimace. "I was doing some research and meeting a friend." Which made it sound as if she'd been having a frolic while her mother languished in hospital and

Anthony waited for her to come home. "I needed a break." That didn't sound much better. "Do you want to come in?"

"I'll just get my case."

"Your case? How – how long are you going to stay?"

Anthony gave another wry smile, his eyes filled with hurt. "Don't you want me to?"

"It's not that. I just thought you'd have work. Catering gigs –"

"I cleared my schedule for the next week."

A whole week. That was kind of him. And yet Rachel wished he'd asked first. She didn't intend to be here for another week. "Thank you," she said after a moment. "Although I'm not sure it was necessary."

"It never is," Anthony murmured, and opened the boot of his car. Rachel walked past him to the front door, afraid they were going to have an argument, and she was far too exhausted and emotionally fragile for it. Although, in reality, she and Anthony rarely argued. It was all veiled comments and pointed remarks, followed by tense or sullen silences – just as it had been with her parents.

Was there no escaping the past? Perhaps by escaping *to* it, thinking about someone who died two hundred and fifty years ago, rather than dealing with her own mess. A mess of her own making, because the truth was she didn't think she knew how to be anything other than she was, and what she was wasn't good enough – not for her mother and not for her husband.

With a sigh Rachel walked into the kitchen, flipping on the lights and gazing around at the looming space, her coffee cup by the sink, everything else empty. Of course, there was nothing in the fridge, and she hadn't eaten all day.

Anthony came in behind her.

"I'm sorry, there's no food," she said.

"That's all right. I figured you wouldn't have had time to shop. I brought some things."

"Oh." She turned around to see him put a plastic crate of food on the kitchen table – a pot of basil, a hunk of parmesan, a bottle of wine, fresh pasta. "That was very thoughtful of you."

"Nothing too fancy," Anthony said with a smile. "Just pasta with fresh pesto and a salad. Some wine. What a view." He nodded towards the window over the sink framing a postcard-worthy vista of rolling hills and barren fells. "You could never get tired of looking at that."

Actually, Rachel thought but didn't say, *you could*. "I think I'm going to run a bath," she said instead. "If you don't mind."

Anthony blinked, looking a little hurt; perhaps he'd envisioned them both downloading their last few days over a glass of wine, but Rachel knew she didn't have the energy for it. Not yet.

"All right," he said after a moment. "I'll get started on the pasta."

Upstairs Rachel lay in the bath, staring up at the ceiling, wondering why she had to be so ridiculously difficult when it came to her marriage. She reminded herself of her mother, and she hated that. Why was she so cold? So… *stony*? It was a default setting and she couldn't seem to flick the switch.

Anthony was lovely. Everyone told her so; Rachel saw it herself. He was so thoughtful, bringing all the trappings for a meal tonight, knowing she wouldn't have had time to shop. Why did it just feel like so much pressure? Why did she resent his kindnesses? Was it because she knew she couldn't return them?

The questions circled around in her brain as they had for years now, with no answers – at least none that she wanted to accept. She didn't know why she was the way she was, only that she was.

Except – perhaps she did know. Perhaps she was stiff and formal with her husband because that was how her mother had been with her father. And while Rachel had resented it as a child, she now found herself falling into the same trap.

He knows why.

Why had her mother said that? What could she have possibly meant? And what might it mean for Rachel – doting daughter of one parent; resented, standoffish child of the other? Caught in the middle, except she hadn't been, really, had she? She'd chosen sides a long time ago, and she'd stayed there, just as her mother had said.

The water was getting cold but Rachel still didn't move. She told herself that once she was downstairs she would make an effort, but she knew that even if she did it would ring false. It always did. Anthony would know she was trying, and he never wanted her to have to try.

"Loving someone shouldn't be difficult," he'd once said sadly, and it had made Rachel feel horribly guilty as well as frustrated. She knew this was her fault. Didn't he realize that? And couldn't he appreciate that she was trying, rather than be cross that she had to? Couldn't love be about trying, rather than not having to?

Loving was easy for him – Rachel knew that. He just opened his arms and his heart, made a shedload of pasta, and called it good. And it *was* good. It was simple. Rachel was the complicated one.

"Rachel?" Anthony's voice floated up the stairs, managing to sound both light and anxious. "Pasta's ready."

"Be down in a minute." She pulled the plug, watching the water swirl down the plughole, the air growing cold around her. Finally she rose and wrapped herself in a towel, telling herself she was ready to make an effort, and perhaps not even seem as if she was. Tonight she'd do better than that.

Downstairs the kitchen was full of lovely smells, the table set for two. Anthony had even brought flowers – purple and white freesias he'd put in a crystal vase.

"I hope that's all right," he said as he caught Rachel looking at it. "I took the vase from a cupboard in the dining room."

"It's fine. It's all going to be packed up anyway. The flowers are beautiful," she added. Too much of an afterthought.

"Packed up?" Anthony raised his eyebrows as he started dishing out the pasta. "What do you mean?"

Rachel sat at the table, her chin in her hand, too weary to explain everything, yet knowing she needed to. "My mother is most likely going to sell the house."

"Just because of the fall?"

"It wasn't just a fall. They've diagnosed her with vascular dementia."

"Oh, Rachel." The look of sympathy on Anthony's face made Rachel want to cry, and yet at the same time she knew she didn't want to cry at *all*. If she started, she might not stop, and she wouldn't even know what she was crying for. Too many things – things she didn't want to have to talk about.

"What happened, exactly?" he asked. So she told him about how Deborah had been found wandering around in her nightgown; how she'd become aggressive and hit her head.

"Apparently, she's been going to a memory clinic for a while, although she didn't want me to know about it. But I gather this is the first time she's had an official diagnosis, and from what I've read online vascular dementia is not the best kind to have, if such a thing exists." She'd forced herself to do an internet search at the hospital, and seen that the medication for Alzheimer's wasn't available for vascular dementia.

The life expectancy from diagnosis was four years or less, despite the consultant's optimistic talk of decades, and in any case she believed her mother had been living with it for a while already. It was all so depressing, and it made Rachel feel far sadder than she'd ever expected to feel, for so many reasons.

"So what happens now?" Anthony asked.

"I don't really know. She's coming home tomorrow. I think she is still able to live independently, for the moment anyway, but who knows for how long?" Rachel's throat thickened. "I haven't discussed options with her. She didn't want to talk to me at all. I think the main thing is getting her into reasonable accommodation."

"This must be so hard for her," Anthony murmured, and Rachel had to resist the impulse to say, *But don't you see how it's hard for me?* Of course it was harder, *much* harder, for her mother. She knew that.

"Yes, it must be," she agreed. She twirled a piece of linguine around her fork. The pesto smelled delicious, and she'd been so hungry, but now she found her appetite had vanished. "I really don't know what the solution is, going forward. I don't think she'd ever want to live with us, but I can't see her in a nursing home either. She's far too independent. Perhaps a retirement flat, at least for a little while."

"Why wouldn't she want to live with us? I know it's different than up here, but Bristol is beautiful –"

"Anthony, she can't stand me," Rachel said flatly. "You never seem to see that, but it's true."

"Oh come on, now, Rach –"

"I'm serious." She leaned forward, her hands flat on the table, as some earnest urgency took her over, wanting to prove to him what she'd always known, or at least believed, to be the truth.

"I know you've always thought she's just a bit distant, like it's some generational thing, but she really doesn't *like* me. She never has. After my dad died, she barely spoke to me. We were like two strangers living together, moving around each other as if we were pieces of furniture. I rang her a few days ago, asking if I could see her, and she made out like it was some great inconvenience." Rachel heard the hurt and bitterness in her voice, and inwardly cringed at them both. She sounded so selfish and needy, but she just wanted Anthony to understand.

"Rachel…" Anthony looked uncertain. "I'm sure it wasn't as bad as that. She was quite nice to me."

"Why don't you *believe* me?" she cried. She sounded so hurt, but she'd never understood why he couldn't seem to accept that her mother didn't like her. Perhaps because his own mother adored him, or because Deborah had been nice to him while he was here.

Anthony was silent for a moment. "Because," he finally said slowly. "Because… I know how you are."

Rachel sagged back against her chair, all the pain and anger leaving her in a defeated rush, replaced by something far worse. She stared at him – his shaggy head lowered, his gaze on his uneaten pasta – and felt as if the tectonic plates of their relationship were inexorably shifting. Cracking apart. And it terrified her.

"What is that supposed to mean?" she asked quietly.

"I don't think we should talk about this now."

That was definitely not a good sign. "You were the one who brought it up, so you can at least explain what you meant." The anger was back, her tone sharp, accusing, because anything else felt impossible. The air between them seemed to crackle, the silence as tense as a wire pulled taut enough to snap.

Rachel wished she hadn't pushed, because she didn't think she wanted to hear whatever Anthony was going to say. And yet she knew she had to. She couldn't leave it like this.

He sighed and put down his fork. "I only meant that you're a bit, well, prickly, Rachel. I love you, absolutely I love you, but you can be… well, hard work sometimes. That's all." He paused while she absorbed what she already knew. It still hurt, almost unbearably, for him to say it out loud. He never had before. "I'm not saying this to hurt you."

"Of course you're not." The words were out before she could stop them.

Anthony sighed again and, picking up his fork, began to eat with methodical determination. "That's exactly the kind of thing I mean."

"What does that have to do with my mum, anyway? Are you saying that her acting as if she can't stand me is my fault, because I'm so very *prickly*?"

"I don't think your mum acts as if she can't stand you."

You've left me alone for the last thirty-seven years. "How would you even know? You've seen us together maybe three times."

He shrugged. "Even so."

"So you think it's me? It's how I act towards her that's the issue? Or are you just assuming –" She bit off the word, unable to finish the question. *Because that's how I act towards you.* Anthony knew what she was going to say anyway. She saw it in his eyes.

He paused mid-bite as he glanced up at her, a resigned look on his face. "Do I think it's about how you act towards her? Maybe. Yes."

Rachel felt winded, as if she'd been punched. "You don't even know," she said, her voice ragged. "You didn't live my childhood."

"No. I didn't." He sounded so weary, and meanwhile Rachel felt as if she were shaking with rage and hurt and fear, her emotions overwhelming her at last. She pushed away from the table hard enough to send her chair rocking back. "You shouldn't have come."

He nodded his acknowledgement. "Maybe not."

"You don't understand –"

"Then tell me, Rachel. For heaven's sake, *tell* me." He leaned forward, his gaze imploring. "Why won't you ever tell me what's bothering you? What you're thinking about, even? I feel as if you're always shutting me out deliberately, and I'm battering and battering at the door, trying to get in." He shook his head. "Sometimes I don't know why I bother. I honestly don't."

"I don't either." She bit her lips to keep herself from crying, her hands bunched into fists at her sides.

"Look, I know it hasn't been easy." Anthony's voice was gentle. "With your dad dying so suddenly when you were young. I understand that, Rachel –"

"No, you don't." She took a measured breath, willing both the tears and anger back. "I know you want to, and I'm sure you think you do, but you don't, Anthony, not really."

Rachel had been to Anthony's childhood home in Queens, outside New York City, several times, starting right after they'd got married. It was a jolly, chaotic place, bursting with energy and love, just like him. She remembered his mother at the stove, stirring a vat of pasta while his father snuck an arm around her waist and planted a smacking kiss on her cheek.

There were grandchildren running in and out, plus two dogs, a cat, and a parakeet. Three brothers and a sister, all teasing him with wide smiles and bright eyes to show how thrilled they were that he'd finally taken the plunge. *We were getting worried. How did you convince her to marry you, Ant? You do know what you're getting into, don't you, Rachel?*

So much laughter. So much love. And all of it had made Rachel feel as if she were shrinking into herself, like some vampire plant desperate for sunlight and water yet unable to cope with either.

"Then tell me," Anthony said again, and she shook her head. She had to, because if she started talking she'd fall apart, and she couldn't have that. She just couldn't, not now.

"All I mean," she said after a moment, striving to keep her voice level, "is that you can't understand it if you haven't been through it." Which made it sound as if she'd survived a war. "I know I sound melodramatic. I probably *am* being melodramatic. Everything feels very –" she drew a ragged breath – "emotional right now."

"Oh, Rachel." Anthony stood up and walked over to her, enfolding her in the big bear hug that she craved even as she felt herself go stiff inside his warm embrace. "I'm sorry. I shouldn't have laid this on you now. Incredibly bad timing on my part."

Her cheek was pressed against his shoulder, her eyes tightly closed. "I'm sorry I'm so difficult," she said in a suffocated whisper. "I know you won't believe me, but I really am."

"I do believe you, and in any case, you're not difficult. No more than I am, anyway." His arms tightened around her. "I'm sorry I'm not more understanding. I'm sorry I barrel in everywhere with my plans and my pasta, thinking a good meal is some sort of stupid cure-all when there's clearly a lot more going on."

"I love your pasta."

"Good."

I love you, she wanted to say, and yet somehow couldn't bring herself to. What was wrong with her? Why did this have to be so hard, *still?*

After another moment and one more squeeze, Anthony released her and stepped back, smiling wryly. "Tell me how I can help," he said as he sat back down at the table and resumed eating.

After a second Rachel did the same. They were going to try to be normal, then.

"Tomorrow, with your mom. Tell me what I can do."

"Come with me to the hospital, I suppose. After that I'm not even sure. I don't know how my mum is going to seem or be. I guess I'll need to start helping her organize the house for sale, but whether she wants me to..."

She needed to call Izzy, Rachel realized, and ask for some extended leave. The only bright side to that was the possibility of returning to Whitehaven and doing some more research. Her friend Soha at the British Library had agreed to send her scans of the Fenton Collection, but they hadn't come through yet.

Rachel knew none of it really mattered, and yet somehow it all did. It was a distraction at least, another thread to pull and unravel rather than gaze hopelessly at the knotted tangle of her own life.

"Whatever I can do," Anthony said. "However I can help. I'll do it."

"Yes." Rachel managed a smile. "Yes, thank you. I do appreciate it, Anthony." Her smile wavered and then slipped off her face. "I think I'll go to bed now, though. I'm absolutely shattered."

"Of course you are. I'll be up in a bit, after I've cleared up."

"Oh." Rachel looked at the mess of their plates, their half-finished food. "I can help."

"No, no. It's no trouble at all."

Why, she wondered, did it so often feel as if they were talking to each other like polite strangers? *After you. No, no, after you.* On and on.

Too weary to offer again, she turned and headed upstairs. She'd been sleeping in the single bed in her old bedroom, but she knew Anthony would want to share a double bed. Of course he would.

Wearily she dug through the time-worn sheets of the linen cupboard for those to fit a double, and made up a bed in another room, this one done in blues and greys, the decor thirty years old. Rachel could not remember a time when this room, or any of the others, had ever been used.

She remembered her mother's words with a prickle of disquiet: *rooms full of children, of love and laughter…*

She'd never heard her mother say anything like that before. She'd wanted more children? Yet she'd seemed so unmaternal for all of Rachel's childhood. As for love and laughter, those were words Rachel associated with her father, not her mother.

And yet.

He knows why.

Outside the sun was starting to sink behind the fells, turning their peaks to vivid orange. Downstairs she could hear the clanking of dishes as Anthony washed up.

The beauty and domesticity of it all should have made her happy and thankful, like a comforting blanket tucked around her, but those emotions felt out of reach, like something she could see in the distance but neither touch nor feel.

A wave of sadness rolled over Rachel like a tide, threatening to suck her under. She thought of the wedding photo of her parents above her father's chest of drawers – Will Barnaby looking so confident and bold, so determined and cheerful, while her mother glanced away, a wistful smile on her face, as if she was already half regretting what she'd done, and wondering when it would all start to go wrong.

CHAPTER EIGHTEEN

Abigail

Whitehaven, 1766

The Fair Lady left on the morning tide one day in the middle of May, when the air was soft and the breeze blowing off the harbour was gentle. It felt like a promise, that day, and James treated it as one, vowing to Abigail that he would make things right, return with their fortunes made and everything set to rights.

Abigail did not know how much had already gone wrong, and she did not dare ask. So she smiled, and kissed him goodbye, and with Adelaide standing a little bit behind her, holding her reticule, she watched the ship sail out of the harbour and towards an unknown horizon. He would not be back for at least a year.

Despite their fond goodbyes at the quayside, their parting had not been the sweetest of sorrows. Over the last month Abigail had felt herself inexorably retreating from her husband, just as surely as she sensed him withdrawing from her.

James had been in a flurry for weeks, in and out of the house, visiting every coffee house in Whitehaven, attempting to secure investors for *The Fair Lady*, insistent that if he captained it himself they would be assured of a considerable profit.

"But you have never sailed to Africa before," Abigail felt compelled to gently point out one evening when she was sitting with Adelaide, teaching her to sew. James was poring over a map of the African coastline, which was covered in dots and squiggles indicating the best trade routes and favourable winds. It was all incomprehensible to Abigail.

"I don't need to have been to a place to know how to get there," James said, his tone sharper than usual, and lacking its usual robust cheer. "And I am quite sure I can drive a better bargain than Phillips did."

"Did he do so terribly?"

"He didn't even fill the hold!" James burst out, shaking his head, before he shot a darkly uncertain look at Adelaide, whose head was bent over her needle and bit of thread. "Really, the man did not know what he was about."

"Why didn't he fill the hold?" Abigail asked.

James shrugged. "He said it was becoming more difficult to get the slaves." He glanced again at Adelaide, and then looked away. "Tribes aren't selling them the way they used to. You know, these people just barter each other away, in exchange for some useless trinkets?" He spoke accusingly, and Abigail held her tongue.

She knew her husband felt she was too affectionate with Adelaide, and undoubtedly thought she needed reminding what her kind were capable of. And yet, was it any better to steal people from their homelands and sell them to someone else?

Such thoughts caused her a level of disquiet that made her heart race and her palms dampen, so she pushed them away. James knew more about it than she did. Or so she kept telling herself, because the alternative felt impossible.

And in truth he could be almost as affectionate with Adelaide as she was; she had seen him take the child on his knee and feed her sweetmeats, patting her on the head as she stared at him with her wide, dark eyes, completely still.

Admittedly, he sometimes tired of her quite quickly, sending her on her way with a firm pat, and he still refused to allow her to sleep anywhere but the warehouse, and had insisted that Abigail continue the practice after he had gone.

He'd at least agreed to summoning the mantua maker to fashion a set of clothes for Adelaide: a lovely little gown of deep blue satin with a frilled petticoat underneath; although the clothes had first seemed incongruous, Abigail finally decided that she looked quite the little lady.

She'd had an unpleasant moment of shock and dismay when she'd presented Adelaide with a dear little pair of heeled boots in brocaded silk and leather; the girl refused to put them on, and when Abigail had insisted, she'd wrenched them off and thrown them across the room.

Abigail had been utterly shocked by the terrible defiance; in the three weeks since Adelaide had come to the house she had been quite docile, learning English and a few domestic arts, as meek and mild as Abigail – or James – could possibly wish for.

"Adelaide," Abigail said severely, brandishing the shoe so the girl cringed backwards. "You must not throw things. And you must wear these shoes."

In the end, Abigail had agreed on a compromise; Adelaide wore the shoes when they went out and remained barefoot inside the house.

"A complete heathen," Jensen muttered darkly when she saw her unshod. "She won't even wear *shoes*."

"I doubt very much she wore shoes in Africa," Abigail said sharply. "They are unknown to her. That is all."

"That is quite my point, ma'am," Jensen answered. She had become quite chilly with Abigail, treating her with a servile formality that Abigail disliked even though she accepted it, and adopted a reciprocal cool authority with the maid she'd once counted as a friend.

The night before *The Fair Lady* was to sail, James took Abigail in his arms; he had not embraced her for weeks, and she came stiffly, unused to the feel of his scratchy coat against her cheek, the musk of his pomade in her nostrils.

"It is a dangerous journey," he told her, "but God willing, I shall return this time next year."

"I hope so," Abigail answered. "I pray so." She felt a wrench of grief for how distant they had become, and what they had lost without even realizing it. She had a sweet yet painful memory of when James had proposed, and she had been so incredulous and joyful as he had listed all her admirable qualities and then kissed her so sweetly.

It felt like a lifetime ago, but it was only three years. Abigail was but twenty-four, and yet she felt like an old woman, her body used up and worn out from too many losses.

James held her for a moment longer, and she wondered if he were thinking the same, if he missed what they'd had and shared. Then he stepped away, his smile in place, his manner one of his usual brisk cheer, if a bit forced.

"Only a year," he said, and Abigail nodded. In truth, it did not seem as long as all that.

Now, as the ship sailed out of the harbour, a lump formed in her throat and fear clutched at her insides. It was but a moment's panic, then she grew calm, reminding herself that it was but a twelvemonth and he would return – with a cargo full of sugar and rum to be sold at the best prices.

Back in the townhouse on Queen Street, it felt very quiet, although all was as it usually would have been; Cook in the kitchen, Jensen upstairs. Abigail glanced at Adelaide, who was waiting a few steps behind her, her eyes dark and watchful.

"You may take off your shoes." She gestured to the boots, and Adelaide quickly undid them and lined them up carefully by the door. Abigail reached out a hand and touched the girl lightly on her head. Her hair was short and woolly, so different from her own, but she'd discovered she liked the feel of it.

"Let's retire upstairs," she said. "I will give you your reading lesson." She reached for Adelaide's hand, savouring the feel of the small fingers twined with her own. She smiled down at the girl, but she did not smile back.

Some weeks later, weeks of quiet days spent in gentle pursuits and the occasional foray to the shops or the park, Abigail's mother paid her a visit.

"My dear, you have withdrawn from society to an unfashionable degree. Now that you are well again, I was hopeful you would be seen out and about."

"I prefer a quiet life," Abigail answered.

Caroline sighed. "I confess, it is modest and proper for you to spend your days quietly now that your husband is gone, but you must not wither away completely! You will be quite forgotten, and that will not do."

"I do not wish to attend any social occasions, Mama," Abigail answered. She was in the upstairs parlour, a book on her lap, Adelaide perched on a little stool beside her, with her chapbook. "I am quite content as I am."

Caroline glanced askance at Adelaide; while she'd admitted the child could be quite sweet, she was not entirely comfortable with her presence.

"I am not speaking of just social occasions," she said. "Although I hope to see you in attendance at those as well.

Mr Wesley is coming to Whitehaven, and I am quite determined to hear him preach. The last time was so very inspiring. I have been waiting for him to return again."

"Indeed," Abigail murmured. She knew her father did not find Mr Wesley quite so convincing; her parents had always been dutiful Anglicans, and the Wesley brothers were known for their impassioned oratory and their desire to stir up the still waters of common society. Abigail had heard more than one gently bred person disdain their so-called "enthusiasm".

"Yes," Caroline continued firmly, "and I would like you to come with me. It is perfectly respectable, Abigail. Mr Hogarth, the Earl of Lonsdale's agent, says he is quite devoted to the cause."

Abigail hesitated, torn between curiosity and a desire to remain as she was, comfortable and hidden. If she attended this, perhaps her mother would not go on so about visiting the assembly rooms or the theatre. "Very well," she finally said. "I suppose I should see for myself what all the fuss is about."

It was a warm evening in June when they assembled in the chapel, only five years old, on Michael Street. Abigail was surprised to see many familiar faces among the several hundred people crammed into the small space, eager to hear the preacher's inspiring words.

As she settled herself on a bench, Abigail could not crack the shell of hardened cynicism she felt around her heart towards whatever the charismatic Mr Wesley intended to say. Faith, so far, had been nothing more than a disappointing wish, her feeble prayers unanswered time and time again, and Providence only named when the winds of fate blew out of control. What use, really, had she for God? Now she wondered with a detached sort of interest what the great man himself would thunder on about; she had heard he was an exceptional orator.

Soon enough, he strode to the pulpit at the front of the chapel, a man of middling height, well proportioned, with a bright eye and clear complexion. He took in every person seated in front of him in one clear, compelling gaze; as it passed over Abigail she squirmed where she sat, feeling as if he'd seen right inside her. What he had seen there, she did not dare to think.

"Awake," he boomed in a loud voice, startling several people. "Awake, thou that sleepest, and arise from the dead." He paused, and Abigail found herself leaning forward, waiting for his next word in a way she had not expected to.

"Now, 'they that sleep, sleep in the night'." He glanced around at everyone again, and his bright gaze seemed to rest for a moment on Abigail, piercing her straight through. "The state of nature is a state of utter darkness; a state wherein 'darkness covers the earth, and gross darkness the people'. The poor, unawakened sinner, how much knowledge so ever he may have as to other things, he has no knowledge of himself: in this respect 'he knoweth nothing yet as he ought to know'."

Utter darkness. The words cut Abigail to the quick in a way she didn't understand. Suddenly, she felt as if she could weep with the force of it, the sheer weight of the knowledge.

"Full of all diseases as he is, he fancies himself in perfect health. Fast bound in misery and iron, he dreams that he is at liberty."

Caroline glanced at Abigail with an approving smile. Abigail's lips twitched in response, but she could manage nothing more. Her heart felt too full, painful and cracked, running over as Wesley's words found their way inside.

His words continued to wash over her, frightening and grieving her in a way she had never felt before, as if he saw all the

216

ugliness and pain inside her that she had not even been able to acknowledge to herself. "He abides in death though he knows it not. He is dead unto God."

Was this her? Asleep, needing to rise? Dead, needing to live? She thought of her quiet, drifting days, time passing without consequence, disappointments hardened into bitter resentment, thoughts and fears that she'd had but refused to allow to take hold, preferring to empty her mind than fill it to overflowing.

"'Having eyes, he sees not; he hath ears and hears not.' He doth 'not taste and see that the Lord is gracious'."

Abigail clenched her hands in her lap, overcome yet not wanting to be, fighting whatever she felt even now, to the bitterest end, because what could possibly be the result?

Others, she saw, were listening as avidly as she was, leaning forward in their seats, hands clenched, faces alight; others still were near to tears or even unabashedly weeping. Abigail had never seen the like. Mr Wesley continued with his oration, his voice rising in a well-pitched and impassioned crescendo.

"Wherefore, 'awake, thou that sleepest, and arise from the dead'. God calleth thee now by my mouth; and bids thee know thyself, thou fallen spirit, thy true state and only concern below. 'What meanest thou, O sleeper? Arise! Call upon thy God!'"

A ripple went through the crowd like a moan; Abigail felt tears start in her eyes and she swallowed hard, willing them back.

"God is light, and will give Himself to every awakened sinner that waiteth for Him; and thou shalt then be a temple of the living God, and Christ shall 'dwell in thy heart by faith', and 'being rooted and grounded in love, thou shalt be able to comprehend with all saints, what is the breadth, and length, and depth, and height of that love of Christ which passeth knowledge'."

Applause broke out, along with cheers, as Wesley came to the end of his rousing sermon; Abigail felt the dampness of tears upon her cheeks. She turned to her mother, grasping her hand.

"Does he mean it?" she asked, her voice choked with urgency. "Does he really mean it? That God will give Himself to every awakened sinner that – that waiteth for Him?"

"Oh, my dear." Caroline's eyes sparkled with tears as she clasped Abigail's cold hand between her own. "Yes, of course he does. He means it utterly, as do I. All you have to do is accept."

"Accept…" She sat back, shaking her head, her mind awhirl. Was this, then, what it was all about? What she'd been striving and aching for, without even knowing why? The empty days, her empty womb, the disappointments and sorrows of her married life, her longing to love. Was this, then, the need that could be filled, at a font that never ran dry? Dare she even think it?

"I do not even know," she whispered. "I cannot know."

"You can, my dear," Caroline urged. "This very day. You have glimpsed truth. Now you must embrace it."

Abigail walked back to the house on Queen Street with her mother, her mind still a whirling blank. She could not think, and yet she had to. Something deeper than reason was compelling her to repeat Mr Wesley's words in the disquiet of her own mind: *What villainies of every kind are committed day by day; yea, too often with impunity, by those who sin with a high hand, and glory in their shame! Who can reckon up the frauds, injustice, oppression, extortion, which overspread our land as a flood?*

She turned to her mother by the door to the house, suddenly fierce. "What would Mr Wesley think to my husband, Mama?"

"Your husband?" Caroline looked startled. "Whatever do you mean, Abigail?"

"He will reach Africa very soon, I should think. He will fill the hold of his ship with slaves – men and women, children like… like Adelaide." Her voice choked. "Would Mr Wesley call that evil? 'A villainy committed by a high hand'?"

"My dear." Caroline shook her head slowly, looking troubled. "I know not," she said at last. "I have not considered such a suggestion. The slave trade prospers all of Whitehaven. Surely it is ordained by God?"

But Abigail could see the confusion in her mother's eyes, the same fearful uncertainty she felt in her own soul. What if it was wrong? What if it was a great evil? What if Adelaide should never have been herded aboard that ship, or brought into her home?

Abigail's chest heaved with suppressed emotion and she shook her head. "Who are we to say what is ordained by God, simply because it suits us?"

"Abigail…"

She closed her eyes briefly against the tumult of her thoughts. "I must think on it."

"Yes, think and pray," Caroline urged. "Perhaps you could ask Mr Wesley himself. He is here another day. He is preaching in the marketplace tomorrow."

Abigail nodded. "But what if…" She could not voice the words.

Caroline placed a comforting hand on her arm. "I am sure he will put your mind at ease. Your husband is an honourable man, after all, and you must obey him in all things."

As Abigail entered the house, she paused by the door to the darkened warehouse, which was locked for the night, knowing Adelaide was within. She pressed one hand flat against the heavy wood, straining to hear something, but all was silent.

What did the child think, spending her days in such gentle pursuits, petted and cosseted like a plaything or a pet, only to be locked away at night, to sleep on a pile of dirty blankets?

Abigail felt a sudden, scorching rush of shame. She had allowed this. She had ordained it, not God, by giving James his way. He wasn't even there, and she'd continued the practice, in part out of obedience, but in greater part out of fear. Adelaide was still a strange creature who did not wear shoes and who muttered gibberish on occasion. Her foreignness made Abigail uneasy, and it had felt safer to keep her in this place. A locked room.

The shame rushed in again, hotter and fiercer this time, and she bowed her head. Surely this was wrong. Surely Mr Wesley would tell her it was wrong.

The next day, with Adelaide at her side, Abigail listened to John Wesley give another stirring sermon in the marketplace, surrounded by mariners and weavers, maids and boot boys, all manner of people with whom Abigail would normally never converse.

Afterwards Mr Wesley was surrounded by admirers, and Abigail had to shoulder her way through the crowd, her heart hammering with both effort and apprehension as she clutched Adelaide's hand to anchor the little girl to her.

"Mr Wesley." Her voice came out far too loud, and the great man turned, eyebrows raised in expectation as he took in the sight of a gently bred woman with her black servant.

"Madam." He gave a slight bow.

"I have been much impressed by your speaking," Abigail said in a lower voice, nerves making it tremble. "Very much moved."

"I am glad for it, Madam, and it is my earnest prayer that this results in your salvation."

"It has," Abigail burst out, surprising herself. "Oh, it has. I feel…" She could not put it into words. "I *feel*," she said again, and Wesley nodded, seeming to understand her perfectly.

Abigail swallowed hard as she gathered her courage. "My husband," she said in a voice so low Wesley had to lean forward to hear it. "He has left for Africa these four weeks past." She waited, watching his brows knit together, before he nodded slowly.

"He is a slave trader?"

"Yes."

"What is it you wish to ask me, Madam? Has your conscience been pricked?"

Tears gathered in Abigail's eyes. "Is it wrong?" she burst out. "All along I have wondered, I have feared, but I have not wanted to *think*. My husband is a good man, and he has weathered such grave disappointments, not least in myself." She paused and glanced down at her stomach, blushing. "I cannot…"

"I believe I take your meaning," Wesley said gently, sparing her any further embarrassment.

Abigail's breath hitched as she made herself continue. "I have been terribly bitter myself, bearing such resentment, but I do not wish to feel that now. Truly, I do not." She lifted her chin and met his gaze unflinchingly. "But I must know. Is it wrong? Is what he is doing, the very livelihood he is engaged in, a sin? An evil?"

"All sin is evil in the eyes of the Lord," Wesley answered, his tone gentle despite the harshness of his words, and it became even gentler as he continued. "As to your question, Madam, I believe you have answered it yourself."

CHAPTER NINETEEN

Rachel

Rachel awoke to spring sunlight streaming through the window, which was a nice change from the rain. Next to her Anthony slumbered on, dead to the world, his chest rising and falling with deep, even, and slightly snuffling breaths.

He'd come to bed last night after Rachel had already crawled beneath the covers and shut her eyes tight, not pretending to be asleep so much as willing herself to succumb to it. She'd listened to Anthony undress and then felt the mattress dip beneath his weight. Part of her had hoped he would reach one heavy arm over and wrap it around her waist, anchor her to him, but he didn't, and she didn't blame him.

Now, in the bright light of a new morning, Rachel was determined to hold on to some kind of optimism, if she could just find it. Her mother was coming home. Anthony was here. They'd argued, she couldn't even say about what, but at least they'd survived it. And today she was going to try, really try, to be what Anthony wanted. To show him how much she appreciated him, how much she loved him, because she did. Underneath all her insecurities and stupid quirks, she knew she did, and that was half the trouble.

But first, a run. She needed to clear her head and get her blood pumping. Blow the dust and the cobwebs out of both her mind and heart.

Outside it was one of those rare dazzling days that made the Lake District feel like the most beautiful place on earth; sun gilded the grey-green fells in gold, and as Rachel started down the narrow road that led from her mother's house towards Windermere, she could see the bright blue glint of the lake in the distance.

Her feet pounded the pavement, her dark hair flying behind her, her heart pumping and her breath coming in rhythm to her fast, sure strides.

Last night, as she'd lain in bed, old, half-forgotten memories had started flitting through her mind like bats on a summer's night, dark shadows going in and out, in and out. She hadn't wanted to catch hold of any of them, and yet they came anyway – raised voices from downstairs, her mother's tears. Holding her father's hand as she turned away from her mother. A phone ringing, a woman's voice.

Rachel ran harder. *Don't think. Don't think about any of it.* Because if she started to think, if she let those flitting memories settle and roost…

She didn't know what would happen.

She ran for nearly an hour, until her lungs burned and her legs felt rubbery, and it still didn't seem like enough. Still, knowing she needed to get ready to collect her mother from hospital, she turned around and headed back to the house.

The house smelled of bacon and coffee as Rachel let herself in. Anthony was in the kitchen, listening to Radio 4 as he prepared them both a full fry-up.

Food was love to Anthony, Rachel knew that, and often she appreciated it. She *did*. Yet sometimes, like this morning, when her stomach was churning and he *knew* she never had more than coffee and a single slice of toast, if that, for breakfast, she felt the weight of his expectation and resented it.

He would be hurt if she didn't eat every single bite of that breakfast – two slices of toast, a mound of scrambled eggs, sausage and bacon, tomato and mushrooms, maybe even a horrid black pudding, because he thought all Brits loved them. He would feel rejected, and do a bad job of pretending he wasn't, and Rachel would feel guilty all over again, and choke the breakfast down besides.

She yanked her earbuds out and tossed her phone on to the worktop. "Wow, you've been busy," she said with a determined smile. She'd told herself she was going to try, so she was.

"Yes, I thought we ought to fortify ourselves. It might be a long day." He smiled brightly as he dolloped portions on plates – all Rachel had expected and more; there was a puddle of baked beans as well. "How are you feeling this morning?" he asked as they sat down at the table. "About your mom."

"I don't really know." Rachel picked up her fork and toyed with a mushroom. The smell of the food was making her nauseous; she'd never been a breakfast person. "I'm not sure what to expect."

"How long do you think you'll stay here with her?"

Rachel shrugged. "Another day or two? I doubt she wants me around, to be honest."

"Do you really think so –"

"Let's not rehash this again, Anthony, please."

"Sorry." He dug into his eggs while Rachel forced herself to eat a mushroom. "About last night…"

Rachel tensed. "We don't have to –"

"No, we do. I do. I shouldn't have brought that all up. I'm sorry. I know you're dealing with a lot right now, and it wasn't fair of me to lay that on top of you as well."

Rachel let out a breath. "Okay," she said, although somehow that didn't feel like the right response. All the things they'd said were still between them, heavy and unspoken.

Anthony laid his hands flat on the table, his gaze lowered, his manner unnervingly solemn. "The thing is, Rachel," he began slowly, and she felt herself tensing up again, as though an invisible hand was turning a crank inside her, making everything tighter and tighter, ready to snap all over again. "We need to have that conversation sometime."

"What conversation, exactly?" she asked, more of a statement than a question, because she really didn't want to know.

He looked up at her, his soft brown eyes filled with something close to despair. "I don't want to go on like this. We've been married for almost three years. I thought at first it was settling in pains. You know, we both married a little bit late, and it was something of a whirlwind romance. I thought we needed to get used to each other. Get to know each other, even, and figure out life together."

Rachel felt frozen, but she forced words through her numb lips. "It feels like there's a big 'but' coming right about now."

Anthony shook his head. "Just what I've said. It's been three years. Growing pains, settling in, whatever. We should have got through that by now, and yet I still feel as if you're pushing me away. As if you're not even trying –"

"You don't like it when I try," Rachel snapped. She couldn't help it. This was all her fault, yet again.

"What?"

"You want it all to come naturally, as easy as breathing, and maybe it does for you, Anthony, but it doesn't for me. I'm sorry, but that's how I am. And so I try, and you look so dreadfully disappointed because I had to." The words were coming faster and faster, so she was practically spitting them out, filled with vitriol. Her chest was heaving. "So it seems like I can't win either way, no matter what I do, whether I try or not, since I'm so very prickly."

Anthony stared at her, looking both bewildered and devastated. "Rachel…"

"And," she threw at him, one last final thrust, "I don't even like breakfast, which you *know*." She pushed up from the table and stormed out of the room, furious and yet also far too near tears.

She went up to the bathroom, putting the shower on full blast, as hot as she could stand it. As she stood beneath the stinging spray, she felt tears running down her cheeks but she pretended, even to herself, that it was just water from the shower. Of course she couldn't fool herself; she couldn't fool anyone. Anthony saw through her, though at the same time he didn't seem to see anything. Or was she the one who was being wilfully blind?

You know why.

Rachel rested her head against the tiles and closed her eyes, but the tears slipped out anyway, determined little blighters. What was she even crying for? Her father? Her mother? Her marriage? The fact that she was in this situation at all, perhaps. Did Anthony think she *liked* things this way? Didn't he understand how much she wanted to be different – how she actually was trying? At least sometimes.

By the time she'd got out of the shower and dressed, Rachel was feeling more like her calm, level-headed self, if a little numb inside. She didn't meet Anthony's gaze as she came downstairs and reached for her car keys.

"Rachel –"

"Don't. Not now. We need to have a conversation. Yes. I understand that, and so we will. But we can't have it now, here, with my mother needing to be fetched, and in any case I think starting one will just cause another argument."

"I'm sorry."

"So am I," she said briskly. "Let's go."

They didn't talk during the drive to Westmorland Hospital,

and that was fine by Rachel. She had to focus on her mother now.

"I'm afraid Mrs Barnaby is in a bit of a state," the nurse told her when she reached the ward. Rachel's heart did an unpleasant little flip.

"A *state*?"

"She became a bit confused when we were getting her ready for discharge."

"What do you mean, confused?" Rachel heard how sharp her voice sounded and strove to moderate her tone. "I'm sorry. I just don't understand what you mean."

"She became a bit agitated – aggressive, even. She wasn't sure where she was or what we were doing, and she didn't appreciate being 'manhandled', as she called it." The nurse smiled ruefully. "We gave her some space, which is what she seemed to want. She's by her bed now."

Rachel swallowed and nodded. "So what needs to happen now?"

"When she's ready to work with us, we'll get her ready for discharge. You can speak to her if you like. It might come better from you."

Rachel doubted that, but she knew she had to try – with this, as with everything else. Battling a wave of trepidation, she headed to her mother's bay, Anthony hanging back a little. Deborah was sitting in a chair by her bed, still in her hospital gown. Rachel saw how it gaped at the back, revealing the bony knobs of her spine, and something in her twisted and broke.

"Mum?"

Deborah turned. "Oh. It's you."

"I've come to drive you back home."

"Very well." Deborah rose from her chair, seeming both dignified and resigned. "Shall we go?"

Rachel hesitated. "Mum, you need to get dressed."

Deborah looked down at herself, annoyance flitting across her face. "And do you think I have any clothes? They found me in a nightdress, or so I'm told. I may have dementia, but I haven't quite lost all my marbles yet." Her voice was waspish, her lips pursed.

Of course. Rachel should have brought her mother a set of clothes to travel home in. She hadn't thought of it.

"I'm sorry," she said. "I didn't realize –"

"No, of course you didn't. You were so busy wondering how I'm going to ruin your life that you didn't think for one second about what I might actually want or need."

Rachel blinked, shocked by her mother's words, even more vitriolic than usual – than her own that morning. "Mum –"

"I can go back," Anthony said quietly, "and get some clothes. It won't take long."

"Anthony." Deborah gazed at her son-in-law appraisingly. "Have you come to save the day?" The mocking note in her voice was unmistakable.

Now Anthony was the one to look startled, as well as a bit wary. "Sorry, Deborah. I should have said hello first."

"Swan in like Superman. We all know how that goes." Deborah shook her head as she sat down. "Fine, fine, go ahead. Get my clothes if it will make you feel better." Anthony gave Rachel an uncertain look and she shrugged. Her mother had always been brusque, blunt, but nothing quite as bad as this. It was as if her dementia – or something – had removed any remaining social filter.

"I'll go now," Anthony murmured, and he retreated, leaving Rachel alone with a mother she felt more wary of than ever before.

"You know," Deborah said conversationally, "Anthony is always going to disappoint you."

Rattled even more, Rachel forced herself to sound level.

"Mum, I don't think we should talk about Anthony right now."

"I know why you married him, of course."

Rachel gazed at her mother uncertainly, feeling horrified by her matter-of-fact statement as well as bizarrely curious. "You do?"

Deborah nodded as she gazed out of the window. "Of course. You wanted your father back again. Anthony is just like him. All charm and expansive bonhomie, everyone's his best friend. The world loves him. How could they not?" She sounded so very bitter that Rachel recoiled.

"Is that how you feel about Dad?" she asked when she trusted herself to speak. "Is that how you saw him? Charm, and nothing else?"

"I know how he was, Rachel." Deborah turned to stare at her, her lips twisted, her eyes narrowed. "You're the one who always had the blinkers on."

"Don't," Rachel whispered. "Don't do this. I know you're ill, and maybe you can't help what you're saying. You don't realize –"

"This isn't illness," Deborah answered with a hard laugh. "Do you think I'm in the midst of some memory lapse? That I'm *confused*? Trust me." She tapped her forehead with one finger. "I know exactly what's going on right now, and the truth is, I can't see the point in pretending to you any longer. Perhaps I never should have but – would you believe it? – I thought I was being kind." She gave another hard laugh, which Rachel hated.

"Don't," she said again. She backed towards the entrance, as if she could escape her mother and her hateful words. She had an awful urge to run from the ward, run and never come back. "Please don't."

Her mother stared at her for another long moment, her eyes narrowed, her lips pursed. "Even now," she said softly, unsettling Rachel all the more, and then she didn't say anything further until Anthony returned with her clothes.

CHAPTER TWENTY

Abigail

Whitehaven, 1766

Abigail heard John Wesley speak twice more before he left Whitehaven, and each time her heart both filled and fluttered, so stirred was she by his words, as well as his forceful and assured manner. She had never heard a man so certain of his own destiny, and so determined to take others with him to that shining, eternal place.

"And in doing good, he does not confine himself to cheap and easy offices of kindness, but labours and suffers for the profit of many, that by all means he may help some. In spite of toil or pain, 'whatever his hand findeth to do, he doeth it with his might'; whether it be for his friends, or for his enemies, for the evil or for the good."

Yes, she wanted to "do with all her might". She did not want to content herself with cheap and easy kindnesses, but to labour and suffer, as Wesley had so passionately declared, for many. Or at least for one.

For Adelaide.

The little girl had, Abigail realized with both wonder and trepidation, become very important to her, and she did not know how to feel about that. She knew that James, along with everyone else of her acquaintance, would consider Adelaide less than a servant, no matter what silks and satins she wore – more of a pet or a plaything than a person. And in her own mind, Abigail did not know how much more she thought of Adelaide than that.

To her wary surprise, Wesley approached her at his last meeting, striding through the excitable crowds to stand in front of her in the market square.

"Madam," he said with a short bow. "Did you decide on the question of slavery to your satisfaction, and more to the point, to God's?"

"I-I think I have," Abigail said, her voice little more than a frayed whisper. "I have certainly considered the matter a great deal."

"And have you prayed upon it?"

Abigail blushed. Of course she should have prayed about it, but all her life her prayers had been either by unthinking rote or in clumsy mutters; she did not think she knew how to do anything else.

"I shall, Sir," she said humbly, bowing her head.

"And what conclusions have you drawn in the meantime? For your husband is still at sea, I presume?"

"Yes, and he will be for another eight months at least."

"And as for your own slave? A little girl, I recall?"

"Yes."

"What will you do with her?"

"Do with her?" Abigail stared at him uncertainly. "What can I do with her, Sir? She is but a small child."

"You could give her her freedom." Wesley spoke matter-of-factly, his gaze alarmingly direct.

"But how? Where would she go? There would be no one to take care of her." As she voiced her protest, she realized she did not want to give Adelaide her freedom. She could not countenance such a thing at all.

"You could make her a servant rather than a slave. Give her a living wage."

"A wage!" Such a thing had never even crossed her mind.

"I see you still have much to consider," Wesley said gently. "And also much to pray on."

Her mind was still roiling with questions she did not even begin to know how to answer when John Wesley left Whitehaven the next day, sailing for the Isle of Man, cheering crowds accompanying him to the quay. They were mainly the poor and simple folk, but with a few gently bred converts as well. Abigail watched the procession from her drawing room window as it headed along Queen Street for the waterfront. She felt like a changed woman, or at least *wanted* to be changed. To be different. If only she knew how.

Some matters, at least, seemed simple. The first thing she did that morning was to move Adelaide's bed from the dark corner of the warehouse to her dressing room, just as she'd once suggested to James. When she asked Jensen to clear the room and bring a mattress of straw ticking in, her maid glowered but obeyed. Abigail knew she would have to be careful how many such requests she made of Jensen; each one seemed to test her goodwill to breaking point.

When Abigail brought Adelaide upstairs to bed that first night, she felt a burst of expectant pleasure at showing the little girl all that she'd done for her.

"Look," she said as she ushered her into the dressing room. "I have given you your own bed."

Adelaide glanced uncertainly at the rough mattress on the floor, made up with a set of old, nearly threadbare, sheets Jensen had dug out of the chest of linens. The washstand, clothespress, and chaise had been pushed to one side, so the room was uncommonly crowded. Still, it was a bed, more than she'd ever had before.

"Do you like it?" Abigail asked, hearing the eagerness in her tone, so wanting Adelaide to be pleased and grateful.

After a second's pause Adelaide nodded.

"Good." She rested one hand briefly on the girl's shoulder. "I hope you will be comfortable here."

Whether Adelaide was comfortable Abigail knew not, but to her own surprise and dismay, she slept restlessly all night long, waking often, straining in the dark to listen for a sound – a creak of the floorboard, a footfall, anything that meant Adelaide was stirring.

It occurred to her, in the middle of a moonless night, how little she actually knew Adelaide. James would have called the girl a savage – dressed in silk, yes, and able to manage some English, but a savage nonetheless, untrained and unable to truly change from her heathen ways. And despite this, Abigail had trustingly put her in the room closest to her own, with only Jensen and Cook upstairs to come if something happened, if they even would, were she to call for help.

They'd both been incredulous when she'd explained where Adelaide would be sleeping. No matter how the little girl grew or developed, the two women still regarded Adelaide as some sort of dangerous beast. At least Cook did; Jensen seemed more to regard the girl as entirely beneath her notice.

"It's her eyes," Cook had confided in Abigail once. "So dark. And that skin! And she doesn't say a word to me, even though you've trained her."

"She is learning," Abigail said patiently. "We must encourage her."

"But she's so *still*, like some wild creature in the forest." Cook shook her head with an unfeigned shudder. "I don't like it, Ma'am. I don't like it one bit."

There *was* something wild about Adelaide, Abigail reflected as she lay in bed, sleep impossible. Something wild and untamed, yet also contained. It scared her, and it also made her sad. It was akin to imprisoning a songbird in a cage, or one of the lions Abigail had read about, chained up in the Tower of London, mangy and prowling. Neither they nor Adelaide, she reflected, were where they should be.

And yet unlike a lion or a bird, Adelaide was cared for. Cosseted, even. She certainly had nothing to complain about, just as she surely presented no danger to her mistress, no matter what horrible stories of poison or savagery James had muttered darkly to her.

Still Abigail lay in bed, staring at the hangings above, eyes and ears both straining in the darkness as the hours ticked their way on to dawn.

When she woke from a troubled doze at last, sometime in the early morning, it was to find Adelaide standing next to her bed, inches away from her face, utterly still and calm, her dark eyes fathomless as she stared straight at her.

"Oh!" Abigail let out a little shriek as she scooted up in bed, away from the little girl and her disconcerting stare. "What – what are you doing, Adelaide?"

"Mistress... want... chocolate?" Adelaide asked in her careful, halting way, searching for the words before she found them.

"Oh. Yes. Thank you, Adelaide." Abigail gave a nod of dismissal, one hand pressed to her racing heart. The girl had given her such a scare, standing so close, looking so... *strange*. Abigail let out a shuddery breath, again questioning their new arrangements.

James would have argued that she'd been comfortable in the warehouse, more comfortable than she'd ever have been back in darkest Africa, where they slept on the ground in mud huts, or so he said.

A short while later, Jensen brought up her morning chocolate, her whole body bristling with obvious indignation as she did so.

"I gave that little baggage a piece of my mind," she announced huffily as she set Abigail's tray down with a bit more of a clatter than usual. "Coming into the kitchen as grand as you please, thinking she's your lady's maid, now she's sleeping in your dressing room."

"She was only trying to be helpful," Abigail protested weakly. She still felt weak and out of sorts, both from lack of sleep and the strange start to her morning.

"Helpful!" Jensen snorted. "She's got airs, Ma'am, terrible airs."

"She is but a child."

"Dressed like a countess!"

Abigail reached for her chocolate and took a sip. "It is merely the fashion," she murmured before rousing herself. "Mark it, Jensen, I do not need to justify any of my decisions to you." She gave the maid a quelling look; Jensen sniffed and then walked out of the room.

Abigail leaned back against the pillows with a sigh. She knew she should not countenance such disrespect from her maid, but part of her understood it. In any case, her head ached and she felt as weary as if it were the end of the day rather than the beginning. She could not deal with Jensen today.

After speaking with John Wesley, and hearing his fervent addresses, she'd so wanted to make a change, not only in her household, but in her own heart. Yet right now it felt like so much effort, and to what end?

A noise at the door startled her; Adelaide had slipped back into the room and was standing against the wall, watching her warily.

"Go back to your room," Abigail said, a querulous note entering her voice. "You may come when you're called." Adelaide simply stared, uncomprehending, and she pointed one trembling finger towards the dressing room. "Go!"

Silently Adelaide went to the little room, gliding on bare feet like a dark ghost. Abigail closed her eyes against her uncertainty and regret, and then took another sip of her chocolate.

Downstairs, dressed and having taken a powder for her headache, she felt a little more herself. Adelaide was sitting in her usual place, on the footstool by her chair, reading a chapbook, as sedate as one could wish. In the late morning, Abigail rang for Cook.

"I have made a list of food I wish to be made for Adelaide," she said as she held out the piece of paper she'd spent all morning deliberating on. "They are all nourishing foods suitable for a child, according to Mrs Glasse." Abigail possessed a copy of the much-vaunted *The Art of Cookery Made Plain and Simple*, but she had never actually opened it until that day.

Cook took the list with a sniff. "Oatmeal and cream, plum cake, suet pudding, fresh fish when it is available!" She looked up at Abigail in disbelief. "She's eating like quite the little lady, if I may say so, Ma'am."

"You may not," Abigail informed her crisply. "She is eating like any child who needs to grow and remain healthy."

"It will cost more," Cook warned her with another sniff. "I can't get all this with what I'm given."

Abigail held on to her temper, knowing she could not further exasperate both of her full-time servants. Next thing the laundry maid who came in three times a week would be up in arms. Still, she could hardly see how the current household budget would not stretch to food for one small child. "How much more do you need?" she asked, and with a long-suffering sigh, Cook named an amount Abigail thought quite excessive, although in truth she did not know much about money.

She was, in name at least, in charge of the household accounts, but since her health had become poor she had left all such decisions to James or to Cook.

"Very well," she said with a brisk nod. "I will agree to that amount." Cook nodded, and Abigail dismissed her. She should really take back the household accounting, she realized with a twinge of unease. She did not even know how much credit was extended to all their suppliers – the butcher and baker, the mantua and the bootmaker, the merchants for tea, and beer, candles and books and gloves. So much she didn't know. And when would the bills be paid? Presumably when her husband returned with a ship full of sugar and rum.

It was not, Abigail soon learned, to be as simple as that. That very afternoon Cook appeared in her sitting room, looking very put out. Abigail's headache had returned and she was feeling decidedly tetchy.

"What is it?" she demanded as the woman harrumphed.

"The butcher won't extend any more credit."

"What!" Abigail stared at her in shocked dismay. "What grave impertinence! What does he mean by such a thing?"

Cook shrugged. "He said the bill has not been paid for over six month, and he will not extend it any further."

"Did you explain to him that Mr Fenton is on a sea voyage, all the way to Africa?"

"He already knew it, Ma'am."

"Then how can he not be willing to –" She broke off, shaking her head, furious with both the butcher and her own seeming incompetence. "Never mind. I shall deal with the matter myself. And we will take our custom to another butcher."

Still bristling with affront, Abigail readied herself to go out, summoning Adelaide with a snap of her fingers. She was full of self-righteous fury as she marched to the butcher on Lowther Street, across from the market, a place she had never needed to enter before, but at least she knew where it was.

"I wish to speak to the proprietor of this establishment," she announced crisply as she crossed the threshold.

A man, solidly built and with a florid face, came out from the back. "I am he, Madam."

His calm voice and knowing manner took Abigail by surprise, and for a second she faltered. "My cook came to you this morning with an order," she said after a moment, bolstering her courage. "And she was informed, quite shockingly, that you would not extend any further credit to my household."

The man eyed her appraisingly, clearly understanding who she was, though she had no prior knowledge of him. "Indeed I will not, Mrs Fenton."

"You are aware my husband is at sea? I assure you, he will return in a few months' time and pay any outstanding amount in full."

The man's chin lifted slightly. "I cannot wait that long."

"But that is how it is done!" Abigail exclaimed. "It is how it has always been done. Everything is supplied on credit and paid later. You must know this."

"What I know is that your husband did not settle any of his bills before he left, although he was asked to do so, more than once," the man replied levelly. "And when a gentleman is going to be absent for as long a time as that, it holds him in good stead to settle his accounts before he departs."

"What?" The word exhaled softly from her, like a sigh, as she stared at him in wilful incomprehension. "You must be mistaken."

"I am not."

"I shall take my custom to another butcher's," Abigail warned, and the man simply gave a nod of assent.

A new and terrible fear was creeping over Abigail like some grey mist. James had not mentioned money to her before he'd left – not in a practical way. He'd talked about making their fortunes and arriving home on a tide of prosperity, but there had been nothing about bills or accounts, and Abigail had not thought to ask.

Anything she bought was on credit. Every shopkeeper and merchant in Whitehaven knew her name, her husband's name. She never troubled herself with any of it, ever.

The only money she had in the house was a few coins for her personal use, to give as alms or in church, or to buy some frippery from a peddler, perhaps. The money from James's shipping enterprises was kept in a locked chest in his study and she did not know where the key was. She had never even looked inside it. Right then, with the butcher staring at her so stolidly, her ignorance shamed her.

"Clearly this was nothing more than an oversight on my husband's part," Abigail said after a moment, as she tried to gather her scattered thoughts and cling to her dignity. "I shall return forthwith and settle your bill. And then, I tell you, I shall take my custom elsewhere."

The man gave her a rather grim smile. "Your attention to this matter is greatly appreciated, Mrs Fenton," he said.

Back in the house Abigail went into James's study, a room she had not spent any amount of time in. It was a man's room, all dark wood and leather, the stale smell of tobacco and whisky hanging in the air, even after all these months.

Now she looked around at the mahogany desk inlaid with leather, the glass-fronted case of books and maps, the locked strongbox where James kept all their coins and banknotes. Taking a deep breath, she began going through the drawers of the desk, looking for the key. She did not even know what it looked like, but she hoped and prayed she'd somehow recognize it when she found it. Why had James not thought to give it to her, in case of some catastrophe or emergency? How could he have left her so woefully unprepared?

She went through the desk, and the bookcase, and the Chinese lacquered cabinet, and found nothing. Fighting a creeping sense of panic, she went upstairs to James's bedroom to look there. She hadn't been in his room since he'd left, and now she breathed in the familiar, lingering smell of his pomade, his person, and felt a pang of – what? Regret? Loss? She wasn't sure.

Taking a deep breath, she started going through his chest of drawers, rifling through his shirts and breeches, stockings and neck cloths. She finally found the key in a small drawer at the top of the chest, at the very back. Although she couldn't remember seeing it, she was certain it was the right key, both from its hidden place and its heft.

She hurried downstairs to the strongbox, her heart starting to beat hard, and inserted the key. She turned it, felt it give way with a mix of relief and apprehension. Then she opened the box and stared down into its dark depths with a sense of incredulity.

There was nothing there but a few coins – a couple of guineas and one half-sovereign. Less, even, than she had upstairs. Abigail stared and stared at the box, trying to make sense of it. Surely this couldn't be all the money they had left. Surely it was somewhere else; somewhere better James had thought of for safekeeping.

Or what if they'd been robbed?

Her thoughts circled her empty mind like a flock of crows, finding nowhere to land. She heard a noise from behind, no more than a breath, and she turned to see Adelaide standing in the doorway, as silent and still as a ghost, her dark eyes giving nothing away.

CHAPTER TWENTY-ONE

Rachel

"I don't know why you're bothering."

Wearily Rachel chose to ignore her mother's words as she unloaded the groceries – microwaveable meals for one, UHT milk, and plenty of toilet paper – she'd bought at Booth's that morning. Deborah Barnaby had been back in her home for two days, and Rachel couldn't wait to leave. Neither, it seemed, could her mother wait for her to go.

She sat at the kitchen table, arms folded, as she crossly watched Rachel continue to put things away.

"I don't need all that."

"Just in case, Mum," Rachel said. "So you don't have to go to the shops too often."

Yesterday she'd spoken to her mother's GP, asking her the question she wasn't sure she wanted the answer to. Was her mother still able to live alone? No matter what the consultant had said, the reality felt different.

"That's a decision that only your mother can make," the GP had answered, and Rachel stared at her in disbelief. Surely she shouldn't trust a person suffering with dementia to make such a decision about their own care?

"In your mother's current condition, I am not overly concerned for her safety," the doctor continued. "And, generally speaking, we always try to give people living with dementia as much independence as possible. It's better for them, both emotionally and physically."

"Yes, I can see that. But what if something happens? What if she leaves the cooker on or wanders off?" Rachel knew she was asking herself as much as the GP. *How could I live with myself?* But what other options were there?

Deborah did not want to go into "some kind of home", as she'd stated flatly, and the possibility of living with Rachel in Bristol had not even come up. Deborah's quelling look was enough to keep her from mentioning it – not that she wanted her mother to live with her. In truth, she couldn't think of anything worse.

Rachel had looked online at some retirement flats in Windermere and also near Bristol, but either way the house had to sell first. Neither she nor her mother had sufficient funds to buy a flat without selling the house in Windermere.

Yesterday she'd had an estate agent round to value the house. He'd exclaimed over its "good bones" and stunning views, but advised ripping out the kitchen and putting in granite and stainless steel for a quick sale.

"We're not ripping out the kitchen," Rachel had said wearily. They had neither the time nor the money for such a thing, and she had a feeling that changing as much as a single tile would upset her mother, as so much did these days.

This morning Rachel had moved the kettle from its corner by the stove closer to the sink, so it was easier for her mother to fill it up. Deborah had been furious.

"How dare you move my things," she'd exclaimed. "This is my house, Rachel. You can't just come in here and change everything."

"I'm sorry, Mum. I was just trying to help," Rachel had said, as humbly as she could, and she'd put it back. Part of her had wanted to snap, Perhaps you'll remember to boil it this time, but she knew that was dreadfully unfair.

Just two days of these constant, snippy interactions made her long to go back to Bristol, to her work – even though Izzy had told her to take as much time as she needed – and to the comforting familiarity of her modern flat.

Anthony clearly wanted to go back too; they'd declared a silent standoff in terms of having a discussion about their marriage, thankfully, and he'd done his best to be helpful, but Deborah's irritable wrath now extended to him as well, and he clearly didn't understand why his mother-in-law was directing so many barbed comments his way.

Welcome to my life, Rachel had wanted to say sardonically, but she'd resisted. There was enough tension as it was – not just with Deborah, but between the two of them. The weight of Anthony's expectations was something Rachel bowed beneath, even as she kept trying to shrug it off. A conversation. Children. Things she couldn't bring herself to think about yet.

At least her mother hadn't mentioned her father again. *You're the one with the blinkers on. I thought I was being kind.* No, Rachel wasn't ready to hear her mother explain what she meant, although, in her darker moments, she had a feeling she already knew.

A phone ringing, a woman's voice. Her father's hand on her head. *Just between us, eh, poppet? That's my girl.*

When had that been? When she was six, maybe seven? Too young to understand anything. She'd just been pleased to be in on a secret, even though she'd had no idea what the secret was, and still didn't really. But she could guess. Of course she could guess.

"There." Rachel turned to her mother, having put away all the groceries. "That should see you through a week or two, at least."

"I told you, I don't need –"

"I know, Mum, but it makes me feel better."

"So are you going, then?" There was a wobble of vulnerability to her mother's voice that was normally never there, and it made Rachel ache with both sorrow and guilt.

"Not yet. I have a few other things to sort out." She was trying to arrange for a carer to come in twice a week to help, but it was taking ages to sort out on the NHS and going privately was too expensive. Plus, she hadn't even mentioned the possibility to her mother yet, whom she knew would bristle at the suggestion she needed that kind of help. "Soon, though," Rachel added, and she no longer knew if it was a warning or a promise.

Later that afternoon, she found Anthony in the living room, finishing a call. She watched him warily as he made breezy assurances and then, having hung up, turned to her.

"That was the Smythes. Do you remember them? I did their daughter's wedding reception last year."

"Did you?"

"They want me to cater a private dinner for eight at the weekend."

"Oh?" That was only two days away. "Are you going, then?" She realized she sounded like her mother, that same awful wobble and defiant look.

Anthony paused, his head lowered, his gaze on the phone in his hand. Then he turned and looked at Rachel, and she wished he hadn't. There was far too much resignation in his eyes. "I think I should. Don't you?"

"What is that supposed to mean?"

"I'm not helping, not really, and… things between us aren't great, are they, Rachel?"

"Do you think they'll get better when you're in Bristol and I'm here?" Rachel closed her eyes briefly. She sounded so spiteful.

"I don't know. I think maybe we just need... a bit of a break. From each other."

"What?" She gaped at him and the ominous finality of his words. *A bit of a break?* Anthony never talked like this. Rachel felt a coldness creeping over her, stealing into her bones, turning her frozen and numb. Her movements felt stiff and jerky as she tried to shrug.

"Fine."

"Is that all you have to say?"

"What do you want me to do? Beg and plead for you to stay?" The words came out of her like a snarling echo, a memory she couldn't bear to think about. Her parents, facing off in the living room, while she crouched on the stairs. Why was she remembering this now?

"No, of course not. I just..." Anthony shook his head. "I don't know what I want."

Welcome to the club. "Go, then," Rachel said, her voice choking, and she turned and walked out of the room.

He left an hour later, without saying goodbye. Rachel could hardly believe it had come to this. She watched him from the upstairs window, squeezing into his little Mini, his shaggy head bowed, the whole effort comical and endearing and terribly sad.

A memory flitted through her mind of the two of them on their wedding day, barefoot on the sand, laughing into each other's faces as a camera snapped.

I'm finally going to figure out how to be happy, Rachel remembered thinking. *This is the way*. She'd been so hopeful – cautiously so, but still. She'd believed things were finally going to change. She was going to start getting things right.

What a joke. And yet even now, especially now, she feared she had no one to blame but herself.

She turned back to the boxes of old photos and papers she'd been going through, although she had neither the stomach nor the heart for the job. She'd already gone through a file of her old school reports her father must have kept. *Rachel is a lovely if rather quiet girl who shows promise when she can be drawn out of her shell.* Amazing how prescient her Year 3 teacher had been.

It made her ache to think of her father reading those reports, putting them carefully in a box. With a sigh of resignation, she pulled another box towards her – more school reports. Rachel picked one up; it was from Year 8. *Rachel has had a very difficult year, but she continues to work diligently.*

A ripple of realization went through her, making her fingers clench the page as her stomach churned. Year 8 – that would have been the year her father died. He couldn't have saved these reports, put them all in a box, along, she saw, with her English essays, her artwork, a project she'd done on deep-sea diving. Her father couldn't have saved her stuff, because by this time he'd been dead.

Which meant her mother had done it.

Rachel sat back on her heels, the crumpled report fluttering, forgotten, from her hand. Why had her mother saved all this? Why do something that suggested she cared, when she so clearly hadn't and still didn't? *You've left me alone for the last thirty-seven years.*

Rachel looked through the rest of the box, and then another and another. They were all filled to the brim. She even found a poster she'd made for a stupid science project in Year 9. Her mother had kept all of it. Why?

She got up, taking the first report with her, and went downstairs to find her mother. Deborah was in her usual place in the drawing room, the position Rachel remembered from childhood – sitting on a blue, floral-patterned wingback chair by the window, her back to the door of the room.

"Mum." Her voice sounded croaky.

Deborah didn't answer.

"*Mum.*"

"What is it?" She sounded tetchy, as usual. Rachel couldn't tell how with it she was; over the last couple of days she'd seemed irritable but cognizant. Mostly. There had been occasional spells of confusion, but her mother snapped out of them quickly and always seemed irritated at Rachel for noticing.

"I – I found some of my old school reports."

"Yes?" *Get on with it*, in other words. *Why would I care?*

"Did you keep them all?" Rachel didn't know why she asked. She'd already found the evidence.

"What if I did?"

"But…" She swallowed. "Why?"

"Why?" Deborah repeated. "Why wouldn't I? You're my daughter."

"Yes, but…" She swallowed again, her throat getting tighter and tighter. "You've never acted as if you cared, Mum." She'd never said such a thing out loud before. She'd never dared. Her whole life had been about pretending she didn't care that her mother didn't care, acting as if it were normal or at least just the way it was, even though it tore her up inside, shredded her self-esteem along with her soul. What was wrong with you when your own mother didn't care about you?

"Oh Rachel, don't be so melodramatic."

Which was exactly the kind of response Rachel would have expected her mother to give. "But why, Mum?" she pressed, even though part of her didn't want to. Surely this wasn't going to lead anywhere she wanted to go. "Why would you keep all that when you didn't even seem to notice while it was going on?" When she'd been growing up, her mother had never asked about her day, or her friends, her worries or fears, dreams or desires. She'd seemed utterly indifferent to the events of Rachel's adolescent life, never mind the inner workings of her mind or heart.

"You're my daughter," Deborah said again, flatly, and some faint, fragile thread Rachel had been clutching on to her whole life finally snapped.

"That's not a reason. It wasn't a reason when I was growing up, it can't be a reason now." Her mother just sighed. Rachel took a step towards her, the old school report now crumpled in her hand. "Why keep all this stuff when you don't care about me?" she asked, decades-old pain throbbing in every syllable.

Her mother stared at her for a long moment, her face utterly expressionless, as blank as marble.

"Why?" Rachel asked again, this time the word a cry.

"Don't be ridiculous. Of course I care about you." Deborah turned away with a dismissive sniff. "You always had a flair for the dramatic, Rachel, just like your father. It's so tedious."

Rachel sank on to a chair, her mind still spinning. Memories of meals eaten in silence, endless weekends drifting around the house like two ghosts, wanting her mother to ask anything about her life but she never would. It had been like that, hadn't it? She was remembering it the way it was, and not just the way it had felt?

It was so unsettling to doubt herself now, to doubt everything. Her father's love, her mother's coldness. Which one was real? Which one mattered?

"I don't understand," she whispered.

"You don't want to understand," her mother replied. "Just like I didn't."

"What do you mean?"

"Better not to understand something than to have to forgive it."

"What is *that* supposed to mean?"

Her mother craned her neck to look out of the window. "When is Will coming back?"

Will? Rachel sat up, jolted as if she'd missed the last step in a staircase. "Mum, it wasn't Will who was here; it was Anthony." *My husband, not yours.*

Her mother tutted impatiently. "That's what I meant, of course. When is he coming back?"

"He's not. He's gone back to Bristol."

"Bristol?" Her mother looked blank.

"Where I live."

"Oh. Right."

Deborah looked away and Rachel struggled to know what to say, how to feel. It was almost as if her mother was playing mind games with her, toying with her fears. Will. Anthony. Two larger-than-life men – one she'd adored and one she was scared to love. Was her mother pretending to be confused, or in her mind had she really morphed Rachel's husband and father into a single person?

Rachel shook her head slowly. She felt no nearer to any answers, and she wasn't ready to ask any more questions. "I'm going back upstairs. Do you want something? A cup of tea?"

"I don't want anything," Deborah said, and with her lips pursed, she turned away, her face set against Rachel.

Back upstairs Rachel stared at the mess of boxes, with papers and photos spilling out. She couldn't cope with any of it right now, even as part of her yearned to dig through all the detritus and see if those forgotten memories held any clues, offered any answers.

Not now, though. She wasn't ready yet. Her brain hurt, along with her heart, so she did what she'd been doing since she could remember – she forgot the present in favour of someone else's past.

In her bedroom, the double bed she'd been sharing with Anthony still rumpled, she reached for her laptop. With pillows propped up behind her she opened her email and downloaded the attachment Soha had sent her a few days ago. The Fenton Collection, which sounded far grander than it was, as the collection comprised only six letters.

She read the short introduction written by an archivist, giving the basic details of James and Abigail Fenton. She was the daughter of a wool merchant, he was a ship's captain turned trader, who had decided to captain his last ship, *The Fair Lady*, which sank off the Caribbean with a full cargo of sugar and rum. All facts Rachel already knew.

> *James Fenton's first letter was written from the west coast of Africa, when he first arrived on The Fair Lady in the summer of 1766, to procure slaves to trade in the West Indies. It is believed he gave the letter to the captain of a ship returning to Whitehaven, to be delivered to Abigail Fenton. As there was no reliable mail delivery service during that period, he would have had to depend on others' goodwill and charity to pass his letters on to his wife. It is not known when Abigail received the letters; it could have been after his death, as often letters were lost, mislaid, or remained in a port until they could be passed on to another ship.*

Rachel felt a little ripple of curiosity and excitement as she clicked on the next page and began to read. "Dearest Abigail…"

CHAPTER TWENTY-TWO

Abigail

Whitehaven, 1766

Abigail stood by the window of the drawing room, oblivious to the cold draught coming from it, her husband's letter in her hand.

It had been five months since he had left for Africa, five long, difficult months. After discovering the lack of funds in his strongbox, Abigail had been left spinning, having no idea what to do. She'd slipped past a silent Adelaide and gone to the parlour, where she'd paced uselessly, completely at a loss.

Was there really no money? Had James left her with no funds at all? Finally, rousing herself as if from a stupor, she'd taken what little there'd been in the box and used it to pay the butcher. It had felt to her a matter of honour as well as a point of pride, and the man's compassionate look had made her cringe.

"Thank you kindly, Mrs Fenton."

It was only afterwards, when she'd returned to the house, that she realized how foolish she'd been. Now she had no money at all. Over the next few days, others came to the door of the house on Queen Street – men with bills and merchants who had no more credit to extend. They must have heard of the to-do at the butcher's, and now everyone wanted what they were owed, except that Abigail didn't have it.

After several days of putting off her creditors and then simply not answering the door, she'd gone, as she'd known she would have to, to her father. She wilted inside with humiliation and grief that it had come to this – that James had allowed it to.

"Clearly it's no more than an oversight," she told her father, sitting in the front parlour, her hands clenched in her lap. "Mr Fenton would have seen to the bills if he'd remembered, but his preparations for *The Fair Lady* were so consuming."

"Of course," her father murmured. Abigail knew she was not fooling him one bit. "All gentlemen make such oversights now and again," he said, and he paid off all the bills, and gave her extra money besides. Abigail had never felt so humiliated, so ashamed, and yet she could not deny the relief she felt at keeping the wolf from the door for a while longer.

Now her gaze flicked to the page she held, with James's schoolboy letters filling it so carefully, his penmanship earned through many painstaking hours of practice. The letter had been delivered this morning, with the arrival of *The Mercy*, a ship returning from Africa through Spain.

Dearest Abigail,

I write these lines from the Slave Coast of Africa, a hot and uneasy place. I thank Providence, who directed the Wind and Weather, to have us land safely near Sinagal. However, I was Much Disappointed to discover that the Trade of which so many speak highly was not the Reasonable Endeavour I had come to expect. In truth there are very few slaves in prime health who would be sold at an Advantage. Many are sickly, although Traders of all kinds use Oils and such Perfumes to hide their great Deficiencies. After several Disappointments, we sailed

on to SereLeon, in the hope of finding Prime Slaves
who will remain in Good Health for the Great Voyage
to the Indies. I confess, My Dearest, that this Voyage has
made me Uneasy in both my Mind and Spirit. I Wonder
at the Stone Prisons where Slaves are Kept – they are
Mighty Fortresses, unlike any you have seen in our own
Pleasant Land. At times it doth seem like a Dread and
Fearful Business, and yet I Trust that God, in Whom all
Enterprises are Ordained, will Bless my Voyage and bring
me Safely back to you.

Yours, as ever,

James

Abigail looked up from the letter, her gaze unseeing. In her mind's eye she saw not the busy harbour prickling with masts visible out of the drawing room window, but a mighty stone fortress built on the shores of some dark and tropical place, filled with the lamentable groaning of those who, in their great misfortune, had become enslaved. She could not imagine it; she did not want to.

But as she read her husband's letter through yet another time, she wondered at what he was not willing to write. Why was he so uneasy in both mind and spirit? Had his conscience been pricked, just as hers had, by the great suffering he was, by his own hand, inflicting on humanity?

She put the letter aside, resenting the ferment of emotions it caused within her. Why was nothing simple? It had been several weeks since she'd removed Adelaide to her dressing room, and it had not brought any great peace to her household. Jensen was still sullen, Cook fearful and suspicious. Adelaide was mostly so very silent, even though Abigail knew her English was much improved.

She, at least, had begun to rest easy with the girl sleeping so close, yet she still felt a vague and restless sense of dissatisfaction; a feeling that the arrangements she'd made were somehow not sufficient. She pictured Mr Wesley speaking to her again, regarding Adelaide's little bedroom with a silent look of censure, and she cringed inwardly with shame even as part of her rose in defiance.

I am doing so much more than anyone else. What would that great man ask of me?

She could hear Wesley's response as if he were standing in the room with her. *It is not I who ask anything of you, Madam, but God.*

Very well, then, Abigail thought petulantly, *why cannot God be satisfied with what I give?*

"Ma'am, Mrs Heywood is here to visit." Jensen stood in the doorway, as polite and proper as ever, yet Abigail sensed the woman's animosity. It had not abated even though Adelaide had been in the household for over six months.

"Show her in, please, Jensen."

"My dear Abigail," Caroline fussed as soon as she entered the room. "I have become so concerned for you of late."

"There is no need, Mama." Abigail knew it was her mother's oblique way of referring to her financial woes; neither of them had ever spoken of it directly, and Abigail doubted they ever would.

"You are faring well?" Caroline asked, eyebrows raised as she took the chair opposite Abigail with a satisfied sigh and a flounce of her skirts.

"I am well," Abigail affirmed, and then lifted her gaze to Jensen. "Will you bring tea, please, Jensen?"

The maid nodded crossly, the sulky swirl of her skirt as she turned away bordering on insolence.

Caroline clucked. "She is getting airs, that one. And to think I trained her myself. She was naught but a scullery maid when she came to us."

"You are right," Abigail agreed in a low voice. "But I am not altogether certain that I can do anything about it."

"Of course you can! Good servants are not as hard to find as all that."

"Yes, but…" Reluctantly Abigail's gaze flitted to Adelaide, who was sitting quietly on her stool, her lowered gaze fixed on her chapbook.

"If Jensen objects on those grounds, it is a nonsense," Caroline said after a moment. "She is perfectly well trained, and when she says anything she speaks well. I must say, you have done marvellously with her, Abigail. Georgiana will have to come to you for all her advice."

"Georgiana?"

"Have you not heard? She has requested a child the same as you, but she wants a little boy. I, for one, could not countenance it, but she is quite determined."

For some reason she could not entirely understand, this bland pronouncement as good as made Abigail's skin crawl. "You say Georgiana is getting a little slave boy?" she asked in a low voice. Adelaide did not move or lift her gaze, but Abigail *felt* her listening. The girl's English was now nearly as good as her own, even though she still said very little, making her question all over again her husband's determined assertion that slaves did not think or feel as they did. How could he believe such a thing, when it was obvious to Abigail that slaves could speak as well as they did?

"Yes. She asked Mr Fenton before he left on *The Fair Lady*, and he promised her he'd look out for a little boy especially. I must confess, I am surprised he did not tell you."

"No, he did not." Abigail felt a coldness steal through her. James had kept such knowledge from her? Why? And yet she knew why. Because he'd known some part of her – a part she could barely understand – would resist. And yet how could she, when Adelaide sat right beside her, and Abigail would have her nowhere else? Why should she protest at Georgiana having the same situation?

"I suppose it slipped his mind," Caroline declared with a little shrug of her shoulders. "He had so very much on his mind, as you remarked."

A silence settled upon them at this unnecessary reminder of James's dire financial straits. Abigail stared into the fire, a sense of disquiet that she'd been attempting to keep at bay threatening to rise up and overtake her yet again.

"Why don't you visit Georgiana?" Caroline suggested after Jensen had brought in the tea tray with a great rattling of cups, and set it down before Abigail. "You could take Adelaide with you," Caroline continued as Abigail began to make the tea, pouring hot water over the leaves with great deliberation.

"Visit Georgiana," she repeated neutrally, not quite a question.

"Yes, you can tell her how you've managed to train Adelaide so admirably. Really, she is quite the little madam, isn't she?" Caroline flicked a glance towards Adelaide with uncertain approbation. "You would hardly know…"

"You would hardly know?" Abigail prompted, a bit sharply, when her mother had trailed off. "What is it you would hardly know, Mama?"

Caroline looked flustered. "Well, I only meant that you would hardly know she is… she is an African." She blushed and bit her lip, looking unhappy. "Of course, I can tell from the colour of her skin, so I could hardly mean that. I only meant as to her manners and suchlike. Oh Abigail, why must you be so stubborn and difficult still?" Irritably she nodded towards the silver teapot, a wedding present from an uncle. "Is it not ready yet?"

Abigail poured the tea in silence.

Later, as her mother was preparing to leave, she urged her to visit Georgiana again. "I know she would look kindly upon a visit from you. She is quite worn out, I think, from her last confinement." Abigail thought she'd kept her face blandly expressionless, but she must not have, for Caroline regarded her unhappily. "I am sorry, my dear. I did not mean —"

"Do not think on it, Mama." Georgiana had had three babies in three years, all still living. Abigail could have had the same if her own pregnancies had come to anything. But she did not think of them any more; she could not.

"Adelaide," she said instead, turning to the little girl, who had been reading her chapbook without a murmur all morning long. "Say goodbye to my mother, Mrs Heywood."

Adelaide looked up, her expression, as it so often was, one of wary blankness. "Goodbye, Mrs Heywood."

"Doesn't she sound like a lady!" Caroline remarked, sounding both impressed and unsettled. "Good heavens."

After her mother had gone, Abigail felt quite restless and out of sorts, although she couldn't have said why. More and more she felt this strange sense of anxious uncertainty, as if part of her could fly even as another part longed to shrink back and hide. Adelaide watched her silently as she paced the room, then picked up some needlework and, after a few minutes, threw it down again, barely touched.

"I suppose I shall have to visit Georgiana now," she said aloud, half to Adelaide, half to herself. "My mother will tell her that I intend to visit, and it would be a great impoliteness not to." She sighed in exasperated frustration. "But I do not wish to." She glanced at Adelaide, her small face so watchful and yet calm. "What do you think, Adelaide? Should I visit her?" The little girl did not answer. "You could come with me." She thought of Georgiana's little slave boy and her stomach curdled. "Would you like to come with me?"

Adelaide's voice was soft and quiet as she answered, "As Mistress wishes."

"That's not what I asked." Abigail heard how sharp her voice sounded, her agitation spilling over. "What do you want, Adelaide?" she asked, leaning forward, her manner turning strangely aggressive. "What is it that you want to do?" she asked again, her voice ringing out.

Adelaide stared at her for a long moment, her smooth face and wide eyes giving nothing away. "As Mistress wishes," she said again, cautiously this time, and Abigail knew she would not get another word out of her.

She visited Georgiana, with Adelaide in tow, a week later, filled with both uncertainty and determination, although in regard to what she knew not. She'd dressed Adelaide in a lovely dress of rose she'd cut down from one of her own, simpler than the first gown she'd had made for her by the mantua maker, and more suitable for a child.

"Abigail, I am so pleased to see you. It has been far too long. And you have brought your little lady's maid! What a sweet little thing she is, but I do wish you'd dressed her up in silks and satins. Didn't she have a dear little ensemble in blue? She looked quite the lady, as I recall." Georgiana let out a gay laugh and clapped her hands. "What can she do? Does she speak?"

"Of course she speaks," Abigail answered stiffly. "She has learned English remarkably well."

"How clever of her! You hear such things, you know, that they can't do very much at all, but I do wonder at it. Mr Riddell has made acquaintances with several Africans on his travels. There are ever so many in London – freedmen and dressed as gentlemen."

"Are there?" Abigail was startled by this news; she had never heard it before, and had assumed that the only Africans in all of England were such as Adelaide, or the Jeffersons' coachman, whom she'd seen from afar, silent and grim-faced.

"Oh, yes. He made the acquaintance of a freed slave – Vassa was his name, I believe. He is a man of letters."

"A man of letters!" Abigail was agape.

Georgiana shrugged. "Some of them are quite clever, I suppose."

"But…" Abigail put one hand to her head, feeling quite suddenly overcome. "But if they can be freed – if they can be men of letters…" She wet her lips, staring at Georgiana helplessly, who frowned back.

"What of it?"

"How can they be enslaved at all?" Abigail whispered. "Surely it is wrong, just as Mr Wesley –"

"Oh, Mr Wesley! Your mother is quite enamoured with the man. I did not realize you shared her enthusiasms."

"He is a passionate speaker."

"Indeed, he is! Working everyone up into a most unbecoming frenzy. My maid of all work went along to one of his speeches in the marketplace, and she has not been the same since. I am quite put out." Georgiana turned expectantly to Adelaide, who was standing by Abigail's chair. "Now, what can this pretty little thing do? Your husband has promised me a little boy to be my page. I would so like someone to fetch and carry!" She rested one hand delicately against her plump stomach. "I believe I am in that happy state once more."

"What, again?" Abigail blurted out, half appalled, half envious. "Your youngest is still with his wet nurse, is he not?"

"Oh, indeed." Georgiana sighed, her hand still on her middle. "I am quite worn out, I tell you. I do not know how I should last without Dr Fothergill's pills. They are the only thing that keeps me standing. I have had such headaches, you know. Of late I have been quite unwell." She pressed one hand to her forehead for what Abigail supposed was effect, although she did indeed look flushed.

"I am so sorry to hear it," she murmured politely.

"In any case," Georgiana resumed, dropping her hand, "I am quite looking forward to having a little page and dressing him in a frock coat and frills. How handsome he will look! Mr Fenton said he would find a healthy, well turned out little lad for me. I am quite depending on him."

"I do not how he will find such a creature," Abigail said before she could think better of it, "when he will have endured the kind of voyage no human being ever should."

"Why, Abigail, you sound almost like one of those abolitionists," Georgiana answered with a laugh. "And with your husband in the trade."

"Well I know it."

"Surely you are not getting such ideas? It would be most unsuitable. Besides, we cannot do without the trade. All of society rests on it." With a little laugh she gestured to the loaf of sugar that had been brought in with the tea tray. "There would be none of this without them, you know."

"Then perhaps we should go without sugar in our tea," Abigail said recklessly. "I daresay it would not be such a great sacrifice."

"And what of the trade? The profit?" Georgiana demanded. "Really, Abigail, you are too much. I thought you would amuse me today, with your little lady's maid, but I am quite put out."

"I am so sorry to disappoint you," Abigail returned with acid in her voice.

"What *does* she do?" Georgiana asked petulantly. "Can you make her say something?"

"No, I cannot." Abigail found she was shaking with rage. "She is not a puppet, or a pet, or a plaything. She is a *person*." Her voice throbbed with emotion as realization rushed through her. She had not always treated Adelaide as such; at least, not as much as she should have. She saw that so starkly now, and it both terrified and shamed her.

She rose from her seat, reaching for Adelaide's hand and clasping it tightly in her own. "I am afraid I cannot stay for tea, Georgiana. I do wish you well in your – your happy state." Without waiting for a reply, Abigail hurried from the room, Adelaide following in her wake.

Back at the house on Queen Street, Abigail could not settle to anything. She paced restlessly, her mind racing. Men of letters, living as gentlemen – how could it be so? How?

She had no further answers to the awful question when, a week later, Caroline visited to fretfully inform her that Georgiana had contracted smallpox. "She'd been unwell for some time, and the spots came out two days ago, poor creature."

"That is terrible," Abigail murmured. She was horrified for Georgiana's sake, but also for her own. She'd seen Georgiana only last week, and everyone knew smallpox was dreadfully contagious. "Will she – will she be all right?"

"Goodness only knows. It is such a dreadful disease."

Over the next few days Abigail waited in apprehension, fearful at every twinge or ache, checking her face in the wavy looking glass in her bedroom, inspecting it for the distinctive and awful spots that accompanied the disease.

None came, but just as she breathed a sigh of relief, she discovered Adelaide lying on her little bed in the dressing room delirious with fever, clutching her stomach.

Two days later, the rash appeared, the spots blooming across the little girl's face. She had smallpox.

CHAPTER TWENTY-THREE

Rachel

My dearest Abigail,

*I write from SereLeon, where we have been Moored these
last few weeks, in the Hope that we will fare Better than
we have thus far. I have been Sorely Tried by this Voyage
in a way I did not Expect. But I do not Wish to Write
of Such Things now, or Trouble you, my dear, with any
Distress. If my Conscience is pricked, then it is I who must
Answer to our Father in Heaven. I have Procured a Young
Boy of good Health and great Charm for your Friend,
Mrs Riddell. She is Quite Determined to have a Page.
I believe he will be Quite Suitable, when he is Trained.
He is a lively little lad, and I have taken Something of a
Shine to him. I call him Nathaniel, which I Believe to be a
Good Name. I eagerly look forward to My Return, and to
see you and Adelaide Once More, away from this Terrible
Business. Yes, it's True, both of you have been my Comfort
and Stay these last few months.*

May God keep you.

As ever,

Your James

Rachel lowered the printout of James Fenton's fourth letter and met Jane's fascinated gaze across the kitchen table of the old vicarage. "What do you think?" She'd spent all last night reading the six letters of the Fenton Collection, transfixed and amazed by this intimate glimpse into the life of a man she now almost felt she knew, as well as his silent wife, her own possible responses lost in the mists of time, if they'd ever been written in the first place.

"He sounds so regretful," Jane murmured. "Tormented, almost – 'this terrible business'."

"Yes, that's what I thought too. I may be reading between the lines, but he does seem to regret getting involved in the slave trade."

"I suppose it must have been a shock, actually being on the ship rather than sitting in your office back in Whitehaven." Jane shook her head slowly. "Such dreadful, dreadful stuff."

"I know." Rachel reached for the printout of the fifth letter. "Yet he continued in it. He could have walked away."

"I suppose his whole fortune rested on it. Not, of course, that it's an excuse."

"No," Rachel murmured. "This one is from when he was about to leave the slave coast, and it's even more emotional. He talks about how he had to build another deck on the ship to take more slaves – I read about that at The Rum Story. And he makes a mention of how closely packed they were, because he needed to make more money. 'I fear the hold will be dreadfully full, yet I can see no other way. The price of slaves is not what I had hoped, and in truth they are becoming more difficult to procure. I do what I must, though it chafes me.'"

"Chafes him! How about the manacles that chafed all those poor people?" Jane exclaimed.

"There's more." She scanned the letter, looking for the relevant bit. "'I have discovered, the only way to make our Fortune on this voyage, is to procure enough slaves that some survive the Dreadful Journey, though in doing so we lose many others. It is a terrible bargain, but it is one I fear I must make.'"

"He likes to justify himself, doesn't he?"

"Don't we all." Rachel sighed and shook her head. "All I have to do is recall that speculum oris, and everything in me shudders. The voyage they made really was unbelievably horrible. Beyond our imagining." She put the printouts down. "But I still feel there is a mystery here. Why is it thought that his ship sank in the Caribbean?"

"What does the last letter say?"

"Not much. It's from the Caribbean, right before he sailed, and it seems strangely cheerful. 'I look forward to seeing you in a few months' time, perhaps before this letter reaches you, when our Fortunes will be restored.'" Rachel put down the printouts. "You know there was no real mail service back then – he would have given it to a ship that was going on ahead to England, but who knows how long it would have taken for the letter to arrive in Whitehaven?"

"And that's the end of it? No more letters?"

"No more letters – at least none that Abigail kept. Just these six. She was the one who decided to donate them to the abolition movement, upon her deathbed."

"When did she die?"

"In 1790, in the thick of the abolition movement. She would have only been in her late forties, but I gather from some of the things James says that she was unwell during their marriage. And they only had the one daughter."

"Adelaide? What happened to her?"

"I don't know. I haven't found much about any Adelaide Fenton online. I've got a friend at the British Library who said she'd look into it for me as a favour, given it's just a pet project now. Who knows what she'll find? Still, there might be something buried deep in some archive or other."

"It's so fascinating. I can understand why you're curious." Jane leaned forward, her expression turning worryingly intent. "But how is real life going, Rachel? Your mum? You said she was back home?"

"Yes, she's been back for a few days now." Rachel had felt guilty leaving Deborah at home for a few hours while she drove to Goswell to have a coffee with Jane, but her mother had rather tetchily assured her she would be absolutely fine, and she most certainly did not need a babysitter. Rachel had been so desperate to escape the confines of the house that she'd taken her at her word.

"Have you decided what you're going to do about it all?"

"I'm trying to sell the house, to start, but it's going to be a long process. It needs updating, and I don't want to have to let it go for a song."

"And what will your mum do in the meantime? Will you stay with her until the house is sold?"

Rachel felt a pressure building in her chest – the same one that had been mounting since her mother had first been diagnosed, or perhaps even since she'd first sensed something was wrong, with that blasted kettle. "I – I don't know," she said on a tired sigh. "I was only planning on taking a week off, but…"

She didn't feel comfortable leaving her mother alone. Just the thought of walking away made her stomach cramp and her head hurt. No matter what the GP said, her mum was barely with it half the time, and rattling around by herself in that big house, anything could happen. And Rachel knew that if it did, she would blame herself. How could she not?

"Could your mum go back with you to Bristol?"

"She doesn't want to." Not that they'd had a conversation about it, but Rachel knew they didn't need to. Her mother was already acting as if she could barely tolerate her presence.

"Maybe she doesn't have a choice," Jane pointed out gently.

"I can't imagine frogmarching my mother anywhere," Rachel said with an attempt at a laugh. "We've never had that kind of relationship. I'm the last person she'd ever listen to."

"Yes, you've said as much, but maybe things can be different now?" Jane smiled hopefully. Rachel wished she could be as optimistic.

"I doubt it. But something has to happen, because I can't leave things the way they are. I do know that." She sighed again, heavily this time, the weight of all her unanswered questions and dilemmas lodged squarely on her shoulders.

"What about your husband?" Jane asked. "Sorry, I forgot his name…"

"Anthony."

"Can he help?"

Rachel's lips twisted. She hadn't spoken to Anthony since he'd left, hadn't texted or emailed or called, and neither had he; a fact that made her thoroughly miserable. They were at an impasse, a standoff, neither of them willing to bend in case they broke. She couldn't help feeling angry that he'd just gone, even though she hadn't wanted him here in the first place. What a ridiculous contradiction she was. "Well, actually," she told Jane, a touch of bitter acid in her tone, "we're taking a bit of a break right now."

"What?" Jane's look of complete shock was almost comical. "Now? When things are so pear-shaped?"

"They've always been pear-shaped," Rachel answered. "We haven't had the... easiest of marriages."

"Marriage is never easy."

"No? Never? Because according to Anthony, it should be a walk in the park." Rachel heard how bitter she sounded and briefly closed her eyes. "Sorry, I must sound awful. I'm just tired and stressed, and it really hasn't been easy lately. It's been ridiculously hard."

"You can tell me about it," Jane said gently. "Whatever it is."

Rachel opened her eyes and looked around the homey kitchen – a tangle of plants on the wide windowsill, dirty dishes piled haphazardly in the sink, a cookbook open to a batter-splattered page on the counter. She wanted a kitchen like this. She wanted a *life* like this. She'd never had it, and she had no idea how to begin to get it. She felt the emptiness of her own life now – from her sterile kitchen in her modern flat to the echo of loneliness whispering through her soul.

"I don't even know where to begin," she finally said in a shaky voice. "There's so much."

"Who decided on the break?"

"Anthony, but I don't blame him." She brushed at her eyes. "I'm terribly difficult to live with. I know that." She let out a laugh that sounded far too wobbly.

"Are you?" Jane asked, sounding both surprised and curious. "Why?"

"I'm prickly and distant and I don't like full fry-ups –"

"I can hardly see what your breakfast preferences have to do with anything."

"Anthony is a chef. Food is love to him." Rachel shrugged, unable to explain it all. "It's not that, though, not really. It's everything. I just feel like such a *disappointment* to him."

Jane frowned. "Is that because of you?" she asked. "Or him?"

"Both, I suppose," Rachel said after a moment. "But mainly me."

"A marriage takes two people, Rachel. Two people working together, giving and taking, not one person pulling all the weight."

"I know that. And I suppose I don't give or take as much as I should. I know I don't. Anthony is upset with me, and I understand why he is. I keep pushing him away – just in little ways, some of them you might not even notice. But he does, he *always* does, and I do as well."

"Why do you do that?"

Rachel shrugged. "That's the million-dollar question, isn't it? I don't know."

Jane, however, would not be put off so easily. "You must have some idea. These things – impulses and feelings – don't come out of nowhere, surely. Even if it's just an inkling."

"No, I suppose they don't." Rachel gazed off into the distance, the room blurring before her as she tried to put her jumbled thoughts and raw feelings into some semblance of coherent order. "I suppose it comes from my childhood," she said slowly. "The way I grew up. But blaming that feels like a cop-out. I should know better. I'm conscious of my past, so I shouldn't let it define me."

"You mean your relationship with your mother? The distance?"

"Yes, and with my father."

Jane looked surprised. "The historian on telly? I thought you got on well with him. The memories you shared, they seemed so special."

"Yes, I did." Her throat was becoming tight as she picked at a loose thread on her jumper, fraying it between her fingers. "Yes, I did," she said again.

Jane didn't reply; just waited.

And that was all it took. Rachel knew she needed to say more. Strangely, she almost wanted to. "All through my childhood, it was me and my dad. A team of two against my mum." The words came out like a confession, the first time she'd ever made it. "I didn't see it that way at the time – I just loved my dad. He was so jolly, so affectionate, so much fun. And my mother was always – cold. Well, cool, anyway. Distant. I much preferred my dad to her, and he made me feel like we were partners. It was only later – recently, actually – that I started to see how my mum had been left out."

"That sounds very tricky," Jane said after a moment. "But why does it seem as if you're blaming yourself for something? Surely it was your father's responsibility."

"Because I should have realized," Rachel burst out. "I should have known. I shouldn't have gone along –"

"Gone along with what?" Jane asked. "Known what, Rachel?"

She took a deep, steadying breath. "I think – I know he was having an affair. Probably more than one, if I'm honest."

Jane was quiet for a moment. "That's not your fault," she said finally.

"I know, but I was – complicit. I overheard my dad talking to a woman on the phone once. He asked me not to tell my mother."

"That wasn't fair."

"And there were other instances. When he took me to Turkey, he was with a woman. I didn't remember it until recently. I've had such happy memories of that trip, and then all of a sudden, it landed in my brain like – like a rotten egg." She let out a trembling laugh. "He had a woman there the whole time. I can't believe I forgot about that for as long as I did."

"It's understandable," Jane murmured. "You were young."

"Not that young."

"So your father asked you not to tell your mother," Jane surmised. "But from the sounds of it, she already knew."

"Yes," Rachel answered slowly, "I think she did. I'm sure of it now. Since she's been diagnosed with dementia, things have come out." She shook her head slowly. "Things I don't want to hear. I loved my dad." She looked at Jane full in the face, her eyes swimming with tears. "I *loved* him. You know that poem, 'You are my sun, moon, and all my stars'? That was my dad for me."

"It's hard to lose a hero," Jane said softly as she reached over to squeeze Rachel's hand. "But your dad's been gone a long time."

"I know." Rachel looked down at their clasped hands, blinking hard. "But somehow that doesn't really make much of a difference."

"The important thing is your mum now," Jane continued. "And your marriage. Don't let the past dictate the present, Rachel. Let it go if you can."

"I think I've been doing that my whole life." A tear slipped down Rachel's cheek and she dashed it away with the heel of her hand. "I've made it my *career*."

"That's different, surely. This is personal."

"I've made this whole foray into the Fentons' lives personal," Rachel admitted. "I don't even know why. I was interested from the first; almost obsessed, in a weird way. But after reading those six letters, I wonder how Abigail felt. Was she able to forgive him?"

"For being a slave trader? How do you know she minded?"

"I don't," Rachel admitted, surprised at the realization. "I don't actually know her at all, and yet I've constructed this personality for her, based on the letters. The way he writes – it's almost like an apology. Like he knew how she felt. Like he knew she minded."

"Perhaps." Jane didn't look convinced.

"But even more, how did he forgive himself? That second to last letter – it almost pulses with pain." She scrabbled for it, grateful to be focusing on something other than her own problems. "'It is my dearest wish and my deepest prayer, wife of my heart, that these matters of conscience do not come between us. Yet I fear they will, for they have come between myself and my own soul.'"

"Yes, I see what you mean," Jane murmured. "And yet he wrote that letter after the one where he seemed so cheerful. Deceiving himself, I guess."

"We all do that, don't we?"

"Yes, I suppose we do." Jane shook her head. "Poor man. Is it wrong to say that, considering what he did?"

"I don't know. But I do feel for him. To know you were the architect of so much pain and suffering, perhaps even murder... How do we forgive anyone, Jane?"

"You mean how do you forgive your father?" Jane said quietly. "And how do you forgive yourself – for what?"

"For giving my mum the cold shoulder for so many years. I know it was mutual, I honestly don't think I'm mistaken about that, but still. I let it happen."

"You were a child –"

"Even after. Long after. I put the onus on her. I know I did. Just as I put it on Anthony." Tears pooled in her eyes once more. "I love him, you know. He might question it, but I really do love him. I'm just not sure I know how to show that to anyone. I don't know if I've ever known how."

"Tell him, then," Jane advised. "Be honest, even if it hurts. Especially if it hurts. And, God willing, the rest will follow."

"And if it doesn't?"

"You need to forgive your father first," Jane said. "And then you need to forgive yourself. And the only way I know of doing that..." She paused, and then glanced out of the kitchen window.

Rachel followed her gaze, jolting a bit at the sight of the church so close to the old vicarage. "Seriously?" she said. "*Church?*"

"Not church. God. Why do you feel this need to be forgiven? That things need to be made better, or even can be? There's a freedom you're longing for, Rachel. Where does it come from except from there?" Jane nodded once more to the church building. "From Him?"

"I don't know." Rachel hadn't had much of a religious upbringing. She'd always viewed religion of any kind from a historian's perspective, an interesting sociological phenomenon, not much more. And yet.

Could she explain away this need and hurt inside herself by mere science or history? She was so desperate and broken now, she thought she might look anywhere, even in a dim church, a dusty pew. Could answers actually be found there, or was she really grasping at straws?

"I should go," she told Jane. "I've taken up enough of your time."

"I don't mind. Honestly, Rachel. Anytime."

"You've been such a good friend." Rachel let out a little laugh as she rose from the table. "It feels strange saying that, since I've known you for such a short time, but it's true."

"I feel the same." Jane reached over the table and gave her a quick, tight hug. "I feel exactly the same."

As she left the old vicarage, Rachel almost turned to the left, down the slate path to the ancient Saxon door to the church. But the thought of that dim, dusty quiet made her shrink inside. She needed space and air to think. To finally feel.

So instead, at the end of the church lane, she turned right, down the beach road, past the B&B where she'd stayed, to the wide stretch of tidal beach. Sea and sky were her only companions as she walked down the beach, head tilted upwards, arms flung out.

Meet me here.

She didn't know what she expected to happen – some moment, some miracle – but nothing did. The earth expanded all around her as she filled her lungs with air and felt something in her start to lighten – only a little bit, but that was enough.

Maybe, just maybe, Jane was right. Maybe, just maybe, it was going to be okay. She'd be honest with Anthony. She'd be honest with her mother, acknowledge her own hurt and let Deborah admit to hers. Perhaps then they could find their way back to each other. And Rachel would find a way forward; she'd leave the past behind in a way she never ever had before. It could happen. It *would* happen.

If she let it.

All during the hour-long journey back to her mother's house, Rachel held on to that barely there yet buoyant sense of hope. It was going to be different this time, not because she'd tried harder, but because she'd let go. Finally.

As she turned into the gravel drive, her heart gave an unpleasant lurch. The front door was wide open, and when she parked the car, got out, and ran inside, she saw that the house was empty. Her mother was gone.

CHAPTER TWENTY-FOUR

Abigail

Whitehaven, 1766

Adelaide was ill, terribly ill, for ten endless days. Abigail nursed her herself; there was no question of anyone else doing it. Not that there was anyone offering such a service. As soon as Adelaide fell ill, Jensen gave in her notice and Cook said she would not return until the illness had left the house. Abigail was on her own, and despite both the loneliness and the fear, she did not mind. It felt right, somehow. It felt ordained, and even sacred.

For during the days and nights she spent by Adelaide's bedside, Abigail began to realize, dimly at first and then with stark, startling clarity, how dear the little girl was to her – not a slave, not even a servant, but a daughter.

When had it happened? In a moment, or over the course of weeks and months? When had the love that she'd barely been able to acknowledge stirred in her heart? Abigail did not know, but all that mattered was she felt it now, and it made all the difference.

Abigail used the last of her money to engage a doctor, who only shook his head and said there was nothing to be done. "When the fever remains and the pustules are flat, it is a terrible thing, and I have seen it only in children. Death is almost certain."

Abigail had stared at him in disbelief. "What do you mean? This is different from ordinary smallpox?"

"I'm afraid so, yes. It is of a much more serious nature." His voice as he spoke was muffled, as he held a handkerchief to his nose, shaking his head as he gazed in distaste at Adelaide lying prostrate on her bed – Abigail had moved her from the dressing room to the best guest bedroom as soon as she'd fallen ill. She wondered at herself for not doing it months ago.

"I have never seen a patient such as this survive," the doctor said, and though he'd done nothing he was happy enough to take Abigail's last gold sovereign.

Despite his grim words, she refused to admit defeat. She applied poultices to soothe the pustules, and wet cloths to help with the fever. She changed Adelaide's sheets and nightgowns, and spooned clear broth into her mouth even when her hands were shaking with fatigue.

And she prayed, as she never had before; not to the impersonal force of Providence, but to the personal, loving Saviour John Wesley had spoken of so movingly, and that she was compelled to believe in now. Only He could help. Only He could save.

The days blurred into nights, the minutes endless and yet the hours speeding by too fast, as Adelaide did not improve, at first twisting and turning, moaning with pain, and then all too listless, as if the very life was ebbing away from her.

"*No.*" Eight days after the fever had first started, Abigail held the girl in her arms, her cheek pressed to hers, heedless of the contagion or the disease. "No, it cannot be. You *must* live, Adelaide, *Adedayo*. You must, because now I know how precious you are." The girl was tiny and fragile in her arms, barely aware of Abigail or her surroundings. Abigail could not bear it.

And she knew she would not be able to bear the worst yet to come – if Adelaide died without knowing how much Abigail loved her, this daughter of hers, as precious as if she'd given birth to her herself. Skin colour was nothing but that: the colour of skin. In those long days and nights of waiting, fearing, praying, hoping, Abigail could have both laughed in incredulity and wept at the utter idiocy of it – to treat someone differently because their skin was a darker shade! It was beyond comprehension; it made no sense at all, and she wondered that it ever could have. It would not, she vowed; she would not let it if Adelaide lived.

If Adelaide lived, Abigail would take her as her daughter. Formally adopt her if she could, if James allowed it. But he had to allow it, because Abigail could not consider anything else.

And then, on the ninth day, Adelaide's fever broke, and she opened her eyes and stared at Abigail, knowing her for the first time in over a week.

Abigail wept.

"Darling girl," she whispered as she touched Adelaide's cheek. "*Darling girl.*"

With the worst over, Abigail washed herself and Adelaide, and burned all the sheets, tainted with illness. She paid a boot boy loitering in the street to take a message to her mother that the worst had passed, and she believed Adelaide would survive. Caroline sent a message back at once, stating that she was of course glad Abigail's slave had been spared, but poor Georgiana Riddell had succumbed to the dreadful illness, along with two of her little children. It was, to be sure, a great tragedy.

Abigail stared at her mother's carefully elegant script for a long time. She was sad for Georgiana, but she ached for another reason altogether. Her slave. Her *slave*. Would Adelaide ever be seen as anything else?

It chafed her sorely, more than anything else she'd experienced, to know that she had only herself – herself and James – to blame for the unfortunate set of circumstances that had brought them to this unhappy place.

If she'd treated Adelaide differently from the start, if she'd just *known*; if James hadn't insisted that slaves didn't think or feel the way they did! Bitterly Abigail recalled it all and regretted every moment. Every mistake, every thoughtless action, every unthinking slight, every careless cruelty. If she could go back and change everything, she would, but as it was, she knew there was only going forward. And so she would, and it would be different. It would all be completely different.

A week later, Abigail attended Georgiana's funeral. Adelaide was not well enough, and she'd engaged the laundry maid, timid thing that she was, to watch over her while she went, promising the princely sum of a shilling – more than she could afford.

It was an icy, grey day as they gathered at St Nicholas to see Georgiana buried; the ground had been frozen, so poor Georgiana's coffin had been stored in a cellar until the ground had thawed enough for a grave to be dug.

Abigail stood with her mother and father as the prayers were said and the coffin was lowered. She felt numb inside, and so very tired; she had barely slept in a fortnight. Even more alarmingly, she felt as if she were viewing the rest of the world from behind a pane of cloudy glass, everything muted and at a distance. Her mother had not even asked her about Adelaide, and Abigail had not offered any information.

As they began to move away from the open grave, Abigail paused by a headstone – that of Mildred Gale, the grandmother of the current Gales, buried here the better part of a century ago. She read the headstone's inscription slowly and with increasing surprise: "d. 1700, Mildred Gale nee Warner of Warner Hall

Virginia, wife of George Gale merchant of Whitehaven. Here also lie with her, her baby daughter and her African slave Jane."

Mildred Gale had had her slave buried with her? Abigail knew that to bury an African in a churchyard was against the law. It was unheard of, an eternal intimacy not to be credited. And yet here they were – Mildred, daughter, slave.

"Abigail, you will catch your death of cold." Caroline grimaced as she reached one gloved hand out to guide Abigail by the elbow. "To think of Georgiana! I am all out of sorts today, I tell you."

"Do you see that, Mama?" Abigail asked as she nodded towards the headstone. "Mildred Gale –"

"Mildred Gale? I don't recall having made her acquaintance."

"That's because she died sixty-seven years ago," Abigail answered. "Look. She was buried with her daughter and her slave."

"Goodness," Caroline murmured, looking discomfited. "Come, Abigail, let us get out of the cold. Come back to Duke Street. Cook will make us a posset."

Reluctantly Abigail let herself be led away.

She returned to Queen Street an hour later, having been unable to mention any of the things that weighed so heavily on her heart, despite her mother's obvious concern.

As Abigail approached the front of her house, her steps slowed, for a man was standing there, looking aggrieved.

"Are you Mistress Fenton? I have come to collect the rent, and I will have it, Madam. Today."

"The rent?" Abigail stared at him blankly. "My husband owns this house outright, Sir. Please leave at once." Yet even as she said the words, she heard their false ring. Here, surely, was another way James had disappointed her.

It soon all came out. The house had been rented, not bought, despite James's assurances of the latter, and the rent was now six months overdue.

"You would surely not turn out a woman on her own?" Abigail said a bit desperately.

"I am sorry for it, Madam, but I am not a charity."

Abigail knew what she would have to do: move back home to her parents' house, until James returned. What would he think, to return to a wife who had been rendered homeless? She felt too despairing to care.

The landlord gave her but one day to vacate the premises. Abigail discovered that all the furniture had been rented as well, save for a single Chippendale chair and the Chinoiserie cabinet James had secured on his voyages.

She packed what little she possessed, and Adelaide's things as well, and sent a message to her mother, via the laundry maid, explaining the situation.

Within a few hours, her father had dispatched a wagon and two brawny men to help carry her things back to Duke Street. Her life, as she had known it, was over.

Yet more was to come, as Abigail had known there would be. Caroline refused to allow Adelaide her own room, insisting she sleep in the kitchen, on the floor.

"It is warm there, and it is more than proper," Caroline insisted. "Really, Abigail, I do not know where these ideas of yours have come from, but they are most unfashionable."

"I do not care for fashion of any sort," Abigail replied staunchly. "And I will not have Adelaide on the kitchen floor –"

"I will give her a blanket."

"You exceed yourself, Mama," Abigail said coldly. "She will sleep with me." Caroline's lips thinned but she made no reply.

Abigail had a bed made up on the settee in her bedroom, and did not think it good enough, although Adelaide did not say a word.

As she tucked her in that evening, Abigail wondered how to begin to talk to this little girl whom she loved. How could she explain how she had changed – how she wanted Adelaide to change? To feel safe, and loved, and yes, even free.

"Adelaide…" She paused in drawing the blanket up over the girl's slight form. "Are you happy here? No, no, that is not what I mean. How could you be?" She sighed. "Would you be happy, if you could? Could you find it… in yourself… to settle here, with me?"

Adelaide regarded her uncertainly and Abigail knew she was not saying all she should or could.

"I have not treated you well, and for that I am sorry." She thought of those first days, of nests of straw and dirty blankets on the warehouse floor, of manacles and a striped back. "I am so very sorry," she choked out, her eyes filling with tears. To her surprise, Adelaide reached out and laid one small hand on hers.

"Mistress… not be sad."

"Oh, Adelaide." Tears spilled over her cheeks as Adelaide gazed at her. "It is you who should be sad. I have no right."

"Please?" Adelaide said haltingly. "Mistress not be sad?"

"I am not sad." Abigail squeezed her hand. "And one day, I hope and pray, you will not call me mistress. You will call me Mama."

The weeks passed quietly then, with Abigail choosing to remain at home rather than go out, despite Caroline's protestations.

"Mama, I am as good as ruined. Our house has been taken, my husband is known to be bankrupt." She shrugged. "Even when he comes back, he will not be able to restore our fortunes to what they were." Although she was realizing more and more that their fortunes had never been what she'd thought they were.

"Even so, it is worse for you to hide away," Caroline insisted. "Your husband's misfortunes are not your fault."

"They are my misfortunes as well," Abigail reminded her. "And I am content."

"It is unnatural," Caroline said in a low voice. "Surely –"

"It is not." Abigail was calm but firm. "It is not," she said again.

In the weeks since Christmas, Abigail had begun attending the little Methodist chapel on Michael Street, much to her mother's dismay. Caroline Heywood had been more than willing to hear John Wesley preach, but she was not amenable to joining the nonconformists who congregated there on a Sunday morning, dissenters who were not accepted by the Church of England.

"Even Wesley himself remains a good Anglican," she insisted. "It is not right."

Abigail was not willing or knowledgeable enough to argue the finer theological points of the matter, so she just smiled and said gently, "Mama, I am happy there."

And she was, somewhat to her own surprise. The members of the chapel were of far humbler stock than the merchants and traders who attended St Nicholas; they were servants and apprentices, tradesmen and mariners, all gathered together to worship and sing. And they accepted Adelaide, not as a slave or even a servant, but as one of their own. Indeed, it was one of the chapel's humble members who gave Abigail a copy of John Wesley's recently published *Thoughts Upon Slavery*.

She read much of it with her heart in her mouth and tears streaming down her face, for Wesley spared no unwholesome detail in describing the gruesome process of procuring and transporting slaves. The reality, depicted so starkly, was horrifying:

*When they are brought down to the shore in order to be
sold, our surgeons thoroughly examine them, and that
quite naked, women and men, without any distinction:
Those that are approved are set on one side. In the mean
time a burning iron, with the arms or name of the
Company, lies in the fire, with which they are marked
on the breast. Before they are put into the ships, their
masters strip them of all they have on their backs: So that
they come on board stark naked, women as well as men.
It is common for several hundreds of them to be put on
board one vessel; where they are stowed together in as
little room as it is possible for them to be crowded. It is
easy to suppose what a condition they must soon be in,
between heat, thirst, and stench of various kinds. So that
it is no wonder so many should die in the passage; but
rather, that any survive it.*

After reading that, Abigail gathered Adelaide in her arms and
kissed her face, so sorry was she that she had endured such an
awful tribulation, and so sorry that her husband was still involved
in the very thing now.

She had had several more letters from James, brought by
various mariners, and they had troubled her soul, for she could see
plainly that her husband did not like his trade, and yet, stubborn
and desperate, he continued in it. He regaled her with stories of
packed holds and terrible filth and disease, yet he seemed unaware
that he was the architect of his own fortunes, as well as those of
the "lamentable creatures" he claimed to feel pity for.

She wished she could write back and assure him that he need
not do such a thing; that she did not want the money made off
those poor, pitiful beings. She would far rather they were poor

and humble, with clear consciences, than make their fortune on the wretched backs of others.

But Abigail had no way of contacting James while he was at sea, and thus no way of letting him know all that was in her heart and mind. In truth, she knew it was something of a miracle that he had been able to write to her at all. Yet during those long winter weeks, she wished she could reach him, and beg him to reconsider his trade.

As it was, January slunk into February and then March, and Abigail began to wonder when *The Fair Lady* would return with its hogsheads of rum and sugar.

"It will be at least a year," said Samuel Jenkins, a mariner at the chapel who had been to Africa twice, before turning away from the trade. "Even with good weather, it cannot be sooner than that."

So Abigail waited, wondering what James would bring with him when *The Fair Lady* finally returned. A fortune in sugar and rum? His battered conscience, still insistent on making his way, or a repentant sinner, determined finally to do what was right? And what would he think about Adelaide, now nearly accepted as her daughter, at least in some circles? The gentler parts of society shook their heads at her eccentricities, but joyfully her parents had come to accept Adelaide's place in her life. They had agreed for her to have her own bedroom and share their meals. They had even engaged a tutor for her, in pianoforte and French, although Caroline worried that they were misleading the girl, since she would have aspirations to the kind of life she could never truly have.

"Perhaps that is not true," Abigail protested quietly. "Things are changing, even now. I have heard stories of freed slaves in London, gentlemen who hold positions of importance."

Caroline shook her head, looking sceptical. "Perhaps in London, and for a man," she agreed reluctantly. "But here, in such a provincial place, and as a woman? A girl? What future can she have, Abigail?"

It was not a question Abigail could answer, yet she hoped and prayed that by God's grace Adelaide would one day have opportunities even she had not known. To work, to marry, to take her place in society. Why should her choices be limited simply because she was of a darker shade? And yet Abigail knew and feared that that time was not yet, and just as her mother had said, she was setting up her daughter to be ground between the millstones of society – too educated and genteel to be a maid, too different to be anything higher.

At the end of April, Abigail began to walk to the quay every day with Adelaide, to look for the arrival of *The Fair Lady*. Some days she thought she could see it on the horizon, its sails billowing in the strong wind off the Irish Sea. She could almost imagine James at the prow, waving to her, ebullient and triumphant. But when she blinked it was gone, nothing more than a mirage, a fantasy of her own mind, and all she could see was flat, grey-blue sea, stretching on and on.

May arrived, with birdsong and flowers filling Holy Trinity Gardens, and still the ship did not come.

"I would not be anxious," Caroline said, sounding just that. "Mr Jefferson's last ship from the Indies took fourteen months."

May dragged by slowly, despite the warm weather and blue skies, and Abigail began not only to wonder, but to doubt and then to fear. Every day she went to the quay with determined hope, only to be disappointed yet again. Even so, mixed with that disappointment was a treacherous relief, for she did not know what would happen when James returned. She was afraid, terribly afraid, that his voyage might have set him firmly in his ways, and he would not countenance Adelaide having a place in their lives. She did not know what she would do then; she dreaded even to think of it.

And then one day in June, upon return to her parents' house, Adelaide's hand in hers, she experienced a disappointment of another kind entirely: a grief far graver than anything she'd experienced before, despite her many losses.

Her mother greeted her at the door, hands fluttering anxiously, her face a picture of distress.

"Mama, what is it?"

"A man has come, quite a rough sort. He says he was on *The Fair Lady.*"

Abigail stared at her, her face draining of colour as the full meaning of Caroline's words struck her with its terrible force.

"*Was…*"

"Oh my dear, he says the ship has sunk." Caroline's face crumpled. "Off the coast of Antigua, months ago now. I am so sorry."

Abigail pushed past her. "I will talk to him myself."

She drew back at the sight of the man standing awkwardly in their front parlour, his narrow-brimmed hat crumpled in his hands, a dirty neck cloth tied about his throat. He wore wool stockings, loose trousers of osnaburg, and a mismatched waistcoat and shirt of stained linen.

"Sir," she said as she stayed at the door. "What news have you of my husband and *The Fair Lady?*"

"I'm sorry, Ma'am, but I am here to tell you the sad news that the ship foundered and sunk off the shores of Antigua. All were lost." He did not look at her as he said it, and Abigail's gaze narrowed.

"All lost save you?" she demanded sharply. "That seems passing strange."

"I left the ship in Antigua. I was thinking to stay on, but when the ship went down, I took another and came here directly."

She frowned. "That was very charitable of you."

He shrugged. "Your husband was a good man, and he – he trusted me."

"Trusted you?" Abigail repeated blankly. It hit her then, what this man was saying, and yet somehow she could not believe it. James gone, *The Fair Lady* beneath the sea. "How – how did it sink?"

"It foundered on rocks. It is a treacherous place, and many ships have been lost." He still would not look at her.

"And every last man was lost?"

He nodded.

"The slaves?"

"They'd been sold already. The cargo was sugar and rum."

"And it's all gone," she said slowly. "Everything…" The ship, its cargo, her husband. In one moment, her life as she'd known it was over, and yet Abigail knew it had already ended, long ago. In some strange way, this man's news was completely unsurprising.

"I am sorry for your loss, Ma'am, truly. I – I have a letter from your husband."

"A letter?" She turned to him in surprise. She had already received six letters from James, and now one more? "Why would he give you a letter if you intended to stay on in Antigua? Surely he would have realized he'd see me first himself."

The man shrugged. "I cannot answer." He thrust out a piece of parchment sealed with wax. Abigail recognized the insignia on James's ring. "Take it, Ma'am, please. I think – I think it will help you to understand."

Abigail stared at the man as he looked her in the eye for the first time, his gaze full of both pity and fear. Wordlessly, her heart pounding, she took the last missive from her husband.

CHAPTER TWENTY-FIVE

Rachel

"Mum… *Mum!*"

Rachel's voice was ripped away by the wind as she half stumbled, half ran from the house towards the road. Where could her mother have gone? How long had she been wandering these narrow, lonely roads, so dangerous for a pedestrian, or even more alarmingly, out on the barren sweep of fells? And how could Rachel have left her?

She scanned the stretch of empty road in both directions, at a loss as to what to do. Ring 999? Or would she be wasting their time if she could find her mother herself? She fumbled for her mobile, her heart pounding, still not knowing what to do.

Then, as she scanned the area all around her, she saw her mother's muddy slipper by a stile at the end of the garden, leading on to the fells.

Rachel slid her mobile into her pocket as she hurried towards the stile. She grabbed the slipper and then clambered over, desperately scanning for the sight of her mother's slight form somewhere among the steeply rolling hills. All she saw was the all-too-familiar grey-green landscape, intersected by meandering dry stone walls, all of it stretching up and up, on and on.

Her mother could be anywhere out here, having fallen in a ditch or valley, or wandered off miles away. Rachel had no idea how long she'd been gone, and her stomach cramped with worry and fear. Should she call 999?

She kept walking, calling for her mother, desperately looking everywhere, before she finally dialled 999.

"Emergency. Which service?"

"I… I don't know." Rachel gulped. "My mother has dementia and she's wandered on to the fells, near Windermere. I can't find her."

"I'll transfer you to Mountain Rescue."

Rachel waited, still walking, searching blindly. "Mum!"

"Mountain Rescue."

"My mum is lost on the fells."

"Can you give me your precise location?"

"Four miles outside Windermere, on the Ambleside road…" Rachel's mind buzzed with panic as she tried to speak calmly and think rationally. "Behind the large grey house of Lakeland stone. Fell view –"

Just then she caught sight of something blue – the deep royal blue of her mother's dressing gown. She started running, barely aware of what the call handler was saying.

"Wait – wait. I've found her. I'm sorry."

"Is she in need of medical treatment?"

Rachel stood in front of her mother, who was huddled against a rock, her knees drawn up to her chest, her face blank. Besides a sore-looking foot from where she'd lost the slipper, Deborah didn't look hurt.

"No, I don't think so. I'm sorry for wasting your time."

The call handler continued to talk about medical assessment and A&E, and overcome, Rachel disconnected the call and dropped to her knees in front of her mother.

"Mum. Mum. Why did you come out here like this?"

Her mother blinked her into focus as she slowly shook her head. "I don't know. I don't remember."

"Let's get you back home, Mum. It's not too far." The panic was leaving Rachel in a rush, making her feel faint and dizzy with relief, on top of the remnants of shock. To think what could have happened. "Let's get you home," she said again, and drew her mother gently to her feet.

Slowly and painstakingly they made their way back to the house, the distance feeling ten times as long as when Rachel had been walking it by herself.

Her mother leaned heavily against her, Rachel's arm around her shoulders, which felt frail and slight to her touch. A wave of protectiveness rushed over her, surprising and yet somehow right in its strength.

Finally they got back to the house and into the kitchen; docile and quiet, Deborah sat at the table while Rachel boiled the kettle for tea and took a warm, wet flannel and wiped her mother's hands and feet with it.

"Thank you," she murmured, and Rachel saw her lips tremble.

"Oh, Mum." She rested her hand gently on top of her mother's. "I'm just glad you're safe."

"I hate being like this," Deborah whispered. "I hate it. I'm losing myself, and I can *feel* it."

"Oh, Mum," Rachel said again. She felt so helpless, and so very sad. "I'm so sorry."

"I don't imagine you care very much," Deborah said, her voice tired rather than spiteful.

"No, I don't imagine that you would imagine I would." Rachel paused, feeling her way through the words, the truth. "Mum, I know about Dad. I've known for a while."

Deborah looked up sharply at that, her expression trapped. "What do you mean?"

"I think I've known all along, but I've pretended even to myself that I didn't know, because I couldn't bear it." She swallowed past the growing lump in her throat. "But I don't think that was very fair to you."

"You loved him," Deborah said after a moment. "And you were a child. I can't blame you."

"Did you blame me? Is that why – we've been so distant? Because I know it's been me too, but –"

"I never blamed you." Deborah looked away, her lips pursed. "I couldn't. But I couldn't try, either. You were always so close; you had this bond and I could never break in. After he died, I couldn't bear to disillusion you. I knew how much that hurt. And I wondered if you'd even believe me. You put him on a sky-high pedestal, Rachel, and I couldn't knock him off even if I wanted to."

"I know I did. I'm sorry."

"You don't need to be sorry."

"I wish – I wish we'd been closer."

Deborah looked at her tiredly. "I wish we'd been closer too. But it felt too hard all the time. You were angry with me for being the one to live –"

"I wasn't," Rachel protested automatically, even as she recognized some truth in the words.

"And I was angry, full stop. I loved him so much, you know, even though. I loved him so much."

Deborah began to cry, softly, like something broken, and Rachel put her arms around her, her heart finally filled with love. Things were going to be different now. She was going to make sure of it.

Just two days later, she was locking up the house outside Windermere, her mother already in the passenger seat of her

SUV. She'd spent the last forty-eight hours in a flurry of motion, packing up her mother's essentials, getting rid of all the food and rubbish she could, and finally dropping off the keys at the estate agent's for potential viewings. Her mother had agreed, with less reluctance than Rachel had anticipated, to move in with her in Bristol. She had left a long, meandering voicemail on Anthony's phone about the plan, but he hadn't got back to her. Rachel had to assume it would be okay.

"I know you value your independence, and I don't want to take that from you," she'd said hesitantly. "But you need care, Mum, and I want to be able to give it to you." She'd already had a first conversation with Izzy about her work hours, and she hoped that she'd be able to be there for her mother. When she couldn't be, there was a day centre nearby with a lovely lady running it, whom Rachel had spoken to on the phone.

"I'm grateful, Rachel," Deborah had said with a tired smile. "Truly I am. It's just… hard."

"I know." Rachel squeezed her mother's hand, still surprised and gratified by how the simple touch felt after having been so sadly absent from both of their lives.

"And you might regret your kind offer," Deborah continued with an attempt at a smile. "I might drive you mad."

"We might drive each other mad." Rachel smiled, and as Deborah's smile widened, she could hardly believe that they had reached this kind of moment, where they could laugh in the struggles they shared.

Even if it was hard, and she knew it would be, but even if it was *impossible*, Rachel was thankful for this moment. She was thankful for everything that had got them here.

Yesterday, while her mum had been at the memory clinic, Rachel had gone to Goswell for the last time to see Jane.

It felt strange, how familiar the little village nestled against the windswept sea had become, and how important Jane had become.

"If it helps, I think you're doing the right thing," Jane said when they were both seated in her cosy kitchen, sipping mugs of tea. "And I'm proud of you."

"Thanks. I think I'm excited and terrified in equal measure. I never thought I'd be at this point. I certainly never thought my mother would reach this point. And yet here we are."

"And things are really better between you?" Jane asked with a smile.

"They're better, yes. They're not perfect, and sometimes they're not even good. We're both still rather prickly people." Her mother could still speak sharply enough to draw blood, and Rachel had a tendency to retreat, but they were working on it as best they could, and that was something. Right now that felt like everything.

"You will come back, won't you?" Jane asked when Rachel had to leave, to pick up her mother. "I know it's a long way…"

"I'm sure I'll have to, when the house sells."

"But even without that."

"I'll try."

"You should," Jane said robustly. "You haven't solved the mystery of the pocket watch, have you?"

"No, I don't suppose I have." James's sixth and last letter hadn't revealed anything more than his growing unease with the slave trade he'd chosen to pursue. Despite that, in the letter he'd detailed his cargo and assured Abigail that he would get a good price for it all. Rachel feared that if his conscience had been pricked, the wound had healed over.

And what of Abigail and her daughter Adelaide? Rachel knew nothing of either of them, and she hadn't received any more information from Soha yet. Nevertheless, she felt as if Abigail's lost voice was one she could almost hear, and she empathized with the unknown woman, even though she didn't know if she had any reason to.

"I suppose it will always be a mystery," she told Jane. The speculum oris and pocket watch had been acquired by The Rum Story. The wreck site had not been deemed worthy of further excavation. That chapter had ended, and the story would remain forever untold. "I'm afraid it's often like that in archaeology," she added with a grimace. "You never find out the truth."

"How utterly frustrating for you," Jane exclaimed with a laugh.

"Yes, but you learn to let go." And she had let go of the past – not the distant, murky past of the Fentons, but of her own. It was liberating, to let her father fall from his pedestal, even as she let herself love and forgive him. It was liberating, but it was also sad.

Now, with the house closed up, the furniture covered in dust sheets, Rachel climbed into the car and headed for home. She'd left a voicemail and several texts on Anthony's phone, but to her annoyance and increasing worry, he hadn't responded to any of it.

She'd been too busy to be overly concerned, but now with five hours of driving in front of her, her mind wandered – and she was worried. It wasn't like Anthony not to be in touch, especially when Rachel's news had been so momentous. In fact, she still hadn't heard from him once since he'd left, a fact that niggled at her. He was all right, wasn't he? Nothing had happened to him? She felt ashamed that the notion hadn't even occurred to her before, so when they stopped at a service station on the M6, Rachel fired off yet another text: "*I haven't heard from you and I'm worried something might have happened. Are you alive??*"

She waited impatiently for an answer, and thankfully her phone pinged just a few seconds later. "*Yes.*"

Yes? That was *it?* She stared at the single word as a deep unease crept over her. Something wasn't right. Of course, she'd already known that, but now she felt it far more deeply and worryingly. Something really wasn't right.

"Anthony, we need to talk. I've been thinking about a lot of things lately and I want to talk to you about them." She cringed at the stilted phrasing, but she was not good at this. At least she was trying though, right?

Except Anthony doesn't like it when you try.

Forcing that thought away, she put her phone in her pocket, desperate for it to ping again. But it didn't.

All the way home, another four hours with traffic, it didn't ping once.

By the time she pulled into the underground parking of her building, she was exhausted and her mother was asleep. Tension bracketed her shoulder blades and a headache threatened to start pounding, but she forced herself onwards. She'd get upstairs, and Anthony would be there, and they would talk. And then, somehow, like a miracle, it would all be okay. It had to be.

But when she roused her mother and headed upstairs, unlocked the door and stepped into the flat, she felt its emptiness echo all around her. Anthony wasn't home.

She tried not to feel disappointed. She'd texted her estimated time of arrival. He could have made an effort to be there, but clearly he'd chosen not to.

Still, she told herself not to mind. "This is your room, Mum," she said, and felt another flicker of annoyance when she saw that the bed was still stripped, the old boxes of files stuck in one corner. She'd asked Anthony to prepare the room, but she supposed he hadn't got that memo, either. Except she knew he must have, because he was still receiving her texts.

She was starting to feel really worried now.

"Why don't you have a sit down, Mum, and I'll make you a cup of tea. Then we'll sort your room out."

She'd just filled the kettle and switched it on when she saw the note propped between the salt and pepper shakers on the little table. Her heart froze and she looked away, as if she could unsee it. But of course she couldn't.

Even so, Rachel waited for the kettle to boil, all the while studiously looking away from that little piece of paper. She made two cups of tea and took one to her mother, who looked ready to fall asleep again.

"I don't know why I'm so tired."

"It's fine, don't worry," Rachel murmured. She looked back at the kitchen. And then slowly, so slowly, she walked over and picked up the note. It was terribly, tragically short. Just five words altogether, and they became emblazoned on Rachel's brain.

"Dear Rachel, I'm sorry. Anthony."

CHAPTER TWENTY-SIX

Abigail

London, 1767

Abigail gazed up at the Foundry in Moorfields, the home of John Wesley's first chapel. Although he still insisted he was part of the Church of England, the homely chapel was the beating heart of Methodism. Now nearly thirty years old, the site possessed a free dispensary, a school, a lending society, and an almshouse. Abigail had no idea what kind of reception she'd receive.

Next to her Adelaide silently slid her hand into Abigail's, fingers squeezing tightly, imbuing strength. Abigail looked down at her daughter and managed a smile.

"It will be all right, my dear."

"I know," Adelaide said softly. Still, she clung tightly to Abigail's hand. It had been an arduous journey from Whitehaven all the way to London, travelling by stage coach. At first, Adelaide had received suspicious looks, especially when it was clear Abigail did not treat her as a servant. At a coaching inn in Leeds, a gentleman had snapped his fingers at her and asked her to fetch something. Abigail had disabused him of his notions most severely. She told the man, in icy tones, that she was travelling with her daughter.

It had been a surprisingly gentle shift in their relationship; a gaining of trust on Adelaide's part, and a need to be forgiven on

Abigail's. When she thought of how Adelaide had slept on some old sacking, locked in the dark warehouse, she could have wept. How could she have been so blind, so unfeeling, yet believing herself to be some sort of angel of mercy all the while? She was ashamed of herself. It was Adelaide who had helped her to leave this behind and forge something new, accepting the love she gave freely, and miraculously giving it back.

The first time Adelaide had put her arms around her, Abigail's heart had overflowed with thankfulness, cracked vessel that it was. The joy had spilled out, and she'd drawn her daughter into her arms, resting her chin on her head, wishing for no more than this.

Now, just over three months after learning of James's death, Abigail still wore widow's black, still grieved the loss of a man she had loved dearly yet still strove to forgive. She still ached for all he'd done and suffered.

She had also struggled with what direction to now aim for in her life. To remain in Whitehaven meant one thing only: to live in her parents' house, as good as a spinster, worse than a widow, at only twenty-five years old. With Adelaide in tow she was most unlikely to form a further connection – not that it was something Abigail either desired or considered. Adelaide was more important.

"You are still marriageable," Caroline had insisted, a month after the seaman had come with his grim news – and his letter. "You are young and healthy –"

"Mama, I am barren." For once the words were not tinged with bitterness; they were simply stated fact. "What man would want me, such as I am?"

"An older gentleman, perhaps a widower himself, one who has already had his children?" Caroline suggested. "If it weren't for this bizarre insistence that Adelaide must be treated as your daughter –"

"She is my daughter." Abigail spoke quietly, without a single shred of uncertainty. Adelaide, who had been sitting quietly in the room, came and stood next to her, leaning her head against her shoulder. Abigail put her arm around her and Caroline sighed.

"If you'd just treat her as a well-regarded servant," she cajoled. "A beloved member of the household, even. I am not without charity, and I have come to see your point of view in regard to the slave trade." She gave Adelaide a fleeting smile, tinged with apology. "Adelaide is lovely, but as for an actual *daughter*..."

"She is my daughter," Abigail repeated firmly. "In every way that matters."

It had taken time and patience to gain her daughter's trust in a way that all of Abigail's small kindnesses as a mistress to her slave had, quite rightly, not earned. Now, as a mother to her daughter, she rejoiced in the spontaneous smile or sudden hug Adelaide had begun to give her. She would not trade them away for the world, and certainly not for a husband.

"I will not change in this," Abigail told her mother. "And in truth, I do not want a husband. I have had one, and I loved him, but I do not need another."

"But a woman alone in this world –"

"I am not alone. And – I do not intend to stay in Whitehaven." Abigail let her mother absorb this statement before she continued. "It is too small a society for Adelaide and me."

Caroline's mouth dropped open with great inelegance as Abigail made that shocking pronouncement. "You will not stay in Whitehaven? But where will you go?"

"I have written to Mr Wesley," Abigail said. There had been no one else she could even think of writing to. "And he has said Adelaide and I may come to the Foundry, in London, where his Methodist chapel and school are located. It is a small, welcoming community, and I daresay I will find a way to make myself useful there." Although she did not know yet how, or if Wesley would welcome such a prospect. She had not made her intentions altogether clear, and he had invited her only to visit. Still, it was a beginning as well as a chance, and she knew she had to take it, for Adelaide's sake as well as her own.

"But all the way to London." Caroline's hand fluttered near her throat, her expression one of hurt dismay. "So far away! And you will return?"

"Perhaps one day. But I cannot stay here, Mama. Not now."

She had lost everything – husband, home, reputation, a future. She was penniless. Although her father had urged her to make a claim on the insurance of *The Fair Lady*, Abigail had refused, and would not be moved on the subject.

After the sale of the few items from their house on Queen Street – the Chippendale chair and the Chinoiserie cabinet – she had just enough for her and Adelaide to travel to London by stage. After that she would be at the mercy of others' goodwill, or else would need to find a way to earn her keep. Either way, her mind was made up. She would take this chance.

And now she was here, gazing at the impressive bustling activity around the Foundry, clutching Adelaide's hand as she considered how to introduce herself. Her body ached with tiredness from three days on a jolting coach, and nights spent in the humblest rooms of whatever inn they stopped at along the way. Her mind burned with purpose. Finally, they were here.

"What do you think to this place, my dear?" she asked Adelaide. "Do you think we might be happy here?"

"It looks like a warm place." Adelaide's voice was quiet, her manner shy. She had seen more in the last three days than in her entire time in Whitehaven. At a coaching inn outside London, an

African, a freedman in a frock coat, had smiled at her. Adelaide had turned back to Abigail, curious and disbelieving.

"Yes," Abigail had answered her question. "It will be different here."

Now she started forward, still holding her daughter's hand. "Come, Adelaide," she murmured. "Let us discover what awaits us."

It took some time and doing, but Abigail finally managed to introduce herself to Mrs Clark, John Wesley's housekeeper, who managed the rooms above the chapel where he resided while in London, along with his wife Molly. Abigail had been a bit surprised at that; she had not realized he was wed.

"It is a hard marriage," Mrs Clark admitted in a low voice. "They are ill suited, to be sure, and have spent months and even years apart. Neither of them are present now, but that should not dissuade you. If Mr Wesley said come, then come. We welcome all." She smiled at Adelaide.

"Thank you," Abigail said. "You are most kind, and my daughter and I will endeavour to make ourselves useful."

Mrs Clark's expression did not change at Abigail's description of Adelaide. "Yes, of course," she said. "Adelaide may attend the school with the other children."

"School?" Adelaide asked once they were alone, sharing a simple room in the Foundry's almshouse. "What is school?"

"It is a place for children to learn together." The Foundry was unique in its willingness to educate boys and girls together, and Abigail hoped the other children would accept her daughter as Mrs Clark had. "Would you like to go there?"

"To learn?" Adelaide looked incredulous. "Yes, please, Mother."

Abigail smiled and drew her into a hug. She would never tire of being called Mother.

Over the course of the next few weeks, they settled into a routine that felt entirely strange yet wonderfully right. Abigail began to help at the school, teaching both needlework and literature, and Adelaide attended, welcomed into the small group of boys and girls as one of their own, without any of the sense of separateness that Abigail had feared.

The first time Adelaide joined in a game in the school yard, Abigail's heart clenched with joy, and she exchanged a look with the teacher, Mr Wiggins, who smiled in understanding. Finally, *finally* Adelaide was beginning to act as any child might.

Even Adelaide's small disobediences were a source of thankfulness that her daughter felt free and safe enough to misbehave. And Abigail steeled herself to offer the proper discipline, not as a mistress to her slave, but as a mother to her child, the bonds of their relationship growing even stronger and tighter.

Then, in November, after they'd been at the Foundry for a couple of months, John Wesley returned, like a conquering hero; he rode into the courtyard while people gathered around excitedly, but Abigail hung back, not yet wanting to attract his attention, unsure of what her reception would be. She didn't want to leave the Foundry, but with Wesley's return she didn't know if she and Adelaide would be invited to stay.

It wasn't until late that afternoon that he sought her out; she was putting chapbooks away in the schoolroom, Adelaide playing outside, when he appeared in the doorway, seeming to fill the space, though he was of but middling height.

"Madam, I am pleased to see you have settled in well here at the Foundry."

"I am very thankful for your welcome, Sir," Abigail replied, a tremor in her voice. "Even when you were absent."

"All who seek succour and comfort shall find their rest here," Wesley replied. "Especially if they are doing the Lord's work."

Abigail prayed she was doing such work as she bobbed a little curtsey. "Thank you, Sir."

"Tell me," Wesley said as he came into the room. "What of your husband and his trade?"

"It is no more," Abigail said quietly. "As I wrote in my letter, he perished on his last voyage when the ship sank." She bit her lip and looked away, hoping he would not ask more, because she did not want to deceive him, but she knew she could not confess the truth.

"And do you believe he came to understand the wretched evil of the trade, before his death?"

She nodded, forcing herself to turn back and meet his penetrating gaze. "I pray so."

"And you, Madam?" Wesley asked softly. "You brought your young slave with you, I have been told."

"She is not my slave, but my daughter," Abigail said, a fierce note entering her voice. "That much has changed."

Wesley smiled. "'Wherefore thou art no more a servant, but a son, and if a son, then an heir of God through Christ.'"

Abigail bowed her head. "It is so."

"And what of you, Mrs Fenton? Are you a servant or a son?"

She looked up, startled. "What do you mean?"

"You have brought one precious child of God into the fold, but what of your own soul? For I sense a disquiet in you that no child of God should ever feel." He cocked his head, his eyes warm, his smile compassionate. "Do I speak true?"

Abigail's eyes filled with tears as she realized he'd seen something in her she had barely been able to understand herself. "You do, Sir," she whispered. "And I do not know how to ease my troubled mind."

"What troubles you so?"

"My guilt," Abigail cried, wretched now, the tears starting. "I am trying to forgive my husband, who acted in ignorance for so long, but I cannot forgive myself. How could I have treated Adelaide so, for such a time? How could I have allowed her so many indignities – to sleep on the hard floor, to eat naught but bread and water, to be dressed up like a lifeless doll. How could I have allowed it, even though I knew deep within me it was wrong? It chafed my spirit all along, and yet still I said yes and amen to it all." She shook her head, tears trickling down her cheeks. "I am bowed beneath the weight of the shame, and I do not know how to lift it."

"It is not you who can lift, but God, through Christ," Wesley told her. "That I know, and have experienced myself with great rejoicing. Do not free your daughter, Madam, and yet live as a slave yourself."

"I do not know how."

"It is not how, but whom. Believe in Him whose blood paid for the sins and shame you suffer under now." He smiled whimsically as he began to sing in a pleasing baritone: "No condemnation now I dread, Jesus, and all in Him is mine; alive in Him, my living head; and cloth'd in righteousness divine. Bold I approach th'eternal throne, and claim the crown, thro' Christ my own."

Abigail let the words sink into her soul. *No condemnation… Bold I approach.*

He had said as much and more in his sermons, and she'd been powerfully moved, but it was an emotional response that had not yet experienced the weight of conviction under it. She had not, Abigail realized in that moment, truly believed. She had still striven to do her best, to change in her own power, by her own will, and then rest on her own shabby laurels. Now, standing in an empty schoolroom, the winter wind rattling the window panes, she felt for the first time, as Wesley's brother's hymn went, the chains fall off, as her heart was free. She let out a laugh of incredulous joy.

"Can it be –"

"It is," Wesley assured her. "It truly is."

From that day on, Abigail lived as one who had been set free. The joy she felt in Adelaide she experienced tenfold, now that it was no longer tainted by her own shame. As soon as she left Wesley, she ran to her daughter, caught her up in an embrace and kissed her cheeks.

"Mama!" Adelaide laughed, throwing her arms around her, and Abigail kissed her again. Mama, not mother. Son, not slave. Free.

CHAPTER TWENTY-SEVEN

Rachel

Anthony was gone. Even with the flat empty all around her, Rachel could scarcely believe it. How could he have just left? How could he have not?

"Rachel?" Her mother's wavering voice sounded from the other room. "Are you coming back?"

"Yes, I am. I'm here." She crumpled the note up and slipped it into her pocket before joining her mother in the sitting room.

Her mind whirled as she sipped her tea and wondered what on earth she could do. Where was Anthony? How could he have gone, knowing she was bringing her mother back and would need help? No matter what the issues in their marriage were, surely now was not the time to just walk off.

Unless he'd simply had enough.

Rachel closed her eyes, longing to block out the thought, but she couldn't. Then she felt her mother's hand on her own.

"Rachel," she said, her voice full of an unfamiliar compassion, "what's wrong?"

"Anthony's left me," Rachel blurted out. "He left a note in the kitchen."

Confusion clouded Deborah's eyes. "Anthony…"

"My husband, Mum." The impossibility of the situation crashed over her yet again. "My husband has left me."

"Oh yes, Anthony." Deborah nodded, her expression clearing. Rachel wondered how many of these kinds of moments she would have to navigate – and now all by herself. "Where has he gone?"

"I don't know. He didn't say." She swallowed, more of a gulp, as the panic that lapped at her senses threatened to overwhelm her. "He didn't tell me anything."

"When is he coming back?" Deborah asked, looking confused again, and Rachel tried to smile.

"Soon, Mum," she said quietly, and Deborah nodded, looking relieved.

"I don't want you to be alone."

"I'm not. But why don't you have a rest? It's been a long day, and you look worn out. Finish your tea and I'll make up your bedroom."

Rachel worked as quickly as she could, her mind both numb and reeling as she shifted boxes and fetched clean sheets for her mother's bed. She opened the windows in all the rooms; the flat smelled stale, she realized. Anthony must have left a few days ago, at least.

Finally, with her mother settled in bed for a nap, her things unpacked, Rachel went out on to the balcony for some privacy. She gazed blindly out at the glinting harbour, her mobile in her hand. If she rang, would Anthony pick up? And what would she say?

She felt angry, but more than that she felt despairing. She'd been finally ready to be honest, to truly try in the way that mattered most, and it was too late. It seemed unfair even as Rachel knew she'd been both waiting for and dreading this day.

Part of her wanted to put the phone down, leave things as they were. *If Anthony was going to leave, then I'll let him*. But that was the voice of the old Rachel, fearful, angry, resistant. She was trying to be different. She wanted to reach out. And she'd learned to forgive.

Rachel looked out at the evening sunlight glinting off the water for several long, silent moments before she finally swiped the screen on her phone and typed out a simple text. "*I got your note. Please can we talk?*"

Then she waited, while the sun sank towards the harbour, and the water flattened out like a shimmering plate, and her phone stayed silent, its screen depressingly dark.

Eventually she went inside to prepare dinner; there was no food in the house, so she would have to make do with pasta, and sauce from a jar. Her body ached with tiredness, from both the drive and the emotional energy expended over the last few days. She wanted nothing more than a hot bath and twelve hours' sleep, yet she knew she wouldn't enjoy either with Anthony's silence hanging over her, a dark cloud of nothingness. No text, no call, no explanation really. "I'm sorry," the note read. If he was walking out on their marriage, didn't she deserve more?

Do you deserve anything?

"Stop!" Rachel slapped her hand on the counter top. She hated that voice in her head; the one that listed all her faults and told her she didn't deserve anything – not her mother's love, not her husband's faithfulness. The voice that kept her from forgiving herself and moving forward. But she wasn't going to live that way any more. She'd made that decision; she needed to live it now.

"Rachel?" Her mother appeared in the doorway, blinking sleep out of her eyes, her normally well-coiffed hair in a flattened muss. "Is everything all right?"

"It's fine, Mum. I'm just getting your supper." Rachel slapped a smile on her face. "Would you like to eat out on the balcony? It's a lovely evening."

"All right."

A few minutes later Rachel brought two plates of steaming pasta out to the little table overlooking the harbour. She saw her mother hunched over, arms wrapped around herself, so brought a blanket to cover her. The breeze off the water was cooler than she'd realized.

As she draped it over her mother's shoulders, Deborah clasped her hand. "Don't make the same mistake I did," she said, and Rachel jolted in surprise.

"What do you mean?"

"With Anthony. Don't stew in resentment, waiting for him to make the first move. Go after him, Rachel, if you love him. It's worth it."

"Is that what you wish you did? With Dad?"

Deborah sighed. "I wish I hadn't been so proud. I stayed angry, but if I was that angry, I should have left him, and I never did."

"I don't want to leave Anthony," Rachel said quickly.

"Then go after him." Deborah glanced at her pasta, her forehead wrinkling. "What's this?"

"Supper, Mum," Rachel reminded her gently, and put a fork into her hand.

An hour later, with her mum back in bed and having settled for a shower rather than a bath, Rachel curled up on her bed and swiped her phone to call Anthony. To her surprise, alarm and relief, he picked up after the third ring.

"Hello, Rachel."

"I thought I wasn't ever going to get to speak you." She'd meant to sound jokey, but it came out sounding bitter, the old Rachel in full force. "Sorry –"

"No, I'm sorry. I know I should have answered your text. I'm sorry that I didn't. I just…" He blew out a breath. "I just couldn't."

"And now?" Rachel asked hesitantly, after a silence had stretched on.

"Now I think you deserve a conversation, at the very least." That didn't sound very promising. "How is your mother?"

"She's okay. She's in the right place."

"I'm glad."

This was all sounding so horribly final. Rachel felt her throat grow tight, her eyes start to sting. *Don't leave me*, she wanted to cry, but she knew she couldn't start there.

"Anthony, please, can we talk?"

"I'm not sure what more there is to say."

"I feel as if I haven't said anything yet."

"Really?" He sounded bitter as well as sceptical. "You said it all back in Cumbria, as far as I'm concerned."

"What do you mean?"

"You're not interested in having a real marriage, Rachel. I saw that clearly for the first time, and I hated it. It hurt." His voice wavered. "But at least I understand that now."

"Anthony, please, wait. Let's talk in person, not over the phone. I – I have things I want to say to you. Things I haven't had a chance to say before. I mean," she amended hurriedly, "I've had the chance, but I haven't taken it. Please." She was begging and she hated it, but she did it anyway, because she couldn't bear him walking away from her now.

Anthony was silent for a long, terrible moment. "All right," he said finally. "But I'm not sure it will make any difference."

They met at a café on the harbour side, a sparkling June morning when everyone was soaking in the sunshine. Deborah was back at the flat, with Rachel's mobile on speed dial, her neighbour on alert, and the front door locked. Still, Rachel felt tense, and she wondered if the rest of her life was going to be like this.

Then she remembered it wasn't, because vascular dementia had a life expectancy of four years, and her mother had most likely lived some of that already, a prospect which felt too awful to think about. How much had they missed out on, because of old hurts and fears and anger? At least these years could count, Rachel told herself. They would matter.

Anthony sat heavily in the chair opposite her, cradling a latte between his big hands. He looked tired, his hair rumpled, his face creased, his clothing wrinkled. Rachel hoped that was a good sign.

"So." He took a sip of coffee. "What are all these things you want to say to me?"

Rachel took a sip of her own coffee, simply to stall for time. Now that they were both here, her mind had emptied and her tongue had become tied. She hadn't even begun, and she was already at a loss.

"I want to say I'm sorry," she began hesitantly. "I know I've – I've been difficult."

"You haven't really, Rach," Anthony said tiredly. "I don't blame you, you know."

His weary tone made panic well up in her and she leaned forward, spilling her coffee in the process. "Don't say that, Anthony."

"What –"

"Don't give up on me." The words came now, faster and faster, suddenly easy to say. "Please don't give up on me. Don't be too tired. Don't stop fighting for... for us. Because I know I'm just starting, but I want to now. I've always wanted to, but I was afraid. So afraid."

"Afraid of what?" Anthony's tone was mystified, but it was also gentle, and that gave Rachel a little hope, at least enough to go on.

"Of losing you. And of losing my hero. My dad." She stopped, took a deep breath, and started again. And then she told him all of it: her father's affairs, how she felt complicit, the distance between her and her mother and how she now understood she had been part of its cause. She told him how she'd been afraid she was unlovable, but also how she'd feared losing her father – not through death, but because of his sins. If she'd made space for her mother to tell her the truth, he couldn't be her hero any more, and she hadn't been able to stand the thought of that.

"I know it's a lot," she finished, her voice choking. "I know I'm a lot. But please, please stay with me. I love you. I know I don't say it enough, or even at all, but I do."

"Oh, Rachel." Anthony looked unbearably sad as he covered his hand with her own. "I'm sorry for everything you've gone through, I really am."

"Please don't let there be a 'but'," Rachel interjected. She felt that one was coming.

"There isn't," Anthony said sadly. "I'm not going to leave you. I believe in marriage, I take our vows seriously. I meant what I said about this just being a break. But..."

There it was. Rachel braced herself for whatever bad news was coming her way.

"But I feel like we want different things," Anthony continued. "And I don't know how we get around that."

"What different things? I want to be married to you –"

"What about children?" Anthony said quietly. "It's not a deal breaker, of course, and if it didn't happen because of biology or whatever, I'd accept that. But it's a big issue for me – I've always wanted a child."

Rachel drew a steadying breath. "I've been scared to have children," she admitted. "Scared that I'd be a bad mother. Cold and distant like... like my own, although I understand more of that now. And like I was with her, and even with you."

"You were scared?"

312

"I still am. But I don't want that to keep me back from – well, from anything." Her heart was pounding as she looked at him directly. "I'm willing to try for children, if you want to."

"Willing to try?"

"Can't that be enough for you?" Rachel asked tremulously. "I know you think love means not having to try, but what if it means the opposite? What if it means trying even when you don't feel like it or you're not sure you can? Forgiving when you still feel angry? Loving when you'd rather be alone? Couldn't that be what love really is?"

Anthony stared at her for a moment, his expression so thoughtful, and yet Rachel had no idea what he was thinking. "Yes," he finally said slowly. "I think it could."

Relief broke over her in a wave. "Then –"

"I'm not trying to put you through the wringer. This isn't some test you have to pass. I love you, Rachel, and I want us to work. And I'm sorry for being so… tired, I suppose." He shook his head. "I shouldn't have walked away like that and left you to it, especially when you had to deal with your mum."

"It's okay," she whispered.

"I thought I was showing you what love was, but maybe you're the one who had to show me." He gave her a lovely lopsided smile. "Because I think you're right. It is about trying, not about not having to. If something is hard, it's worthwhile."

"And I'm jolly difficult," Rachel said with a little laugh.

"No, you aren't." Anthony looked at her seriously. "No more than me, anyway. We're coming to this the same, Rachel – we are both flawed, even if it's in different ways."

Rachel nodded, her throat too tight for her to speak, her heart too full to do more than reach over and clasp Anthony's hand. And that was enough. It was everything.

As they were leaving the café together, a text pinged on to Rachel's phone. Worried it was her mum, she reached for it and then let out a little gasp of surprise when she saw the message from Soha.

"Found Adelaide Fenton!"

"It took some doing and digging," Soha told her excitedly when Rachel called her later that afternoon. She was back in the flat, and so was Anthony; when he'd arrived, Deborah had confused him with Rachel's father, but the moment had quickly passed and now things felt, more or less, as if they were on an even keel. Life wasn't going to be easy, but it was going to be okay.

"So what happened to Adelaide?" Rachel asked as she opened her laptop to look at her notes. "All I have is the mention of her from the Fenton Collection. Otherwise, it's as if she didn't exist."

"Well, she didn't exist, not until after James Fenton's death," Soha said, and Rachel frowned.

"What?"

"There are no birth or baptism records, and no indication that the Fentons had children."

"But –"

"Plus, Abigail's father, Daniel Heywood, died without heirs, in 1791, a year after Abigail, when he was eighty-seven years old."

"I'm confused," Rachel said with a laugh. "How can this be?"

"I think this image might help make things clear. It's a portrait of Adelaide Quicke, with her husband Josiah, a lawyer and member of the abolitionist movement. I'm sending it now."

A few seconds later it pinged into Rachel's inbox, and then she opened it, letting out a soft sound of surprise when she saw the photo of an elegant, soft-eyed woman, one hand resting on her husband's arm.

"Adelaide was black," Rachel said in wonder.

"I think she must have originally been a slave, since I can't find any records, and Abigail adopted her at some point after James's death."

"But he was a slave trader." Rachel shook her head. "He mentions her in one of the letters – that he misses her as well as Abigail."

"As I'm sure you already know, possessing young slave children was considered something of a status symbol. People dressed them, had them act as pageboys and such. My guess is Adelaide had that role, and then, as their relationship grew in affection, she became more like a daughter."

"But to adopt her in the 1760s," Rachel said slowly. "That would have been a bold move. The abolition movement hadn't really started then."

"I know. It is extraordinary. And I've found some correspondence between John Wesley –"

"John Wesley? You mean, the Methodist?"

"The very man. He mentions Abigail Fenton in a letter to another young woman. From the context, I'd say she was working at the Foundry, the Methodist headquarters in London until 1778. After that, I'm not sure where she went, but I'm guessing she stayed in London, associated with the Methodist community, and then later the abolitionist movement, based on what I've learned of Adelaide."

"Wow." Rachel shook her head slowly. "I assumed Abigail just faded away from history, a merchant's widow in Whitehaven."

"Apparently not," Soha answered with a laugh. I haven't been able to find where she is buried, but I do know where Adelaide is buried – the old churchyard of Holy Trinity Church in Clapham Common. It was the church of William Wilberforce, leader of the abolitionist movement, built in 1776. They used the churchyard from the old site."

"Do you know more about Adelaide?"

"A bit, although none of it fully explains why *The Fair Lady* sank off the coast of Whitehaven instead of the West Indies."

"No, although we could guess, perhaps." Had James Fenton been attempting insurance fraud? Or had something deeper and darker been going on? Rachel shook her head slowly. "Maybe some things are meant to always be a mystery."

"Yes, that's part of it, isn't it? We'll never truly know, but I feel like I know more about Abigail now."

"And what about Adelaide?"

"Her husband was involved in the abolitionist movement all the way up to 1833, when slavery was finally abolished. She lived until she was eighty-five, and she had four children and eighteen grandchildren. She lived a good, long life, as far as I can tell. She and Josiah were part of the Clapham Sect – have you heard of it?"

"Vaguely."

"It was a group of Christians, including Wilberforce, who all lived in Clapham and promoted abolition as well as charitable and missionary works. They were quite influential."

"Wow. That's amazing. Thanks, Soha."

"So is the riddle solved?" Anthony asked with a smile when Rachel got off the phone.

"Yes and no. I've learned more about the Fentons, which is great, but I don't know any more about the ship." Her mind was still full of Abigail and Adelaide, slavery and Methodism. She was glad Adelaide had lived a long, seemingly happy life. Eighteen grandchildren…

Rachel slid her arms around Anthony's waist and he pulled her close. "I don't mind, though. I feel as if the questions I needed to be answered have been." And more importantly, Rachel knew, she had a sense of peace settling in her soul, in her very bones, that she hadn't felt in such a long time, thanks to Abigail.

The restless desire to lose herself in the past didn't have the same hold over her. She felt free. Free to love, and be loved. To forgive and be forgiven. Free, finally, to live.

"It's finished," she said softly, and laid her head on Anthony's shoulder.

Epilogue

Whitehaven, June 1767

Abigail held the letter in her hands, half afraid to open it. The rough-looking mariner had gone, leaving her with her shock and grief, and this – James's last letter, written just before he'd died. How? Why? What would she find in these lines? Did she want to know?

Abigail ran her finger over the familiar seal, an ache twisting her insides as it hit her again that he wasn't coming back. He was gone, had been gone for weeks, and she'd never known. Or had she? Some part of her was unsurprised; some part of her had been waiting for this.

But what had he wanted to tell her?

Taking a deep breath, she broke the seal and, unfolding the piece of parchment, began to read her husband's last words.

Dearest Abigail,

I write this from the West Indies, where my Heart has been tried sorely, so sorely! I do not know if you will ever read these lines, or indeed, if we shall ever see each other again. I think we will not, this side of Eternity, although I pray that I will see you on that Distant Shore. God only knows how He will judge me.

I love you, my Darling, and I always have. I hope, despite my Lamentable Failures, you can find it in your heart to still love me, even amidst all my Weaknesses that the Lord has shown me Full Well these past Weeks and Months.

I fear, by this time, you have realized the Sorry State of my Affairs. It was my Greatest Hope to return to you, Victorious, our Fortunes Restored, but I know now that cannot come to pass. Forgive me, Abigail, for not telling you how Dire it had become. I was Afraid, and I did Believe things would come to Pass as I had worked and Hoped for. Now I know that they cannot.

I have seen Sights I cannot bear to describe to you; sights I have brought about Myself, and I am so Ashamed. We had Seven Hundred Slaves sailing from the Slave Coast, and when we Arrived in Antigua we had but Two Hundred. Two Hundred! I Need Say No More. Indeed, I cannot, for it Grieves me Beyond All Measure even to Confess my own Part in this Grave Tragedy. Even Nathaniel, the Young Lad I Wrote to You of before, Succumbed to Disease and was in Terrible Agony that I could not Bear to See.

Knowing This, and my own Culpability in this Dread Trade, I cannot Bear to return to You. I dare not look upon your Face, but only Pray that our Lord and Maker might, in His Great Love, have Mercy upon My Soul, for when I began it, I knew not, but I cannot Account for All I Did since Knowing, and for that I may only Cry "Mercy, Mercy", though I did not Extend such Mercy to Those who surely Needed it Most.

I leave for England on the Evening's Tide. I have paid most of my crew, and Sail with only those I Trust. When I am Able, I will Release them, and, if I Possess the Courage, My Own Soul. For the Sake of Your Reputation, I have asked my Trusted Crew to put about that The Fair Lady Foundered on Rocks near this Terrible Shore. I pray you will not be Shamed by me in this action as surely as what I have done Previously has Shamed Me.

Forgive me, my Dearest. For my love of you which never wavered, forgive me.

For ever,

Your James